THE WIFE IS THE LAST TO KNOW

At 3:00 A.M. he paid the cab and let himself into the house. She was waiting in the family room and watching a movie on the VCR.

"I couldn't sleep," she said. "What took so long?"

"They had to pump her stomach, run a tox screen. She's going to be fine."

"That's good." She walked over to him and kissed him, ran her hands down his chest. "Are you tired?"

"Not tired. A little keyed up. Let's go to your room."

"No, I want to go to your room, to her bed."

"The kids might get up."

"They won't. We'll lock the door."

"Have you no shame?" He grinned.

"No, and neither do you. That's why we work so well together. . . ."

WHERE'S MOMMY NOW?

ROCHELLE MAJER KRICH

Rochelle Krich

PINNACLE BOOKS
WINDSOR PUBLISHING CORP.

PINNACLE BOOKS

are published by

Windsor Publishing Corp.
475 Park Avenue South
New York, NY 10016

First printing: June, 1990

Printed in the United States of America

To my husband, Hershie,
for believing in me and encouraging me to write,
and to our children—
Eli, David, Sabina, Chani, Meira, and Daniel—
for giving me the time and space to do it.
R.M.K.

ACKNOWLEDGMENTS

My thanks go to the detectives of the Wilshire Division of the L.A.P.D. and to the Los Angeles County Medical Examiner's Office for answering my numerous questions; to Dr. David Fox for graciously providing me with insight into the practice and theory of psychology; to Frieda and Len for their professional and personal encouragement; and finally, to my unofficial "editors" for their valuable comments and invaluable support.

R.M.K.

Chapter One

He was one of the first passengers off the plane, and he was all at once inordinately glad that he had taken his briefcase and two-suiter on board with him. Quickly, he made his way past the LAX terminal doors and across the street to the parking structure where his black BMW was waiting.

He wondered again whether he should have gone to the conference in Las Vegas. He certainly hadn't gained much from the medical lectures he'd attended. But then, he hadn't really been listening. He had been preoccupied, anxious about what was happening in his absence. He had called home twice in the early evening, had exchanged long-distance kisses with Kate, with his family, had at first accepted, then turned down, a barhopping offer from some colleagues ("Come on, Mark; cut the matrimonial cord!"). After packing his few belongings, he had watched a pathetically tedious X-rated cable T.V. offering in his room.

At 11:10, she had called.

"What's wrong?" he had asked, instantly alert.

"Nothing's wrong. I just wanted to hear your voice again. You sounded so tense before. I know you're worried, Mark, but you don't have to be. I'm fine."

"The kids?"

"Sound asleep. Stop worrying."

After the phone call, he had checked the room quickly to make sure he hadn't forgotten anything. Five minutes later he was downstairs in the lobby of the Las Vegas Hilton, paying his bill. He made it to the airport for the 11:50 P.M. flight to Los Angeles with four minutes to spare.

At one o'clock in the morning, there was no traffic. The BMW made swift progress along the main boulevards, and twenty-five minutes after he had fastened his seat belt, he turned the corner with a mixture of eagerness and a nameless dread that suddenly overwhelmed him, even before he saw the ambulance occupying his spot in the newly cemented driveway, its sepulchral whiteness illuminated by the arching streetlamps, before he saw the flashing red lights on the two black-and-white police vehicles that welcomed him home.

He braked sharply in front of the house and jerked the ignition off. The car came to a shuddering stop. In seconds he was running up the carefully tended lawn and almost collided with the white-clothed paramedic who was sliding the stretcher and its silent occupant past the gaping doors of the ambulance.

A uniformed policeman approached. "Dr. Bauers?"

"Oh, my God!" Mark cried. "Kate! Kate!"

10

Chapter Two

Five weeks after she opened the gift shop with her best friend, Laney Tolbert, Katherine Bauers came to the conclusion that she needed additional household help.

"I think we should get an au pair," she told her husband, Mark. They were lying in the antique king-size bed that had belonged to her parents. Kate had waited patiently until he had finished watching a TV sports wrap-up.

"A what?"

"An au pair girl," Kate repeated, "Pay attention, Mark. You're the one who gave me the idea. Don't you remember? You mentioned a few times that one of your patients keeps raving about her au pair and how great she is with her kids."

He looked puzzled. "Oh, yeah. Mrs. Brockner with the colitis and the mustache. So you want to get an au pair?"

"I've been giving it a lot of thought. It's French, by the way. I looked it up; it means 'in exchange.'"

"In exchange for what?—or shouldn't I ask?" His hazel eyes crinkled with laughter.

"Be serious." She smiled and ran her fingers lightly through the dark brown hair, always a little too long, that curled at the nape of his neck.

She loved his instant good humor. It was one of the first things that had attracted her to him, that had drawn her out of the shell of her misery after Evan's fatal car accident two and a half years ago had transformed her, with brutal suddenness, into a twenty-nine-year-old widow with a bewildered four-year-old boy and an infant daughter whose very existence and dependence had magnified her fear and loneliness. But Mark had changed all that.

"Okay, I'm serious. You want to hire a European girl to live with us and help with the kids. But I thought you didn't like the idea of having a stranger living in the house."

"I don't. But with the shop keeping me so busy, I have to consider it. And I'm not being fair to Laney. She hasn't complained, but she can't be thrilled."

Laney had been staying at the shop every weekday until five-thirty with a part-time saleswoman; a car pool took her children home from school (Laney did the morning shift), and she felt comfortable leaving Ned and Kimberley, her two younger ones, with her twelve-year-old daughter Abigail.

Kate's schedule was more complicated. She had been leaving the shop at eleven o'clock to take Dana home from play group, and again at a quarter till three to pick up Jeremy from school; she didn't like the idea of having someone else take either of her children home on a steady basis. Her original plan to return to the shop every day after she settled Jeremy at home with a snack and checked on Dana had never materialized.

"I don't understand the problem," Mark said. "I thought Louisa agreed to stay until six every day and to come in on the alternate Saturdays that you go to the shop."

"Didn't I tell you? Her husband said no more Saturdays. But that's not the main problem. Mark, the woman barely understands English! I'm nervous about leaving the kids with her for long periods of time. What if there's an emergency? I'm not sure she'd know how to handle it. The way things are, Laney probably thinks I spend more time on the phone than with the customers."

"Okay, so you need more help. Why don't we contact an agency and get a live-in maid who *does* speak English?"

"I don't know, Mark. Somehow, I like the idea of an au pair. They're more educated, for one thing. And most of them speak English. Sybil Blackwood says her au pair speaks English better than she does. She was telling me about her at the gym last week. Sybil's very pleased. Her kids love her."

"Must be pretty classy if Sybil has one, huh? So what would you do, get rid of Louisa?"

"Of course not. Au pairs do only light housekeeping, if at all. But I want someone responsible to take care of Dana—and Jeremy, too, when he's home from school."

"I don't know, Kate; maybe the shop wasn't a good idea. Maybe you should sell your half if it's so complicated."

"No! I won't do that!"

"Come on, Kate. Don't bite my head off."

"I'm sorry. I didn't mean to get so excited. But you know how much the shop means to me, Mark. I really think it's going to be a success. And Dr. Zuroff says it's important for me to get out of the house and do something I enjoy. You thought so, too."

"I know that. And I want you to be happy. But the whole idea of starting the business was to take your mind off things, not give you something else to worry about. It's not as though we need the money."

"I'm *not* worrying about it. I just want to find a solution to the afternoons, and I think an au pair is it."

"What if she doesn't work out? What do we do, just ship her back air freight—'Return to Sender'?"

13

"That won't happen. I'm going to check very carefully before I hire anyone. References, background—everything. And by the way, Mark, I intend to pay all her expenses myself. Don't try to argue about it."

"Why should I argue? You can afford it a hell of a lot more than I can. My ego is strong enough to take it." He laughed. "So how do you go about getting an au pair?"

"Sybil advertised in a few local papers in some small towns in Austria. That's where she finally got hers."

"Austria? As long as we're going European, I was thinking more along the lines of a tall Scandinavian with blonde hair, long, long legs, and big, firm breasts—" He traced an imaginary silhouette with his hands.

"Forget it." She laughed, punching him lightly in the shoulder. "We're looking for a girl to watch the kids, not a playmate for their thirty-five-year-old daddy."

It took Kate several weeks to make preliminary inquiries. She received answers from several young women, all between the ages of eighteen and twenty-two, from Austria and from Switzerland—Mark had asked the mustachioed Mrs. Brockner for the name and address of the newspaper in Geneva through which she had found her au pair. Kate studied their résumés carefully and contacted the references they gave her. Some she eliminated on instinct, others because they had little or no experience with children. Finally, with Mark's help, she made her selection: Janine Panetierre.

Janine was twenty years old, a secretary for a pharmaceutical firm in Geneva, with wonderful references and extensive child-care experience. Orphaned when she was ten, she had lived with her mother's younger sister and her husband in Chatel St. Denis, a small town near Lausanne, Switzerland, and had helped care for their three boys and the four infant girls who had arrived during the next eight years.

After graduating from a Catholic girls' high school, Janine had gone to Geneva to take a secretarial course and had moved in with a family named Gauthier, who had offered Janine a reduced boarding fee in exchange for her part-time help with their three children.

The arrangement had been satisfactory; Janine had sent Kate a highly favorable recommendation from Mme. Gauthier. But when, two years later, one of Janine's friends had secured a position as an au pair with a family in New York, Janine had been fascinated with the idea of living in America, even for a short while. After careful contemplation, she had taken a course in conversational English (she had done well in her high school English classes; everyone had always told her that she had a flair for languages) and had pursued leads in the local newspapers.

She had explained all this in a charmingly phrased letter full of quaint near-translations that made Kate smile.

"Do not to worry," the girl had written in a neat, rounded, schoolgirl script. "I will not get sick-to-home; I am used to being on my own."

She was obviously well qualified, but it was more than that. There was something about the earnest expression on the sepia-toned graduation photo the girl had enclosed with her letter that had immediately appealed to Kate. Mark had been impressed, too.

("I know what you're thinking," Kate told Dr. Zuroff in one of their sessions, "that I chose her because I'm identifying with her, because she's an orphan, like me."

"Is that what you think you're doing?" the older woman asked.

"Maybe. Probably. Is there anything wrong with that?"

"Not necessarily. Especially if you're aware of your

15

feelings. But you've suffered several traumatic losses during the past few years, Kate—first your father, then Evan, and just recently your mother. That makes you rather vulnerable, I should think. I wouldn't want you to create an emotional attachment that may be one-sided."

"I'll be careful.")

In addition to room and board, Kate had agreed to give Janine a weekly stipend of one hundred dollars. Sybil had disapproved, insisting that seventy-five dollars was more than ample, but Kate had remained firm. The au pair would be off every Sunday and two weekday evenings.

Sybil had warned Kate to make sure that the au pair girl obtained a tourist's visa; technically, Sybil had explained, it was illegal for her to work here, but going through formal immigration channels was a difficult and lengthy process.

"If you go that route," Sybil had argued, "by the time the girl gets here, Dana and Jeremy will be in college."

At first, the thought of bringing someone into the country illegally had made Kate a little nervous, but then Laney had reminded her that Louisa was just as illegal.

"El Salvador just seems closer to home," she had reassured Kate. "Stop worrying."

Kate had agreed to pay for half of Janine's airline ticket. Privately, she had decided that if she and the children liked Janine, she would reimburse her for the other half as well; she hadn't dared tell Sybil that. She had mailed her a personal check and waited anxiously until Janine sent her the flight information. She would be arriving in Los Angeles on Wednesday, March 16, on TWA's Flight 122.

Waiting always made Kate nervous.

She sat on a vinyl bench in the passenger lounge and checked her appearance in a pocket-size mirror. She was

16

still surprised whenever she saw her hair; the body perm, and the abundant blonde highlights her hairdresser had added at Mark's suggestion, were only a week old. The new me, she thought, and decided again that she liked it. It made her look softer, less anxious. She smiled into the mirror and noticed that her lipstick was gone; she had unconsciously chewed it off in the car. She applied a new coat.

Kate was about to check her watch again when she sensed some movement in the corridor that led from the aircraft. Sure enough, the queue of arriving passengers, its pace a little sluggish, had started its uneven procession. Some travelers, exhausted but smiling, detoured into the welcoming arms of waiting relatives or friends; a few with extra reserves of energy even tossed squealing toddlers into the air and rummaged immediately through hand luggage to find the all-important toy souvenirs. Others headed past the lounge toward the baggage-claim area. Kate stood up, smoothed her camel wool skirt and sweater, and scanned the first group of passengers carefully, but she didn't recognize anyone.

A minute later, though, she spotted her: she was a little taller than Kate had expected, but she looked exactly the same as she had in her graduation picture. She had a sweet, almost heart-shaped face and clear, light skin. Her dark blonde hair was smoothed into a long, sleek braid that hung against the back of her simple brown shirtwaist dress.

The girl was looking around the lounge uncertainly. Kate hurried over to her, a smile on her face.

"Janine? I'm Katherine Bauers. Kate. Welcome to Los Angeles—I guess I should say to America."

Blue eyes peered seriously from behind plain, silver-toned metal frames. A shy smile. "Hallo." A navy blue wool coat was draped over her right arm; she switched it to her left one, took Kate's extended hand, and shook it

17

warmly. "I hope it is not long that you are waiting, Madame Bauers. The plane, it is taking a long time to come down."

"Not long at all." She noticed the large vinyl satchel that the girl was carrying. "You must be tired. Let me take your bag and we'll go get the rest of your luggage." Kate spoke slowly, careful to enunciate each word.

"*Non, non.* It is not heavy, Madame." She shifted the wide brown straps more firmly onto her shoulder.

"You're sure? Okay, then; let's go. It's a good thing you went through customs in New York; this way, we can get out of here much quicker. You must be very tired."

"A little. It is a long trip from Geneva. But I am happy to be here," she added quickly, and smiled again.

Miraculously, there was no congestion around the baggage-claim area, and Janine's tan valise was among the first pieces to come hurtling down the chute. The girl quickly hoisted it off the carousel, deposited it near Kate and the waiting satchel, and indicated that she was ready to leave.

"That's it?" Kate asked. Since Janine would be staying for a year, Kate had expected her to come with a minimum of several suitcases. She had even worried about how to arrange them in the smallish trunk of her Mercedes station wagon.

"Yes. Many of my things I have left in Geneva," she said quietly. "I did not think they would be good in California."

Great! Now I've made her self-conscious; that's probably all she has. Nice going, Katherine! "You're absolutely right, Janine. The weather here is so different. And you can buy what you need once you've settled in."

"Oh, it is no problem, Madame. I can manage for a while." A hint of pink had crept into her pale cheeks.

And a hundred dollars a week won't exactly give you carte blanche at Saks, will it? "I'm sure you can," Kate

18

told her firmly, resolving to think next time before she spoke.

Once in the car and out of LAX, the girl seemed avidly interested in everything around her. Kate dutifully pointed out all the sights they were passing: the grasshopper-like oil pumps pecking rhythmically at the earth in the Baldwin Hills; the few remaining elegant eateries along La Cienega, testimonies in elaborate stucco construction to the winding boulevard's former fame as Restaurant Row; the Beverly Center, a huge, dark taupe behemoth that occupied an entire city block.

"It has department stores and shops and theaters, and a wonderful produce market—for fruits and vegetables," Kate explained. "I think you'll enjoy seeing it."

They passed the white, sprawling CBS building on Beverly Boulevard, sitting unperturbed on a wide expanse of newly misted, plush, emerald green lawn, primly isolated from the ethnic traffic, just a street away, of neighborhood pedestrians who milled among fruit stalls, bakeries, shoe-repair shops, "bargain" stores, and independent grocery markets.

"Sometimes, you can get free tickets to the shows there," Kate said. "It's fun. My sister Barbara and I used to do it often during the summer when we were kids."

Five minutes later, Kate pulled into the driveway of the spacious, two-story house on South Las Palmas.

"Well, here we are." She looked at Janine, noticed the awed expression on her face, saw the house as she must have been seeing it.

"It was my parents' home," Kate told her as they were getting out of the car. "We moved in after my mother died." Now why did I do that? she thought. Why do I constantly feel the need to apologize?

"It is beautiful," Janine murmured.

Kate insisted on taking the valise, and with Janine

19

following, she headed up the driveway to a side entrance and opened the door with a key. "My housekeeper—her name is Louisa, by the way—is here, but I don't want to ring the bell. Dana's probably napping, and I'd like to help you get settled before she gets up."

"Oh, but I am so looking forward to meeting her. And your son."

"Well, they're dying to meet you, too, Janine! And Jeremy should be home soon from school. A neighbor is bringing him. But believe me, once Dana sees you, we won't get much done." She laughed knowingly.

Passing through a service porch to a door that led into a wide hall, Kate ushered Janine to a room on the right, opened the door, and stepped aside.

"This is your room, Janine. I hope you—"

"Mommy?"

The voice, thin and high, was accompanied by a pudgy little girl with wispy blonde hair who padded barefoot on the bleached hardwood floor. Her face—rosy, still creased from sleep—was nestled against a nubby pink blanket with a frayed satin edging that she held, bunched up, in her left hand. With her right fist, she was rubbing her eye in a slow, circular motion.

Kate walked toward her quickly, swooped her up into her arms, and nuzzled her neck. Just then, a car horn honked a greeting and the doorbell rang insistently.

"Excuse me a minute," she said to Janine.

Hitching her daughter onto her hip, Kate hurried to the side door and returned a moment later with a tow-headed, freckle-faced boy carrying a blue nylon backpack and a Sesame Street lunchbox. The little girl's right thumb was anchored in her mouth.

"Janine," said Kate, "this is Dana and Jeremy. Kids, this is Janine."

He stared at Janine unabashedly. "Is she the opera girl?"

20

"The *au pair* girl," Kate corrected as discreetly as she could, making a mental note to tell Jeremy to avoid using that label. Not that it was offensive, but still . . .

She heard the side door open and Mark's cheerful hello.

"In the hall," Kate called.

A moment later he joined them.

"I am so very honored, Dr. Bauers," the girl said softly. "Janine Panetierre." She extended her hand.

"I don't know about 'honored.'" He laughed uncomfortably, shook her hand, and released it quickly. "Well, you're finally here."

"Welcome to the family, Janine," Kate said. "We're so happy you've come, aren't we, Mark?" She was a little embarrassed by the way he was staring at the girl's waiflike appearance.

"What?" He sounded startled. "Oh, yeah. Definitely. Really happy. It'll be great."

Chapter Three

"So how's the opera girl working out?" Laney asked the following Monday morning. Kate had told her about Jeremy's misnomer, and somehow the term had stuck.

It was early and no customers were in the shop. Kate was cleaning and polishing the crystal, silver, and porcelain giftware; she enjoyed lavishing attention on the objects that she and Laney selected with such care. Laney was sitting at the small, almond-colored, lacquered desk near the front of the store, entering into the inventory ledger all the items sold during the previous day.

"Great!" She returned a crystal bowl to the glass-and-brass baker's rack, picked up a vase, and examined it for spots. "Dana liked her immediately, and Jeremy's warming up to her, too. She played handball with him a few times, and that seemed to impress him."

"Men are such pushovers!" Laney entered some more figures in her books. "What about Mark? How does he like her?"

"He's still noncommittal. Actually, he's more or less uninterested. 'As long as you're happy, I'm happy'—that kind of thing. He thinks she looks like a nun."

"Does she?"

"Well, she does look plain, and her glasses make her look serious. Severe, almost. She doesn't wear any make-up."

"I wish I could say the same for Abby."

"Abby? You're kidding! She's only twelve!"

"Don't let her hear you say that. According to her, that means she's in her thirteenth year and almost a mature woman. I caught her sneaking out of the house a couple of days ago with some purple eyeshadow and this godawful coral lipstick hidden in her bookbag. Maybe I should bring her over to your house and let your Swiss miss influence her."

"You could try." Kate smiled. Both women knew that Abigail Tolbert had inherited more than a little of her mother's independence and stubbornness.

"Not a drop, huh? Not even lip gloss?"

"Not as far as I can see. I guess it's because Janine was brought up in such a strict environment. Her aunt and all her family are Catholic, you know. And she always attended Catholic private schools."

"So what does she wear, a uniform?"

"Almost. Her clothes *are* kind of dowdy."

During the past week, Janine had worn a shapeless gray flannel dress as plain as the brown one in which she had arrived and a navy blue pleated skirt with a succession of somewhat pilled turtleneck sweaters in drab colors. Her shoes were sensible black flats. Kate was sure there were other dresses and skirts, other shoes, but somehow she doubted that any of them looked any better.

"But she has great skin and good cheekbones," Kate continued, "and she'd probably look better if she didn't wear her hair pulled back in a braid. She's not unattractive; she just doesn't do anything to make herself look pretty."

"Be happy! At least you don't have to worry about

23

Mark lusting after her."

"Laney!" Kate laughed.

"Just kidding. Everyone knows how much he adores you; considering that you're not newlyweds any more, it's almost indecent."

Mark and Kate had celebrated their first anniversary in September, but Kate still marveled at the way coincidence had brought them together. Mark Bauers had been her mother's internist, and six months after Evan's death, when Kate was still overwhelmed by exhaustion from insomnia and an enervating depression, Claire Simpson had insisted that her daughter make an appointment to see him.

Mark had prescribed daily exercise and a caffeine-free diet; instead of medication, he had offered friendship. Five months later they had admitted to each other that there was nothing casual or platonic about their relationship and were married in a quiet ceremony in the chapel of Kate's church.

Only Kate's immediate family had been present. Mark's elderly parents, Ernest and Sarah, had been unable to come from Minnesota on such short notice, but they had telegraphed congratulations and sent a quaint soup tureen. Kate had worried needlessly about Evan's parents' reaction to her remarrying so soon; Marion and John McCallum had been wonderfully supportive, even insisting on taking care of Jeremy and Dana while Kate and Mark honeymooned for three days in Lake Tahoe.

It meant a great deal to Kate that Laney and Brian had accepted Mark so easily. She knew that it hadn't been easy; Evan's death had been a sharp loss for them, too. He and Brian had been childhood friends, had gone to law school together. And even though their careers had taken them in different directions—Brian became a prosecutor, while Evan made a fortune in private practice and oil drilling syndications—the friendship had remained

24

close, and had expanded to include their wives.

"You have nothing to complain about with Brian," Kate told Laney. "In fifteen years of marriage, he's never given you any reason to be jealous."

"That's because he's a deputy D.A.; he's seen first hand what wives do to husbands who cheat on them! Anyway, I always make sure that all my friends have heavier thighs and kinkier hair than I do. You're the exception."

"You look fine, and you know it."

"I guess," she said grudgingly.

Laney was always complaining about her height, weight, and thick, curly brown hair. She had once jokingly told Kate that she had been attracted to Brian primarily because he was six feet, two inches tall and had absolutely straight hair. Actually, her weight was well distributed along her large frame—she was five feet, nine inches tall—but she yearned to look like the pencil-thin *Vogue* models who looked elegant in contorted positions.

("They're taller than I am, but they're so goddamn skinny! And don't tell me they don't have boobs—I'd trade mine in to look that svelte!")

Her hair was no longer a problem. As a teenager, she had tried different tactics, all with limited success: she had straightened it and ironed it; she had wrapped it nightly, wet, around her head. Later, she had tried wearing it long and pulling it back in a ponytail, but it had fanned out like the feathers of a startled bird. And then perms had become the rage, and Laney had, *au naturel*, what women across the country—including her best friend Kate—were paying sixty dollars every three months to acquire: crimped, frizzy hair. She had cut hers short, washed it every day, and let it dry into unrestricted curliness.

"What about Louisa?" Laney asked. "How's she getting along with Janine?"

"I haven't seen them interact much, but Janine's very polite and low key. I suppose Louisa must have been a little nervous at first, even though I explained that Janine's coming wouldn't affect her job in any way. But she's probably happy she doesn't have to take care of the kids; that leaves her more time to take care of the house."

"Imagine that! More time to clean the house. How exciting for her!" She grinned mischievously.

"No, really; you know what I mean."

"How do they communicate? Does Janine speak Spanish?"

"No, but she's quick with languages, and I left her a Spanish-English dictionary and a list of words I usually use."

"But who's in charge when you're gone—Janine or Louisa?"

"No one. Not really. I haven't given that any thought." She sounded a little unsure. "Why, do you think it's a problem?"

"Not necessarily. Unless the opera girl turns out to be a prima donna!"

"No way, Laney. Janine is very unassuming. And shy. But there's something very real about her. I don't know how to explain it."

"You really like her, don't you?"

"Yes, I do. She's trying so hard to please us. And I feel very secure leaving the kids with her. She's terribly conscientious. She must have asked me a hundred questions about their schedules, what they like and dislike—and that was the first night she got here! What with the time difference and having been on an airplane for all those hours, she must have been exhausted, poor thing. And the next morning, she made sure to be up early to see how I prepare Dana's cereal and what I make the kids for lunch."

"Well, I have to admit it's nice having you here full

26

time. Mrs. Margolin's okay with the customers, but she gets on my nerves after a while. And she has no sense of humor."

"It seems to be working out," Kate agreed.

On Wednesday, Kate had taken Janine along to pick up Dana from her play group. On Thursday and Friday, Janine had walked the six blocks to the play group and taken Dana home in the stroller she had brought with her. Kate still had to drive Jeremy home, since the private school he attended was more than two miles from the house, but she felt no qualms about returning to the shop—she had called home only four times the first afternoon, and twice the second.

"So how does she like the house?" Laney asked. "Her eyes must have popped out, huh?"

"Sort of," Kate admitted, a little uncomfortable.

She was invariably uncomfortable about her house. Her parents' house, really. She and Mark had moved into it less than a year ago after her mother, a widow of five years, had died. Before her death, Claire Simpson had made her intentions clear.

"I don't plan to die for quite some time," she had told Kate. "But when the times comes, I don't want you to sell this house. I want you and Mark and the children to live in it, enjoy it. Your father worked very hard to earn the money to buy it and make it beautiful, and he'd hate the idea of strangers living in it. Frankly, so would I."

"What about Barbara?"

"Barbara certainly doesn't need it. She may be two years your senior, but she obviously hasn't settled down yet, and I don't see any signs of her marrying again and starting a family in the near future. You're not to worry about that, Katherine. Believe me, I intend to be fair. Barbara will have nothing to complain about."

The "time," tragically, had come prematurely, though not without warning. Claire, only fifty-three years old, had been under a cardiologist's care when she suffered a major heart attack and died en route to the hospital. At first Kate had violently resisted the idea of moving into her parents' home. But Mark, and then Laney, had gently argued with her, reminding her of her mother's wishes, wishes that had been formally stated in her will. Even Barbara had agreed.

"Don't be an ass," she had said with characteristic bluntness. "Mom left it to you, so why the hell shouldn't you live in it? You're not going to get any points for being a martyr, Katherine."

Finally, Kate had yielded, and although it had taken her time to dismiss the elusive ghosts that tenanted the rooms, in the end, she was happy she had allowed herself to be persuaded. But she still felt uncomfortable, not because of its memories, but because of its size.

Even in a neighborhood renowned for the grand dimensions of its homes, the lot was oversized. The almost-Olympic-size swimming pool and the hot tub occupied only a small part of the backyard, leaving ample room for the beautiful, well-tended formal gardens, a gazebo, a two-bedroom guesthouse, and a large cultivated plot, discreetly hidden from view, where Claire Simpson had enjoyed growing a variety of vegetables and herbs.

The house itself had two stories. There were enormous formal living and dining rooms on either side of a wide, marbled entry hall; a modern kitchen and connecting breakfast room that faced the pool; a custom-paneled library, family room, guest bedroom with adjoining bath, an office, maid's quarters, and a beautifully appointed powder room.

Upstairs, there were six spacious bedrooms—each with a separate bath, dressing room, and balcony—and a small den. The master bedroom had an adjoining sitting room with a fireplace. Mark had added a mini refrigerator-freezer that sat camouflaged behind the carved doors of a French cabinet.

Laney had been genuinely delighted for Kate's good fortune, but she hadn't been able to resist teasing her about her "mansion."

"If you're looking for a full-time maid, I'll take the job," she had told Kate the first time she had seen the house. "Your maid's room is bigger than my bedroom, for God's sake! I can always see Brian and the kids on my day off; I'm sure they'll understand. As a matter of fact, Brian won't mind a bit. He's always complaining that I take up all the closet space, and the kids'll get to eat all the junk cereals he always lets them buy."

Laney was by no means poor. She lived in a lovely Spanish two-story home with four bedrooms and a family room, but even though Formosa Avenue was only nine blocks away from Las Palmas Avenue, it was leagues removed from the luxury and wealth and status of Kate's Hancock Park address.

"Anyway," Kate said thoughtfully, "Janine seems happy. I think she's a little homesick, but she's trying to hide it."

"So everything's perfect, huh?"

"Just about. Well, there is one little problem. I'm not sure what she should call me. 'Mrs. Bauers' sounds so formal. I asked her to call me Kate, but she seemed uncomfortable with that."

"What does she call you?"

"'Madam Kate.' I guess she heard Louisa call me Señora Kate and figured it's the French equivalent."

"Madam Kate, huh?" Laney grinned.

"I know. Even with her accent, it makes me sound like a brothel owner."

"You could make more money at that in a week than we grossed in the last month. In the last two months, probably."

"Laney!"

29

"It's just a thought—Madam Kate."

Kate was still chuckling at six o'clock when she drew up in front of her house. Mark's BMW was already in the driveway, and behind it, usurping her place, was her sister's green Jaguar. Kate parked on the street and hurried into the house.

"Where is everybody?" she called.

Janine materialized immediately. "Hallo, Madame Kate. Did you have a fine day?"

"Yes, thanks." She took off her leather jacket and hung it up in the hall closet. "Where are the kids?"

"Jeremy, he is putting on his pajamas after his bath. He tells me he would like his privacy. Dana is in the television room. She, too, is bathed. I am reading her a story, the one with Lyle, the crocodile. She knows all the words."

"I know." Kate smiled. "She loves that book. Is my husband around?"

"In his office. And your sister, she is here. She is upstairs."

"Thanks." She found Dana in the family room, ensconced on the couch, the book lying open on her miniature lap. Her thumb was in her mouth. "How's Mommy's best girl?" Kate asked, bending down to kiss the top of Dana's head.

The little girl jumped up, slipped her arms around Kate's neck, and planted a noisy kiss on her cheek. "Hi, Mommy." She looked at the book that had toppled to the floor.

Kate bent down and retrieved it for her. "I'm going upstairs to say hi to Jeremy. Janine can finish reading the story to you. Okay?"

"'Kay."

Upstairs, Jeremy was playing with a Lego castle set that

Mark and Kate had bought him for Christmas. She kissed him and tickled him through his Spider Man pajamas, but he seemed anxious to get back to moats and knights.

"Where's Aunt Barbara?" she asked.

"Dunno."

"Dinner in about a half-hour, okay?"

"What?"

"Never mind." She left his bedroom and made her way down the hall. "Barbara?"

"In here." The voice came from Kate's bedroom.

Barbara was standing in Kate's almost-room-size walk-in closet, flipping with expert fingers through Kate's dresses. She didn't turn around when Kate entered.

"Looking for something?" Kate asked. She tried to keep her annoyance from showing.

"A simple black dress. Simon and I are having dinner with these old geezers, real conservative types. We have to make a good impression. Boring, but what can you do? We need their money."

Simon Leicester, Barbara's latest boyfriend, was a British expatriate of five years and a self-proclaimed artist who had recently abandoned his own promising career and hoped to open a gallery on La Brea Avenue. Kate had never seen any of his work and could only take the word of a smitten and hardly objective Barbara that he was "Fabulous, absolutely fabulous. Ahead of his time."

Barbara had met him several months ago at an art show in Laguna Beach. She had been so taken with the blond, slightly balding though long-haired, thirty-nine-year-old ex-Briton's amazing depth of knowledge that she had unceremoniously dumped her escort and ended the evening in Simon's somewhat rickety twin bed.

A week later, he had moved into her Century City condominium. His apartment was a tiny one-room affair in West Hollywood; he could never impose those conditions on her, he had told her. Ever since then, Barbara's conversations revolved almost entirely around Simon. It was always "Simon says this" or "Simon says that."

"Barbara has her own 'Simon says' game," Mark had commented to Kate one night; it had become their own comic password and the source of a great deal of private laughter.

Barbara had supplemented Simon's somewhat meager artist's wardrobe and introduced him first to a good hair stylist and manicurist and then to some prospective investors who might be interested in financing his gallery.

"Artists can look scruffy and poverty-stricken and walk around in torn jeans looking full of *angst*," she had told him. "Businessmen can't afford to. They have to look dependable and bankable. And they all use deodorant."

Barbara had already committed a large sum to the venture—she had every confidence in him—but Simon needed two hundred thousand dollars before he could open the doors. They had even sent out subtle feelers towards the Bauers. Over Irish coffee in a café on Melrose Avenue, Simon had carefully explained to Kate and Mark that, although he hated the commercialization of art, he felt it was his duty to battle the philistine element in the States and, in particular, in Los Angeles, which was "drowning in the swamp of Hollywood's superficiality." His gallery would do this by helping real artists express themselves, while simultaneously educating the public.

Kate had gently but firmly declined to participate.

Mark had paid for the coffee.

"I think I've found something," Barbara said, pulling out a simple black wool crepe dress. She slipped out of her jeans and her rhinestone-studded sweater, put on the

32

dress, and modeled it in front of the full-size mirror in the closet. "Christ, do you really wear this thing? It's awful!"

"Thanks. I'm not forcing you to borrow it, you know."

"Oh, come on, don't be so damn sensitive! No, it's perfect. I don't want to get these people nervous, if you know what I mean. A little cleavage might send the old man into cardiac arrest. If his wife doesn't kill him first for looking. Anyway, it fits."

The sisters were slim and almost the same size. At five feet, seven inches, Barbara was a little taller and bustier; Kate's angles were more softened by the last five pounds of her pregnancy that she had never been able to lose.

Barbara wiggled out of the dress, hung it up haphazardly on the hanger, and stood musing in her French underwear. "I guess I should probably buy something like this in case I need it in an emergency, huh?"

"Like castor oil," Kate muttered under her breath.

"What?"

"Nothing."

From the time that they were teen-agers, Barbara had helped herself, without asking and without the hint of a thank-you, to underwear or panty hose (always her newest pair) or shoes or sweaters or purses from Kate's closet and drawers. Sometimes she criticized them as boring or outdated, but she took them, and rarely returned them. And if she did return them, they needed either mending or cleaning, or both.

Several months ago, Kate had complained about an expensive, oyster white, angora sweater from Neiman Marcus that Barbara had returned with a conspicuous cigarette burn in the sleeve.

"Christ, Kate, it's just a *thing!* I can't believe you're getting so upset about a stupid sweater. You could take anything I own and never return it and I wouldn't care."

33

Kate knew that was true, and just because she hardly borrowed anything from Barbara—and on the rare occasion that she did, she made sure to return it immediately in perfect condition—it seemed beside the point. Kate had felt foolish and petty and terribly small and somehow not entitled to be angry. And that was before United Parcel had delivered three angora sweaters from Neiman's.

Since then, she had decided to keep silent. She couldn't even complain to Mark. He wanted her to tell Barbara in no uncertain terms that she couldn't borrow Kate's things. But how could she do that? She was her sister. And in a way she wished that she could be like Barbara, more casual about her possessions, about life.

"Did you see Mark?" Kate asked.

"No. He hid in his office the minute he heard me come in. I played with the kids a while. Jeremy beat me at hand wrestling, and Dana showed me her latest finger painting masterpiece. I think even Simon would be impressed." She grinned. "God, they're more delicious every time I see them, Kate! They look more and more like Evan, don't you think? Those blue eyes!" She sighed. "How is it that they didn't get brown eyes? I thought brown is dominant."

Barbara's eyes were also brown, but today cosmetic contact lenses had made them a startling blue. She also had pairs in green and violet.

"Lucky, I guess. You should come by more often and spend time with them."

"I know; you're right. Oh, yeah, I met your au pair. Kind of frumpy, isn't she?"

"She's sweet," Kate said defensively. "I wasn't looking for glamour, you know. I need someone good with the kids."

"Well, if you want my opinion, she looks a little intense to me. Like a Salvation Army recruiter, know what I mean?"

"No, I don't know what you mean. And in any case, that's not important. We're all very pleased with her."

"Mark, too? I doubt it, Katherine. I'll bet he was kind of disappointed when she showed up looking like Little Orphan Annie on your doorstep, huh?"

"It doesn't matter to him one way or the other, Barbara."

"I'll bet." Dressed, her cognac suede boots pulled over her jean bottoms, she went into Kate's bathroom, found the lipstick she wanted, then tousled her thick, layered, mahogany red hair. Last month it had been more carroty; the year before, platinum blonde.

"I'm going downstairs," Kate told her. "I have to get supper ready." Without a backward glance, she left the room.

She was angry with Barbara and her tedious insinuations about Mark, but that was one more thing that Kate didn't want to make an issue of. Of course, only this morning Laney had teased Kate in much the same way— what had she said again? Something about Mark lusting after the au pair? And that hadn't bothered her one bit. Now why was that?

She found him sitting at his oversized desk, poring over a file. She went over, wrapped her arms around him, and kissed his neck. He swiveled around in his chair, grabbed her, and pulled her onto his lap.

"I didn't even hear you come in," he told her.

"I just came home a few minutes ago. I was upstairs talking to Barbara."

He grimaced.

"She claims you hid from her."

"That's silly. I was in my office when she got here. I called out a friendly hello."

"Okay. I guess she'll be staying for dinner." Kate had taken out some lamb chops before she left for work,

35

enough for Mark, Janine, the kids, and herself. But she had a microwave, and if Barbara invited herself to dinner (and what, after all, was the big deal if she did?), she could quickly defrost another few chops.

"Fine."

"Is it?"

"I said it's fine, didn't I?" He sounded a little annoyed. "Don't push it."

"Okay." She slipped off his lap. "About twenty minutes, I think."

"Great." He went back to his papers.

By now, she should have been used to the friction between her husband and her older sister. In fairness to Mark, he was always congenial to Barbara, always tried to make her feel welcome. Barbara, for some reason, seemed to enjoy needling him whenever she could, and constantly criticized him to Kate.

("He has a bump on his nose," she had told Kate the night Kate announced she was marrying him.

"So?"

"So maybe your kids will have bumps on their noses."

"I'll take the risk. I think he's very handsome. And I'm not marrying him just for his looks, you know."

"Have you considered the possibility that he's marrying you for your money? I mean, between your share of Daddy's estate and one or two million Evan left you, you're not exactly a poor, struggling widow."

"That's idiotic! Mark has a successful medical practice. He doesn't need my money. And I think it's disgusting and mean of you to suggest it!"

"Well, just don't say I didn't warn you."

"Shut up, Barbara, will you?")

In calmer moments, it was clear to Kate that Barbara was lashing out because her own life was less than fulfilling—two failed marriages and nothing to show for either one. At those times Kate ached for her, longed to recapture the easy closeness they had shared, to penetrate the brittle shell she had erected around herself. But she resented the tension that Barbara created whenever Mark was present, and she found it difficult to excuse, again and again, behavior that was, after all, inexcusable.

Barbara decided not to stay for supper ("Lamb chops! Ugh! You know I hate lamb chops!"). She played a few minutes with Dana, nibbled cucumber and carrot slices from the salad that Kate was preparing, and was about to leave.

"Don't forget the dress," Kate reminded her quietly, happy that Mark was still in his office, out of earshot. "Put a plastic bag around it, okay?"

"Right!" A minute later she was back with the dress (no plastic bag) slung over her arm. "See ya."

One of the best things about having an au pair, Kate decided that night as she was slipping into bed next to Mark, was having someone to clear and rinse the supper dishes and put them in the dishwasher. Kate hadn't known what to expect—Sybil's girl helped out in the kitchen, but then, Sybil was pretty assertive—but she needn't have worried. From her second night with the Bauers, Janine had insisted on taking over that chore. That released Kate to spend time with her children—"quality time," educators and psychologists called it; in any case, she really enjoyed it.

"What did Barbara want?" Mark asked.

"Nothing. Just chatting. She and Simon are going out to dinner with some prospective investors."

"Did she borrow something?"

Kate hesitated. "Yes. It's a dress I hardly ever wear."

"That's good, 'cause you'll probably never see it again."

"Don't start, okay?"

"Okay. How was business today?" Mark asked.

"Fair. I'm hoping sales pick up more for Easter. Laney and I think we're doing okay for such a short time. I mean, we're not breaking even yet, but that's unheard of so early in the game, isn't it?"

"Uh-huh. Just don't worry, okay?"

"No problem. What was that file you were looking at before dinner?"

"Nothing special. Ned's new patient." Ned Korman was Mark's partner. "Ned wanted me to take a look at the case. Seems this guy's been hopping from doctor to doctor with a strange stomach ailment. Ned wants us to solve it."

"Think you will?"

"Everybody knows we're the best."

"Oh, really?" She smiled.

"Don't you agree?"

"I don't know." She moved closer, touched him, felt his immediate response. "Why don't you prove it to me."

"You didn't say the magic words."

She laughed. "Simon says."

Afterward, Mark fell asleep first. Kate got out of bed, put on her nightgown, and walked down the hall.

Dana lay sprawled on top of her comforter. Kate adjusted her sleeping form and kissed her lightly on her forehead. She left the thumb in place. Jeremy was bundled up, tentlike, under his cover. She lifted a corner of his comforter and stole a kiss. When he was awake, all too often he squirmed out of reach.

She was halfway to her room when she remembered that she had told Janine to leave the lights on in the kitchen and family room when she went to sleep. Kate went downstairs, shut the lights, and started walking up the back stairway when she thought she heard sounds from Janine's room.

38

The girl's door was open, and the bedside lamp was on. Janine was kneeling in front of her bed, saying her prayers, her long hair splayed along the back of a flannel nightgown. Kate waited until she had finished.

"Janine?" she said softly from the doorway.

Janine turned around, startled, and rose quickly. "Madame Kate! Is something wrong? The children?"

"Oh, no. Nothing's wrong." Kate walked over to her. "I thought I heard something. Are you all right?"

"No. Really, Madame. I am fine." She averted her eyes.

Even in the half light, Kate could see the redness and slight puffiness around the girl's eyes. "You've been crying, haven't you?" Kate said gently.

She nodded. "It is just that I am thinking about home a little bit, you know. My aunt, and my cousins. It is a long time until I will to see them again. And I was thinking that I am so grown up, too old to be sick-to-home."

"Homesick," Kate corrected. "No one's too old to be homesick, Janine. When I was in college, I was homesick, too. And I was older than you are."

"Really?"

"Really. I promise."

"Well, that makes me feel a little better."

"Good. Promise me that if you feel homesick, or if anything else bothers you, anything at all, you'll tell me about it right away. Will you do that, Janine?"

"Yes. Thank you. You are so kind. How can I repay you, Madame Kate?"

Kate laughed. "That's easy. Just call me Kate." She saw the girl's hesitation. "Please. And think of us as friends, all right?"

"All right." She smiled shyly. "All right, Kate."

Kate hugged her lightly and went upstairs.

*　　　*　　　*

The girl locked the door. She walked into the bathroom off her bedroom and splashed cool water onto her face. Her eyes looked terrible. She found the witch hazel among the toiletries she had placed in the medicine chest and used a cotton ball to daub some onto her eyes.

Back in the bedroom, she slipped out of her flannel nightgown, tossed it aside, and examined herself in the brass-framed mirror hanging over the dresser. Using both hands, she twisted her long, thick hair and pulled it high above her head, chignon-style. She turned to see her profile, then back.

The elevation of her hands accentuated the firm, high thrust of her full breasts and the tininess of her waist. Her nipples were a little larger than she liked, but that was a side effect of the birth control pills, she knew. There was nothing she could do about it.

Suddenly, she released her hair and shook her head swiftly back and forth until her face was framed with dark blonde strands. She ran her tongue slowly across her lips.

She shut the light and lay on top of the down quilt. She closed her eyes, traced the smooth expanse of her neck and chest, stroked her breasts lightly, followed the curves of her body, murmured a name.

Chapter Four

"Simon said the dress was perfect," Barbara told Kate at dinner. Three weeks had passed since the all-important meeting with the elderly couple.

"So how did it go?" Kate asked. "Are they interested in investing in the gallery?"

"Maybe. They didn't commit to anything. Simon says all they need is a little push."

Mark caught Kate's eye and winked.

"What's so funny?" Barbara asked sharply.

"Nothing," Kate said, nudging Mark under the table. "I hope everything works out. By the way, why the suitcase?"

Barbara had called Kate at the shop in the afternoon and invited herself for dinner, and when she had showed up at the house, she had deposited a Louis Vuitton overnighter in the entrance hall.

"Oh, didn't I mention it? There's some stupid problem with the plumbing in my condo, and all the water has to be shut off for a few days. I figured I'd stay in your guest room. Simon's place is really too awful."

"Janine is in the guest room," Kate said. "I can put you in the maid's room." The three spare upstairs bedrooms were completely unfurnished.

41

Barbara glowered. "Can't you move her into the maid's room for a couple of nights?"

"No, I can't. That would be terribly rude. You can stay in the guest house, if you want, but it may be a little musty."

"Oh, forget it. Put me anywhere you like. Where is she, by the way?"

"Putting the kids to bed. She ate with them earlier." Kate had invited Janine to eat later, with the adults, but she had nervously declined.

"Hmmm. So, Mark, how do *you* like Our Lady of Perpetual Dowdiness? Not exactly what you expected, huh?"

"I hadn't really noticed."

"Oh, really? That's surprising." She tasted the vegetable quiche. "This isn't bad," she told Kate.

"Thanks," Kate said dryly.

"So how's your practice coming along, Mark? Killed any patients lately?"

"Only two this week. Things have been slow."

"At least you don't have to worry about paying the mortgage on this place. It's nice to have a wife who's independently wealthy, isn't it?"

"I'm sure that's what Simon must be thinking," he said.

"What the hell do you mean by that?" Barbara asked.

"Mark," Kate said quietly.

"Nothing. What could I possibly mean?"

"Simon is interested in *me,* not my money. Or do you find that impossible to believe?"

"Not at all. I think you're an attractive, unique woman who could give a piranha fish fierce competition." He rose. "Well, I'd love to continue this conversation, but I have to figure out who my next victim is. I'll see you girls later."

"Why did you have to do that?" Kate asked as soon as

42

he had left the room. "Why can't you be civil?"

"Oh, come on, Kate. I just enjoy kidding him. I don't think he really minds."

"Well, I mind." She got up and started to clear the table.

"I thought you told me the girl does that."

"She's not my maid, Barbara. She's here to help with the kids. I don't want to take advantage of her."

"Well, just make sure she doesn't take advantage of *you*. You're not very assertive, Kate. You let people step all over you."

Like you, Kate thought. "By the way, did you bring the dress?"

"It's in my suitcase. The zipper broke. You know, I wish you had told me there was a problem with it. I had a hell of a time getting out of the dress. I don't know what I would have done without Simon's help."

"I'm *so* sorry."

By eleven o'clock the house was quiet. Janine had disappeared into her room; Barbara was unpacking. Kate turned off the television in the family room and walked to Mark's office.

"Coming to bed?" she asked.

"Soon."

"Don't be too long."

"I won't." He grinned.

Walking down the hall to say good night to Barbara, she heard loud music. She knew it wasn't coming from Janine's room—the girl was discreet about everything—and when Kate passed her open door, she found her in bed, reading.

Kate poked her head in. "Should I shut the door? I'm sorry about the music."

"Oh, no. It is all right." She smiled.

"Good night, then."

Barbara was in the tub, smoking, surrounded by hills of iridescent bubbles. Her eyes were closed, and she was humming along with the music emanating from the large transistor radio sitting on the edge of the tub.

Kate walked over, grabbed the radio, placed it on the sink counter, and lowered the volume.

Barbara's eyes flew open. "What exactly do you think you're doing?"

"I've told you a hundred times how dangerous it is to leave anything electrical near the tub! *Mom* told you a hundred times!"

"And I've told *you* a hundred times that I'm careful. Give me the radio, Kate."

"You can hear it just as well from the counter."

"Christ, you are so paranoid! I'm surprised you let your kids eat food without chewing it for them first. They *could* choke."

"Cut it out, Barbara."

"You've been impossible since Mom died. Not everyone's going to die on you, you know. Your shrink was supposed to explain that to you." She sighed. "Oh, hell, never mind; leave it there, if it makes you happy. But raise the volume before you go, will you?"

"The music was too loud. I heard it all the way down the hall, and Janine's room is right next to yours. It's after eleven, Barbara."

"What is this, a dormitory? Or are you worried the au pair won't get her beauty sleep?"

"Lower your voice. Look, I don't want to argue. I just came to see if everything's okay."

"Everything's perfect. So are you having bed check in an hour, or what?" She grinned, then saw Kate's expression. "Loosen up, will you? I'm just joking."

"What's wrong with you tonight?"

"Nothing." She hesitated. "I bumped into Greg

44

yesterday. It's been years since we split up, but it still shook me up a little to see him."

Gregory Podell was Barbara's first husband. She had been a senior in college when she met him in a political science seminar at USC. It had been love at first debate—or so she had been convinced at the time.

"He told me he gave up teaching a year ago and bought a car dealership in the Valley. He's married, has two and a half kids. He showed me a picture of the wife and kiddies standing in front of a cute little ranch house. No picket fence, though."

"Are you sorry you divorced him?"

"No. Greg was nice, but aside from political science and sex, we had nothing in common. And even in that department, he was a little boring. And Daddy was right. I was spoiled and immature, and I couldn't get used to living on a teacher's salary. That's what all our fights were about." She sighed.

"What is it, Barbara? Are you having problems with Simon? Is that why you're upset?"

"Did I say that?" she asked, suddenly irritated.

"No, but I just thought—"

"I don't want to talk about it, Kate, all right?"

"All right." She started to leave.

"Kate."

"What?"

"I'm sorry I'm being such a bitch. I'm just a little on edge, okay?"

"It's okay. Good night."

"And Kate, can you raise the volume a *little* bit?"

As she entered the hall, she heard Janine's door click shut. Obviously, the loud music *had* bothered her. She wondered suddenly whether the girl had heard her argument with Barbara.

When Mark came to bed, Kate told him about her conversation with Barbara.

"Do you think I'm paranoid, Mark?"

"No, I do not. I think you're a perfectly balanced mother who exercises normal caution. Your sister, on the other hand, is courting disaster."

"I hope not. Anyway, let's forget about Barbara."

"Yeah, let's. Maybe we could call the plumbers and slip them a little extra to get the job on her condo done faster."

"Come on, Mark. It won't be so bad."

"It already is."

"Barbara finally left, huh?" Laney asked Kate several days later. The plumbing job had taken longer than expected.

"*Finally* is right. I feel like I just survived a war."

"Are you and Mark still married?"

"Barely." She laughed. "Actually, he stayed late at the office almost every night just to keep out of her way. The kids loved having her around, though. She brought them new toys every day and spent hours playing with them. It's amazing how sweet she is with them, like a totally different person." She paused. "You know, she never gets along with Mark, but this time she was snippier than usual. Tense, too. I think it's because Simon hardly called."

"You think they're having problems?"

"I tried to get her to talk about it. I really think she wanted to confide in me. Once or twice, I thought she was going to open up, but then one of the kids or Mark came into the room, and that was that."

"Well, maybe now that she's back in her condo with Simon, things'll work themselves out." She looked at Kate appraisingly. "New outfit?"

"Uh-huh. To celebrate Barbara's departure. Just joking. Actually, I took Janine shopping last night at the

46

Beverly Center. She asked me for advice on where to go, but I couldn't really see her lugging things home on the bus. We had fun."

"So how did she do?"

"Okay. You know, I never really think much before buying something. But I could see that Janine was worried about getting the best value for her money."

"She should've been able to save up quite a bit, though, during the past month. She doesn't have any expenses, does she?"

"No, but she's been sending most of her pay to her aunt in Switzerland. She told me she wants to repay her a little for all her kindness during the years."

"So she didn't get much stuff, huh?"

Kate hesitated. "Actually, I bought her a few things, too. She really didn't want to let me, but I insisted. I mean, it's so easy for me, and she's been such a help with the kids. And they adore her." She had bought more than "a few things" for Janine but was reluctant to tell Laney just how much she had spent.

"You're just a softie, Katherine Bauers. I guess that's one of the reasons I like you so much. I have just one question."

"What?"

"Can you take me shopping, too? Brian's threatening to take away my charge cards." She laughed.

In the morning, after she returned from escorting Dana to play group, after she modeled her new clothes again in front of the mirror, she derived an almost sensual pleasure from the simple act of rehanging the skirts, blouses, and slacks in the closet, of refolding the sweaters and storing them in the dresser drawers.

She decided to wear the Calvin Klein jeans and a *Guess?* sweater. On Sunday, she would go to the Sanrio shop they

47

had passed last night and buy some trinket for Dana and Jeremy. Kate would be pleased.

"I'm very pleased with your progress," Dr. Zuroff told Kate in her office in early May. "I think we'll be ready to talk about ending our sessions soon. How do you feel about that?"

Two months ago, the idea of terminating therapy would have sent Kate into an emotional tailspin. She had begun seeing the Russian-born psychologist almost a year ago, soon after her mother's fatal heart attack had shattered the delicate equilibrium that Kate had painfully reconstructed after Evan's death.

When Evan had died, Kate had been devastated, but, although she had been overwhelmed by the responsibility of being a single parent, she had been determined to hide her panic, to subordinate her grief to her children's needs. Claire's death had reduced her overnight to a helpless, almost childlike state. Kate had abdicated her role as mother, depending on Mark and Laney and a series of nurses and sitters to tend to the children while she went through days and then weeks in a valium-induced fog.

Ironically, it was Barbara who had mentioned Irene Zuroff.

"My shrink recommended her. Roger's the best, of course, but I don't think it's a great idea for both of us to share him. Anyway, we should spread the Simpson wealth and neuroses, don't you think?"

And when Kate had shrugged off the suggestion, Barbara had been extremely annoyed.

"If Laney or Mark had told you about this Dr. Zuroff, you'd be there already, lying down on the couch. Just because it's my idea, it's no good, right?"

Kate had made the appointment.

To her surprise, she had felt an immediate rapport with the tall, graying, middle-aged doctor, had felt comfortable talking to her in the cozy, country French room, with its bleached oak armoire and chintz-covered sofas, that looked more like a sitting room than an office. Initially, Kate had met with her twice a week, sometimes three times. After six months, the sessions had tapered off to once a week, then to once every other week.

The nightmares had stopped several months ago. The pain no longer had the power to immobilize her, but she supposed it would always be a part of her, ready to strike a sudden, unexpected blow in the guise of a tender memory. She still woke up sometimes in the middle of the night, still leaned over to feel Mark's warm breath on her cheek, still stole out of bed to check on Jeremy and Dana's quiet forms. She still rushed to the pediatrician at the first hint of a cold, and it had taken all her willpower not to take Dana into the Emergency Room at Cedars when the little girl started running a fever of 104 degrees at three o'clock one morning. But she no longer felt that someone was waiting in the shadows, ready to snatch Dana or Jeremy, or Mark, or someone else she loved, if she relaxed her guard.

"I think I'm ready," Kate said slowly. "I mean, I have to admit it's a little unsettling to think that I won't be coming to see you, to share my feelings. And I'm sad that our relationship is ending."

The woman nodded. "It's natural, of course, for you to have some separation anxiety. We have spent quite a few hours together, Kate, in this room. But the important thing is that you realize that you *are* capable of handling your life, that you are *not* helpless. You've made some major decisions during the past six months—starting a business, hiring an au pair—and you made them on your own. I'm proud of you." She smiled.

The truth was that Kate couldn't remember when she

49

had felt so relaxed, so in control. Even Mark had commented that she seemed happier than she had in a long time, and she knew he was pleased that she had joined a health club and had started caring about her appearance again.

The gift shop was humming with activity. Since Kate no longer had to take Dana home from school, or to worry about how both children were faring at home without her, she really enjoyed spending the days with Laney, dealing with the customers (except for a few difficult ones—Laney was better at handling those), ordering new merchandise, displaying it to advantage. Easter sales had been excellent, surpassing both women's expectations, and with the growing number of returning customers, attracted by the shop's friendly atmosphere and its extensive variety of beautiful objects, Kate and Laney felt the heady excitement of imminent success. For the first time since the shop had opened, the books reflected a profit.

At home each day, the minute Kate walked past the side door, she felt enveloped by a harmony that was almost tangible. By six o'clock, Louisa was gone for the day, and all the machines of household efficiency were quiescent. Jeremy and Dana, already bathed, were invariably absorbed in play; the table was set (Janine had carefully watched Kate once and committed the American pattern to memory); and supper was warming in the oven.

For the first three weeks after Janine's arrival, Kate, now putting in full days at the shop, had attempted to do some of the meal preparations early in the morning before she left the house or, sometimes, late the night before. It had been difficult, though, and several times she had stopped on the way home for a pizza or some take-out Chinese food. No one had complained, certainly not the children, but Kate had felt guilty, inadequate. Yet when Janine had volunteered her help, Kate had felt obliged to decline.

"I couldn't possibly let you do that, Janine. I don't want to take advantage of you."

"Oh, but I enjoy cooking. Often I have prepared supper when my Aunt Renee is busy. I will prepare some French recipes that she taught me, if you like. And I would like to learn from your cookbooks, too, if I may."

They had agreed to take turns: gradually, though, except for weekends and special occasions, Kate had gratefully relinquished the kitchen to Janine.

More and more, Kate felt that she had been incredibly lucky to find Janine. The girl was quiet and considerate, often anticipating Kate's needs. With the children she was warm, loving, and wonderfully patient. They probably remind her of the young cousins she had to leave behind in Chatel St. Denis, Kate realized; Janine often talked about them wistfully.

At the dinner table, Dana and Jeremy often reported the day's activities to Kate and Mark—how Janine had delighted them with pantomines and French fairy tales and folk songs, or had taught them a few French words (they were still working on *"Je t'aime, Maman, Papa"*), or had read Dr. Seuss aloud together with Jeremy.

"He is helping me to practice my pronunciation, are you not, *cher* Jeremy?"

So far, Kate had seen her flustered only once, when her glasses broke. Janine hadn't been upset because of the glasses—they were certainly replaceable. But she had been obviously uncomfortable when Jeremy told Kate that Dana had broken them.

"She twisted them to death, Mommy! Truth! Janine made me promise not to tell you, but I didn't say 'Scout's honor' so it doesn't count."

"Where did you get them, Dana?" Kate asked.

"'Neen gimme dem to play."

"Oh, Dana." She sighed, exasperated. "Janine didn't

51

give them to you to play." She turned to the au pair. "I'm so sorry. I guess she went into your room and found them."

"Please, do not be angry. I would feel terrible if you were angry with her." She looked near tears.

Of course, Kate was adamant about paying for a new pair of glasses. But at the optometrist's office, when she saw Janine's eyes linger on the posters advertising contact lenses, she had a better idea. It took a little convincing, and when they returned home, Kate was almost more excited about Janine's new contact lenses than Janine was.

It was Janine, not Kate, who remembered to ask the optometrist for balloons for the children.

Janine was affectionate without being cloying, helpful but never intrusive. She never trespassed on Kate's maternal rites, never tucked the children into bed or read them their bedtime stories or recited their prayers with them. When the Bauers had company, she would immediately disappear after clearing the dinner dishes, and even if there was no company, Kate often had to coax the girl into staying in the family room instead of hurrying to her bedroom on the pretense of writing home. Kate knew she was simply trying to give her some privacy with Mark.

It was simplistic, Kate knew, and probably silly to say that Janine's arrival had provided the answer to all her problems; often, though, that was exactly how she felt. But she never mentioned it to anyone. Mark and Laney would laugh at her; Dr. Zuroff would disapprove.

And there was still Barbara and her constant sniping at Mark. Kate doubted that she would ever stop. Then again, she could think of only a few people who escaped her older sister's caustic tongue—Jeremy and Dana (Kate believed that Barbara loved them unreservedly),

52

and for now, Simon. And who knew how long that would last? Kate had noticed that Janine tried to stay out of Barbara's way as much as possible.

Smart girl.

"I don't like her," Laney announced to her husband.

"Who? Cher?" They were in their bedroom, watching a video starring the singer-actress.

"I didn't mean her, although come to think of it, I don't like her either. She's everything I hate in a woman—tall, thin, and beautiful! No, I mean Kate's au pair."

"She seemed very nice when I met her—when did we have that dinner at Kate's, a month ago?"

"Just about."

"Anyway, I thought you said you liked her."

"I did, sort of. But since then I've seen her a few more times, and she's getting on my nerves."

"Why?"

"I can't put my finger on it. I just get the feeling that there's something fake about her. Kate brought her to the shop a few Saturdays ago, to show her around the place, you know? The girl remembered all our kids names and ages and asked about them."

"So what's wrong with that?"

"Why would she care about our kids, Brian? She never met them, and I remember for a fact that I never discussed them that night at dinner."

"So she's being polite, Laney. Give her a break, will you?"

"Uh-uh. She's trying to impress me or Kate, probably both of us. And that's another thing. I hadn't really planned on being the three musketeers. I'm getting a little tired of having Kate drag Janine along to the health

53

club every time we go."

"The bottom line is, how does she look in a leotard?" He grinned.

"Good. Too damn good, if you want to know the truth. I think Kate was kind of surprised the first time she saw her in it, too. Little Janine is built. Half the guys in the class probably have pulled muscles from straining their necks to see her. And it was Kate's leotard."

"Was?"

"She told Janine to keep it, said it looked better on her."

"You sound annoyed."

"I am. I think Kate's indulging her too much. Two months ago she bought her some clothes; practically every week since then, she picked up something that's 'just perfect for Janine.' Now she's talking about buying a small car and letting Janine use it to pick Jeremy up from school. This way, Kate says, she won't have to leave the shop in the middle of the day, and Janine can take care of the grocery shopping and run some errands while Dana's at play group or napping."

"Makes sense. It's not like Kate can't afford it."

"Maybe. Kate claims this was her idea, but I doubt it."

"You're making a big issue out of this, Laney. It's not your business."

"It *is* my business, Brian. Kate is my best friend."

"Maybe that's what's really bothering you."

"What?"

"Maybe you're upset because you think this girl is coming between you and Kate. You know, horning in."

"That's ridiculous!"

"Think about it. In the meantime, I'm going to watch the movie. It's getting interesting."

"No way! I want to talk about this, Brian. You brought it up."

"Later."

54

She took the VCR controller and shut off the movie. "Aw, shit, Laney!"

The second Saturday morning that Janine had accompanied Kate and her partner to the health club, she had immediately sensed the other woman's pique. She had known from Kate that they were best friends as well as partners, and she had guessed that Laney saw Janine as a threat.

She had been a little surprised by Laney's reaction. Janine had never felt the need for an exclusive friendship with another girl, not even when her fellow classmates were pairing off periodically in elementary school, and later in high school. Oh, she had been approached several times, but she had always politely turned down the offers; after a while, the other girls had stopped asking. And that had suited her fine. She had no desire to confide in anyone else, to exchange girlish giggles and double entendres and whispered recountings of first dates, first embraces. That grown women would need that kind of relationship, would depend on it, puzzled her.

It amused her, too. Because she knew that it would be so easy to insinuate herself into Kate's personal life, if that's what she wanted to do. They were both orphans, and from the beginning, Kate had obviously been uncomfortable treating her like an employee; in a detached way, Janine admired her generosity of spirit, although she couldn't identify with it and saw no use for it in her own life. Janine wasn't sure exactly how Kate viewed her (as a younger sister, perhaps?), but the nuances of beginning friendship were there, waiting to be cultivated.

For now, though, Janine didn't want to upset Laney and possibly precipitate a confrontation. So on the following Saturday morning, when Laney came to pick up Kate on the way to the health club and Kate invited Janine to join them, the au pair declined.

"Thank you, but I must say no. I think I have pulled a muscle in the exercises."

"You're kidding! Why didn't you say something? Do you want Mark to take a look at it?"

"Oh, no. I am sure it will be all right; I will just have to take it easy for a while."

She had almost laughed aloud at the look of relief that had flashed across Laney's face. Really, it was almost pathetic.

Chapter Five

For the first time in her life, Janine had her own room, and she reveled in the luxury of an almost intoxicating privacy, of knowing that the only face she would see upon awaking would be her own, that there would be no sticky fingers touching her clothes; no accidentally spilled lotions, smeared lipsticks, scribbled-on magazines; no acrid smell of wet or soiled diapers, of soured milk curdling in a forgotten bottle hidden under a tangle of dirty clothes.

In Chatel St. Denis, she had shared a small room, cramped bureau drawers, and microscopic closet space, first, with her two youngest male cousins, then with one, two, and finally three girls. Her Aunt Renee was a kind woman, almost always dressed in a housecoat, who tried to be affectionate when she wasn't exhausted from taking care of the house and the children and doing alterations late into the night on other people's clothing to earn a little extra money. Her Uncle Charles was a little more stern, somewhat self-involved, an auto mechanic who liked his quiet and a long daily bath after supper to soak off the stains of his trade.

Both—Renee more than Charles—tried to make her feel welcome, to compensate for her pain of being suddenly orphaned. But with the arrival of each new child, Janine felt more and more like a parasite who was usurping space, food, air. At first, she had been bitterly resentful toward her parents, railing against them silently for having allowed themselves to be killed in a railway accident without providing for her and her younger brother, Claude. When she was older, she pretended to accept her situation, but the bitterness was always there, camouflaged by a brave smile. And when she thought of Claude (she had missed him terribly the first months, the first year; gradually, he had faded from her memory), it was invariably with sharp envy, for he was living with paternal relatives in the north of France who had only two children, both girls.

When her Aunt Renee gave birth to a fourth daughter, Janine was not surprised to be asked, somewhat guiltily, to sleep on the living room sofa. There really was no alternative. And although it was inconvenient having her clothes and possessions in the girls' bedroom, and she felt more than ever like a transient, uninvited guest, she had welcomed the escape from the nocturnal contata of sniffling and whining, of whistling baby-snores, of midnight squalling that had all too often interrupted her sleep.

At the Gauthiers', her accommodations had improved slightly. She had shared a clean, modest-sized downstairs room with the oldest daughter, ten-year-old Mathilde, a pleasant though often annoyingly inquisitive child whose best feature was her willingness to be bribed into keeping Janine's late-night returns a secret from her parents. Still, living with a family was far from ideal, and she had been looking for a roommate to share a small apartment, when everything had changed. Overnight, Kate Bauers's need for an au pair had fortuitously solved all her problems.

Here, at the Bauers's, in a spacious, airy bedroom

with French doors that opened onto the garden and pool, Janine had not one but two full-size beds with padded headboards.

"I think one mattress is firm, the other extra firm, but I'm not sure which is which," Kate had told her. "I asked Louisa to make up both beds, so you can choose whichever one you like. Or switch off, if you want to."

Oh, yes, she wanted to.

Everything in the room whispered of subtle, effortless beauty. There was a handsomely crafted dark mahogany dresser with brass accents and more drawers than Janine could ever hope to fill; a French secretary where a drawer revealed fine linen stationery, an assortment of pens, and a roll of stamps; and a comfortable armchair whose fabric repeated the wallpaper design, a watercolor floral in mauve, mint green, and slate blue. Plush mauve carpeting caressed her bare feet.

The room was fragrant with the musky scent of expensive woods, of lemony polish, of a refined elegance that permeated every corner like an exotic perfume. And although she was still somewhat overwhelmed by the grandeur and vastness of the Bauerses' home, when she was alone in this, her private sphere, she found it easy to relax into a proprietary complacency, to pretend that the room and the furnishings were hers, really hers.

Not Kate Bauers's.

Janine wondered whether Kate realized how lucky she was. She seemed unimpressed by her house, by the wealth that was its silent companion. Or maybe she was being careful not to flaunt her fortune in front of the au pair. Janine had tried to detect condescension in her employer, but she had to admit that Kate was pleasant, genuinely kind, almost audibly ticking with a nervous desire to please, to invite friendship.

And she was a caring, affectionate, almost doting mother. Well, why wouldn't she be? How difficult was it to lavish attention on well-groomed, obedient, picture-pretty children with scrubbed, smiling faces when you had time and money and the confidence born of wealth at your disposal? When you had it all. Including a handsome husband. A doctor.

She wondered what went on in their bedroom. Was making love on crisply ironed designer cotton sheets different? More exciting?

Janine's first sexual experience had been less than spectacular, a hurried encounter in the apartment of her math instructor in her junior year of high school. Hurried because the wife was due back at any moment from work. Unspectacular because the instructor was as passionless and unimaginative in his methodical groping as he was in front of a blackboard illustrating equations and isosceles triangles.

But she had achieved her goal: she had been inducted painlessly into adulthood, and more importantly, she had guaranteed herself a A in math even though she had barely passed her last two tests.

Living with her aunt in Chatel St. Denis had circumscribed Janine's sexual activity but hadn't eliminated it completely. And when she graduated from high school, with honors, and the nun handing out the diplomas dimpled in pleasure and wished Janine well, there were several members of the faculty who were particularly sorry to see her go.

Including the principal.

Once in Geneva, she was intimate with more than a few men, all usually quite a bit older than she. She was always cautious—she may have had difficulties with mathematics, but her grasp of biology was perfect, and she had no intention of being betrayed into pregnancy by carelessness or the excitement of the moment. Of following in her aunt's labored footsteps.

Some men she found intensely attractive, and that was

enough for her, to lose herself in the spiraling intensity of physical pleasure; most offered her a glimpse of a more appealing world: dinner in an exclusive restaurant, tickets to an opening-night theatrical performance, a leather purse, a cashmere sweater, an expensive piece of jewelry. She never allowed them to pick her up from the Gauthiers', always insisted on meeting them elsewhere. It helped her keep her worlds separate, helped sustain what was for now a fantasy.

Someday, though, she would leave the world of boardinghouses and secretarial jobs and her sensible, secretarial wardrobe far behind her. And she would never look back.

In the mornings, Janine rose early with spartan regularity, exercised for twenty minutes, showered, and dressed. She was always careful to braid her thick hair, to resume the identity of the serious, spectacled girl in the high school portrait. Then she dressed Dana, peeled carrots, helped assemble lunches for the two children, coaxed breakfast past unwilling lips. Made herself cheerfully indispensable.

She enjoyed walking Dana to play group, grasping the chubby fingers in her hand, listening to the little girl's lisping chatter. As they strolled past the stately homes set far back on unblemished lawns, she wondered about the people who lived behind the ornate doors, and about the lives they led.

The spring semester was almost over. In August, she would enroll in a few classes. Computers, maybe. She hadn't really given it much thought. In the meantime, she didn't really need her two weekday evenings off, and she hadn't quite planned what to do with her Sundays. It was still too chilly to go to the beach, and museums didn't interest her.

Kate had encouraged her to get out of the house, to explore the city. On her second Sunday, Janine had taken a bus to Hollywood, had walked to the Mann's Theater (formerly Grauman's Chinese), had played the tourist, trying to match her handprints with those of the female celebrities she had watched on the movie screen.

Another evening she had passed by the Hard Rock Café at the Beverly Center. She had told Kate a half-lie, that she was going to see a film in one of the theaters there. The crowd had looked young, exciting, but in the end, she hadn't gone in, not the way she was dressed. Like somebody's maiden aunt. (She had considered carefully before packing for Los Angeles, had decided it would be wiser to leave her more sophisticated outfits locked in a trunk in the Gauthiers' basement.) Maybe, in a week or so, she would go to the Hard Rock again. She had some pretty things now; Kate had been extremely generous.

She smiled, remembering how easy it had been. On their first shopping venture, she had allowed Kate to steer her to the stores she frequented, had tried on two outfits that Kate had pulled from the racks. Then it had simply been a matter of one or two wistful stares, followed by a brave suggestion of finding "some place less expensive."

Of course, if she wanted to, she could buy a few special outfits with her own money. Just last night she had counted the bills she kept in an envelope in the back of a narrow desk drawer. She had over six hundred dollars. She had never sent money to her Aunt Renee, had no intention of sending her anything.

Not even a return address.

Mornings, the house was Janine's. She was Goldilocks in a strange home, and there was no one to stop her from sampling its wonders. Janine loved exploring the

62

different rooms, studying the arrangement of the furniture, opening cabinets, touching the fabrics and the carefully selected bric-a-brac, reclining on the various sofas, absorbing the essence of the house.

There was a large color television in the family room, recessed into the oak-paneled walls, and Janine found it extremely instructive to watch different programs, to listen carefully to the dialogue on the sitcoms, to the often banal exchange between guests and host on talk shows. She hadn't lied about her skill with languages. Her A's in English had been earned legitimately, in the classroom. Within a few weeks, she had mastered intricate pronunciations, grammatical constructions, idiomatic expressions. But she had no intention of permanently erasing her accent. She knew that Americans—especially the male variety—found it charming, sexy.

True, the house wasn't completely empty. Louisa was there. But Janine was able to trace her progress by the sound of her footsteps and the noise of the vacuum. And the housekeeper's routine was fixed. Louisa always went directly upstairs, straightened the bedrooms and baths, laundered the clothes; after lunch, she worked downstairs, beginning with the more formal rooms and ending with the kitchen.

Louisa was a short, thin woman, industrious and obliging, a whirlwind of activity; she was friendly to the children, periodically dispensing hugs and tickles, but Janine guessed that she had welcomed being relieved of the responsibility of caring for them. Louisa had been understandably wary when Janine had first joined the Bauers, but the au pair had taken pains to be pleasant, to avoid even a hint of superiority in her speech or manner, to indicate that she had no intention of interrupting the woman's routine.

But she had not invited friendship, either. For the most part, the two women operated in separate orbits,

63

and although they were often the only adults in the house, they rarely conversed, and never ate lunch together. Some days, after a polite exchange of morning greetings (Janine had easily mastered a few Spanish phrases), they would hardly see each other until five o'clock, when it was time for Louisa to leave.

So at two o'clock on a Tuesday afternoon in late May, after checking on Dana, who was fast alseep, exhausted by an hour's sojourn to the park, Janine, instead of returning downstairs, entered the master bedroom.

Of course, she had seen it before. Kate had pointed with pride to the large antique bed, dresser, and armoire. ("This furniture has been in our family for three generations.") And Janine had passed by frequently on the way to Jeremy or Dana's room, had stolen several short, private looks, always armed with a toy that she could produce ("Dana will be so happy! Can you imagine—I found her doll under the bed!") just in case she had to explain her presence.

Today, though, there was no risk of Louisa's coming upstairs. Minutes ago, when Janine had surreptitiously checked on her, the woman had just begun emptying the refrigerator as a prelude to washing the bins and shelves, and the dishes were still waiting in the sink.

Janine was inexplicably bored. It was another forty-five minutes before she had to pick Jeremy up from school. (She enjoyed driving the new Volkswagon that Kate had bought, although she would have preferred pulling up in front of the school in the Mercedes. Or the BMW.) Besides, she owed herself a reward. She had been such a good girl, the perfect au pair.

There were few surprises in Kate's large walk-in closet. Except for several pairs of jeans and some casual sweatshirts, almost everything—blouses, sweaters, dresses, skirts, all made of the finest fabrics in soft, appealing colors—was well tailored, clearly expensive, neatly preserved in a heavy opaque plastic bag, not in the thin, commercial variety that came from a dry cleaner. A little boring, actually. Timid.

She wondered whether Kate's wardrobe had been in the family for generations, too.

There were a few evening dresses that looked more promising—a strapless black tafetta gown, in particular—but she decided to leave it for another time.

In the lingerie drawer she found a white Christian Dior nightgown. She knew without looking at the label that it was one hundred percent silk. The fabric felt wonderful as she slipped it on over her bare skin.

She tested the two perfume bottles sitting on the vanity in the bathroom. The Joy was more expensive, but she chose the Opium. It was muskier, sexier. She was surprised that Kate had bought it.

Maybe he had bought it for her.

She undid her braid, watched in the bathroom mirror as the afternoon sun bounced off her unleashed mane. She walked languidly back into the bedroom with an almost vamplike affectation.

Which side of the antique bed was Kate's—Mama Bear's?

She laughed, decided she would try them both.

She stretched out on the bed, traced the heavy outline quilting on the floral bedspread with her fingertips, wondered how much fabric it took to make a king-size bedspread.

She didn't hear Louisa coming up the stairs, didn't see her until she was standing in the open doorway, a basket of laundry in her arms.

Janine gazed at her with calm, icy blue eyes.

Neither woman said a word.

After Louisa backed out of the doorway and shut the door behind her, Janine got dressed and carefully replaced the nightgown in the drawer.

In all likelihood, the woman wouldn't say anything to Kate. And even if she did, what were the chances that Kate would believe her? Would *want* to believe her?

There was, after all, nothing to worry about.

Kate had spent two hours on a precious Sunday morning looking for it, but she hadn't been able to find it.

"Give it up for now," Mark told her. "It'll show up."

"Not yet."

Kate found Janine in the backyard, supervising Jeremy and Dana while they played on the redwood swing set.

"Something is wrong?" the girl asked.

"Not really, just puzzling. Do you remember a green cotton knit sweater that I have? It's a dark green, actually, almost like this leaf." She pointed to a shrub nearby. "And it has some embroidered flowers on it."

"But of course. I remember thinking that it looked so very nice on you."

"Thanks, but I can't find it. I know I put it in the laundry last week, but it's not in my closet or in any of my drawers. I checked the laundry baskets, too, to see if Louisa still didn't get around to ironing it yet, but it's not there."

"Oh."

"So I was wondering if maybe Louisa put it with your things, by mistake. Maybe you could look."

"I see." She avoided Kate's eyes.

Oh, God! She thinks I suspect her of having taken it herself!

"Janine—"

"Kate—"

They both stopped.

"Look," Kate said, "forget the whole thing. Mark says it'll show up; he's probably right." She started to leave.

"Kate, wait."

66

Kate turned around.

"The reason I did not say anything is that I am trying to understand before I speak. And I am not sure if I should say anything."

"What are you talking about?"

She looked embarrassed. "The sweater you are talking about? I saw it last week."

"Where?"

"I went into the service porch to find some shoe polish, and Louisa was there. She was putting the sweater into a brown bag—you know, the kind from the market?—along with some other things."

"What other things?"

"There was a brown belt that I have seen you wear, and some children's clothes. The little dress with red dots that Dana likes? That one. When Louisa saw me, she told me that you gave her some clothes that you no longer needed."

"But I never—" she stopped.

"I am sorry. If I had known . . ."

"Well, there was no way you could have known. I can't believe it! This is so unlike her!"

"Perhaps there is a mistake. Maybe I have seen a different sweater. I do not want to get Louisa into trouble, Kate, but I thought I should tell you."

"Of course you had to tell me! What if there are other things missing? God, I hate this!"

"What's wrong?" Mark had joined them in the garden. Kate explained. "Nothing is certain, but it does seem as if she helped herself to some things."

"I wonder if she took that twenty-dollar bill, too."

"What twenty-dollar bill?"

"I left it in my top drawer a few weeks ago, near my cuff links. When I came home from work, it wasn't there."

"Why didn't you say anything?"

He shrugged. "I figured it would show up. But now, I don't know . . ." He turned to Janine. "Are you missing anything?"

She hesitated. "I am not sure."

"You are, aren't you?" he demanded.

"A locket," she admitted quietly. "But I thought that I might have lost it someplace. The chain was thin, you see."

"You think I should fire her, don't you, Mark?"

"I don't know what to tell you."

"But we're not sure about any of this. It could be a mistake."

"Then why did she tell Janine that you gave her some clothes?"

"I don't know." Kate sounded miserable. "What should we do?"

"Ask her about it. See what she says."

"Okay, I will. I'll ask her about it tomorrow morning."

"I could barely understand her," Kate told Mark on the phone. "She was hysterical."

"So what did she say?"

"Basically, from what I could make out, she claims that she found the clothes in the trash and figured I didn't want them."

"Did you tell her what Janine said?"

"No. What's the point? She obviously lying, so why make it worse? You know, Mark, in a way I feel sorry for her. She must be desperate if she has to steal."

"I guess. So what do you want to do, give her another chance?"

"It's too late for that."

"What do you mean?"

"After we talked, she told me she couldn't work for someone who suspected her of stealing. That's what I

68

think she said. Anyway, she just grabbed her purse and ran out the door."

"Look, Kate, I know this was awful, but you don't want to have someone in the house who you don't trust, do you?"

"No, absolutely not."

It made sense for Janine to help Kate interview the young women who applied for Louisa's job; after all, they would be dealing with the au pair more than with Kate. It was Janine who asked them about their references, their experience, the hours they preferred. And it was Janine who suggested to Kate that they hire someone for four days, not five.

"Often I have seen Louisa with very little to do," Janine said. "Why should you pay for an extra day if you do not need it?"

"I don't know, Janine. It's a big house."

She smiled. "I promise you, if it does not work out, I will be the first to complain. We can always add one more day, no?"

With Janine standing by her side, Kate hired Anuncia Gutierrez, a nineteen-year-old mother of two from Guatemala.

She would work Monday, Tuesday, Thursday, and Friday.

Wednesdays, she would be free.

So would Janine.

Chapter Six

"You look great in that bathing suit," Barbara told Kate. "Did you lose weight?" She applied more tanning lotion to the wide expanse of exposed golden skin between her hot pink bikini bottom and bandeau.

It was a warm Sunday afternoon in June, and the two women were sitting at the edge of the pool, their feet dangling in the water. Kate was keeping a cautious eye on Jeremy, who was paddling with his floaties. Dana was sitting on the top step of the pool, slapping the water delightedly with her hands to create waves around her plastic sailboat.

"Inches, actually, more than pounds. Thanks for noticing. I've been working hard at the club, thanks to Laney; she won't let me miss a session. But I do feel great."

"How was San Francisco?"

"Wonderful. Mark and I haven't been alone since our honeymoon. As a matter of fact, it was so nice that I'm thinking of going in late to the shop one day this week so that we can spend some private time together. Wednesday is probably best for him, but I'll have to check with him, and with Laney, too. Jeremy, not in the deep!" She nodded approvingly as he inched his way back toward the shallow end of the pool.

"Weren't you nervous about leaving the kids?"

"Not at all. Janine's great with them. And I left Laney's number with her just in case."

"You could have asked me to watch them, you know. I wouldn't have minded at all."

Kate looked at her, surprised. "I know you've been extremely busy, between taking interior design classes and trying to get the gallery open. And believe me, Barbara, watching the kids is a full-time job."

"I know that, Kate. But I'd like to do it. Don't you think I can handle it?"

"Of course you can. I've always thought you'd make a wonderful mother."

"Right." She sighed. "Anyway, I'm glad you called. It's been ages since we've had time to talk alone."

Kate had invited Barbara to spend the afternoon ("Just you and me and the kids," she had told her). Mark had gone to play racquetball with a friend.

"I noticed Janine on my way in, by the way. Where was she going?"

"Shopping."

"She's dressing better. I see she started wearing makeup."

"Only a little. Estee Lauder was having a free make-up demonstration a few weeks ago at Saks. I decided to go and I took her along."

"Something else is different, too, but I can't figure out what."

"You mean her hair? She's not wearing it in a braid any more. I suggested it."

"Playing Dr. Higgins, huh?"

"So? What's wrong with that?"

"So nothing. She's very pretty, or hadn't you noticed?"

"So when *is* the gallery opening, Barbara?"

71

"Changing the subject, huh?" She laughed. "Who knows? Simon's still short about $120,000. I'm beginning to wonder whether he'll ever open the doors. I could write a check, but I've already committed more than I probably should have."

"Having second thoughts?"

"Simons knows his art—I have no doubts about that. But I'm not sure he has any business sense. Oh, well, what the hell. At the worst, I'll just have a tax write-off."

"What's wrong, Barbara? You sound strange."

"Nothing's wrong, exactly. But nothing's right, either." She sighed. "Oh, shit, I don't know why I'm bothering you with this. It's not as if you can do anything about it."

"About what? Can't you talk to me?"

"I'm thirty-four years old, Kate. I have two ex-husbands, a few good friends, a shrink who's beginning to run out of reasons to continue seeing me, a condominium that I'm tired of redecorating, and a boyfriend who I suspect is cheating on me. I have enough money to live in luxury for the rest of my life, and I'm feeling just a little bit sorry for myself right now."

"Are you sure about Simon?"

"He's been extremely chummy with this woman who works for one of the major auction houses. Her name is Monica Blendheim. He says it's strictly business, but we were at a party together last week and his hand was practically inside her dress."

"I'm sorry." She didn't know what to say.

"Don't be. Frankly, I'm not sure we're right for each other anyway. I mean, he's brilliant and amusing and he's great in the sack, but I can't see myself living with him permanently. He doesn't want kids, for one thing."

"Do you?"

"Yes, damn it! I'd trade my white silk couches and Villeroy and Boch china in a minute for a sofa covered in some awful plaid, Olefin, kidproof fabric and a service for eight of melmac from Sears. Right now, even stretch marks sound good to me—as long as they're matched, of course."

"Barbara!" Kate laughed.

"But Simon's definitely not interested. He's got two sons from his first marriage back in Liverpool, and they're more than enough for him."

"Maybe he'll change his mind."

"I doubt it. And to tell you the truth, it's just as well. The charm is wearing a little thin, and not just because of Ms. Blendheim. And as much as I hate to admit it, I think Mark is right. Simon's interest in me is probably motivated more than a little by my ability to help finance the gallery."

"Oh."

"You're supposed to say, 'Oh, no, Barbara; I've seen the way Simon looks at you. He's madly in love with you.'" She laughed morosely.

"Of course he likes you, Barbara. How could he help it? But you know I've felt all along that you rushed into this relationship."

"It seems to be a habit with me, doesn't it? First Greg, then Lionel. God, Kate, how could you have let me marry someone named Lionel? Did I ever tell you he used to leave his toenail clippings all over the place?" She shuddered.

"If you remember, Evan and I tried to talk you out of marrying him, but you weren't about to listen to anyone."

"Not exactly," she agreed. She trailed her fingers through the water. "Roger says I married both of them to get Daddy's attention."

"Well, you certainly did that."

"Yeah, I guess I did." She grinned. "Remember his face when Greg and I came back from Vegas, all legal? I know

73

Dad thought I was pregnant, but he never asked me. Mom kind of hinted delicately. She asked me whether we'd be renting a one- or two-bedroom apartment." She paused. "Roger also says I was trying to hurt Daddy because I thought he loved you more than he loved me."

"That's silly!"

"Come on, Kate, he thought you were perfect. So did Mom. Your grades were better than mine were, your friends were more polite, your hemlines were never too short, your make-up was never too loud. Living with a sister like you, it's a miracle I didn't turn out deeply disturbed." She made a grotesque face.

"So it's my fault you married Greg and Lionel?"

"Absolutely." She grinned. "Okay, I'll take full responsibility for Lionel. I must have been drunk or in a trance when I agreed to marry him. Actually, if you want to know the truth, it was his body and his saxophone. That was before I found out about the toenail clippings. Not to mention the girlfriend he had all along on the side. Can you believe his gall, using my money to buy her gifts?"

"You never told me that."

"I was too humiliated. And as far as Greg is concerned, looking back, I can see now that I was damn lonely, and you and Evan were engaged, and there I was, two years older, and, well, I don't know . . .

"But I knew Daddy didn't approve. 'What kind of living can a university professor make?' he asked me. 'You're used to having everything you want, Barbara.' And it didn't help that I knew he thought the world of Evan, treated him as if he were his own son, and that was way before Evan made gobs and gobs of money. Daddy liked him just because you chose him."

"Barbara, be reasonable. Mom and Dad were friends with Evan's family for years. The McCallums were over our house all the time, ever since we were kids. And it

74

wasn't exactly a big surprise when we decided to get married—we started dating in high school. You married Greg out of the blue."

"I guess."

"But Dad liked Greg, Barbara. You know he did. He was very disappointed when you divorced him."

"Maybe." She sighed.

"What happened to that guy you were seeing after you left Lionel? It was just around the time Evan died, and I guess I wasn't a very good listener, but I seem to remember that you said he was special. But later, when I asked you about it, you didn't want to talk about it."

"There was nothing to tell; it just didn't work out. I just seem to pick the wrong men. Except for Jeremy. You love Auntie Barbara, don't you, sweetie?" she called.

He kicked an enthusiastic spray in response.

They sat a while in silence.

"Barbara, do you realize this is the first time in ages that we're having a real conversation?" she asked suddenly.

"I know. I bared my soul. It must be premenstrual tension." She laughed a little nervously.

"I'm serious, Barbara. You know, I thought that after Mom died, well, that we'd be close again, the way we used to be. I really wish you'd come over more often."

"Come on, Kate. Let's be honest. You don't want me over when Mark's home."

"Why don't you like him? I wish you'd tell me what's wrong."

"Maybe I'm just jealous of your happiness."

"I don't believe that. You were never like that when Evan was alive, even when you were having problems."

"What can I tell you? The chemistry's just wrong between us." She got up. "I'd better be going."

"Stay a little longer. We don't have to talk about Mark, if it makes you uncomfortable."

"No, it's not that. I'm meeting a friend for an early dinner. Oh, I almost forgot. Simon and I are going to the theater on Thursday night. I'm planning on wearing my red Valentino suit, but I can't find the black lace camisole I always wear with it. You have one, don't you?"

Kate suppressed a smile. "Yes. Do you want to take it now?"

"No. I'm going to check through my drawers one more time. I can always stop by during the week if I can't find it."

"Okay. Janine is here, except for mornings. She usually runs errands or goes to the market when Dana's at play group. But you have the key I gave you, don't you?"

Barbara nodded. "And look, about Mark, I'll try to behave the next time I see him, okay?"

On Wednesday morning at ten o'clock, Barbara pulled into the Bauers' driveway. She was a little surprised to see the BMW there—Kate had told her that Mark usually used that time to visit post-op patients—and less than pleased. She wasn't really in the mood to see her brother-in-law.

She was about to ring the front doorbell but changed her mind. Instead, she used the key she kept in her purse. Mark was probably in his office. If she was very quiet, she could get the camisole and leave without seeing him. Janine was nowhere in sight. Kate had said that the girl usually ran errands in the mornings.

Upstairs, she made her way quickly to Kate's dresser and rummaged through the drawer where she knew she kept her lingerie. The camisole was on the bottom, a little wrinkled, but she would iron it at home. No problem. The contents of the drawer were messy from her search. She put the camisole on the dresser and quickly straightened

76

the underwear before she shut the drawer.

The French doors that led onto the balcony facing the pool were partially open. She heard the sound of water splashing, and noticed for the first time the slacks, shirt, and underwear lying on a pile on the floor near the bed.

So he was swimming. Why not? It was his pool, his day off. She didn't know why she was so annoyed. Was it because he was relaxing while Kate was at the shop? That wasn't fair, she told herself; it was Kate's choice to work. But she was still annoyed.

She walked to the balcony, stood behind the lace-curtained door, and looked down. He was there in the pool, lying on a raft. She eased the curtain to one side. Even from a distance, his body looked lean and muscular, and she felt a familiar ache spread through her. Stop it! she told herself.

Suddenly, he jumped off the raft and made his way out of the pool. He was grinning, and Barbara couldn't figure out why until she saw Kate emerging from the patio area and walking toward Mark. Quickly, Barbara released the curtain. Kate was wearing the same bathing suit she had worn on Sunday, and Barbara thought again how good she looked in it.

But what was Kate?—and then she remembered; Kate had mentioned talking off a morning to spend time with Mark. Roger would say Barbara had subconsciously chosen to come today, knowing she would see them together. But that was ridiculous.

She knew she should leave quickly, that she had no right to trespass on the privacy of this special moment that they had taken out of what was just an ordinary Wednesday. But she couldn't leave, and as Kate walked slowly over to him and his arms closed around her, Barbara felt sad, so terribly sad, because it had been a long time since any man had held her like that.

They were kissing. He lowered first one strap and then

the other of Kate's bathing suit, then peeled it down, all the way down, and helped her step out of it. Now Kate was pulling his head down, and Barbara could see only her bared back, but she knew he was kissing her breasts, her sister's breasts, and she almost moaned. And when he released her, and she reached for his trunks that clung, wet, to his body, Barbara finally averted her eyes in belated shame and despair. But she couldn't stop her memory, impassively cruel in its accuracy, from thrusting his naked image against the dark screen of her sealed eyes.

She heard a splash and turned back, pulled the curtain aside. They were both in the pool, Kate's legs straddling his waist. Her arms were locked around his neck, and he was spinning her around and around and around, and Barbara felt dizzy, almost nauseated, and then he suddenly stopped, with his back toward the balcony, and slid her body up against his until it was high above his head. Her neck was arched backward, and Barbara waited stoically to see her face, to punish herself with the joy she knew she would find on it.

It was Janine.

She released the curtain quickly, as though the fabric had singed her fingertips. The blood was pounding in her ears and she could barely think, but she knew she had to leave immediately. She was certain that they hadn't seen her, but she had no idea how long they would stay in the pool.

When she got into her Jaguar, her hand was shaking so badly that she had difficulty inserting the key into the ignition.

"You looked bushed," Mark told Kate when she came

home from the shop. "Rough day?"

"You could say that. I spent all morning on the phone with UPS trying to trace two important deliveries that should have been here last week. So much for my romantic plans, huh?"

"Maybe next week."

"Right. Anyway, while I was busy showing a customer every piece of cobalt we have, her bratty kid was playing with the crystal like it was tinker toys."

"Did he break something?"

"Only a four hundred-dollar Lalique sculpture." She sighed. "On top of that, the air conditioning system went on the blink. What I'd love to do is go upstairs before supper and shower. You don't have to wait if you're hungry."

"Go ahead. Take your time."

Fifteen minutes later, Kate, wearing shorts and a tank top, joined Mark and Janine at the breakfast room table. The children had already eaten.

"That's funny," she mused aloud as she sat down.

"What?" he asked.

"I found my camisole on top of my dresser. I wonder how it got there. Can you pass the salad, please, Mark?"

"Sure."

"Unless," she said slowly, "Barbara came by to get it and decided not to take it after all."

"What are you talking about?" he asked.

She explained about the camisole. "I think she said she needed it for tomorrow night." She turned to Janine. "Did you see her stop by, Janine?"

"No, I did not."

"Well, she has a key to the house, so she could have let herself in. You were probably out running an errand. But I still don't understand why she didn't take the camisole, or put it back." She shrugged. "Oh, well, you know Barbara. She's very unpredictable. I don't think she

79

knows herself from one minute to the next what she's going to do. I'll solve the mystery when I talk to her."

"Do you think she saw us?" Janine asked coolly.

They were in the kitchen. Kate had gone upstairs to put the children to bed.

"Maybe."

"What do you think we should do?"

"Nothing yet. Let's wait and see what she does."

The following Tuesday, Barbara found Laney alone in the shop with a customer.

"How've you been?" Laney asked after the customer had left and the two women had exchanged greetings.

"Okay. Medium, actually. I just left the doctor's office. I've had this stupid bladder infection for weeks. He changed the antibiotic and told me no baths for a few months. I *love* baths!"

"So cheat a little. I won't tell."

"No way. I want this to clear up. I guess I'll live." She grinned. "Kate isn't here?"

"She went to make a bank deposit. She should be back any—oh, here she is. Kate, you have a visitor!" she called.

"Barbara!" She walked over and hugged her. "I was beginning to think you were avoiding me, you know. Didn't Simon give you my messages? I called at least four times."

"Of course he did. I'm sorry; I've just been so busy." She smiled weakly. "I thought maybe you and I could go to lunch."

"That's a great idea! I'd love to." She looked at Laney.

"No problem. I can manage for an hour or so. Just give me a minute to go to the bathroom before you leave,

80

okay?" She walked to the rear of the shop.

Barbara absent-mindedly fingered a porcelain vase on an *étagère*.

"So are you going to tell me the truth about Wednesday, Barbara, or what?"

"What?" She almost knocked over the vase, caught it just in time.

Kate didn't notice. "You were there, weren't you—in my bedroom, I mean."

"How did you know?"

"It didn't take much detecting. You left the camisole on the dresser. But why didn't you take it? Did you decide to wear something else?"

"Something else? Yes, yes I did. I thought maybe a dress would be better than a suit." She hadn't realized until she had gotten home that she had left the camisole in the bedroom.

"How was the evening?"

"Very nice. Really. I'll tell you about it at lunch."

"I'm glad you came by the shop," Kate said after they had ordered. "I feel so close to you since we talked on Sunday. I guess you feel the same way. That's why you came by today, isn't it?"

"I do, Kate. I may not always show it, but you have to know that I love you."

"Of course I know that." She studied her face. "Are you okay? You sound a little tense."

"It's just the heat. And I have a bladder infection. I just came from Dr. Siegal." She played with her fork.

"That's funny. I'm thinking of making an appointment to see him. And not about my bladder." She smiled.

"Why? You're not pregnant, are you?" she asked sharply.

She looked at her, surprised by her tone. "No, I'm not

81

pregnant, but to tell you the truth, I've been thinking about having a baby. Why do you sound so upset?"

"I'm sorry, you just took me by surprise. Have you and Mark talked about it?"

"Not in specific terms. He loves Jeremy and Dana as if they were his own, but every man wants to have his own child. I'm sure he hasn't suggested it till now because he was worried about my health. I was certainly in no condition to think about having a baby after Mom died. But now . . ."

"I don't know, Kate. Maybe you should wait a while. You're just getting back on your feet. And what about the shop?"

"I feel fine. And I'll work something out with Laney. Other women juggle pregnancies and careers. I'm going to talk to Mark, and then I'm going to make an appointment with Dr. Siegal to have my IUD removed."

"I saw Mark, you know."

"Really? When?"

"At the house, on Wednesday."

"What are you talking about? Mark wasn't there."

"Yes, he was, Kate. He didn't see me, though."

Kate waited.

"He was swimming, you see. I noticed him from the balcony in your bedroom. Janine was there, too." She avoided Kate's eyes. "And, well, it looked to me like she was being a little too friendly."

"What the hell are you talking about?" Her tone was frigid.

"I'm trying to tell you, Kate. The girl is trouble. She was coming on to Mark, and a man would have to be made of stone not to respond."

"Are you saying he kissed her?"

"I don't know. She put her arm on his, but then they walked under the patio overhang, so I couldn't see what was happening."

"You mean you're not going to tell me that he ripped her clothes off, that they made passionate love on the grass? I'm surprised at you, Barbara. Disappointed, really."

"Kate, I don't want to hurt you, but I thought you should know."

"Come off it, will you? You and I both know that you're making this whole thing up just to get me angry at Mark."

"Kate, I swear—"

"You know, you were obviously telling the truth the other day when you said you were jealous of my happiness. So what is it now? You can't stand the fact that Mark and I may have a child? Is that it?"

"You don't understand, Kate. I'm *not* lying! The truth is—"

"The truth is, Barbara, that you're mean and vicious and I don't know why I've been making excuses for you till now. But I'm finished. You really need help. I mean that, Barbara. I don't think Roger's doing you any good. Find someone who won't indulge you, someone who will make you face the truth."

"And what is that?"

"That Evan is dead, Barbara. That we all loved him, I more than anyone—God, you *know* how I loved him! But he's dead, and I won't let you make me feel guilty any more. I didn't betray Evan by marrying Mark. I am getting on with my life, Barbara. And if you want to be a part of it, if you want to come to the house and see Jeremy and Dana, you're going to have to stop harassing Mark. You don't have to like him, but you're going to have to accept him and treat him with respect."

"But Janine was—"

"Stop it! You're picking on a sweet, lovely girl, an orphan, goddammit, who never harmed you, and I won't have it, do you hear me? I simply won't have it!"

"Please, Kate. You're making a terrible mistake."

But Kate had already pushed her seat away from the table. Barbara sat dully as she stormed out of the restaurant."

"Barbara, thank you for seeing me."

"What do you want, Mark?" She didn't try to hide the revulsion she felt.

"Can we sit down someplace?"

She had stayed in the hallway after opening the door.

"I don't plan to have a long conversation, Mark."

"Please, Barbara."

"Oh, all right."

He followed her into a spacious, all-white living room.

"The place looks nice. Where's Simon?"

"Probably out looking for starving artists. I wouldn't know. He's moved out temporarily, if it's any of your business, which it isn't."

"I'm sorry. I hope you two work things out."

"Cut the crap, Mark. You don't give a shit about me. Why don't you say what's on your mind and get out?"

"Okay." He paused. "You saw us, didn't you? I mean me and Janine."

She didn't answer.

"Kate told me about your lunch yesterday. She said you told her you saw Janine flirting with me. She doesn't believe you, by the way. She thinks you made the whole thing up."

"*Flirting* isn't exactly what I saw, Mark. Although what the two of you were doing starts with the same letter."

"Barbara, I want to explain. I know you could have told Kate everything, and I just want to tell you how much I appreciate your discretion."

"You bastard! I didn't do it for you. As far as I'm

concerned, you can drop dead tomorrow and the world would be a better place. I didn't want to hurt Kate. I knew she'd be devastated."

"You're right. I don't think she could handle it. Look, I don't blame you for being angry at me. I'm not very proud of myself. What can I say, Barbara? I'm human. I gave in to temptation. But I swear it'll never happen again. You have my word."

"Your word? That's a laugh!"

"I love Kate, Barbara. You have to believe that much."

"Prove it."

"How?"

"Get rid of that girl. Send her back to the Alps."

"I'm not the one who hired her, Barbara. Kate did. And Kate really likes her."

"Kate will find someone else, someone a little less accommodating."

"You don't understand. What would I say to Kate? If I tell her to fire Janine, she'll wonder why. She'll think there's something to what you told her."

"That's your problem, Mark. You figure it out. If you care about Kate and your marriage—and frankly, in my mind, that's one hell of an if—then you'll see that you don't have a choice."

"Well, let me give this some thought, okay? I don't want to rush into anything."

"Oh, don't I know that, Mark! Everything you do is deliberate and planned. But let me make things real clear for you. I'll give you two weeks to get that girl out of the house and on a plane to Europe."

"Come on, Barbara. Be reasonable."

"And if you don't," she said slowly, "if you don't, then I'll tell Kate everything. And I mean everything, Mark."

He smiled. "Barbara, she doesn't believe you now. Why do you think she'll believe you next time? What you're forgetting here, and I think you'll see this is an important point, is that Kate loves me. She depends on me. I'm the one who saved her from depression after Evan died. I'm the one who makes her feel secure, who makes love to her, who holds her at night and makes all the demons go away. What do you do for her, Barbara?"

"She'll believe me. I know she will."

He shook his head. "If she listens to you at all, which I highly doubt, she's going to hear a jealous, vindictive, lonely woman who has never been able to hold on to a man. A woman who's so miserable that she can't see anyone around her happy, not even her sister. That's what she'll hear, Barbara."

"You're despicable!" she hissed.

"Face it, Barbara. You'll lose her. She'll never talk to you again."

"I'll tell her about us, Mark. She'll listen then. She'll see what a sterling character her husband has. Dr. Mark Bauers. Healer of the sick. Pursuer of wealthy, gullible widows. Jilter extraordinaire."

"I didn't marry her for her money."

"Like hell you didn't! Obviously, my inheritance from my father wasn't enough for you!"

"Barbara—"

"You talked about marriage. You said you loved me."

"I thought I did. I didn't plan on meeting Kate, falling in love with her. Do you think I enjoyed hurting you like that?"

"Well, how do you think I felt when she called me up and told me she was getting engaged to the man I'd been sleeping with for almost six months? You didn't even tell me you knew her! How do you think I feel every time I see you together?"

"I'm sorry, Barbara. I know it's been hard on you. What can I say? Kate started out as my patient, and then, well . . . I know I handled things badly. But these things happen, Barbara. Maybe in time you'll understand."

"It didn't happen, goddammit! You *made* it happen. You just figured out that my newly widowed sister was a better investment than I was. After all, she had Daddy's money *and* Evan's millions. Were you sleeping with both of us at the same time, Mark? Did you get a kick out of doing two sisters?"

"You're crazy, you know that? You should be committed."

"Well, why don't we let Kate judge, okay, Mark? Why don't we see who she believes."

"She'll believe me, Barbara, because I'm telling the truth, and because she has to believe me. And if you use this to try to get rid of Janine, it'll just convince Kate that you're trying to get back at me for dumping you. That's it, isn't it? That's why you're doing all this?" He got up.

"Two weeks, Mark. Or I swear I'll call Kate. And I'll get proof that she *will* believe."

"Think about it, Barbara. Be smart. You're the only one who's going to lose."

"We'll have to be more careful, Janine."

"But of course; I understand perfectly. She told you two weeks?"

"She's bluffing. She knows Kate won't believe her. She won't say a thing."

"Perhaps. And if she does?"

"I'll think of something."

"As long as I do not have to go back to Geneva." She smiled and ran her hand lightly along his thigh.

Chapter Seven

"Laney, it's for you," Brian said as he entered the kitchen. "Barbara."

"Barbara?" She shut the faucet, wiped her hands on a towel, and picked up the phone extension.

"Don't be too long, okay? I'm expecting an important call." He went back to the den.

"Hi, Barbara. What's up? Is everything okay?"

"Is someone else on the line?"

"Brian didn't hang up yet. He should be—oh, there's the click. Why, what's wrong? You sound so mysterious."

"I have to talk to you, Laney. It's very important. It concerns Kate."

"Oh."

"Did she say anything to you after our lunch last week, Laney?"

"Well, I knew when she came back that you and she must have had a fight. But she didn't seem to want to talk about it, so I didn't press it. To tell you the truth, Barbara, I don't feel comfortable discussing Kate with you. Why don't you call her, see what she—"

"Laney, I wouldn't have called you, but I don't know who else to talk to. I think Kate could be in serious trouble, but I'm not sure she'll listen to me. But I know she'll listen to you. She trusts you."

"Trouble? What kind of trouble?"

"It's hard to explain over the phone. Look, can you meet me someplace where we can talk privately?"

"Right now?"

"No. I still have some things I want to check out. What about tomorrow night?"

"I can't. I told Abigail I'd take her to a movie. How about Thursday?"

"Okay. How about coffee at the City cafe? Nine o'clock?"

"Fine. What's this all about, Barbara? I have to admit you're making me curious as hell."

"All I can tell you is that it concerns the au pair."

"Oh, her."

"You don't like her?"

"Not much. But what about her?"

"I'll tell you when I see you. But it's more than just her. You see, I found out that Ma—what was that click?"

"We have call waiting. The click means that someone's trying to get through. It must be for Brian; he's expecting a call. Hold on a sec, will you?"

"No, it's okay. I'll tell you everything on Thursday."

Like many of the art galleries and shops that had sprung up on La Brea Avenue, the City was a relatively new establishment. Laney often observed the clientele sitting at the crowded sidewalk tables as she drove by on her way to do late-night marketing at the Ralph's on the same street and wondered what had made the un-decorated, rather spartan gray building a trendy, overnight L.A. success.

It was 9:05 by the time Laney parked her Volvo, and she hurried toward the restaurant. She hadn't noticed

Barbara's Jaguar while she had circled around the block looking for a parking spot. Barbara had probably parked on the next street.

The place was moderately noisy. After Laney's eyes adjusted to the dim lighting, she scanned the room. Barbara wasn't here yet. She chose a small table toward the front where she would be able to see her entrance, and ordered a diet lemon Coke.

By 9:20 she was annoyed. Brian had been against her coming in the first place, and they had quarreled about it.

"You're getting mixed up in family stuff," he had warned her. "Kate won't appreciate it."

"But Barbara said this has to do with Janine, not just Kate."

"Butt out, Laney. Let them handle it themselves."

There she was. Laney got up to wave to her, but Barbara looked at her blankly, and then Laney saw that it was someone else with layered mahogany hair.

The long-haired, miniskirted waitress came over again. "You ready to order?"

"My friend isn't here yet. I wonder if she called to say she'd be late?"

"You want me to check?"

"Please." She gave her the name.

She was back a few minutes later. "Nope." She looked at her expectantly.

"I think I'll give her a few more minutes. I'll have another lemon Coke, though."

She gave Laney a suit-yourself-honey shrug and disappeared.

While she was waiting for the Coke, Laney decided to call home. "Did Barbara call?" she asked Brian.

"No. She didn't show, huh?"

"She's probably delayed."

"Forget it, Laney. You know what a flake she is. She

probably just forgot. This wouldn't be the first time."

At 9:55, Laney decided Brian was right. She left a large tip for the waitress. She had a few things to say to Barbara the next time she saw her, and none of them were complimentary. If she hurried, at least she would miss only a few minutes of "L.A. Law."

"Where were you last night?" Kate asked Laney. "Brian sounded very mysterious when I called."

"Oh, you know Brian. He makes a trip to the market sound like a covert operation. It's the lawyer in him." She laughed. "I just had an errand to run."

"Oh. I'm going to the back to unpack the Lennox vases that came in, okay?"

"Fine."

The doorbell rang and both women looked toward the front. Two uniformed officers entered.

"These guys must be here about the alarm going off the past couple of days," Laney said. "You go ahead. I'll talk to them."

Kate stood where she was. There was something in their slow approach that told her they weren't here about anything as innocuous as alarms. She had seen the same we-hate-to-tell-you-this reluctance three years ago in the young faces of other men who had come to tell her that Evan had been killed, his car forced off the road by a drunk driver.

She knew instinctively that they had not come for Laney, knew they had come for her. She was a magnet for death.

"Mrs. Bauers?" the blond officer asked.

"Yes." She was amazed at how steady her voice was.

"Mrs. Bauers, I'm afraid we have some bad news. There's been an accident—"

"Who?" She felt Laney's arms gripping her.

91

"I'm sorry. It seems that your sister . . ."

"I feel so awful, Brian," Laney told him that night. "I mean, here I was, cursing out Barbara for standing me up, and all the time she was lying dead in the bathtub. The police don't know how long she was there, but they think it was a few days." She shuddered. "The officer said the cleaning woman found Barbara this morning. God, I pity her! It must have been gruesome."

"What do they think happened?"

"Apparently, she accidentally electrocuted herself. There was a large radio in the tub; it must have fallen in. Will they have to do an autopsy, Brian?"

"Of course, even though it's an accident. Did Kate have to identify the body?"

"The police said Mark could do it for her. I don't think she could have handled it."

"How's she doing?"

"I don't think it's hit her yet. She's acting a little weird—not hysterical at all, very quiet. Too quiet, actually. Mark gave her a sedative and took her home. I spoke to him a little while ago; he said she's resting."

"How did they get Kate's name, by the way?"

"I asked the officer. They found her doctor's name on some prescription medication she had in her purse and contacted him. He told them Kate was her next of kin. When she wasn't at the house, they called Mark's office. He wasn't in, but his secretary had the number of the shop."

"Poor Kate. It never seems to end for her, does it?"

She had become an expert at funerals. She slipped with ease into the simple black linen dress she had hoped never to wear again, stepped into the black medium-heeled pumps, adjusted the veil of the black straw hat that she had set at a somber angle over blonde-streaked hair pulled into a tight bun.

It was a short service. Reverend DeWitt clasped her hand with both of his and murmured soothingly to her after he had delivered his eulogy. She acknowledged him with a grateful nod. There were quite a few people, Kate's friends as well as Barbara's. She hadn't seen Simon, but maybe he had stayed toward the back. Jeremy and Dana were with Mark. Kate had no idea what they were wearing. Janine had dressed them.

All she really wanted to do was sleep. She wasn't ready to think about Barbara, about the finality of their last angry parting. Mark had given her a valium tablet this morning, and she still felt its numbing effects. Maybe he would give her another one later.

"She's not really up to talking to anyone yet, Laney," Mark told her. "And she absolutely doesn't want any visitors. But I've been giving her all your messages. I told her you've been calling every day for the past two weeks."

"I understand. I'm sorry I'm bothering you at the office, but every time I call, Janine answers. I just wanted to find out from you what's going on."

"I'm glad you did call. I know how much you care about Kate."

"Tell her not to worry about the shop, by the way. Mrs. Margolin says she can fill in until Kate feels like coming back."

"I'll tell her. To tell you the truth, Laney, I have no idea when that will be. Right now she doesn't want to leave her room. She's just like she was after her mother died." He sighed.

"Have you talked to Dr. Zuroff? Maybe she would

come see Kate. She helped her so much the last time."

"Kate doesn't want to see her, Laney. I suppose I should encourage her, but I don't want to push her right now. She's so fragile."

"Right. Well, let me know if there's anything I can do. Tell her I love her, Mark. Tell her we all do. I'll call again tonight after I get home from the shop."

Laney sighed and replaced the receiver. She was grateful when the shop filled up with customers. Helping them choose giftware helped take her mind off Kate, at least temporarily.

Mrs. Margolin had left early, and at 4:55 Laney was about to close up. The doorbell rang and a short, slight man wearing a brown tweed three-piece suit entered the shop.

"I'm sorry, but we're closing." She smiled apologetically. "Look, if you can find something quickly, fine. But I really have to get going."

"Are you Kate Bauers?"

"No. I'm Laney Tolbert. Her partner. What can I do for you?" She looked at him more closely. His smooth-shaven skin, a little shiny, gave him a boyish look that contrasted with his neatly combed, thinning brown hair. He was wearing too much aftershave lotion.

"Well, I need to speak to her."

"And your name is?"

"Dupard. Franklin Dupard."

"Can you tell me what this is about, Mr. Dupard?"

"I'll just come back tomorrow."

"Mrs. Bauers won't be here tomorrow. She's taking some time off for personal reasons."

"I take it you're referring to the sister's death?" He didn't wait for an answer. "Read about it in the paper. Society page. That's why I'm here, you see. I had some business with Miz Simpson, and now that she's dead, well, I figured I'd better see her sister, Mrs. Bauers. I waited two weeks—it's only decent, right? Anyway, the obituary said she's the only surviving kin, so I called the house 'bout ten times, but this girl with an accent who keeps answering says Mrs. Bauers isn't available. I thought I'd try here. Miz Simpson told me her sister owned this place."

"Mr. Dupard, if you leave me your card, I'd be happy to have Mrs. Bauers call you. I'm in touch with her husband all the time."

He shook his head. "Not a good idea. This is kind of confidential-like, you see. I have some information for her, information that I wouldn't like to get into the wrong hands. If you see what I mean."

She didn't see what he meant. "Look, I happen to be Mrs. Bauers's best friend. I was also a friend of Ms. Simpson. Are you sure you can't tell me what this is all about?"

He hesitated. "I don't know. See, Miz Simpson hired me to get some information. Now she gave me a retainer, but she was supposed to pay the balance when I finished the job. So now here she went and died, and I'm real sorry about that, but my problem is that I got this information and I don't know who's going to pay me for it. If you see what I mean." He smiled.

A private detective? Laney couldn't believe it. "Can I see a card, please?"

"No problem." He reached into his jacket pocket, found his wallet, extracted a glossy card, and handed it to her.

"How much money did Ms. Simpson owe you?"

"Look, I wanna be fair. I mean, I could tell you all kinds of hogwash, and there's no way you'd know if I was telling the truth, right? The fact is, she gave me twenty-two hundred dollars up front, which is a lot, but I only charged her one seventy-five per day plus expenses. That's a pretty good deal, but I'm just starting out, and she hired me for a minimum of two weeks, so I figured we could work something out. Otherwise, it would've been two hundred per day plus. Which is cheap, if you check around.

"I started on Thursday, June 30, and I read about her death on Monday, July 11. So naturally, I didn't do any surveillance on Monday. The thing is, though, that the one seventy-five was for two weeks. So now I'm afraid I have to figure on the basis of two hundred per day, plus expenses. If you see what I mean."

Laney stared at him. "How much?"

"Two hundred seventy dollars should do it. I have an itemized list for my hours and everything I spent. Phone calls and such."

"And if I pay you this money . . . ?"

He cocked his head to the side. "Well, I'm not rightly sure what to do in a case like this, but I guess the information would belong to you. If you see what I mean."

"How do I know there's anything valuable in what you're selling me?"

"Well, you don't know, obviously. And to be honest, you might not find it all that valuable. Miz Simpson was pretty interested in what I had to say when I talked to her on the phone a couple of weeks ago—I was keeping her posted on my progress. But it might not mean anything to you. If you see what I mean."

"What did your work for her involve?"

"Well, again. I don't think I can tell you that. You'd just have to take your chances."

"I don't think so. I mean, I'd have to know a little bit about what I'm buying, Mr. Dupard. If you see what I mean." The phrase had leapt unconsciously to her lips. She hoped he wouldn't think she was mimicking him.

He didn't seem to notice. "Well, I can see your point there." He nodded judiciously. "All right. I can tell you this much. Miz Simpson asked me to do some surveillance on her brother-in-law. She thought he was fooling around with this Swiss girl who's living with them."

"Mark?" She was stunned.

"Mark Bauers, M.D. That's him. That's why I couldn't exactly have you telling him that I was calling. If you see what I mean." He waited. "Miss?"

"What? Oh, yes. I'm sorry. You just surprised me, that's all. And did you find anything . . . ?"

"Well, that I can't tell you. But all the information's in here." From an inner pocket of his jacket, he withdrew an envelope.

"Okay." She had made up her mind. "I don't have much in the register, Mr. Dupard. Can I write you a check?"

"Well, I don't know. What if you decide you don't like what's in the envelope and decide to cancel the check?"

"I won't do that. If you like, I'll sign a paper saying that I'm paying you $270 for information delivered. And you obviously know where to find me."

She waited until the kids were asleep and she was in bed with Brian to tell him what she had done.

"You're crazy, you know that, Laney! This is not some cop show you're on. What the hell do you think you're doing?"

"Don't you want to know what his report says?"

He looked at her.

"Barbara asked him to investigate Janine and Mark. She told him that she knew they were having an affair, that she had seen them together once at the house, but that she needed proof so her sister would believe her."

"So did he find this proof?"

"Well, not exactly. But Barbara also told this detective

97

that she confronted Mark, and that she figured Mark would be careful, at least for a while."

"Laney, this is idiotic! Barbara never liked Mark. You know that. Everybody in L.A. knew that. So she got this insane idea into her head—how can you believe any of this?"

"I don't, really. And I admit that Barbara didn't see clearly when it came to Mark. But why would she hire a detective unless she thought there was something to find?"

"Who knows why? She was a rich, bored woman with nothing to do with her money. Maybe it was a diversion."

"Maybe. But this detective did uncover some interesting information. For one thing, Mark's been staying home most Wednesday mornings. Dupard talked to some construction workers doing a major remodeling job on the house across the street from Kate. They noticed that one day a week he leaves early in the morning, comes back around nine-thirty, then leaves again in the afternoon."

"Why would they notice that? Are they keeping a log or something?"

"They like his BMW. And they admitted they watch the house to get a glimpse of Janine. They think she's cool. She won't give them the time of day when she comes out, but they think she likes to get their attention."

"I still don't see the point. He's a doctor, Laney, or did you forget that? Doctors usually have Wednesdays off. Unlike deputy D.A.'s."

"Mark used to do morning hospital visits on Wednesdays, then work out at the Sports Connection and play a couple of sets of racquetball. Mr. Dupard found that out from Mark's secretary. He told her he was doing a survey for the American Medical Association on doctors' leisure routines."

"So?"

"He called the Sports Connection. Asked them if Dr. Bauers still had Wednesdays reserved for the Nautilus machines and for the racquetball court. They said he switched to evenings a little more than a month ago. Then he talked to the head of nursing at Cedars, asked when was the best time to reach Dr. Bauers on a Wednesday. They said Mark was making mostly afternoon visits."

"I still don't see what you're getting at. So he's home? What's the big deal?"

"Janine is home. And there's no one else there."

"What about the maid?"

"She doesn't work on Wednesdays. That was Janine's suggestion. I remember that clearly because Kate was so impressed with how Janine was trying to save her money."

"That's still not proof that anything was going on between them."

"Maybe not. Brian, did you know that Mark was married before?"

"No. But since when is that a crime?"

"Kate never mentioned it, and we tell each other everything. I wonder if she knows."

"Was that in the report?"

She nodded. "He married Ellen Kringle in Northfield, Minnesota, in 1975. That was thirteen years ago, just before he went to medical school."

"So what happened? Divorced?"

"She died, less than a year after they were married. Dupard checked the Bureau of Records."

"Well, that explains why Mark didn't mention that he was married. Something tragic like that, he probably wanted to put the whole thing behind him. And we don't know for sure that he didn't tell Kate about it. Maybe he just asked her not to say anything."

"I guess you're right. But what do we really know

about Mark, Brian? I mean, we accepted him because Kate accepted him."

"I don't believe this. You're determined to find something wrong with him, aren't you? What are you saying now, that you've been suspicious of him from the day you met him?"

"No. I've always liked Mark, right from the start. He's a lot of fun, and he's been wonderful to Kate. But I never really thought much about his background. Who are his parents? Why haven't they ever been here?"

"They're elderly people, Laney. You told me that. You said yourself that it's hard for them to travel."

"So why haven't Kate and Mark gone to visit them? Now that I think about it, every time they planned a trip to Minnesota, Mark would get a letter or a phone call saying that it wasn't a good time."

"So?"

"It's funny, that's all."

"You never thought it was funny before."

"That's because a private detective wasn't investigating him. So what do you think?"

"I think you have a lot of suppositions that don't really add up to anything. The fact that he's home Wednesdays doesn't mean that he and Janine are messing around."

"You men always stick together, don't you?"

"Come on, Laney. Be fair. You just don't want to admit you threw out three hundred dollars."

"Two hundred seventy dollars. I'm going to investigate this a little more, Brian."

"Not tonight, though, okay? Tonight, how about investigating me?"

"What do you mean?"

"Come here and I'll show you."

On Sunday morning, Laney decided not to call first. "I am so sorry, Mrs. Tolbert," Janine said when she

100

opened the door. "Kate is still sleeping. But I will certainly tell her that you have been here."

"Where's Dr. Bauers?"

"He has taken the children to Kiddy Land to go on some rides."

"Well, I think I'll check on Kate myself. Maybe she's up by now." She moved past Janine into the hall and walked quickly up the stairs.

The room was darkened by the closed drapes. At first Laney thought Kate was asleep, but then she saw her eyes flutter open.

"Laney? Is that you?" She yawned.

"Who were you expecting, Robert Redford?" She walked over and sat on the edge of Kate's bed.

Kate smiled weakly. "What time is it?"

"Eleven."

"Really?" She sat up and yawned again. "I'm so tired all the time."

"Do you want me to get you some breakfast? I could run downstairs and have Janine prepare something."

"No thanks. I'm not really hungry. I'm glad you came, Laney. Mark told me you called, but I was a little surprised that you didn't stop by."

"I'm sorry. I got the impression you weren't up to seeing anyone."

"You're not anyone; you know that." She squeezed her hand. "People have been so kind, calling, sending notes. Evan's parents called from London. They offered to come home and help with the kids, but I told them everything's under control. They've been planning this year abroad for so long; I don't want to ruin it for them."

"Have you heard from Mark's parents?"

"Mark said they called. And they sent flowers to the chapel with a lovely note."

"You didn't speak to them?"

"No. Frankly, I'm just as glad. I feel uncomfortable talking to them on the phone. They always sound a little strained. I guess it's because we've never met." She sighed. "I still can't believe Barbara's dead. Can you?"

"I know this is rough, Kate. I wish I could help."

She shrugged. "There's nothing anyone can do, really. It was an awful accident. But it didn't have to happen. I don't know how many times I warned Barbara about leaving a radio near the tub. A hundred, at least. But there isn't much comfort in saying 'I told you so' to a grave, is there?

"What really hurts is that the last time we were together, we had a horrible fight." She hesitated. "She said some things about Janine and Mark—stupid things, really; I never believed them for a minute. And instead of seeing how lonely and miserable she was, I got angry, and I said some terrible, cruel things. And I can never make it up to her."

"Sisters fight, Kate. Believe me, Barbara has forgiven you. And she'd be the first one to admit that she wasn't always the easiest person in the world to get along with."

"I guess." She yawned again.

"Maybe I'd better go, let you get some rest."

"That's all I'm doing, is resting. I'm not really tired. It's the sleeping pills, I think. Mark doesn't like giving them to me. He wants me to stop taking them."

"Why don't you?"

"I will, soon. I'm just afraid of the nights. Dreams. You know."

"Why don't you call Dr. Zuroff, Kate?"

"I probably will. I was going to call her last week, but Mark feels I should wait a while, give myself a chance to handle this on my own. He thinks I can do it. I get the feeling he thinks I was too dependent on Dr. Zuroff."

"I don't think so, Kate. She did wonders for you."

"I guess."

* * *

102

"So were you a successful little snoop, Laney?" Brian asked when she returned.

"Don't make fun of me. Kate looks awful, Brian. Pale, listless. I tried to encourage her to get out of bed, to go for a walk in the backyard, but she said she was too tired."

"She'll be okay. She pulled through this before. With Evan, with her mother. It'll just take a while."

"This is worse, though, in a way."

"Why?"

"She's blaming herself for Barbara's death. She's convinced herself that if Barbara hadn't been upset with her, she would have been more careful with the radio when she was taking the bath—you know, that line of thinking. I told her it's ridiculous."

"Maybe she should talk to that shrink she was seeing. She'll straighten her out."

"Funny you should mention that. When I suggested that she see Dr. Zuroff, she told me that she wants to, but that Mark thinks she should wait a while."

"So?"

"So when I mentioned the same thing to Mark a few days ago, he told me that *he* suggested it to Kate, but that she doesn't want to go yet."

"You probably heard him wrong."

"Maybe. And did I also hear him wrong when he said Kate wasn't up to seeing anyone, including me? When I was there this morning, she asked me why I hadn't come over sooner."

"He's probably trying to protect her, conserve her strength. There's nothing sinister in that."

"When are you going to admit that there's something odd going on?"

"When you prove to me that there is."

On Monday, Laney didn't have much time to think

103

about Mark, or Franklin Dupard's report. Mrs. Margolin called in sick, and the shop filled up quickly with customers. Laney suspected that half of them came in just to get out of the heat.

She was in the middle of preparing supper when the phone rang. It was the nurse from the day camp her younger children attended, calling to tell her that she thought five-year-old Kimberley should see a doctor.

"I don't know whether Kimberley mentioned anything to you, but I thought you should know that she's been complaining all day of pain when she urinates. We gave her lots of juice, but if it's a bladder infection, she'll need antibiotics. It's pretty common in young girls, you know."

"Thanks. I appreciate your calling. I'll certainly take care of it."

But after Laney hung up, she remembered that with Kate still at home and Mrs. Margolin sick, she wouldn't be able to leave the shop.

"Brian, you'll have to take some time either in the morning or during lunch to take Kim to the doctor."

"I'll try, Laney. I don't know if I can get away."

"A bladder infection isn't something to fool around with. What do you want me to do, close the shop? I can't—" She stopped suddenly.

"What's wrong?"

"I just remembered something," she said softly. "Brian, a week before Barbara died, she stopped by the shop to see Kate. She told me she had a bladder infection."

"I don't think she's worrying about a bladder infection now, do you?"

"No, let me explain. She told me that her doctor said she couldn't take baths for a while. A few months, I think she said. So what was she doing in the tub?"

"Maybe she didn't follow doctor's instructions. Isn't

104

that possible?"

"It's possible. Anything's possible. But why *wouldn't* she follow instructions? And if she was—" She stared at him.

"So what are you saying, Laney? That someone put her in the tub and threw in the radio? That someone killed her?"

"I don't know what to think."

"Why would anyone want to do that?"

"I don't know. But what if—" She shook her head.

"What were you going to say?"

"No, it's stupid. It's just this detective business. And Barbara saying that Kate was in trouble, that she was going to tell me all about it. And she never showed up."

"Laney, come on. Even if Barbara's death wasn't an accident—and I still think it could be—it's just a coincidence that she died before she was supposed to meet you."

"I know. I told you this was stupid."

"But you don't think it was a coincidence, do you?"

"I don't know. What if she was killed because of something she was going to tell me? It's crazy, right?" *Tell me it's crazy, Brian.*

"You're talking about Mark? Or the girl?" He looked at her in disbelief. "Because from what I can see, they're the only ones who would have wanted to stop Barbara from talking to you, right?"

"I haven't thought it out yet."

"But what did Barbara possibly have to tell you? Look, I'll admit that from what this detective found out, it looks like Mark was fooling around with the girl. But can you honestly see him killing Barbara just to keep her from telling you that? Don't you think it's a little extreme?"

"Maybe he was afraid Kate would divorce him if she found out. Maybe he doesn't want to give up the lifestyle he has. Barbara always said he married her for her money; maybe he did. What if Mark suspected that Barbara knew about Janine and was checking into his background? And if Kate didn't know that Mark was married, and if Barbara planned to tell Kate about it *and* show her proof that Mark and Janine were having an affair . . ."

"But why would he care if Barbara spoke to you?"

"There's too much animosity between Barbara and Mark. Barbara told me that she didn't think Kate would listen to her, but she knew Kate would listen to me. So if Mark found out Barbara was planning to meet me, he would've been worried that I'd believe her and help expose him and—" She frowned. "But that doesn't make sense. Because Mark didn't know I was going to meet Barbara. Neither did Janine." She grinned. "God, I feel so much better, Brian!"

"Mark knew."

"What?"

"He called here the night before you were supposed to meet Barbara. You were at the movies with Abby, remember? Anyway, he invited us over for a barbecue the next night, and I told him you already made plans. To meet Barbara."

Chapter Eight

Brian called Laney from the office the next morning. "I checked with Records. The coroner's findings show that Barbara's death was accidental. The guy who went out to investigate is Sam Ryker. He's usually with Wilshire Divison, but he happens to be on loan to West L.A. Seems one detective there quit—stress; two others are on extended sick leave."

"Did you speak to him?"

"He wasn't in. I left a message. He'll probably call back some time today."

"Do you know him?"

"Not personally. I've heard his name. But I checked with Ray Paluzzo." Ray was a bailiff. "Ray says Ryker's a good cop. Thorough. Doesn't embarrass our office in court."

"You'll call me when you hear from him?"

"Yeah. Are you sure you want to pursue this, Laney? I mean, if you meet with Ryker and he thinks there's merit to your theory, he'll go after Mark. If you have second thoughts later, you can't just say, 'Oops, I changed my mind.'"

"I know that. But you agreed there was a lot of coincidence here. You said yourself it might not be a bad idea to talk to the police."

"I know."

"What should I do, Brian, drop it? Pretend I don't know anything? I can't do that. Because if the worst is true, Kate is living with a killer."

The uniformed officer at the front desk recognized her name immediately.

"Detective Ryker's expecting you." He escorted her upstairs to Robbery-Homicide and pointed to a tall man at the far wall of the large room. "That's him."

The room was filled with regulation beige metal desks and plain-clothes detectives who were sitting at them, typing or writing or shuffling papers. No one paid attention to Laney as she made her way to Ryker, who was leaning against his desk, his arms folded, a phone nestled between his left ear and shoulder. He was wearing navy twill slacks and a beige oxford shirt. He had loosened his navy-and-burgundy-striped tie.

"Just a sec'," he said into the phone when Laney approached. "Mrs. Tolbert?"

She nodded.

"Be right with you. Have a seat."

He was even taller than he had appeared from across the room—almost as tall as Brian, she thought—and had a muscular build that showed only the slightest hint of a pot belly. Laney guessed he was in his mid-forties. He had a square jaw, a rugged complexion, a short nose set slightly off center between warm hazel eyes, and wavy brown hair. Laney thought he was very attractive.

"Sorry I kept you waiting," he said after he had hung up.

"That's okay. I appreciate your seeing me, Detective Ryker. I wasn't sure you would."

"Frankly, I'm interested to hear what you have to say.

Your husband told me what's bothering you, but I'd like to hear the details from you, if you don't mind."

"Of course." She hesitated. "I suddenly feel so foolish, Detective. I hope I'm not wasting your time. I mean, what if this is all a product of my overactive imagination?" She smiled nervously.

"Why don't you let me be the judge of that, Mrs. Tolbert. And don't worry about my time. Your tax dollars are paying for it anyway." He smiled genially.

"Okay. Well, to put it simply, I'm not sure that Barbara Simpson's death was really an accident."

"Why not?"

"Several reasons, actually." She told him about Barbara's bladder infection. "The more I think about it, the surer I am that she was definite about not taking baths. And then there's her phone call to me just a few days before she died. You see, she asked to meet me, to discuss her sister, Kate Bauers. She told me she thought Kate was in trouble."

"She didn't say what kind of trouble?"

"No. She didn't want to discuss it over the phone. But she did say that the problem concerned the Bauers' au pair."

"That's a live-in baby-sitter, right? From Europe?"

"Right. Janine is Swiss. Truthfully, I don't think I would have thought anything was wrong if that detective hadn't showed up."

"Which detective is that?"

"His name is Franklin Dupard. He told me that Barbara had hired him to investigate Janine and Mark, Kate's husband." Laney described Dupard's findings. "So you see, that's why I'm here. It just seems like too much coincidence—Barbara's hiring the detective, her dying before she was supposed to meet with me, her being electrocuted in the tub when she told me she wasn't allowed to take baths."

"This is interesting," Ryker said thoughtfully. "Very interesting. Let me tell you what we have. Ms. Simpson's cleaning woman, Mavis Johnson, found the body at nine o'clock on Friday morning. She works for her Mondays, Wednesdays, and Fridays. Taking into account the effect of the water on the body temperature, the decomposition of the body, and the digestive state of the food products found in the deceased's stomach, the medical examiner fixed the time of death from 11:00 P.M. Wednesday to 4:00 A.M. Thursday.

"We talked to the sister. She said Ms. Simpson had a history of carelessness with electrical appliances, that she herself had repeatedly warned her specifically about leaving a radio near the tub. So that supports the finding of accidental death."

"But Detective Ryker, if Kate knew that Barbara was always leaving the radio near the tub, isn't it possible that the killer knew that, too? Maybe that's why he decided to kill her that way, because people who knew Barbara would naturally assume that her being electrocuted was just an accident."

"It could be. But the autopsy showed no signs of any foreign substances that would indicate foul play—drugs, chloroform, anything of that nature that a person would have used to subdue the deceased before placing her in the tub. There were no signs of any adhesive on her mouth, arms, or legs. There *was* blunt force trauma at the rear of the base of the skull—that means a contusion. No blood, though."

"Doesn't that mean anything?"

"Not really. You see, someone who's being electrocuted is going to do a hell of a lot of thrashing around. That's a reflexive action of the involuntary nervous system. So it's extremely likely that Ms. Simpson hit her head against the back of the tub. And that would be entirely consistent with the accidental death finding."

110

"But the injury *could* be the result of someone hitting her on the head?"

"Yes. With a blunt instrument. Because the skin wasn't broken, you see. But if you're right, and this is homicide, how did the murderer get into the house? There was no sign of forced entry. And if she let the murderer in, and he struck her on the head to make her unconscious, there would probably be some sign of struggle—scratches, abrasions, skin under the nails. But there was nothing. That's another point in favor of accidental death."

"But what about the bladder infection and the fact that she wasn't supposed to take a bath? Doesn't that change the picture?"

"It might. But we have no way of knowing that she was being careful about following her doctor's instructions. There's no way we could prove that, you see."

"And the fact that she hired a detective? And that she was planning to meet me, probably to talk about the fact that her brother-in-law was having an affair with the au pair?"

"Again, it's interesting. Unfortunately, it doesn't necessarily add up to homicide. Let's assume this man *was* cheating on his wife, and the sister-in-law found out about it and was going to expose him. Why would he kill her?"

"That's what Brian—my husband—said. Mrs. Bauers is very wealthy. She inherited quite a bit of money from her parents and even more from her late husband. Millions, in fact. Mark makes a fine living—he's an internist in private practice—but I happen to know they use her money to live the way they do. She bought him a BMW for his birthday, for instance, and a while ago she bought a vacation home in Big Bear."

"He's not the proud type, huh?" Ryker smiled.

"No. He told her from the start that it didn't make any

sense for her to live more modestly than she did before just because of male ego. Kate found his attitude very refreshing, as a matter of fact."

"You think he married her for her money?"

"I never thought so before. Now I'm not so sure. Barbara always alluded to it, but I used to think she was just trying to get under his skin. They never got along. I don't know if I mentioned that."

"I see. So what you're saying here, Mrs. Tolbert, is that Dr. Bauers wouldn't want to risk losing the comfortable lifestyle to which he had become accustomed?"

"Yes. I know that sounds flimsy, but with everything else . . ."

"You'd be amazed at what we see. People kill for less. I had a case a number of years ago where a guy killed his neighbor because he wouldn't clean the mess he made every time he pruned the hedge that separated their houses. Thank God most people are more reasonable. I'll tell you the truth, though, ever since then, I've been damn careful with my neighbor!" He grinned. "Let me ask you something, Mrs. Tolbert. How long have you known Dr. Bauers?"

"About two years. Brian and I went out with him and Kate a little while before they were engaged."

"And you liked him?"

"Yes. He has a good sense of humor, and he always seemed devoted to Kate. Kate is very much in love with him."

"Yet overnight you're willing to believe he's capable of murder? Just because he was fooling around with some girl?"

"Brian asked me the same thing. And I've been asking myself that question since I read Mr. Dupard's report. I don't have an answer, Detective. Look, I really *was* thrown by the idea that Mark was having an affair. But

112

you're right; it's a major leap from adultery to murder. I guess it's just a feeling I have. I wish I didn't have it, but I do." She looked at him. "So am I crazy, or do you think there may be something to this?"

"I'm not sure—hey, I don't mean about your being crazy." He grinned. "You sound normal to me. And I can follow your thinking. Hypothetically, it makes sense, but I don't think I have anything to go to the D.A. with. If I went to your husband, he'd throw me out of his office." He paused. "Tell you what. You've got me interested enough to do some checking. The problem now is that I don't know whether the crime scene has been disturbed. You see, since the finding was accidental death, there was no reason to seal off the place. As far as I know, Mrs. Bauers has been there ten times by now."

"She hasn't left her house. She isn't feeling well; she's taking her sister's death very hard. And I don't think she'd want anyone else to go through Barbara's things."

"So maybe no one's been there." He nodded. "That's good. That would certainly be important in regard to any physical evidence we may find. Okay. The first thing I'm going to do is contact Mrs. Bauers, see if we can get another look at the apartment."

"You're not going to tell her why, are you?"

"Not exactly." He smiled. "I'll call you in a day or so, all right?"

"Fine." She rose. "I don't know whether I should be happy that you think there's something to look into or depressed. I feel guilty even suspecting that Mark's involved with this. But then I think about Dupard's report, and, well . . ."

"I understand. It's a tough spot. For your friend's sake, I hope Ms. Simpson had an irresistible urge to take a bath."

* * *

Two days later Ryker called her at the shop.

"I don't have anything specific yet, but I wanted to show you some photos of the bathroom where Ms. Simpson was found and get your impressions. Don't worry," he added quickly. "The ones I'm going to show you were taken after the body was removed."

"When do you want me to come down?"

"Monday afternoon would be fine. I'm planning on going to Ms. Simpson's place Monday morning. I called Mrs. Bauers and told her we had to make a routine final check of the premises. She told me she hasn't gotten around to clearing out her sister's things. Anyway, I figured I'd have the cleaning woman meet me there, see if she can spot anything out of the ordinary. We didn't ask her before because we were going on the assumption of accidental death."

"Can I come with you?"

"That's pretty unusual." He paused. "But since technically we've already finished with the investigation, I guess I wouldn't actually be breaking a rule. And being a woman, you might notice something that I'd miss. *And* since you're the wife of a deputy D.A., I guess I could make an exception. All right. I'm having Mrs. Johnson meet me at Ms. Simpson's at ten o'clock tomorrow morning. Can you make it then?"

"Definitely." Mrs. Margolin could handle things by herself for a while.

Laney hadn't seen Mark since Franklin Dupard had dropped the report with all its Pandora-like ramifications into her lap. She had spoken to him several times when she called to inquire about Kate, but it wasn't difficult to filter her confused feelings—suspicion, awkwardness, a trace of fear—from her voice. Standing in front of the Las Palmas house, she hoped she would be able to present

114

a normal face to whoever opened the door.

"Kate's upstairs," Mark told her. "She ate a little supper tonight, which is an improvement, let me tell you. She's really taking this hard, Laney. Harder than I thought she would." He shook his head.

"Have you encouraged her to see Dr. Zuroff?"

"I don't want to pressure her. I mentioned it a few days ago, and she seemed anxious. I'll bring it up again soon."

"Is she still taking tranquilizers?"

"Yes. And I'm not happy about that at all. She panics when I tell her she should stop taking them. I've decided to cut the dosage in half, for starters."

"Maybe she should get out, come into the shop, at least part-time. It would do her good to be around people, to take her mind off things."

"I don't think she's ready for that Laney. And frankly, I'd appreciate it if you wouldn't even suggest it. I think she'd feel anxious about it, you know? Let's just wait a while, give her a chance to get back on her feet."

Kate was lying in bed, her head propped up on two pillows, looking much the same as she had on Sunday.

"The police called today," she told Laney. "They have to check Barbara's place one final time before they file the report. That's what the detective told me. I guess I should make plans to go through her things. I just can't face it yet."

"I suppose the building manager has a spare set of keys."

She nodded. "I have a set, too. Barbara and I exchanged spare keys long ago. It seemed like a good idea."

"Are you sleeping better?"

"A little. Janine's been fixing me hot chocolate with whipped cream almost every night. I mentioned that my mother used to prepare it for me when I was a little girl whenever I had trouble sleeping. It does help me relax,

115

although it probably isn't doing much for my figure. How's the shop?"

"Boring without you. But don't worry, I'm making both of us rich. How are the kids doing?"

"Fine, I guess. Dana's still in play group; Jeremy seems happy in day camp. To tell you the truth, they don't come in that often. I think they're nervous to see me like this. Kids get frightened when they think a parent is sick. But I just don't have the energy to get out of bed." She yawned, and smiled ruefully. "See what I mean?"

Every night, Kate told herself that she would try to sleep without a pill. But the minute she closed her eyes and faced the dark, she began to feel her chest constrict, and she could barely breathe, and she knew she wouldn't be able to sleep, not with so many turbulent thoughts bombarding her, not with anguish hovering nearby, ready to smother her.

The pills made her so calm. Sometimes, she took one in the afternoon, too, just to soften the edges. Mark would be terribly upset if he found out. He had left a bottle of the blue pills on her nightstand, but he would become suspicious if they disappeared too quickly.

It wasn't really a problem, though. Because she was going to stop taking them altogether soon. Maybe tomorrow.

On Monday morning Laney was standing in front of the entrance to the condominium complex when Ryker showed up.

"Am I late?" he asked.

"No. I'm a little eager, I think. By the way, I saw Kate yesterday, and I managed to find out that she had a key to Barbara's condo."

116

"You want to join the force?" He grinned. "Wait here while I get the key from the manager."

When he returned, they took the elevator to the sixth floor. Ryker opened the door to the condominium and they stepped inside. Mavis Johnson arrived a few minutes later.

"I'm not 'zactly sure what you want me to do." The woman looked at Ryker with intelligent brown eyes.

"Well, I thought you could just look around, see if anything strikes you as wrong or odd. Don't touch anything, though. If you notice something, just tell me."

"Okay." She sounded dubious. "I'll start in the bedroom, I guess."

Ryker and Laney followed her in and watched as she looked around the room for a few minutes.

"I don't see nothin' strange. Except whoever made her bed didn't do a very good job."

"What do you mean?" Ryker asked.

"Didn't one o' your men fix it when they was here?"

"Why would you think that?"

"Well, 'cause that's not the way I do it. Look't the seams o' that bedspread. They's nowhere near the edge o' the bed. An' see the way that there pillow's tucked? Sloppy." She clucked disapprovingly.

"Maybe Ms. Simpson took a nap and fixed the bedspread herself after she got up."

Mavis Johnson chuckled, and suddenly stopped. "No offense to Miz Simpson, 'specially now she's dead. But in all the years I been workin' for her, I never seen her fix her spread. Oh, sometime she'll shake out her quilt, and she hardly did that, either. But pick up that bedspread? No way. It weighs more'n thirty pounds." She shook her head and sighed, as if remembering the weight. "Where do you want I should go next?"

"The bathroom, I think," Ryker said. He looked around.

"That there door." She pointed.

She followed Ryker across the plush expanse of white carpet and waited patiently while the detective covered the doorknob with a handkerchief and opened the door. Ryker moved aside to let her enter. Laney stood next to him.

"Real pretty," Mavis said. "Looks like it was set up for a magazine, don't it?"

"Does anything look different than it should?"

"Not that I can see." She looked around again. "Can I just fix that hamper? Bothers me no end to see somethin' stickin' out like that."

"I'll do it. Could you please get me a fresh towel, Mrs. Johnson? I don't want to touch the surface of the hamper."

She looked at him strangely before she left the room. In a minute she was back with a towel from the linen closet and handed it to him.

Ryker lifted the hamper lid. Using the towel, he emptied the contents onto the floor. There was a turquoise cotton blouse, a pair of pink lace panties, a white terry bath sheet, and a violet cotton nightgown.

"Mrs. Johnson, could you look at these items a minute?"

"I'm lookin'."

"On the last Wednesday that you were here, did you do all the laundry?"

"'Course I did. The washin' an' the ironin' too. Miz Simpson was real particular 'bout havin' her things ironed. Even her nightwear. I know I ironed that there purple one on Wednesday. See all them eyelet ruffles? Took me 'bout ten minutes alone just to get them lookin' right."

"And you're sure the hamper was empty when you left on Wednesday?"

"I said so, didn't I? I wouldn't leave nothin' in the hamper."

"What about the towel? Why would that be in the hamper?"

"I dunno. But Miz Simpson, she didn't like to use a towel more'n once. That wuz just her way. Didn't bother me none." She shrugged.

"Mrs. Johnson?" Laney said. "I was wondering whether you put that bar of soap in the recess in the tub."

"Not this time, I didn't. I usually do, but Miz Simpson, she told me she wasn't takin' baths for a while. I put a new one in the shower, though. I remember that."

"Are you sure she wasn't taking baths?" Ryker asked.

"How can I be sure of that? I didn't live here with her, did I? I can't say what she did an' what she didn't do."

"Can you take a look at the shower, Mrs. Johnson?" Ryker asked. "See if everything looks right. Again, please don't touch anything."

She walked over. "Looks all right. Shower door's got water'n soap spots on it. I know I didn't leave it lookin' like that. Is that it?"

"I think so. Could you look around the rest of the apartment, though? I really appreciate your cooperation."

"Fine with me."

Fifteen minutes later they were done. Mavis Johnson hadn't found anything of interest, and she was relieved when Ryker thanked her and told her she could leave.

"Why were you interested in the contents of the hamper?" Laney asked him.

"I was wondering about the nightgown. Did you notice there was another one on the counter?"

"That's where I would put it if my bathroom counter was long enough. I usually end up leaving it on the toilet seat."

119

"Okay. Mavis Johnson clearly remembers that she ironed the purple nightgown that Wednesday. So why was it in the hamper? And why did Ms. Simpson prepare another nightgown for after her bath? How many nightgowns does she use in one night?"

"Maybe she was hot and decided to change."

"The place is air-conditioned. I checked. The only way to explain the two nightgowns is that she got into her nightgown, changed her mind, decided to take a bath, and prepared a fresh nightgown. Do you see any problem with that scenario?"

"I think so," Laney said slowly. "If she decided to take a bath *after* she went to bed, why was there already a bath towel in the hamper? That would suggest that she'd already bathed or showered. And the water and soap spots on the shower door would point to that, too."

"Good! Remember, too, that Mrs. Johnson said somebody fixed the bed, and she doubted that Ms. Simpson was that someone. And if you think about it, why would she remake her own bed in the evening?"

"Which means what?"

"That if you're right, here's what could have happened. She went to sleep. The killer struck her at the base of the skull to knock her out, undressed her, and put her in the tub. Then he or she—"

"She?" Laney exclaimed.

"It could have been a woman. We can't rule that out. It wouldn't be easy to drag the body to the bathroom, but it isn't far, and it's certainly possible."

"I never thought about that, but I guess you're right."

"Okay. Where were we? Right. The killer assembled all the things Ms. Simpson would normally prepare before she took a bath. And the killer couldn't use the nightgown Ms. Simpson was wearing—that was already wrinkled and looked slept-in, and it obviously wasn't fresh. Then the killer goes back into the bedroom and fixes the bed so that it won't look as if Ms. Simpson had been sleeping."

Laney stood silent.

"What's wrong? Doesn't it make sense?"

"It does. It's amazing how much you deduced from a bedspread and the contents of a hamper. I would never have figured out any of this."

"You noticed the towel, and the soap. Given time, you would have thought about the nightgown, too. What else is bothering you?"

"I guess I was hoping that I'd come here and see that my theory was crazy. Can we take another look at the bathroom?"

Ryker followed her. She looked around for a minute.

"Do you think the police moved anything?"

"Let's take a look. I happen to have those photos I told you about. I wanted to show them to you anyway." He took two black-and-white snapshots out of an envelope that he removed from his jacket pocket and handed them to her.

Laney studied the room, then the photos. "Everything looks the same. Something's bothering me, though, but I don't know what."

"Take your time."

She looked at the room again, at the nightgown, slippers, and talcum powder all sitting on the counter; at the neatly folded bath sheet and washcloth lying on a stool near the tub.

"Is something missing?"

"No, that's the problem, I think. Everything's too perfect. Remember what Mrs. Johnson said when she walked in here? Something about the room being pretty as a picture. For a magazine, I think she said. You know what this reminds me of? A hotel room. The only thing that's missing is the wrapped glass and a miniature bar of soap. Everything is so neat. The slippers are lined up next

121

to the nightgown. It's as if someone was setting the scene for a bath. Do you see what I mean?"

"Yeah. I do. I think I'd better watch out before you go gunning for my job." He grinned. "Okay. I think we're done here. I'm going to have the lab boys check for prints and pick up the laundry and a couple of other things, do some tests."

"So you think she was murdered, Detective?"

"It's a definite maybe. I can't tell you more than that."

"But what about all the clues?"

"Nothing is real evidence. Everything is just supposition. Here's another way of looking at the same clues. Ms. Simpson takes a shower, puts on a nightgown, but doesn't go to bed. She's restless, bored. She watches TV or something. Later, she decided she needs a bath to relax, in spite of what the doctor told her. She puts her nightgown into the hamper because she plans to use a fresh one, just like she always uses a fresh towel. She's electrocuted, hits her head on the tub. End of story."

"What about the bedspread?"

"She took a nap in the afternoon, decided to fix the bed afterwards. Maybe she was having someone over. See what I mean? It could make sense either way."

"But what do *you* think, Detective?"

"I'm inclined to agree with you, Mrs. Tolbert. But that doesn't mean my boss will. I'll run this by him and let you know what he says. By the way, do you have any idea who inherits Ms. Simpson's estate?"

"I guess her sister would."

Ryker called her two days later.

"Sorry I didn't get back to you sooner. I've been real busy."

"I understand. Are they going to reopen Barbara's case?"

"Maybe. Something interesting came up. Do you know someone by the name of Simon Leicester?"

"Simon? He's—he was Barbara's boyfriend. They were living together until just recently. Why?"

"I called the bank where Ms. Simpson has a checking and savings account. It seems she wrote a check to Simon Leicester on the Tuesday before she died. The amount was $150,000. Interesting, isn't it?"

Chapter Nine

"I can't believe Barbara gave Simon that much money for the gallery," Laney told Ryker.

"What gallery?"

"Simon is an artist turned businessman. Barbara was trying to help him raise the capital to finance an art gallery on La Brea, and I know from Kate that she personally invested some of her own money in it."

"Wouldn't she be likely to give him more, if she thought it was a sound venture?"

"Maybe. Kate would know more about it. But I *do* know that Barbara and Simon were having problems. Kate told me about it. She said Barbara didn't sound too hopeful about their relationship."

"Well, I think we'll have a talk with Mr. Leicester."

"It's pronounced 'Lester,' by the way."

"Oh? Thanks. Was he at the funeral, by the way?"

"Yes. I saw him there."

"I may have to talk to the sister, Mrs. Bauers, and see what she thinks."

"Do you have to talk to Kate, Detective Ryker? I just saw her last night, and she's still extremely depressed about Barbara's death. I don't think talking about her relationship with Simon will help matters."

"I'll see if I can work around it."

Laney had stopped by in the evening. Secretly, Kate had been relieved to see her go. Laney had tried to encourage her to get out of bed, to come into the shop, and even though Kate knew she was trying to be helpful, trying to transfuse her with some of her own vitality, she had sensed an unspoken "why-don't-you-get-a-handle-on-yourself" disapproval in all her suggestions.

Maybe she wasn't being fair. Maybe it wasn't Laney's disapproval she was sensing, but her own disappointment. She had expected that by now she would be stronger, that she would be able to emerge from the cocoon of grief and accept her role as wife and mother. Instead, she was helpless; the assurance and serenity that had been erected, layer by layer, in her many sessions with Dr. Zuroff had crumbled, like a fragile figurine, into fine dust.

Mark was wonderfully supportive about her slow recuperation. He hadn't pressured her to resume their love-making, had encouraged her to wait until she was ready. Ready. When would that be? she wondered. She was still so tired much of the time. Mark had given her a different tranquilizer, half the dosage of the earlier one, and he had warned her that he would be taking those away soon, too. She didn't know how she would manage without them. Well, she would have to.

Janine understood her. Janine knew the deadening pain of bereavement, of feeling like a flower whose petals have been torn off, one by one, until it stands defenseless, alone. Janine understood that Kate needed time to heal, to form, once again, the beginnings of a protective scab over the wound that death had left, understood that she wasn't merely indulging herself in misery.

Janine never insisted that Kate come downstairs for meals, never complained about the countless trays she prepared so cheerfully with food that was more often than not left uneaten. She didn't complain, either, about the extra responsibilities she had assumed since Barbara's death, the fact that she had to spend more time with the children, bathe them, put them to bed. She bandaged their scrapes, admired their arts-and-crafts projects, played with them. She comforted Dana when she had nightmares. Kate never even heard the crying.

In every action Janine was considerate, trying to help Kate maintain the illusion of maternity. Even though Kate didn't have the strength to read to Jeremy and Dana before they went to sleep, Janine always made sure to consult with her about which book to read to them. And when Jeremy's first tooth fell out, she made him go directly to Kate to display the tissue-wrapped trophy and collect a weak hug.

But Kate knew she was wasting the daily material of which precious memories are forged. A few nights ago she had decided to surprise everyone and come down for supper. She had found them sitting at the breakfast room table—Mark, Janine, Jeremy, and Dana—and for a moment she had felt like an intruder, and she had been sharply jealous of the intimacy of the family tableau they presented.

It was Janine who had seen her first, who had jumped up and helped her into her seat, who had rushed into the kitchen and brought another place setting. The children had looked at her curiously but soon resumed their chatter. Kate had tried to listen intently, to follow the recital of their day's activities, but their conversation had seemed muffled somehow, and she had been tired, so tired. After the soup, she had excused herself and gone back upstairs.

Maybe she would try again in a few days.

Richard Bristol of Bristol, McKay, and Lederman received Detective Ryker graciously in his book-lined office but was reluctant to discuss the financial affairs of his late client, Ms. Barbara Simpson.

"Frankly, I don't see your interest in Ms. Simpson's estate," the white-haired senior partner told Ryker. "From what I understood, her death was ruled accidental. Are you saying that you're reopening the case?" He peered at the detective through rimless bifocals.

"Not at this time, Mr. Bristol. There *are* some suspicious circumstances which have come to light surrounding her death, nothing concrete enough, however, to warrant reopening the case. I'm speaking confidentially, you understand; I've got to have your word that you won't mention any of this to any member of Ms. Simpson's family."

He nodded. "You have my word, of course, Detective."

"I *did* contact Ms. Simpson's bank and learned that she had written a check in the amount of $150,000 to a Simon Leicester. I was wondering whether you could tell me whether you had any prior knowledge that she planned to do so."

He pursed his lips. "I find that rather strange, to say the least. You see, just before her death, Barbara called me and asked me how she could recover money that she had already placed into an escrow account for the gallery that Mr. Leicester was planning to open."

"Did she say why?"

"Yes. She told me that on second thought, she had grave doubts as to Mr. Leicester's business acumen. I also read between the lines that their . . . ahem . . . relationship had hit a snag. But I can't attest to that. In any case,

Detective, it is completely illogical that she would have contributed *more* money to the venture."

"Is it possible that she reconsidered? That he convinced her that he *could* make a go of the gallery with her help?"

"Even then, she would never have written a personal check, Detective. I've known Barbara since she was an infant. The Simpson family has retained us for over forty years, you see. And while Barbara was hardly conservative in her dress or decorum, and she liked to indulge herself in the luxuries she could well afford, she was not a rash woman when it came to business affairs. If she had intended to give Mr. Leicester additional funds, she would have simply notified me of the fact and asked me to handle it in the proper legal fashion."

"Do you find it strange that she had so much money in a savings account?"

"Unwise, certainly, from a more traditional fiscal viewpoint. The money could have been working more to her advantage. But as I mentioned, Barbara liked to spend her money, often on a whim. She enjoyed knowing that she had a considerable sum at her fingertips. Frankly, I had given up arguing with her about it."

"So in your estimation, Mr. Bristol?"

"In my estimation, Detective, Barbara Simpson didn't write that check. But I don't know whether you'll be able to prove it."

Simon Leicester took a seat across the desk from Ryker and crossed his right leg over his left knee, careful not to ruin the crease of his gray pleated slacks. He had left the top two buttons of his mauve silk shirt undone, and had artistically draped a print silk scarf around his neck. Ryker wondered why he had omitted the beret. It would have camouflaged his thinning blond hair.

"Thank you for coming in, Mr. Leicester. I appreciate your cooperation."

"Your officers didn't give me much choice, actually." His small gray eyes studied Ryker coolly.

"I'm sure they told you this was voluntary, didn't they?"

"Well, yes, they did. But the implication was that I had no choice."

"I'm sorry you got that impression. You're not under arrest. We'd just like to ask you a few questions about Ms. Simpson. I understand that the two of you were romantically involved?"

"That's correct."

"Were you living with her at the time of her death?"

"Barbara and I had decided to live apart for a short while, just to give ourselves time to think. We thought we would both benefit from a temporary separation before we made a formal commitment."

"You were planning on getting married, then?"

"Oh, yes. Absolutely. Barbara was a wonderful woman—warm, beautiful, caring. She had a fabulous personality, a great sense of style. I can't believe that she's really dead." He shook his head sadly.

"She told her sister that you and she had been having some problems recently."

"An exaggeration, Detective. Barbara was a tad jealous because I was showing attention to a woman who works for a major auction house. She calmed down, though, when she saw that our relationship was just professional."

"I see. When was the last time you saw Ms. Simpson?"

"I can't remember exactly. I believe it was several days before she met with her awful accident, but I can't recall the exact day."

"Maybe I can help you there, Mr. Leicester. We have a canceled check from Ms. Simpson's bank that she wrote to you in the amount of $150,000. The check is dated Tuesday, July 5. That's just a day before she died."

"Yes, that's correct. Barbara had called me, you see. She had decided to invest more money in an art gallery that I'm planning to open. She was very generous, I must say, and she was totally committed to the gallery."

"Well, I'll tell you the truth, Mr. Leicester. We're having a little problem with the check. First of all, the number is out of sequence. The check she gave you is 407. But 405 and 406 are dated Wednesday, July 6."

"She probably just tore off the wrong check on Tuesday. That's happened to me once in a while. It can really complicate one's personal bookkeeping, can't it?" He smiled.

"It certainly can. I also noticed that the ink used to fill in the check seems identical to the ink you used to write your endorsement. It's a rather interesting shade of blue."

"I don't see—oh, yes. Of course. I remember quite clearly now. Barbara's pen was on the blink. She was rather upset about it, as a matter of fact; it was expensive, and she had just purchased it. But you know how inferior workmanship is today, Detective." He shrugged. "Anyway, I loaned her mine."

"Thoughtful of you. Mr. Leicester, I should tell you that one of our handwriting experts is examining the writing on that check and comparing it with some correspondence we obtained that bears Ms. Simpson's signature. We're looking into the possibility that the check is a forgery. As a matter of fact, I'm expecting a call any minute from SID—that's Scientific Investigation Division—with the results of that comparison."

"That's absolutely impossible! What can you possibly mean by this? Barbara wrote the check while I was there."

"I don't think so, Mr. Leicester. You see, Ms.

Simpson's prints are nowhere on that check. Don't you find that odd?"

"That check has been handled by several people, Detective. By myself, for one. By the teller to whom I presented it and by various bank personnel thereafter. Isn't it possible that Barbara's prints could have been eliminated in the process?"

"Smudged, maybe. But not eliminated. It would be interesting to see whether your prints stayed clear, wouldn't it? Do you have a key to Ms. Simpson's apartment?"

"Yes, I do." He shifted slightly in his chair.

"Where were you on the night of Wednesday, July 6?"

"I don't understand why you're asking me that. What difference could that possibly make?"

"We have new evidence which suggests that Ms. Simpson was murdered. That someone placed her in the tub, filled it with water, and threw in the radio to simulate an accidental electrocution. Now who do you think would have wanted to do that?"

"I find your implication abhorrent, Detective. To suggest that I would kill Barbara is insulting and preposterous. I loved her!"

"You and she had separated, Mr. Leicester. You needed additional financing for your gallery, but Ms. Simpson's attorney told me that she wanted to retrieve the money she had already invested in the gallery. Did Ms. Simpson tell you that she wanted out of the gallery? Did you get scared, Mr. Leicester? Did you see all your dreams disappearing right in front of your eyes?"

"This is absurd!"

"What happened, Mr. Leicester? Did you come in when she was sleeping? You had a key to the apartment; you could easily have entered at any time. And then, when you killed her, you figured you might as well make it worth your while, so you wrote yourself a little check.

131

You're an artist, aren't you? It would be relatively easy for you to imitate Ms. Simpson's handwriting."

Leicester sat silent.

"Or maybe you didn't plan it. Maybe you had a fight, hit her in a fit of anger? You still haven't answered my question, you know. Where were you on Wednesday evening, July 6?"

"I have absolutely nothing to say to your outrageous allegations. And I think I should see an attorney before I answer any more questions."

"Good idea. I'd do it if I were in your shoes."

"Am I free to go, Detective?"

"Certainly, for now. But don't leave town, Mr. Leicester. You understand." Ryker pressed a button on the phone, but just then another line rang. He answered it. "Wait just a minute, will you, Mr. Leicester?" He turned back to the phone. "Yeah, I'm listening. Is that right? Yeah. Okay, thanks a lot. I owe you one."

He hung up and turned to Leicester. "You know, it's amazing what the lab boys can do nowadays. I mean, I could look at two samples of writing and think they were written by the same person because of their superficial similarities. But these experts, they study every curve, every slant, the heights of the characters, the pressure." He shook his head in wonder. "I find it fascinating, don't you?"

"Detective Ryker."

Ryker waited.

"Detective Ryker, if I can prove that I was somewhere else that evening, where would that leave me?"

The starched assurance of his previous tone had wilted. Ryker wasn't sure if it was his imagination, but the folds of his silk scarf seemed to have drooped, too.

"Well, assuming that you could prove that to our satisfaction, I guess it would eliminate you as a murder suspect. That's the good news. The bad news, Mr.

Leicester, is that you'd still be accountable for the forgery. It *is* forgery, isn't it?"

"I'd like to make a statement."

Ryker picked up the phone, dialed an extension, and asked for a stenographer. After she had come in and seated herself, he read Leicester his rights. "Don't you want to speak to an attorney?"

"I don't see that it will matter. You were right, Detective. I forged the check. But I didn't kill Barbara." He stopped.

"I'm listening, Mr. Leicester."

"I went to the apartment on Thursday morning, to pick up a few things. I hadn't moved everything out, you see. I found Barbara dead in the tub. It was frightful. Absolutely frightful." He shuddered. "She was bloated and discolored. She would have hated the disfigurement more than the death, I think."

"Why didn't you call the police?"

"I was about to, but then . . . look, Detective, Barbara was an enormously wealthy woman. And she was dead. Calling the police wasn't going to bring her back."

"So you decided to take advantage of her death?"

"I didn't see the harm in writing a check to myself. The truth is, we would have gotten back together, and in spite of what her lawyer suggested, she would have helped me with the remainder of the financing for the gallery. As far as stealing the money, whom did I hurt? Her sister is wealthier than she is. She certainly wouldn't miss a mere $150,000."

"I'm not sure that she would see it quite the same way."

"And you know, Detective, you may not believe this, but I don't think Barbara would have minded. In fact, had she been able, I'm convinced she would have told me to write the check. I really am."

"Well, unfortunately, we'll never know, will we? So

133

you predated the check because you didn't want anyone to know you had been there on Thursday, is that right?"

"Correct. But I didn't touch anything in the apartment."

"Where were you on Wednesday night, Mr. Leicester?"

"With Monica Blendheim." He hesitated. "She's the woman that aroused Barbara's jealousy."

"The one with whom you were having a strictly professional relationship?"

Leicester flushed. "I am not a saint, Detective. While Barbara and I separated, I needed some female companionship. I do have needs, you know."

"That's quite apparent. How long were you with her?"

"We had dinner together at a restaurant with another couple. After that, we all went for drinks at the Four Seasons. We returned to her apartment quite late—after two o'clock, I think—and we went to sleep. Not right away, you understand." He coughed delicately.

"Ms. Blendheim will, of course, corroborate what you're saying?"

"Absolutely. And not to protect me, Detective. We have a casual relationship. Look, call her now if you want. She doesn't even know that you're questioning me, so she'll be totally unrehearsed. Ask her anything you want about the evening."

"I plan to."

After a uniformed policeman had taken Leicester away to book him, Ryker picked up the phone.

"Joe, your timing was perfect. He was just about to leave."

"Well, I got your signal. It worked, huh?"

"Like a charm. Leicester assumed you were the lab guy, calling in the report about the handwriting comparisons."

"Didn't anyone ever tell him not to make assumptions?"

"I guess not." He grinned. "In the long run, I'm sure the tests will show that it was a forgery anyway. I just thought we'd give him a little push and see what happened."

"Think he killed the Simpson woman?"

"That's a different story. He seems pretty confident. That doesn't mean he didn't do it, of course. Maybe he knows the woman will protect him. If she does, it'll be hard to break his alibi."

"So Leicester's alibi holds, more or less," Ryker told Laney the next evening. He had called her at home. "We spoke to the other couple; they confirmed that they were out with this Blendheim woman and Leicester, although they don't remember it being such a late night. And Monica Blendheim says she and Simon were otherwise occupied until pretty late."

"But he could have left while she was sleeping?"

"It's possible. She admitted she's a heavy sleeper. But it'll be hard to break his alibi. We have him on the forgery, though, and on theft. He hasn't spent the money, and if he returns it, considering this is a first offense, he might not get off too badly. Maybe even a suspended sentence with some community work. He's already out, by the way. The Blendheim woman posted bail."

"What about Barbara's death, though? Are you going to reopen the case anyway?"

"Sorry. My chief doesn't think we have enough real evidence. Unless we come up with something tangible—not just clues based on personal habits—he won't give me the go ahead."

"Won't they even talk to her neighbors? Maybe one of them saw someone that night going to her apartment. You could show them a picture of Simon."

"He doesn't want to assign any manpower to it. And I don't have the time right now."

"Oh."

"Maybe something will come up. You never know. For what it's worth, Mrs. Tolbert, I think Ms. Simpson was murdered. Maybe Leicester is the guy, maybe not. But for now, my hands are tied."

Laney had read Franklin Dupard's report so many times that she practically knew it by heart. But she read it again after she hung up with Ryker, looking for something that she might have missed.

She was terribly disappointed about Simon Leicester's alibi. She had felt infinitely better casting him instead of Mark in the role of Barbara's murderer—because there *was* a murderer; she was positive of that.

She was about to put the report away in her nightstand drawer when she suddenly had an idea. She didn't know why she hadn't thought of it before.

The following morning she dialed the number she had found at the top of the report.

"Mr. Dupard, this is Laney Tolbert. You remember, Ms. Simpson's friend?"

"Oh, yes. What can I do for you?"

"I'd like you to do some investigative work for me. It has to do with Ms. Simpson's death, as a matter of fact."

"Oh, really? I thought it was an accident."

"Well, I'm not convinced that it *was* an accident. There's some evidence to support my theory, but right now the police aren't interested. But I am. What I want you to do is talk to the people who live in the condominium complex where Ms. Simpson lived, see if

136

they saw anyone going to her place late Wednesday night."

"Is there someone you're thinking of?"

She hesitated. "Actually, there are two people. But this is really confidential. It's only a theory."

"I would never betray a confidence, Mrs. Tolbert. After all, discretion is the name of my business. If you see what I mean."

"All right. I have an idea that a man by the name of Simon Leicester may have been involved in Ms. Simpson's death. He was living with her until just before her death. He benefited rather substantially from her death, I think."

"I see. You mentioned two people."

"Yes. The other one is Dr. Bauers, Ms. Simpson's brother-in-law. It's just an idea, you understand. It may turn out to be nothing. I can get you a picture of Dr. Bauers. I don't have one of Mr. Leicester, but I can give you a good description. Do you think you can you handle this for me?"

"Why, of course. No problem."

They agreed that Dupard would come to the shop some time that day so that Laney could fill him in on the details.

"Now as far as fees go, I'd be happy to make the same arrangement I had with Ms. Simpson. $200 a day or $175 if you retain my services for two weeks or more."

"Actually, Mr. Dupard, I don't think so. You see, with my $270 in addition to the $2,200 that Ms. Simpson paid you, you received $2,470 for eleven days' work. Now $175 per day at fourteen days comes out to $2,450. So what I'd like to do is go back to Ms. Simpson's original two-week arrangement. According to that, you owe her—and now me—three days' work. If you see what I mean. Of course, I'll be happy to pay any additional expenses."

"Mrs. Tolbert, I'm afraid you've figured this out

137

wrong. I don't think I can do that."

"Really, Mr. Dupard? That's funny. I explained my thinking to my husband—he's a deputy district attorney, you know? He thought it made a lot of sense."

"I see. Well, maybe we could work it out that way, seeing as how you were willing to help me out before and you were such a good friend of Ms. Simpson's. But anything over the three days would be at the other rates, right? 'Cause otherwise I'd be losing income."

"Absolutely. And I definitely see what you mean."

Chapter Ten

Franklin Dupard was hungry and depressed.

He was hungry because a careful examination of his refrigerator had revealed only three cans of beer, a half package of square black pumpernickel, a jar of Miracle Whip sandwich spread, a chunk of moldy Monterey Jack cheese, and three suspicious-looking slices of pepperoni and pastrami that he had picked up at the deli two days ago.

He was depressed because he would have to wait to go out to eat. His landlady, Mrs. Rosetti, was out front, watering the balding plants and the narrow strip of yellow-green that served as lawn, and he wanted to avoid her as long as he could. His rent was ten days overdue, and she had already spoken to him about it twice.

He took one of the beers, found a can of sardines and an open package of Saltine crackers in a cupboard, set his feast on the formica table in the dining area of his one-bedroom apartment, and sighed.

The fact was that he needed money badly, not only for the rent on his apartment, but also for his second story office on Hollywood Boulevard and for the alimony he owed his ex-wife Lorraine. If business didn't pick up, he might have to give up the lease and work out of his apartment for a while. Or maybe he would just give up the detecting business for good.

He had lied when he had told Laney Tolbert that he was just starting out. The only new thing about his profession was the hundred glossy business cards he had just had printed. He still had thirty or so of the old cards he had ordered six years ago; some were bent at the corners, others stained, and they all seemed permeated with the yellow dinginess of failure.

Six years ago, becoming a private investigator had seemed like a good idea. After an undistinguished stint in the army, he had applied to and been rejected by the police academy (too short) and had quit a Sears training program for appliance repairmen after two weeks. He had held several jobs—door-to-door salesman for a private line of cleaning products; sales clerk in a sporting goods outfit, then in a succession of shoe stores—but had decided that working for himself was the only way to make any money. Now he wasn't so sure.

The Simpson woman's coming to him had been a real break. She had told him she'd found him in the Yellow Pages, had liked his name. Funny. Here he'd been thinking about not renewing the ad. When she had walked into his office, he had seen from the expression on her face that she thought she'd made a mistake. But he'd jumped right up, helped her into a chair, told her he'd been planning to relocate to a bigger place for some time, but he was so busy, so many clients, blah, blah, blah. He wasn't sure if she'd believed him, or if she had just been in a hurry to get started.

He had lied, too, about the money he'd received from the Simpson woman. She had given him three thousand dollars, practically insisted on paying up front to insure better service, but he had thought he could make a little extra money from the sister. Not a lot—he knew it didn't pay to be greedy, or he might get nothing at all. So he had brushed off his suit and his manners and gone to the fancy gift shop that the sister owned.

All the money was long gone. He had used part of it to pay the back rent on both places, most of it to repay his bookie. Franklin Dupard liked to bet the horses, but he invariably bet the wrong ones. He had kept a little of the money to buy some low-grade coke from a connection he had made a while ago. He knew it didn't solve his problems, but when he was high, he could forget about the godawful drabness of his apartment and his life.

Franklin had been pleasantly surprised when the Tolbert woman had called and hired him to investigate Barbara Simpson's death. And then she had told him that he owed her three days' work. And she had pulled that "My-husband-is-a-Deputy D.A." shit. The bitch. Well, he would try to string her along, tell her it would take longer than three days to see all the neighbors. But she wasn't stupid. Maybe she wouldn't buy it.

The boyfriend and the brother-in-law. He wondered which one was involved. Maybe neither one. Maybe the Tolbert woman had it all wrong and it *was* an accident. If not, why weren't the police interested?

But if it *was* murder . . .

He frowned. If it *was* murder, from what the Tolbert woman had explained, it could've been one of these two guys. They both had keys to the Simpson place, both had motives. What if he called them up, told each one that the Simpson woman had hired him to tail him?

Night *and* day.

What if he said that he'd seen someone at her place late on the night of July 6? That he hadn't thought anything of it at first, because the woman had electrocuted herself, right? But that he'd gotten to thinking that maybe somebody had just made it look that way. He wasn't sure. He didn't want to go the police, but it was bothering him, you know? Maybe somebody could explain it to him so it could make sense.

Franklin nodded, drank some beer.

The question was, who to call first? The doctor or the artist?

By morning, he had made his decision.

". . . so I don't want to put you out or anything, but I thought it would be a good idea if we could meet. If you see what I mean."

"I have no idea what you're talking about, Mr.—?"

"Dupard. Franklin Dupard. Look, maybe you had a perfectly good reason for being there. The thing is, I'm a detective. If I sit on something like this, and it turns out to be important, I could lose my license. If you see what I mean."

"Mr. Dupard, you obviously have the wrong man. Maybe you saw someone who looked like me, but I can prove that I was somewhere else all night. I don't think—"

"Listen, I'll be at a little bar on Sunset called Gino's from 10:00 till 11:30 tonight. It's right near my house, so it's no big deal for me. I'll be wearing gray slacks, a red and white striped shirt, and a blue blazer with a red kerchief in the pocket." His best outfit. He'd just gotten it out of the cleaners.

"Mr. Dupard, you're wasting your time and mine."

"Till 11:30. Think it over. I'm only trying to help."

At 11:25 that night, Franklin Dupard decided that once again he had bet the wrong horse. Or maybe they were both duds. He had nothing to show for the evening, and he had spent $16.50 that he couldn't afford on watered-down drinks to accompany the stale peanuts that sat in front of him.

The place had been half full all night. Some regulars, a couple that had come in around 10:30, probably stopping in for a drink after seeing a movie. Laughing, smiling. Franklin had looked at the two enviously. He hadn't had a real date in ages.

He had noticed a young woman sitting at the bar when he came in. She wasn't bad looking, he had decided. Cute, with short brown hair, and a hell of a lot prettier, actually, than some of the women he came across at the singles' bars he went to when he scraped a little dough together. And she wasn't flashy, not painted like some of the hookers he saw on Hollywood or Sunset, carrying God knows what disease. He had tried catching her eye once or twice, but she hadn't seemed to notice. She kept looking at her watch. Probably waiting for her boyfriend. Weren't they all?

At first he didn't realize the girl was speaking to him.

"I'm sorry, miss. I didn't hear you."

"I just wanted to know what time it is."

He checked his watch. "11:40."

"Oh." She looked crestfallen. "I was supposed to meet my brother. I guess he's not coming."

"I was waiting for someone, too. I guess we're both out of luck." He smiled. "Can I buy you a drink?"

She shook her head lightly. "Thanks anyway, but I don't think so."

"Hey, just a drink. No strings attached, see?" He lifted his arms, pushed up his jacket sleeves and turned his wrists outward with a flourish. "What do you say?"

She smiled hesitantly. "I guess it's okay." She paused. "My name is Sally. Sally Pearson."

"Nice to meet you, Sally Pearson. Franklin Dupard. My friends call me Frank. So what'll you have?"

"Well, Frank." She smiled, showing even, white teeth. "I'd like a strawberry dacquiri, if that's all right. I don't like anything too strong."

"A strawberry dacquiri it is." He signaled to the bartender with studied nonchalance, ordered her dacquiri and a whiskey sour for himself. Maybe the evening wouldn't be a total loss after all. He'd charge the drinks to the Tolbert woman as an expense. She deserved it for the crap she'd pulled.

They stayed at the bar until 12:30. Franklin helped her down from her barstool and escorted her outside.

"Well, thanks," he said. "I enjoyed talking to you. I hope you won't take it wrong if I say I'm glad your brother never showed."

She blushed. "To tell you the truth, Frank, there *is* no brother. I was waiting for a male friend. I just didn't want you to get the wrong idea. And if you were the wrong kind of guy, well, I could always say my brother was coming soon."

"I see. So, Sally, can I see you again sometime? Take you to a movie or something?"

"I'd like that." She rested her hand lightly on his arm. "Could you give me a lift to my car? It's a few blocks away."

"I walked. I live just a couple of blocks away. On Fountain near Vista." He looked at her. "Would you like to come to my place for some coffee? I don't have much else to offer you, I'm afraid. I've been meaning to do some grocery shopping for days, and I haven't gotten around to it."

"I don't know, Frank. Maybe another time. It's a little late."

"Hey, Sally. When I say coffee, I mean coffee. No games, honest. I'm not that kinda guy."

She hesitated, then smiled. "Coffee sounds nice, Frank. Real nice. But I can only stay a little while."

Maybe his luck had changed. And if Sally Pearson turned out to be worth the effort, Franklin Dupard decided he wouldn't charge the evening to Mrs. Tolbert after all.

* * *

Laney knew it was ridiculous to expect instant results, but when five days had passed with still no word from Franklin Dupard, she became annoyed. She called him again at his office. Again, he wasn't there, and she left a message on the answering machine asking him to call her as soon as possible. This time she didn't bother to hide her impatience.

She called Ryker next. He *was* in.

"What can I do for you, Mrs. Tolbert?"

"I was just wondering whether there was anything new on Barbara's death."

"Sorry. Nothing's come up. To be honest, we're not really pursuing it at this time."

"I see. Well, I guess that's it, then."

"Right. Oh, yeah, there was something I wanted to ask *you*. What was the name of that detective Ms. Simpson hired?"

"Franklin Dupard."

"I thought I recognized the name, but I couldn't remember where I'd heard it. When you called I made the connection."

"Why do you ask? Are you going to speak to him?"

"Not exactly. Actually, I'm afraid no one is. Dupard is dead."

"Dead!"

"He was found in his apartment yesterday. His landlady was planning to evict him for nonpayment of rent, and she wanted to see what shape the place was in."

"How did he die?"

"From the looks of it, he shot up with some stuff and got more than he bargained for. He either overdosed or got some bad stuff. We won't know until we get the lab results."

"I don't believe this! This can't be a coincidence, Detective Ryker."

"I'm afraid it's just that, Mrs. Tolbert. Eerie, I'll admit, but a coincidence. After all, Dupard didn't have any further connection with Ms. Simpson, did he?"

"As a matter of fact, he did."

"What are you talking about?"

"I hired him to talk to Barbara's neighbors and see if they saw anyone come to her place the night of her death. I gave him a picture of Dr. Bauers and a detailed description of Simon Leicester."

He sighed. "When was this?"

"On Saturday, August 13. I was frustrated and I wanted some answers. Do you still think his death is just a coincidence?"

"Frankly, I don't know. I'm not handling this; West Hollywood Division is, but I know some guys there and I'll see what I can find out. In the meantime, don't mention any of this to anyone, okay?"

Ryker asked to be present at Franklin Dupard's autopsy. Lou Morelli, the forty-eight-year-old detective from West Hollywood in charge of the case, didn't mind. He and Ryker had been in the same division seven years back and had worked several cases together.

Morelli was inches shorter than Ryker and pounds heavier. He had coal black, thick, wavy hair with only a few trespassing strands of silver, and large, onyx, marble-like eyes that were almost, but not quite, lost in the generous contours of his slightly florid face. Standing next to each other, Ryker and Morelli resembled Mutt and Jeff; but there was nothing cartoonish about their relationship or the professionalism with which they had apprehended numerous killers and handed the district attorney's office the irrefutable evidence with which to convict them.

There had been no competition between the two men, simply mutual admiration for each other's expertise. And although they had had only sporadic contact after Ryker had transferred to Wilshire Division, whenever they saw each other, they fell into the good-natured banter of their earlier camaraderie.

The acrid smell of formaldehyde greeted Ryker as soon as he walked off the elevator. He made his way down a long hall past a series of pathology labs, exchanged hellos with a few familiar faces. Standing outside the doors to the autopsy room, he located two Tums tablets in his pants pocket, popped them into his mouth, and crunched them quickly, hoping to offset the all too familiar churning that his stomach promised.

When he entered the room, Morelli and the Medical Examiner, Lee Kanata, were already there. "Doc, Lou. Hope I didn't keep you waiting."

Kanata, a short, dapper man in his mid-forties, was busy preparing his instruments and didn't answer.

"Just got here myself," Morelli said. "Lost a little more hair, huh, Sam? Linda's probably not too thrilled." He grinned, patting his own full head of hair.

"Still short, huh, Lou?" Ryker grinned back at Morelli. The two men smiled at each other genially.

"So how's Linda, beautiful as ever? And the girls? Your older daughter, she must be in—what, junior high?"

"Kelly's in tenth grade already, Lou. Becky's in seventh. They're great." He smiled, not bothering to hide his pride. As if he could. "How about you? How's Rose and the family?"

"The family's growing. I guess you didn't hear, huh? I'm gonna be a grandfather, Sam. Can you beat that?" He shook his head in wonder. "My daughter Carol's due in January. Rose says I look bigger'n she does." He patted his paunch and laughed. "They're turning me into an old man before my time." He looked ecstatic.

"Mind if I interrupt this little reunion?" Kanata asked with mock gruffness. He had finished arranging his

147

instruments to his liking. "If I had known this was going to be a social event, gentlemen, I would have ordered coffee and doughnuts. I happen to have a backload of cases, you know."

"Ready whenever you are, Doc," Ryker said easily.

"So what's your interest in this, Ryker?" Kanata asked as he slipped on his gloves. "What's the matter, don't you have enough stiffs in West L.A.?"

"I just love watching you work, Doc. You know that." Ryker grinned. "Actually, there's a possibility this may be tied in with a case I'm interested in." He told them briefly about Dupard's connection to Barbara Simpson.

"Slim," Morelli said. "It may just be an overdose."

"Maybe," Ryker admitted.

"Okay," Kanata said. "Let's get on with it."

He made his first bloodless incision into chalky gray skin that parted obligingly under his deft, masterly stroke. Ryker glanced quickly away until he was sure he had his stomach under control, then forced his eyes back to the cadaver. He was careful to avoid Dupard's eyes. Morelli watched, fascinated, until Kanata had finished.

The autopsy itself didn't show anything suspicious.

"The liver's a little enlarged," Kanata said. "Probably drank too much. Heart looks okay. No signs of trauma. No damage to the larynx. You say you found a syringe near the body?"

"Uh-huh," Morelli said. "With some rubber tubing for the arm. We also found a small white packet with a powdery residue that looks like coke. It was sitting on a counter near the stove, next to a pot that smelled like it had ordinary alcohol in it. I think Dupard liquified the coke in it. We're doing an analysis of the packet and the pot, too. So what do you think, Doc? Is it an overdose?"

"Maybe. Could be a poison, though. We'll have to take tissue sections and body fluids and do a base screen toxin analysis. I only see the one needle mark, by the way, so

148

if this guy was a user, then this was probably the first time he injected the stuff."

"First and last," Ryker said. "Which arm shows the needle mark, by the way, Doc?"

"Left arm. Which would mean he's right-handed."

"Anything else?" asked Morelli. "You think he used coke before?"

"Nasal passages look irritated, so could be he sniffed the stuff, if anything. Anything else, you'll have to wait till we get the lab results. Did you get anything from the syringe?"

"The lab is backlogged, but I'm hoping they'll get to it within the next few days," Morelli said.

"No rush," Kanata said. "This man isn't going anywhere. I'm going to send the lab a blood sample and tissue from the liver, heart, and spleen."

"Can you get a sample from the throat, too, Doc?" Ryker asked.

Kanata looked at him and nodded. "Good idea."

The lab results of the powder in the packet and the liquid residue in the syringe and the pot came through two days later, on Wednesday. The surface of the syringe and rubber tubing bore only Dupard's fingerprints, as did the white packet. An analysis of the traces of the liquid in the syringe and pot showed a mixture of cocaine and strychnine.

Morelli and Ryker checked with narcotics detectives in the other precincts. So far, nobody else had O.D.'d on a coke-strychnine mixture, but that didn't mean that somebody wouldn't.

"Let's hope this is just an isolated incident," Morelli said. "I'd hate to think some maniac was putting this stuff out on the street."

"Right. And if it *is* an isolated incident, then it looks like Dupard was a specific target. Good news for all the junkies; bad news for Dupard."

On Thursday, Kanata called Morelli and then Ryker with the results of the analysis of the tissue samples. The blood sample and tissue sections from the heart, liver, and spleen showed traces of cocaine and strychnine. The sections from the throat and palate showed only strychnine.

"What do you think?" Ryker asked.

"Looks like two different episodes. The cocaine-strychnine mixture was injected; that's clear. The results from the throat and palate tissue indicate that the strychnine was ingested orally, probably with a liquid. We found coffee in his system, and a considerable amount of alcohol. Ordinarily, I might not have taken a throat sample, so we might not have noticed the discrepancy."

"Could someone have given Dupard coffee with the strychnine first, then waited until he was almost dead and injected the other stuff?"

"Very possibly. Say the killer puts ten milligrams of strychnine in the coffee, saves another fifteen to twenty milligrams for the coke mixture. After Dupard drinks the coffee, he starts thrashing around, convulsing. Then the strychnine attacks his central nervous system, shuts down the respiratory system, the heart, the brain. The killer would have had to inject the stuff while Dupard's heart was still pumping, though; otherwise, the stuff wouldn't circulate in his system. Did you find anything in the guy's place with traces of only strychnine?"

"Morelli says no. So are we looking at homicide, Doc?"

"Definitely. There's no way this guy could have shot up after he ingested the strychnine. Does that make you happy, Ryker?"

"Tickled pink."

* * *

150

With Morelli's go-ahead, Ryker went to Dupard's apartment after work. The place had been sealed after Dupard's body had been removed, and Ryker waited for the officer on duty to let him in.

Since the autopsy had revealed large traces of alcohol in Dupard's system, the first thing Ryker did was look for liquor. There were empty cans of beer in the trash can under the kitchen sink, but no discarded bottles. Dupard must have gone out for drinks.

There was a terry kitchen-towel on the sink next to an empty dish rack. Ryker took a plastic bag he had brought with him and carefully placed the towel inside it.

The bedroom didn't reveal anything. Dupard wasn't a meticulous housekeeper, but the room was relatively tidy. Ryker noticed that the bed hadn't been slept in, although the somewhat frayed white cotton chenille spread had been neatly folded down. He looked under the bed and found several days' worth of dirty laundry. Dupard's scent was still alive even if his body wasn't.

Some legacy.

Based on the temperature of Dupard's liver and the absence of rigor mortis, Kanata had estimated that death had taken place between twelve o'clock and five o'clock Tuesday morning, August 15. If Dupard had consumed liquor, it was likely that he had gone to a neighborhood bar.

Ryker had obtained a photostat of Dupard's driver's license and enlarged it. Not a great picture, but it was better than flashing around one of the crime unit photos. Ryker had brought one of those along, too, though, just in case.

One hour and six bars later, Ryker entered Gino's on Sunset. The bartender, Jerry Silva, recognized Dupard immediately.

"Yeah, sure. He's a regular. What's he done, skipped without paying the rent?"

"What makes you think that?"

"Just that he's always complaining that he's short of cash, and that his landlady's always threatening to evict him. Anyway, I usually let him run up a bar tab, but no more than thirty dollars. He always pays up, sooner or later."

"Do you remember if he was here late Monday night, the fifteenth of August?"

"Say, what's going on?"

"Mr. Dupard is dead. We're trying to trace his whereabouts on the night he died. So was he here?"

"No shit!" He whistled. "Frank? Jesus! How'd it happen?"

"We're trying to find out. Do you remember if he was here?"

"Well, I can't hardly say. I mean, he comes here often, being that he lives nearby. But I don't know if he was here that particular day. I don't exactly keep track. But I know he was here towards the beginning of that week."

"Is there anything special that you remember? It might be important."

He frowned. "Well, now that you ask, Frank told me he was expecting someone to meet him here. Must'a been someone important, 'cause Frank was wearing a jacket with one of them handkerchiefs stuck in the pocket— 'Mr. Executive,' I called him. Anyway, he seemed pretty excited, kept lookin' at his watch every five minutes. Had about four, five drinks, but the guy never showed up."

"He said he was expecting a man?"

"Yeah. He asked me if I'd mind putting the guy's drinks on his tab and could they sit at a booth. Said he had something private to discuss."

"Did he talk to anyone at the bar?"

"Not till just before he left. He was eyeing this chick sitting across from him. He bought her a drink, and they left together."

152

"Did you ever see her before?"

"Not that I remember. But I can't say for sure. I see a lot of faces, can't keep track of all of 'em."

"What did she look like?"

"No glamour girl, but not bad looking. Cute, kinda. Curly brown hair, kinda short. Good body, too, but she wasn't giving away any free samples, if you get my drift. Tell you the truth, I was kinda surprised she went for him. He's not a real ladies' man, Frank."

"Did she make any moves toward him?"

"Not really. Well, I know she asked him for the time. I was right near 'em, you see. I wasn't sure if she was talking to me or to him, but then she looked right at him, so that let me out. Maybe I'll have better luck next time."

"Maybe you already *had* better luck, Mr. Silva."

"What?" He looked puzzled.

"Nothing. Just a little black humor. By the way, you mentioned that Mr. Dupard's landlady was upset with him. Did Dupard mention anyone else? Someone who might have had it in for him?"

"Well, he was always griping about his ex-wife. Said she had her claws in him for alimony. And I know he played the horses. Usually lost quite a bit, from what he told me. Maybe he owed his bookie. I don't know." He shrugged. "That's about it, I guess."

"Okay. Thanks for your time, Mr. Silva. If you think of anything else, please let me know." Ryker handed him his card.

Mrs. Rosetti, Dupard's landlady, told Ryker that she hadn't seen or heard Dupard come in on the night in question. She made no move to invite Ryker in but stood firmly planted in the doorway to her first-floor apartment, her arms folded sternly against her ample bosom.

153

"Maybe he comes in late, maybe not. How do I know? I don't stay up like his mother watchin' out for him. All I know is, I'm out two months' rent!" She glared at him. "So when can I have the apartment, Detective?"

Ryker told her it would be soon. He stopped off at the West Hollywood precinct, told Morelli about his conversation with the bartender, and gave him the plastic bag containing the towel from Dupard's kitchen.

"I hope you don't mind," he told Morelli. "If the killer gave Dupard coffee, he or she probably washed the cup and put it away. I thought maybe we could run some tests on the towel, see if it shows anything."

"No problem. I'll ask them to rush it through. Maybe we'll have something by next month." He grinned. "So you think it's this woman from the bar?"

"Could be. It's the only lead we have so far."

"Yeah. It fits. Especially with what Dupard was wearing."

"What was that?"

"I thought you knew. Some fancy jacket with a satin lapel—you know, like the ones these Cary Grant types wear in the movies when they want to impress the ladies?"

"A smoking jacket."

"Right. Only I never seen anyone do any smoking in it." He grinned. "Anyway, Dupard's wasn't too classy—kinda ratty looking and full of spots. Grease, probably. Pretty pathetic, huh?"

"Pretty pathetic," Ryker agreed.

"When we found him, I didn't think much of the outfit. Some users, they have a whole ritual they go through when they're shooting up. The same music, the same lighting, the same clothes. Heightens the experience and all that shit. Whatever." He shook his head in a mixture of perplexity and disgust. "But it makes more sense that Dupard was dressing for company. And it

154

figures he'd put that jacket on for a dame, more than for a guy, right?"

"Right. By the way, Lou, where'd you find the body?"

"He was lying on the floor in the living room, near the sofa. Way I see it, this woman offers to make some coffee. He goes into the bedroom to change into the jacket. Real smooth."

"And to clean up his room." Ryker told him about the laundry under the bed.

"Oh, yeah? My kids do that all the time when they hear Rose on the warpath. Tell you the truth, sometimes so do I." He grinned. "So where was I? Right. He comes back into the living room; she brings the coffee. They get nice and cozy on the sofa. He drinks the coffee, the stuff hits him, and boom! he's thrashing around. She shoots him up with the coke-strychnine mixture, and it's good-bye, Franklin Dupard." He frowned. "But when does she prepare the syringe? She can't count on him being in the bedroom more than a couple of minutes."

"She brought the syringe along in her purse. She had to. And after he's dead, she—or he—liquifies the strychnine-coke mixture in the pot to make it look like Dupard prepared his own syringe. I figure she used gloves to prepare it. And before she leaves, she wipes her prints off the syringe, places it in Dupard's hand, and lets it fall out and roll near his arm. She also has to get his prints on the rubber tubing."

"How does she know which arm to shoot? Maybe he's a lefty?"

"According to the bartender, she asked Dupard for the time in the bar, so she noticed what arm he wears his watch on. That's the arm she shoots."

"Clever bitch."

"Could be a guy, Lou. We can't forget that."

"Yeah. But for what it's worth, my money's on the girl. Yours too, right?"

155

Ryker shrugged.

"The thing I don't get, Sam, is if this girl knew Dupard was drinking all night, why didn't she just slip a few pills in his coffee? With the booze, that would've finished him off. Why go to the trouble of getting the strychnine and coke?"

"That puzzled me too, Lou. But one, she couldn't be sure how much he'd had to drink. And even if he had a few drinks, and she put some drug in his coffee, he still could've called 911. With the strychnine, he never had a chance."

It took SID three days to run the tests. Morelli called Ryker with the results.

"A break for us," he told Ryker. "There are traces of strychnine on the towel. No coke."

"That clinches it. I can't see a corpse getting up and washing and drying his coffee cup."

"You haven't met my mother-in-law."

Ryker called Laney on Tuesday.

"You were right about Dupard. He was murdered. But the only possible suspect is the woman he left the bar with that night. And we can't even be sure about her. We don't know that she went to his apartment."

"What does she look like?"

Ryker repeated the bartender's description. "So that could be anyone. I don't know where to start. And I don't know why a total stranger would want to kill Dupard. If it was an unhappy client, he'd know her, be on his guard."

"Maybe it wasn't a stranger, and not a client either."

"What do you mean?"

"Maybe it was the au pair. Janine."

Chapter Eleven

"How can it be the au pair?" Ryker asked. "Dupard must have seen her when he had Dr. Bauers under surveillance."

"I don't think so. Remember, Barbara warned Dupard that Mark would probably be careful, because she'd confronted him. And even if Dupard saw Janine when he was watching the house, it would have been from a distance."

"This Janine fits the bartender's description?"

She hesitated. "Actually, she doesn't. Janine has long blonde hair."

"So how—?"

"She was wearing a wig, Detective! I'm sure of it. There are plenty of wig shops around where you can get something to wear right out of the box, especially if it's a short, curly style. I bought a wig once when I damaged my hair trying to straighten it."

"I don't know. We can't be sure that Dupard never saw her. And even if she *was* wearing a wig, she'd look pretty much the same."

"She could have changed her appearance in other ways, not just the hair color."

"How different could she look?"

"*Very* different. When she first came to L.A., she looked dumpy. But then she starting fixing herself up, using make-up, doing something with her hair, wearing contact lenses instead of glasses. You wouldn't believe it was the same girl. Maybe she used a modified version of the 'before' look when she went to see Dupard. She didn't want to look unattractive; that would defeat the purpose. The more I think about it, Detective, the more convinced I am that she's the woman in the bar!"

"Wait a minute. She's Swiss, right? What about her accent?"

"Kate told me Janine does a great American accent; she entertained Mark and Kate one night with her imitation of some American stars, or something like that. Anyway, Kate said she was incredible. Let me ask you something, Detective. Why would a total stranger kill Dupard? That doesn't make any sense, does it?"

"There are psychos—male and female—who get their kicks out of killing people just for the fun of it. But odds are Dupard was killed by someone he knew. Frankly, I sure as hell hope so, 'cause if the killer *is* a stranger, we'll be looking for a needle in a haystack. The bartender said Dupard was waiting to meet someone that night, but the guy never showed up. I doubt that we'll be able to find out who that was.

"Anyway, we're checking into Dupard's background. So far, we haven't come across anything interesting. We know Dupard was married before. His ex isn't too shook up about his premature departure. Seems Dupard owed her quite a bit of alimony. But she claims she was with her boyfriend on the night in question. We'll check it out. Also, we're trying to get a lead on Dupard's bookie, see if Dupard was into him for a large sum of cash."

"But Detective, why would his ex-wife kill him? Then she'd certainly never get her back alimony. And if he had gambling debts, why would a crime organization send over a woman to kill him and make it look accidental? I thought crime bosses want to publicize the way they punish people who welch on them as a warning to others."

Ryker laughed admiringly. "I see there are two D.A.'s in the Tolbert family. Look, we don't even know for sure that the woman killed him. Just because he left the bar with her doesn't mean that she went to his place. And even if she did, someone could have come in after she left."

"How was he killed?"

"This is confidential. You can't discuss this with anyone, all right?"

"All right."

Laney listened carefully while Ryker explained about the strychnine and the coke.

"But don't you see, Detective? This sounds like something a doctor would engineer—the timing of the injection, for one thing. How would anyone else know that?"

"Anybody could read up about strychnine in a medical encyclopedia. The rest would be easy." He sighed. "Okay. I'm not saying I'm buying this yet, but let's assume this Janine is the one. Why did she kill Dupard?"

"Obviously, she did it to protect either Mark or herself. The way I see it, after I told Dupard that I suspected Mark of killing Barbara, Dupard tried to blackmail him."

"We don't know that."

"No, but it's the only thing that makes sense. And according to the bartender, Dupard was expecting to meet someone. I think that someone was Mark. But even here, I can see two possibilities. One, Mark told Janine that he killed Barbara. When Dupard contacts him, Mark tells her about the meeting. Mark can't go; Dupard will be on his guard. Janine agrees to meet Dupard and get him to

159

take her to his apartment. Mark prepares the syringe and tells Janine exactly how and when to inject the contents—meaning, after Dupard drinks the coffee but before he's dead. He could have written a prescription for the cocaine, and you can pick up some strychnine-based rat poison anywhere."

"Forget the prescription. Dr. Bauers would be stupid to write one out for the cocaine; it would leave him wide open to risk. But getting the coke is no problem. Unfortunately, it's all too easy to pick some up on the street. What's your next possibility, Mrs. Tolbert?"

"Call me Laney, okay? I'd feel more comfortable."

"Fine, if you'll call me Sam. Go ahead. I'm interested."

"All right. What if Mark *didn't* kill Barbara? What if Janine killed her. You said yourself that a woman could have put her in the tub, right? Then, Mark innocently mentions Dupard's call to her; it means nothing to him, just a crank call. But she's nervous and decides she has to kill Dupard, too."

"Why would she kill Barbara in the first place?"

"Because she's in love with Mark or she doesn't want to go back to Geneva. Maybe a combination of both. Look, she has a great life here: an easy job, beautiful surroundings. Kate buys her stuff all the time. And she's having an affair with a handsome doctor. Maybe it was a fling for Mark, but she sees a future in it for her. Why would she want to give that up?"

"But would she kill for that?"

"Remember the guy you told me about who killed his neighbor because he left a mess on his property? I don't know what Janine's home life was like, but I can imagine it must have been pretty bleak. She's an orphan, you know. Okay. She decides to poison him and make it look like an overdose. From what you just told me, she could read up on everything she needed to know. Again, getting

160

the strychnine is no problem, but I don't know if she'd know how to go about making a connection to get the cocaine, or if she had enough money to buy some."

"I think I like the first scenario better, that Bauers was in on it. In any case, why would she risk a murder rap?"

"She didn't plan on being caught. And if she got away with it, the rewards were high. So what do you think, Detective Ryker?"

"Sam."

"Right. Do you think there's enough here to start an investigation?"

"I'm not sure. I don't know if the chief will let me go after this. Everything hinges on Dupard's death. If we can't connect Janine with it, then we can't connect Dupard's death with Ms. Simpson's death. See what I mean?"

"I guess." Her disappointment was obvious. "So you're just going to drop it?"

"No. But I need something concrete. Is there some way you can get me a picture of Janine? Maybe the bartender could I.D. her from it even though her hair looks different. I can get a police artist to sketch her with curly hair if I get a decent photo."

"I could try, but I have no idea how to go about it. I mean, what would I say? Smile for the camera?"

"I have confidence in you, Laney. Somehow, I'm sure you'll figure out a way."

"Okay."

"There's another thing we haven't considered. What about Simon Leicester? What if Dupard tried to blackmail him? What if he's the one who sent a woman in his place to meet Dupard and dispose of him?"

"What woman would he send?"

"He's very friendly with this Monica Blendheim, the one who gave him an alibi for the night Ms. Simpson died. Or maybe he just hired someone. Hit men aren't always 'men,' you know. The point is, we have to consider Leicester as a possibility."

"You're right, of course. I forgot all about Simon. I don't know why."

"Maybe you're fixed on this au pair. You don't sound as if you like her very much."

"I don't; I've thought all along there was something wrong about her. Brian said I was jealous of Janine's friendship with Kate. Maybe I was, but I honestly thought Janine was up to something. But you're right. I have to think logically."

"Okay. Let me see if I can get a picture of this Blendheim woman to show the bartender. Call me when you get Janine's picture. In the meantime, unofficially, I'll check into Ms. Simpson's personal papers. I'm assuming her sister hasn't removed anything from the condominium yet."

"Not as far as I know."

"Good. Maybe I'll come across something that'll give us a lead. Also, I'll find out if the crime unit picked up any wig fibers in Dupard's apartment. Keep your fingers crossed."

When Laney called Kate Wednesday morning, Janine answered the phone.

"I think Kate is still asleep," the girl said.

"Could you check for me, please?" She gritted her teeth.

"I can have her call you back, Mrs. Tolbert. That might be simpler."

Bitch. "I don't mind waiting while you check." Her tone was calm but firm.

"As you wish."

Laney heard the receiver being put down. A few minutes later, Janine was back.

"As I told you, Mrs. Tolbert, Kate is sleeping. She had

a restless night, I am sorry to say. But of course, I will tell her—"

"Oh, I'm sorry Janine; I didn't know you were on the line." It was Kate.

"Kate? Hi! It's Laney. I called to see how you are, but Janine said you were sleeping."

"I am so sorry, Kate." Janine sounded flustered. "I went upstairs, but your eyes were closed, so naturally, I assumed you were asleep. Shall I bring you some breakfast now?"

"Something light, if you don't mind."

"Not at all. And then, if it is all right, I will do the shopping."

"That's fine. I'll be all right here."

"Well, if that is all," Janine said tentatively.

Time to hang up now, Janine, Laney thought, and she smiled when she heard the satisfying click of the receiver being returned to its cradle.

"She worries about me so much," Kate said. "I feel guilty about it. It isn't the job she bargained for."

Then again, little Janine's not exactly what you advertised for either, Kate. "I hope I didn't wake you," Laney said. "It's past ten, so I figured you'd be up."

"I was just resting. I know I should get out of bed the way you keep telling me to, Laney, and I have every intention of doing just that. But then I feel so tired, and somehow the day slips away. Today I'm going to make a real effort, though."

"Great!"

"Why did you call? Is something wrong in the shop?"

"No, not at all. Just checking to see how my partner's doing. By the way, have you given any thought to coming back, Kate? Maybe part-time, to start? It might do you a world of good. And it would save me from Mrs. Margolin and her little homilies." She groaned. "An adage a day . . ."

"Oh, I don't know, Laney. I'm not ready to think

about that yet. Mark feels it would be too taxing."

"Well, he's the doctor," Laney said brightly. "I don't want to pressure you. So what's your plan for today? Is Mark spending the day home?"

"No, he'll be out all day. He has too many post-op patients to see today. Jeremy and Dana are spending the day at friends' houses; Mark dropped them off on his way to the hospital and he'll pick them up on his way home. I'll be pretty much by myself. Janine's going to do some grocery shopping and take care of some long-overdue errands. She keeps putting things off because she doesn't want to leave me alone when I'm asleep, even when the maid is here. I guess I'll walk around in the garden a little, get some fresh air. My skin looks so pasty. Maybe I'll lie down on a lounge chair near the pool and read."

"Sounds good. Do it! Oh, damn. Mrs. Margolin's waving furiously. I think she's having a problem with the register again. Talk to you later, okay?"

Thirty-five minutes later, Laney parked her Volvo behind a Sears van down the block from Kate's house. She waited impatiently until she saw Janine walk down the driveway, enter the Volkswagon, and back it onto the street. As soon as the girl had turned the corner, Laney left her car and walked to Kate's front door. She rang the bell and waited.

Was Kate sleeping, or was she too tired to come downstairs and open the door? Laney could come back later, but then Janine might be back. Or Mark. She hesitated, then took out her key ring from her purse, selected a key, and, feeling decidedly uncomfortable, opened the door. Laney and Kate had exchanged house keys a long time ago, "in case of emergency."

Well, this was an emergency.

"Kate?" she called when she entered. "It's Laney. Are

164

you downstairs?"

No answer. Maybe Kate had actually followed through on her plan to walk in the garden. That would be an encouraging sign. But a quick look in the backyard showed that she wasn't there, either.

Kate was in her bed, sound asleep.

Laney was momentarily annoyed—how could she be sleeping again?—and was about to rouse her, but stopped herself. She had brought along some new catalogs of porcelain and ceramic *objets d'art* from two of the major giftware houses that the shop dealt with. That was to have been her reason for coming to the house—she needed Kate's opinion on which pieces to order, how many of each, etc. And then, while Kate scanned the catalogs and penciled her selections, it would have been a simple matter for Laney to hunt for the picture she needed.

Now, with Kate asleep, it was much easier. And much more difficult. Not only was Laney tricking her best friend, but she was taking advantage of her bedridden condition to do so.

Are you proud of yourself, Laney?

But what else could she do? She *had* to get the picture. Laney stood watching Kate for another moment; then, burdened with the guilt of subterfuge, stole out of the bedroom and down the stairs.

Laney knew where Kate kept her albums. She switched on the light in the closet at the far end of the family room and located a row of leather-bound albums standing on a tall shelf. She took a few, settled herself on the couch, and started flipping through pages filled with snapshots of Jeremy and Dana until she found an album with pictures that were current.

There were several pictures of Janine, some alone, some with Jeremy and Dana, Kate and Mark, some with only Kate.

A member of the family, Laney thought bitterly. *And this is not jealousy, damn it!* she insisted furiously to herself.

She found an excellent close-up shot of Janine and carefully removed it from behind its protective plastic sheet. The gap left by the removal of the picture stared at her accusingly, and she was suddenly nervous. What if Kate noticed that it was missing? Or Mark? Or Janine. Improbable, but possible. At the thought, she felt a frisson of fear ripple through her. Quickly, she peeled back the plastic sheet and replaced the snapshot.

It took her several minutes to find the yellow Kodak envelopes with the negatives. Kate had stored them in a large box on an upper shelf that Laney had barely been able to reach. Carefully, she maneuvered the box off the shelf and into her arms and was on her way back to the sofa when she heard the front doorbell.

Quickly, she placed the box on the sofa and rushed to the entry hall, casting a nervous glance towards the stairway.

"Yes?"

"Hello, ma'am. I'm with Rid-All Exterminators. We happen to be in your neighborhood today, and we're offering free termite inspections with absolutely no obligation."

"No, thank you."

"Well, why don't I just leave a card, then. If you change your mind before the end of the week—"

"Fine, fine. Just put it in the mail slot, please." She walked to the foot of the stairway and listened. It had only been the one ring. She returned to the family room and the box of negatives.

It was tedious holding up the dark amber strips to catch the light, and she had examined over twenty strips from several envelopes before she finally spotted the picture she wanted. She returned the other negatives to

166

the envelopes, replaced the envelopes in the box, and set the strip she wanted on the blotter of the antique cherry wood desk in the room.

In the process of returning the box to its place on the shelf, she toppled several board games. In an instant, black and red checkers, assorted game pieces, game cards, and dice lay in scattered confusion on the floor of the closet and room. Laney spent ten minutes locating all the game pieces and distributing them into their respective cardboard boxes. She gave a final check to make sure she hadn't left anything on the floor and returned to the desk.

Careful not to touch any of its surface, she picked up the strip of negatives and slipped it into a small envelope she had found in the right-hand desk drawer. Now she placed the envelope into her purse and sighed with relief. Hopefully, the bartender would be able to identify Janine as the woman who had been with Dupard even though she had been wearing a wig.

The wig! Why hadn't she thought of that before? As long as she was here, shouldn't she take the opportunity to look through Janine's things? Maybe the girl had kept the wig. And if Laney could find it . . .

Leaving her purse on the desk, she walked quietly down the hall to Janine's room and opened the door. She had no idea where to look.

The closet? There were two pairs of neatly aligned shoes on the carpeted floor next to several shoe boxes. Laney opened each one but found nothing. The shelf above the rod looked empty, but she ran her hand along it just to make sure there was nothing hidden from view. Nothing there either.

There was no sign of a wig in any of the drawers that she checked (she was careful not to disturb any of the contents), or in the dresser, the desk, or the nightstand. She would have liked to go through the nightstand more

167

thoroughly. Maybe she could find something incriminating—a letter? But she was too jittery in her debut as a sleuth.

The bathroom cabinets held the usual toiletries and feminine paraphernalia. She found some birth control pills, but they were hardly sinister and didn't prove anything other than Janine's lack of innocence. Laney was sharply disappointed and then annoyed with herself. Had she expected to see a bottle of strychnine and a hypodermic syringe sitting in the medicine cabinet? What on earth had made her think that Janine would hold on to evidence that would implicate her in murder? Only a fool would do that, and if Laney was right, Janine was far from foolish.

She had probably disposed of the wig immediately, dumped it in somebody's trash. And now there wasn't so much as a strand to connect her with Dupard.

Her eyes narrowed.

Maybe there *was* a strand.

She hurried back into the bedroom. There was a hairbrush on the dresser. She took it into the bathroom where the light was better and examined it carefully. Blonde hair. Long, blonde hair.

But hadn't she seen another brush? Yes, she was sure she had, in one of the bathroom drawers, next to a blow dryer. She opened one drawer, and then another, and yes! here was the brush. And there were some darker, shorter strands mixed in with blonde ones. It wasn't her imagination, or wishful thinking. She would remove some of the strands and give them to Ryker. If the police found some wig fibers at Dupard's apartment, and these strands matched those fibers—

"Who's there?" the voice demanded from the hall.

Laney felt as if her feet were nailed to the ground. Her heart thudded. There was no place to hide. Janine must have come back early. Damn, damn, damn! Quickly, she

168

opened the drawer, tossed the brushes in, shut the drawer, then went into the bedroom.

"Janine? Is that you? Where are—Oh! *Laney?* What on earth are you doing here!" She stared as her friend emerged from the bedroom.

"Surprise!" Laney said with forced cheerfulness. "I hope I didn't startle you."

"Well, of course you startled me! You scared me half to death! First I heard a bell, but it only rang once, so I figured whoever it was went away. Then I thought I heard a noise downstairs and decided I'd better check it out. You're lucky I didn't call the police!" She stared at her, waiting for an explanation.

"I feel so stupid, Kate. Actually, I've only been here a few minutes. I went upstairs, but you were sleeping so I figured I'd wait in the family room until you woke up. I'm really sorry, Kate."

"But what were you doing in Janine's room?"

"Oh, that. I needed a nail file. I couldn't find one in the guest bathroom, and I figured Janine wouldn't mind if I used hers." She felt her blood rushing to her face, felt as if her face were burning. *Liar, liar, pants on fire.*

"But how did you get in? Was Janine still here when you arrived?" She sounded puzzled.

"Well, no. Actually, I rang the bell, but I thought maybe you were in the bathroom or something, so I used the key you gave me."

"Oh." Kate looked at her strangely.

"You're not mad, are you?"

"No, of course not." She smiled. "Forget it. I'm glad you're here. But you really gave me a start. The last thing I need is more drama in my life." She frowned suddenly. "Is something wrong? Why *did* you come?"

"Nothing's wrong, silly. I just decided that I can afford to take off an hour every now and then to spend with you. Besides, it's been a slow morning, and Mrs. Margolin can definitely manage by herself. Actually, I think she prefers it. Oh, and I brought a few catalogs to show you. They just came in today's mail. They're in my purse in the family room. I want you to see them." She had been so flustered that she had forgotten all about her props. She walked into the room, with Kate behind her, got the catalogs, and handed them to Kate.

"Thanks. I think I'll look at these later, if that's all right." Kate put the catalogs on the desk and walked toward the sofa. "What's this?" She pointed to the albums.

"Oh, I was looking for something to do while I was waiting for you. I thought it would be fun to look at some pictures. Then I noticed that I must have chipped my nail, and I wanted to take care of it before I snagged something or before the chip turned into a crack, because I just had these acrylic nails done—you know, at Susan's Nails on Beverly?" *You're talking too much, Laney. Drop it.* "By the way, you have some great pictures of the kids."

"I know. There are tons more in my room that I haven't put into albums yet."

"You haven't? Shame on you! You're always so organized! I'm sorry," she said quickly when she saw Kate's face. "I wasn't thinking. I guess you've had a lot on your mind."

"It's all right. I'll get around to it soon. I can't avoid seeing pictures of Barbara forever."

"What happened to that morning walk and all that outdoor air you were going to inhale?"

"I don't know. I started feeling so sleepy again."

"Did you eat anything? You look awfully thin, Kate."

"Tea and toast with marmalade, and a few bites of a soft-boiled egg. Janine fixed me a tray." She looked at her friend. "You seem a little nervous. Do you have to get back to the shop?"

170

"Trying to get rid of me, are you? I'd suspect that you were meeting a lover, but you don't seem to have the energy for it."

Both women laughed.

"Kate, can I ask you something? Don't get mad, all right?"

"What is it?"

"Why are you so tired all the time? I mean, are you still taking all those tranquilizers?"

"Not so many!" she said quickly, and flushed. "I'm sorry. I guess I'm a little sensitive on the subject. But I've really cut down. The truth is, Mark didn't give me much choice; he took away all my old pills and gave me new ones with smaller dosages. He's worried that I'll become addicted, the way I was after my mom died. It's just that I'm not ready to give them up. I know you think I should be strong like you—"

"Kate, I—"

"No, let me finish. You *are* strong, Laney. You seem so . . . competent. I used to think I was, but after my mother died, and now Barbara . . ." She sighed. "But I know I have to get hold of myself. Camp ended last week, you know, and there was a major performance. Jeremy and Dana had parts in it. All the kids did. I planned on going; I really did. It was just for an hour and a half, and the auditorium is so close by. Mark couldn't make it, but Janine was going to drive me there. You should have seen how excited the kids were when I told them I was coming to see them.

"The play was supposed to start at ten-thirty. I forced myself to eat a good breakfast so that I'd have energy, you know? And then I took a short nap to rest before the drive, and I only took a half a pill, just to relax. And the next thing I knew, it was noon, and I was still in the damn bed."

"Why didn't Janine wake you?"

"She tried to. I remember hearing her voice, telling me that I had to get out of bed, that we'd be late. But the voice seemed so far away. I tried to get up, to reach the voice, but I couldn't, Laney. I just couldn't!" Her eyes filled with tears. "So after a while, when Janine saw that she couldn't get me up, she went by herself. At least she was there for the kids even if their mother wasn't."

"I'm sure they understood, Kate."

"They didn't even ask me why I hadn't showed up. I'm not even sure it mattered to them. They probably expected me to disappoint them. That's all I've been doing lately."

"Look, kids are resilient. And maybe Jeremy and Dana are too young to realize what you're going through, but they see that you're hurting. And they know you love them."

"Do they? They hardly see me at all. School's starting soon. Jeremy needs clothes and supplies; Dana needs a few outfits and new shoes. They both need haircuts. I always enjoyed shopping with them, doing things with them, but I'll probably have to ask Janine to take them. Thank God she's here! They need a full-time mother, Laney, not some doped-up, self-pitying failure of a—" She broke off abruptly. "That's the essence of self-pity, isn't it?"

"Kate, I've never heard you talk like this. Even after your mother died—"

"I'll be okay. I just need a little more time, Laney. I know I'll be fine. And about the pills, I *am* trying to stop. This morning I didn't take anything, even though I usually do just to take the edge off the day." She yawned. "I guess my heroic measure didn't make much of a difference, though, did it?" She smiled ruefully.

"You're being awfully hard on yourself. Maybe it's not just the pills, Kate. You're not getting any exercise. You lie in the house, cooped up. You hardly see anyone. I'm

172

not a psychologist, Kate, but you sound depressed, not just tired. Have you given any more thought to seeing Dr. Zuroff? What could it hurt?"

She shook her head. "Mark says we can handle this on our own, and I think he's right. After all, look how I fell apart the minute Barbara died, and that was after countless sessions with Dr. Zuroff. I don't blame her," she added quickly, "but sometimes I think Mark does. But then, he's just so worried about me. He thinks I need to get away from all of this—a real vacation, he says, with a change of scenery. Big Bear or something. Maybe he's right."

Laney wanted to stay longer, but she really had to get back to the shop. Besides, she didn't relish being in the house when Janine returned, and she had no idea when that would be.

"I'll call you later today," she told Kate on her way out. "If you have time, look at the catalogs. I really need your opinion on what to order."

"I think you're managing just fine without me. Maybe you should look into getting another partner."

"Kate—"

"I'm sorry. There I go again. Self-pity can become a habit."

"Do you want me to stay? I can call Mrs. Margolin, tell her I'll be a while longer." And she would deal with Janine, if she had to.

She shook her head. "Go ahead. Janine will be back soon anyway with Dana. If I really work at it, maybe I'll muster up enough energy to give my daughter a hug."

With a heavy heart, Laney made her escape from the house and walked quickly to her car, clutching the purse that contained the stolen negatives with renewed determination.

*   *   *

173

"Lou? Sam Ryker. How are you?"

"You really wanna know, or you just making conversation?" He laughed. "I'm drowning in paperwork, Sam. What's up?"

"I wanted to find out if there was anything new on the Dupard investigation. Any leads on his ex-wife or the bookie?"

"Zip. The ex-wife's alibi checks out. We haven't located the bookie yet. Don't know if we will. By the way, we checked out Dupard's place of business. Some business! He was just a small time P.I., Sam. Had a crummy ad in the Yellow Pages, but from the looks of his office, the ad didn't bring in too much business. We found a letter from the DWP threatening to shut off the electricity, and another letter from the phone company giving him three days to pay his bill. The phone is dead."

"Where's his office?"

Morelli gave him the Hollywood Boulevard address. "We had to ask the manager to let us in. Seems Dupard's keys are missing. We looked all over his apartment. Nothing. Interesting, isn't it?"

"Very. Maybe the killer took the keys and went to Dupard's office to look for something. Any sign that someone disturbed the office?"

"If you mean papers thrown around, no. Nothing like that. All he had was one file cabinet. We had to break the lock on that to open it. Nothing much inside. I brought the folders back with me."

"Was there a folder for 'Simpson' in there, Lou?"

"Lemme check. Hold on." He was gone a few minutes. "You still there?"

"Yeah."

"Sorry, no 'Simpson.' Is that good news?"

"I'm not sure. See, this Simpson woman is the one who was electrocuted in the tub, the one who hired Dupard to tail her brother-in-law and his girlfriend."

"So if the killer removed the Simpson file, then the killer has to be connected with Simpson. And that means that Simpson's death wasn't an accident, right?"

"Right. But no file isn't proof of anything. Maybe Dupard didn't have a file on Simpson. Maybe all he had was the report he gave Laney Tolbert."

"What report? And who the hell is Laney Tolbert?"

"You know Brian Tolbert, in the D.A.'s office? She's his wife." Ryker explained her involvement with Barbara Simpson and Franklin Dupard and her theory about Janine.

"You enlisting civilians to do our work, Sam? Does the chief know about this?"

Ryker ignored him. "Or maybe Dupard kept the file in the house."

"If he did, it's not there. My boys would've found it."

"That reminds me, do you know if they picked up any synthetic hair fibers?"

"What do you mean?"

"I'm looking for a strand from a wig. Brown."

"Thinking about buying a rug, Sam? You don't need it—yet." He chuckled.

"Seriously, Lou. The thing is, the bartender saw Dupard pick up a brunette, but what if she was wearing a wig to disguise herself?"

"Where'd you come up with that idea? Don't we have enough trouble trying to find this woman without worrying about her hair color? Jesus!"

"It wasn't my idea," Ryker admitted. "Laney mentioned it."

"Oh, it's *Laney*, is it? What does Linda say about this?"

"Tell me when you're finished ribbing me, Lou. But I have to warn you, I don't have all day."

"Okay, okay. I know you wouldn't mess around anyway. You're a good boy, Sam, even if you're not

175

Italian. So wig fibers, right? I'll have the boys check through the stuff they got."

"When do you think you'll have something, Lou?"

"Yesterday."

On the way back to the gift shop, Laney dropped the strip of negatives off at an hour photo place. She dealt politely with customers all afternoon, but even Mrs. Margolin noticed that she was preoccupied. At 4:45, Laney told Mrs. Margolin that she was leaving and asked her to lock up. She drove to the photo place. The prints were ready.

She called Ryker from a pay phone to make sure he was in the station and told him she was on her way. Twenty minutes later she was sitting in front of his desk.

"This is good," Ryker said, looking at the snapshot of Janine. She had a half-smile and was gazing directly at the camera. "Pretty girl."

"Are you going to show this picture to the bartender?"

"Yeah. But I'd like to wait until I hear from Lou. Lou Morelli. He's running the Dupard investigation. Anyway, he's checking to see if the crime unit picked up any wig fibers in Dupard's place."

"I see. And if they didn't?"

"Not conclusive. But it would help if they found something." He smiled. "Soon as I hear from Lou one way or the other, I'll have the bartender come in to look at this picture. Then I can have our artist sketch a likeness, add a wig. By tomorrow, I should also have a picture of Monica Blendheim."

"How will you get that?"

"I went over to her office during my lunch hour, told her I needed a photo of her so the bartender at the Four Seasons could confirm she was there with Leicester the night of Ms. Simpson's death. She didn't seem thrilled,

176

but she said okay. I arranged to meet her at her apartment tonight to get the picture. Anyway, we'll see what happens."

"Okay." She got up to leave. "Oh, I almost forgot to tell you! While I was at Kate's, I looked through Janine's things."

"Technically, what you're describing is 'breaking and entering.' I'm not sure you should be telling me this." He smiled.

"Guess what I found?"

"Don't tell me—a wig!"

"Unfortunately, no. But it suddenly dawned on me that if she was wearing a wig, she'd have to style it, at least a little bit. So I looked at her brushes, and there were short, brown strands on one of them." She looked pleased.

"I take it you took some strands off the brush?"

"I was about to, but I heard someone calling, and I was frantic because I thought Janine was back. Anyway, I shoved the brushes back in the drawer. In the end, it turned out to be Kate. But I'll go back again, maybe tomorrow; I'll make sure to go when Janine is out. It shouldn't be too hard."

"Look, be careful. If you're right, we're dealing with a dangerous woman, someone who's involved in two murders. Does your husband know what you're doing?"

"Yes. To be honest, he's not thrilled. Now that I've convinced him that Mark and Janine were responsible for Barbara's death, he's worried."

"I can't blame him, Laney. Frankly, I'm surprised he's not objecting to your activities."

He admired her eagerness to help—there was a vitality about her that reminded him of Linda—but when he thought of Linda, he was grateful that she never became overinvolved in his cases. But then, Laney Tolbert wasn't becoming involved in a "case," he reminded himself. She was helping a friend. Linda, he knew, would do the same.

"Brian understands that I have to do this." That wasn't exactly true. They had argued last night about her going to Kate's house to search for the picture, Brian insisting that she leave the investigation to the police; in the end, she had worn him down with her persistence. But she had no intention of telling him about her discovery of the brown hair, or her plan to get a sample. "Anyway, you said that your chief doesn't think you have enough to go on. And you can't get a search warrant to look through Janine's things, can you?"

"No," he admitted. "And frankly, I don't know that we'd find anything."

"I can't just sit around doing nothing, waiting for a lucky break; I'm too worried about Kate. And you have to admit I'm really in the best position to help you. Since I'm Kate's friend, it's not unusual for me to be at the house often. And Janine has no idea that I suspect her."

"I hope so, Laney. I sure as hell hope so."

Chapter Twelve

"The veal is delicious, Janine," Kate said. "And so was the soup. Wasn't it, Mark?"

"Delicious," he agreed.

"It is just a simple recipe my Aunt Renee taught me. It is the leek that makes it different, I think. I am glad that your appetite has improved."

"What's a leek?" Jeremy asked. "It sounds yuck." He grimaced.

"Leek, leek," Dana squealed, and giggled. "Leek."

"It's a kind of onion, and it's not yuck. So did you have fun at Barry's house today?" Kate smiled at him.

"Uh-huh." He slid off his chair and moved away from the table.

"Where are you going?" Kate asked.

"To play."

"You didn't finish your vegetables."

"Janine doesn't make me eat my vegetables if I don't want to. Can I go now, Daddy?"

"Jeremy, your mother made a special effort to have supper with us. I think you can stay a little while."

"Why?"

"It's okay, Mark. I'm going to try to spend more time with all of you from now on." She took Mark's hand and

179

squeezed it. "Go ahead, Jeremy. Have fun."

"I saw you got some giftware catalogs in the mail. Don't they usually go to the shop?"

"They did. Laney brought them by mid-morning. She said she needs my advice about what to order, but I think that was just an excuse to come by."

"What do you mean?"

She didn't notice the sharpness in his tone. "Nothing really. Just that she's worried about me, and she wants me to feel needed. I saw right through her." She smiled. "Still, it was fun looking through the catalogs. I didn't realize how much I miss being in the shop."

"So how long was she here?" Mark asked.

"Not very long. Actually, I was asleep when she arrived, but she let herself in with the key I gave her."

"Isn't that a little presumptuous, Kate?" Mark asked. "I know she's your best friend, but she shouldn't go barging in whenever she feels like it."

"She wasn't barging in, Mark. Why are you so upset?"

"I'm not upset. I just think it was rude, that's all. So what was she doing while you were sleeping?"

"Nothing special. Looking through some albums to keep busy. We had a good talk. I miss seeing her."

"All gone, 'Neen!" Dana announced, and showed the au pair her plate.

"Good girl, Dana," Kate said.

Janine took the plate and patted Dana on the head. "Shall I give her a bath now, Kate?"

"No, I'll do it tonight."

"Are you sure you're up to it, Kate?" Mark asked. "I don't want you to overexert yourself."

"I think I'm capable of giving my daughter a bath, don't you?"

"Don't be so sensitive. I'm just concerned for your welfare."

"I'm sorry. But I've been planning this all day." She

rose and approached her daughter.

"I want baf wif 'Neen."

"Come on, Dana," Kate said cheerfully. "We'll have fun. Bubbles and everything."

"I want 'Neen!" she insisted. "I want 'Neen!"

"I'm really sorry, Kate." Janine was visibly embarrassed.

"It's not your fault," Kate said. "Go with Janine, Dana."

Janine lifted the little girl off her seat. "Give Mommy a kiss good night, Dana."

"Night, Mommy."

"Good night." Watching her daughter leave the room with the au pair, Kate felt suddenly depressed and eager to get back upstairs to the comfort and security of her bed.

When Mark came upstairs a half hour later, he found Kate lying on her back, staring at the ceiling. An open book lay on her quilt.

"Why don't you rest?" he suggested. "Close your eyes."

"I will. I want to read a little bit."

"You're still upset, aren't you? About Dana, I mean."

"No, not really."

He sat at the edge of her bed. "Talk to me. Come on; tell me what's bothering you."

She looked at him. "It's just that I wanted the evening to be so pleasant—all of us together, a family. I didn't take a pill all day so I wouldn't be sleepy. And I thought the kids would be happy to see me. I don't think they care one way or the other."

"They're just kids, Kate. You're reading too much into this. Dana loves you; she's just used to having Janine cater to her needs."

"I know. I guess I'm being silly. It's just that I felt—"

"What?"

"I can't even say it, I'm so embarrassed."

"Tell me." He took her hand.

"For a split second, I was jealous of Janine, and I think I resented the way the kids take to her. That's awful, isn't it?"

"It's understandable, Kate. You're their mother. Do you think she's doing anything to take their affection away from you?"

"No, of course not! I know it's my problem. And I'm ashamed of the way I feel. I know she's only trying to help us out, and she's been wonderful since . . ."

"Since Barbara died," he finished for her. "Kate, we have to talk about this; I think it's important."

"Talk about what?"

"What Barbara told you, about seeing me with Janine. You said you believed me when I told you Barbara was making all that up to hurt me."

"I did. I do! Why are you bringing this up?" she cried.

"Let me finish. You didn't seem bothered by it at all. But if there's any part of you that isn't comfortable with having Janine here, any part at all, well then, I think we should find someone to take her place."

"Mark, that's not—"

"Let me finish. Because no matter how wonderful she is with the kids, no matter how attached they are to her, your health and emotional well-being are the most important things in the world to me. I hope you know that. And I won't let anything, or anyone, jeopardize our marriage."

"Mark, I don't want to get someone else. You know how I feel about Janine. She's like a sister to me."

"Maybe. But I saw how you looked at her tonight. If you think she's taking your place with the kids, maybe you'll start imagining that she's trying to seduce me."

"That's ridiculous! I told you, I know that nothing went on between you."

"You're sure?"

"Of course I'm sure. Look, I don't want to discuss this any more. Please. I just overrreacted; it's nerves."

"Try to relax, Kate. I hate seeing you so upset." He stroked her hair.

"I'll try." She forced a smile.

"I brought some files home from the office that I have to go over. Will you be all right by yourself?"

"Yes." She paused. "Will you be long?"

"An hour or so. Why?"

"Nothing, really. It's just that, well . . . it's been a long time since we've . . . made love." She didn't know why she felt so awkward, but she did.

"You haven't been well, Kate. I didn't think you were in the mood, and I certainly didn't want to add any pressure."

"I know; you've been wonderfully patient. But it's been almost two months and you haven't even . . . you know, tried."

"I guess I figured you'd show me when you were ready, Kate." He stared at her. "You don't think it's because I don't want you, do you? Because that's crazy! I want to make love to you. God, I think about it all the time!" He hugged her fiercely. "But I don't want you to rush things because for some reason you've gotten it into your head that you've been neglecting my needs."

"Maybe that's part of it," she admitted. "But I miss you, Mark. I need you."

"Of course, you need me. We need each other. But as far as making love, I want us to wait until you're sure, until the time is right for *you*."

"But Mark—"

He put his finger on her lips. "Shhh. Trust me. And don't feel guilty." He got up. "Maybe you should take a pill tonight, just to make sure you'll sleep well. You've had an upsetting evening."

"Are you sure?" From the moment she had come upstairs after supper, distraught, confused, she had been acutely aware of the vial with the pale yellow tablets lying on her nightstand.

"I think it would be a good idea for tonight." He filled her glass with water from the carafe on her nightstand. "Here."

"Thank you," she whispered. "Mark, I'm going to be okay. I know it. And thank you for being so understanding. How did I ever find someone as wonderful as you?"

He leaned over and kissed her softly. "Just lucky, I guess."

Afterward, she walked him to the door of her room. Pressing her naked body against him, she kissed him and felt his instant arousal.

"Tomorrow," she whispered. "I need my sleep, you know. Don't forget that I'm a working girl." She laughed and pushed him out the door.

The black silk nightgown he had bought her was lying on the armchair. He had made fun when she had insisted that he drape it carefully over the back of the chair, had grumbled good-naturedly; but then, he couldn't understand that she was still new to luxury, that it would be a while before she could adopt the casual, "I-can-get-a-new-one" attitude of the wealthy toward their possessions.

She slipped on the nightgown. It felt cool against her skin, and she liked the way the thin fabric skimmed her curves. She stood in front of the dresser mirror and reached for the tortoise-shell brush so that she could begin her nightly ritual.

It wasn't there.

She frowned, puzzled. She walked into the bathroom, and after opening several drawers, she found the brush.

It didn't belong there; she always left it on the dresser. Neither did the styling brush that she kept in another drawer together with her blow dryer. She had no idea how the brushes had gotten there.

Kate would never dream of entering her room without permission. And as for the children, they had long ago discovered that her living quarters held little of interest for them. Besides, if Dana had wandered into her room, she would have been attracted to make-up, not brushes.

Anuncia? The housekeeper always straightened Janine's room. Today had been her day off, though, and Janine remembered using the brush in the morning.

But someone had put the brushes in the drawer.

Laney. Laney Tolbert.

The woman had been in the house by herself for some time—how long? Ten minutes, a half hour? Time enough to explore and poke through her things? Looking for what?

Something to discredit her with Kate, no doubt.

She went into her bathroom, opened all the drawers to see if anything had been disturbed, detected nothing. But she was convinced that her things had been touched.

Why would Laney be interested in her brushes? She went back into the bathroom, picked up the circular styling brush, and examined it. She started pulling absent-mindedly at the strands of hair entwined around the bristles and was about to toss a matted clump into the trash when she noticed that some of the strands were brown. Brown and short.

So what? What could that possibly mean to anyone? The more she thought about it, the more convinced she was that Laney couldn't have been interested in the brushes. Because that would mean that Laney knew something about Dupard. And that was impossible. The woman had probably just been snooping around and had moved the brushes by accident.

185

She stood for a moment, lost in thought, tapping the brush lightly against her fingertips, and nodded. Methodically, she removed the remainder of the strands until the bristles were completely bare. She took all the strands and flushed them down the toilet. Then she picked up the tortoise-shell brush, returned to the bedroom, and drew the brush with slow, even strokes through her long, blonde hair.

On Thursday, Sam Ryker found a note on his desk when he returned from a quick lunch. "Call Morelli."

He dialed the detective's number and was connected with him immediately.

"Morelli."

"Lou? It's Sam. You called?"

"Yeah. Seems the crime unit didn't find anything when they checked, but they weren't looking for wig fibers. So I sent one of my best guys, Steve Purcell—you remember him? He was a rookie back when you were here. Anyway, I sent Steve back to Dupard's, and he found something that could be what you're looking for. A couple of nylon blend fibers. Brown, wavy. Could be from a wig."

"Where did he find the fibers?"

"In the john. Couple of strands in the sink, a couple of others on the floor. But there's no way of telling how long the fibers were there. Could have been days, weeks. From the look of the place, Dupard wasn't exactly into housekeeping. So does this help you?"

"Maybe. Thanks, Lou. I'll keep you posted."

"You'd better. Dupard is my investigation, remember? Not that I mind your help. Matter of fact, I'm shorthanded right now, and we've got two other homicides that the chief wants solved first. Just one thing, Sam."

"What's that?"

"Don't even try to put in for overtime." He chuckled, and hung up.

Ryker called Gino's, but the bartender who answered wasn't Jerry Silva."

"Jerry don't come on till six o'clock," he told Ryker.

"Would you ask him to call me, please? I'll give you my number."

"I'll tell him when I see him, but that'll be Tuesday. He's takin' off for a couple'a days, it bein' Labor Day weekend an' everything. Goin' up the coast."

"Shit. Look, do you have a daytime number where I can reach him? Maybe he hasn't left yet."

"I can't give out his personal number. And don't bother calling information; it isn't listed."

"I'm a police detective. This is important."

"Could be. How do I know you're who you say you are? I can't see no badge over the phone, right?"

Ryker sighed. "Okay. Call this number and ask for me. I'll be waiting." He hung up and waited impatiently until the phone rang.

"Homicide. Detective Ryker."

"This is Ed Loomis. From Gino's." He gave Ryker the phone number. "Sorry, but I was just playin' it careful, for Jerry's sake, you understand."

"Thank, Mr. Loomis."

"No sweat, Lieutenant."

First he doesn't believe I'm a detective; now he gives me a promotion.

Ryker dialed Silva's number and let it ring about ten times. He was about to hang up when someone answered.

"What is it now?"

"Mr. Silva? Sam Ryker here with the L.A.P.D. I talked to you last week about Mr. Dupard's death."

"Right. I remember. Sorry; I thought you were my girlfriend."

"Mr. Silva, I'd like you to come down to the station

this afternoon. I have some pictures to show you. I'm hoping you can identify the woman Dupard met in the bar."

"Gee, I'd like to help you out, Detective. The thing is, I'm just on my way out of town. Goin' fishing and scuba diving for the weekend with my girlfriend. Matter of fact, I was all the way down the hall when I heard my phone ring. I thought it might be her, calling to remind me to take something else, so I came back. Women, they gotta have everything perfect."

"This is important, Mr. Silva. I don't want to interfere with your vacation plans, but I'd appreciate your cooperation. It shouldn't take very long."

"The thing is, Rosanne—she's my girlfriend—well, she's kinda the impatient type."

"An hour, Mr. Silva. I promise."

He hesitated. "Okay."

Ryker thanked him and gave him the address of the West Los Angeles precinct. He had just put down the receiver when the phone rang again. It was Laney.

"I just wanted to know if you heard anything about the wig fibers," she said.

"As a matter of fact, I did." He repeated what Morelli had told him. "Jerry Silva, the bartender, is on his way here now to look at the pictures. I wish we could find the wig, though. A fiber isn't going to do us much good if we can't match it up to anything."

"I'm still going to try to get the hair from the brush that I told you about. Today's not good; I called Kate. Janine and the kids are going to be home all day. But tomorrow morning, Janine is taking them to the park for a few hours. I'll go over then."

"Look, remember what I said. Be careful."

"It won't take more than a few minutes, Sam."

Twenty minutes later, Ryker spotted Silva making his way toward him. He was dressed in stone-washed jeans and a shirt, unbuttoned almost to the waist, that displayed a chest-full of blond hair. His bare feet were in sandals. Without his bartender's uniform he looked bigger, clumsier.

"Thanks for coming in, Mr. Silva. I appreciate it."

"Yeah, well, I hope it's worth something. Rosanne's madder than hell."

Ryker withdrew eight pictures from an envelope. Among them were snapshots of Janine and Monica Blendheim. He handed them to Silva.

"Take your time, Mr. Silva."

Silva shuffled through them, looked up at Ryker, and shook his head. "Nope."

"Could you go through them again please, one at a time? If there's a possibility that one looks at all familiar, put it aside."

Silva sighed, checked his watch. "Okay." He discarded the first two, studied the third. "This one has the right hair color, but she's older than the girl who was there that night."

Ryker looked at the picture. It was Monica Blendheim.

Silva continued going through the pictures. When he got to Janine's, he hesitated.

"Do you recognize her?" Ryker asked casually.

"She's not the girl from the bar, if that's what you mean. There's something about her, though. Anyway, she's blonde. The girl I saw had brown hair."

"What if she was wearing a wig?"

"What?" He looked startled, then shook his head. "No, I don't think so."

"Wait here, please." Ryker left and returned a minute later with another man. "Mr. Silva, this is Officer Brancusi, our police artist. Tony, this is Mr. Silva, the bartender I told you about. Show Mr. Silva what you've done, Tony."

Tony Brancusi placed two sketches on Ryker's desk.

"See, I drew the face from the photograph you saw, Mr. Silva. Then I changed the hair—color, length, and style. What do you think?"

Silva leaned over the sketches. "This is the same woman in the photo? No shit! She looks so different!" He scrutinized the sketches again, then pointed to the one on his right. "The hair's too curly."

"What about the other one?" Ryker asked.

"The hair is right, but too far back from her face. She had more bangs or something, you know?"

"Give me a minute," Brancusi said. With a charcoal stick, he quickly added a fringe of wavy hair to the forehead of the woman in the sketch. "Is that more like it?"

Silva squinted. "Yeah. Yeah, I think that's better."

"Is that the woman you saw with Mr. Dupard, Mr. Silva?" Ryker asked.

"Yeah, that could be her."

Ryker smiled. "Would you be willing to swear to that in court?"

"Well, that's a whole other thing. I said it *could* be her, but I don't think I can say a hundred percent that she's the one, know what I mean? I'd like to help you out, but I'm just not sure. Maybe if I saw her in person or something." He shrugged. "I don't know." He checked his watch again. "Listen, I really have to get going, okay? I told Rosanne it wouldn't take long, and I want her to be in a good mood this weekend, if you get my drift." He winked. "Anyway, I'll be back Monday night. You get anything else to show me, I'll be happy to help you out. That's the best I can do. I'm sorry."

Not as sorry as I am. "Thanks again, Mr. Silva. Happy fishing."

"Thanks. Hey, you too, Detective. Get it? I'm going fishing, and so are you!" He grinned, pleased with his quip, and waved as he left the room.

"Everybody's a comedian," Ryker said glumly.

Ryker called Morelli and told him about the bartender's tentative I.D.

"So where does that leave us, Sam? Nowhere, that's where."

"Not exactly. If we could get Silva to look at her in a line-up, maybe he could give us a positive I.D."

"Yeah, but if he doesn't identify her as the woman in the bar, you have nothing to charge her with. You can't even bring her in for questioning. For all you know, she may have a solid alibi for that night."

"I'll have to check it out. Listen, Lou, can your boys check the wig stores in the area, see if anyone remembers that this Janine bought a wig?"

"Jesus, Sam! You've gotta be kidding! You know how many wig shops there must be in L.A.?"

"How many, Lou?"

He sighed. "Too many. And we don't even know for sure that this woman bought a wig. This could be a total wild goose chase, Sam."

"Maybe. Then again, it may open the case wide open."

"And what if she did buy a wig? Is there a new law on the books that I don't know about against owning a wig?"

Ryker waited.

"All right, all right. I'll send out a few of the boys tomorrow. Where does this Janine live?"

Ryker gave him Kate's address.

"Hancock Park, huh? Fancy neighborhood. Okay. We'll check some shops around there, but chances are she'd go farther away from home. Less risk. Maybe downtown; maybe Hollywood Boulevard. I know there's a lot of wig places there. You got a picture of this woman?"

"Laney Tolbert made several copies of a snapshot she

191

was able to get. I'll drop some off on your desk some time today."

"You do that, Sam."

Kate had mentioned that Janine was taking the children to a park program that started at ten thirty. On Friday morning, Laney arrived at Kate's house at eleven o'clock. She rang the bell and waited for Anuncia to let her in.

"*Ah, Señora Laney. Lo siento. Pienso qué la Señora Kate esta dormiendo.*"

Sleeping again. So what's new? Laney sighed. "Anuncia, I need a book that I left here yesterday." She saw the woman's puzzled expression. Laney's housekeeper spoke passable English, but Laney had retained a few phrases of her high school Spanish class. "*Ayer, yo dejé aqui un libro, que tiene fotografías.*" How the hell do you say "catalog" in Spanish? she wondered.

"*No entiendo, señora.*" A frown creased her forehead.

"I look for *el libro*, okay?" She pantomimed searching.

"*Ah! Usted va a buscar el libro.*" She smiled and nodded her head rapidly. "*Bueno.*"

She followed Laney into the family room.

"*Es* okay, Anuncia. *Yo busca sola*, okay?"

The woman nodded again. "*Con permiso.*" And she was gone.

Laney waited a moment, then walked across the hall to Janine's room and into the bathroom. She found the brush and its companion blow dryer in the second drawer she opened (funny, but she had been sure that she had returned the brush to the other drawer). But when she picked up the brush, she almost cried aloud with frustration. It had been stripped of all its telltale hairs, almost as if Janine had known that they could weave her in a web of crime.

But that was silly. Obviously, Janine had simply

decided that it was time to clean the damn brush. Even a quick glance around the immaculate rooms proved that the au pair was extremely neat. Fastidious, almost.

The Swiss, Laney decided irritably, took cleanliness to an extreme.

Dejected, she left Janine's room quickly and returned to the family room. The catalogs were on the coffee table in front of the sofa, not on the desk where she had left them. Maybe Kate had looked at them. Laney picked them up and was heading up the stairs to find Anuncia and say goodbye when the chubby woman popped into view carrying a basket of laundry.

"*Yo voy.*" Laney waved the catalogs to show that her search had been successful. "*Gracias.*"

"*Ah, de nada. Pero la Señora Kate se ha despertado.*"

Not only was Kate up, but she was even out of bed. Laney found her in her robe, standing on her balcony.

"This is a nice change!" Laney said.

"Look at the sky. It's beautiful. I think I'll go downstairs, have breakfast, and spend the day outside."

"Famous last words. Sorry," she said quickly.

"No; don't apologize. You're right; I deserve that. But maybe today I'll really do it! You can come back and check up on me if you want." She smiled.

"I should keep my mouth shut. I have no business criticizing you, Kate. You've been through so much lately. If you need more time, you need more time. What do I know?"

"But you think I should get a hold of myself and get on with my life, don't you?"

Laney didn't answer.

"Maybe you're right." She sighed. "Mark and Janine treat me with kid gloves; I think they're afraid I'll have a breakdown or something. Maybe they're *too* caring."

Laney hesitated. "Look Kate, if you want me to be honest, I think you're a lot tougher than you give

193

yourself credit for. And I don't think you need the damn pills. They messed you up when your mother died, and you're letting them do the same thing now."

"It's hard to stop. I feel panicky when I think I can't have one. I don't know how to explain it."

"Then get some help, for God's sake! There are lots of places that treat chemical dependency. The television ads are full of them. Just pick one. If you want, I'll help you."

"No, I don't think I *need* a special place. And I don't think Mark would like that. But I *am* going to stop."

"When? You keep saying that."

"I've already cut down. I told you, my new pills have a lower dosage. And I've been taking half-pills instead of whole ones. I haven't even told Mark. I want to surprise him."

"Are you feeling better?"

"Sometimes; other times, I can barely stay awake. Mark says it'll take a while until I adjust to the new pills—it's a different kind of tranquilizer. Also, it'll take time for the old pills to get out of my system. Look, let me brush my teeth, and I'll walk downstairs with you. Then you'll see that I'm serious about going outside."

"Okay. But I can't stay long. Mrs. Margolin is waiting. I came by to pick up the catalogs, by the way. I found them in the family room. Did you have a chance to look at them?"

"Uh-huh. I circled a few items. Maybe you can come over one evening. I'd really like you to fill me in on what's happening in the shop."

"I'd love to! Does that mean you're thinking about coming back?"

"Oh, I couldn't do that." She sounded alarmed. "I mean, I'm just not ready yet. But soon," she promised.

The phone rang while Kate was in the bathroom.

"Get that, Laney, will you please," she called with a mouth full of toothpaste.

Laney picked up the receiver on Kate's nightstand. "Hello?"

"Who is this?"

"Oh, hi, Mark. It's Laney. Kate's brushing her teeth. Hold on a sec', will you?" She wondered if he'd noticed how eager she was to get off the phone. Probably not. She walked over to the bathroom. "Kate, it's Mark. Tell you what, since you'll probably be on the phone a while, I'll just go downstairs and let myself out. I'll talk to you later, okay?"

Laney was somewhat encouraged by Kate's attitude, but she had more important things on her mind. She had to phone Sam Ryker and tell him that the "evidence," if that's what it had been, had disappeared. She hoped he wouldn't be too disappointed in her.

"Don't worry about it, Laney," Ryker said. "You did the best you could. And we probably wouldn't have been able to prove anything from the wig strands anyway. See, human hair has individual characteristics that can help us identify the owner—in a sense, like the whorls on a fingerprint. But with synthetic wigs, well, there could be hundreds of wigs made from the same fiber. Thousands, maybe. And under a microscope, they'd all look alike."

"So the strands didn't mean anything?"

"Not in a court of law. But the fact that you saw what you did *is* important—don't forget that. That, plus the fibers the police found in Dupard's apartment, convinced me that Janine *did* have a wig. Morelli's sending out a couple of guys to check out some wig shops, see if anyone can identify Janine. He's using the pictures you gave me, by the way."

"Really? That's a great idea!"

"Well, don't get too excited yet. It's a long shot. I just spoke to Morelli a while ago. They went to several shops in the downtown area. Nothing yet. And because of the Labor Day weekend, his men won't get back to checking out the wig shops till Tuesday."

"Tuesday! But we'll be losing so much time! What do we do in the meantime?"

"We wait, Laney. I do it all the time."

Chapter Thirteen

It was completely impossible, Laney decided, to sit around doing nothing until Tuesday. If she couldn't do anything to help with the investigation, maybe she could help Kate.

She sighed. She knew she'd been neglecting Brian and the children lately. They had all noticed her preoccupation ("What's with Mom?"; "Laney, for God's sake, I'm talking to you!") and its disruptive effect on their home life: Laney had forgotten to buy a gift for Kimberley to take to a friend's birthday party; to relay an important message to Brian; to set the timer for a pot full of boiling eggs. The eggs had exploded; the pot was probably ruined.

Her marriage would be ruined, too, she thought glumly, if she didn't pay more attention to it. The other night, after she and Brian had made love, she had made the mistake of wondering aloud whether Mark was having sex with both Kate and Janine.

"Shit, Laney! Can't you stop thinking about the Bauers for ten minutes?"

"I'm sorry; you're right."

"You're obsessing, you know that?"

He had every right to be upset. And maybe she *was*

obsessing. But she didn't know how to control her troubled thoughts, how to forbid them access to her consciousness when she was functioning as wife, mother, lover, and gift shop owner.

Maybe if she could accomplish something with Kate, she'd be able to concentrate on enjoying the holiday weekend with her family.

Laney called Kate Friday evening—"Did you go outside?" she had planned to tease her. But Mark answered and insisted that Kate was sleeping and had given instructions not to be disturbed.

"She overexerted herself today, Laney. And then, because she felt so tired, she became depressed and took an additional tranquilizer. I wasn't home at the time, of course; Kate admitted to me later what she'd done."

"Is she all right?"

"Luckily, it's a small-dosage pill, and she took only one more pill. But I have to be honest. I *am* worried. If she's careless because she's anxious, who knows what she might do? Without meaning to point a finger, Laney, I think you could be doing Kate more harm than you realize."

"What do you mean?"

"Kate told me about her conversation with you, how you're encouraging her to get out more, go back to the shop. You and I have talked about this before, Laney. I know you mean well, but frankly, I don't think you understand the delicate condition Kate is in."

"I'm sorry."

"No need to apologize. I felt I had to tell you, Laney. I knew you'd understand. And I *will* tell her you called."

The call filled Laney with a mixture of confusion and alarm and not a little guilt. Maybe Mark was right. Maybe Kate needed an extended period of pressure-free recuperation, not the return to activity that seemed so sensible to Laney. Laney was certainly no expert on emotional healing.

But she suddenly remembered who was.

The following morning, Laney sat waiting in the room that Kate had described, the room where Kate had rediscovered peace and strength after Claire Simpson's death.

The chintz sofa didn't seem that long. What did tall patients do? Laney wondered. She slipped off her flats, stretched out on the sofa, and found that her toes just met the rolled arm. It was, she had to admit, comfortable.

"Mrs. Tolbert? I am Irene Zuroff." A short, gray-haired woman wearing a rose-colored linen skirt and a pale pink silk blouse had entered the room.

"Oh! I'm sorry." In one startled movement, Laney lifted her head and swung her long legs off the sofa. She stood up, and as her feet searched for their shoes, she shook the psychologist's extended hand.

"Don't apologize." She smiled warmly. "That's what the couch is there for—your comfort. Shall we sit, or would you prefer to lie down?" There was a twinkle in her gray eyes.

"Sitting will be fine." She felt like an Amazon, towering over the diminutive doctor, and quickly sat on the sofa.

A lovely French country desk and cane-back chair sat in front of a large, square-paned picture window that faced a small garden. The doctor made no move to sit there; instead, she chose an upholstered arm chair near Laney. She had a clipboard with paper on her lap, and a fountain pen which she immediately uncapped.

"So. It is 'Mrs. Tolbert,' yes? I think that is what you said."

"Yes. Please call me Laney. Kate has told me such wonderful things about you, Dr. Zuroff. I really appreciate your seeing me on such short notice. It's very important."

"Yes, well, I am happy that I was able to fit you in this morning. You sounded quite distressed when I spoke to you last night on the phone. So, shall we begin?" She smiled reassuringly. "Now then, can you tell me what is troubling you?"

"Actually, Doctor, I'm not here about myself. I'm here about someone else."

"I see. Laney, before we go any further, I feel I must interrupt. Very often, people come to doctors or ministers and talk about 'a friend with a problem.' And always we—the doctors or the ministers, as the case may be—know that it is the person himself who has the problem. Now if you want me to help you, the first step is to admit that you have a problem. You do see that, yes?"

"Oh, absolutely; I see what you mean. But you don't understand. The person I'm talking about is Kate. You see, Dr. Zuroff, Kate is having a very difficult time right now, and I think she needs help. I know you helped her before, so I thought I should tell you what's happening to her."

"Mrs. Tolbert—Laney—I'm afraid I must stop you right here. It would be completely unprofessional for me to discuss Kate with you."

"But I know she was your patient. She told me about her sessions with you."

"I cannot comment on that either, Laney." She rose. "I'm afraid you're wasting your time. Considering the circumstances, there will be no fee."

"Dr. Zuroff, please. What if I do all the talking? You don't have to say a word, just listen."

"I don't see a problem with that. But what can you gain from my just sitting here?"

"Please."

Dr. Zuroff seated herself again. "All right. I am listening."

"Okay." She took a deep breath. "You may not know this, but Barbara, Kate's sister, died recently."

The woman's eyes revealed her surprise. "No, I did not," she said quietly. "I am extremely saddened to hear that."

"Kate has taken it very badly. She's depressed; she's basically confined herself to her room. She's back on tranquilizers, sleeping pills—I don't know exactly what's she's taking, but I know she's constantly tired. Almost every time I go there or call, she's sleeping." She glanced at the doctor expectantly; her face remained impassive.

"I've suggested that she call you, Dr. Zuroff. But Kate says that Mark, her husband, doesn't think it's a good idea. I have an idea why, but I'll get to that later. In the meantime, I wanted to know if you would call Kate. Maybe if she heard from you, she'd decide to come see you. I'm convinced she has to." She paused. "Well, that's about it. Will you do it? Will you call Kate?"

"Laney, I made my position clear before: I cannot and will not discuss Kate Bauers."

"She needs you, Dr. Zuroff! If you saw her, you'd see what I mean."

"I'm sorry. I admire your loyalty to your friend, but you must see that I am bound by the ethics of my profession. I really *am* sorry."

"But Dr. Zuroff—" She broke off. "Dr. Zuroff, can we speak hypothetically?"

The woman reflected. "There are some clinical psychologists who would advise against a hypothetical discussion; I think you can see why. But yes, I will agree to it."

"All right, then. Let's say I had a friend who needed help with an emotional problem and I asked you to call that friend and offer that help. Would you do it?"

"Unfortunately, again, according to the ethics of my profession, I cannot initiate the therapy. That would be the equivalent of soliciting a client. Your friend would

201

have to contact me and request treatment."

"But you wouldn't be soliciting a client, not if my friend has already undergone treatment with you. Doesn't that make a difference?"

"Possibly. Still, the nuances of placing such a call are very subtle and can be subject to misinterpretation. Frankly, I would far prefer to have the friend call me."

"What if my friend is being advised against her better judgment *not* to undergo therapy?"

"Then again, I'm afraid my actions would be circumscribed. I could call and indicate that I am aware that she has been having a difficult time; I could tell her that if she feels that talking will alleviate her distress, I am available. Some therapists, by the way, would frown even on this type of overture. I myself am not comfortable with it. And in no way could I urge her to see me. All these codes of professional conduct are for the protection of the client. I hope you see that."

"I'm not sure. And even if that's so, there have to be exceptions to the rule. Dr. Zuroff, what if I told you that Mark—that my friend's husband is deliberately sabotaging her recovery? That he is discouraging her from going back to a job that she enjoys, that he is insidiously abetting her dependence on drugs? What if I told you that this husband is attempting to limit my contact with her, that while he tells my friend that he doesn't want her to see a psychologist, he insists to me that it's my *friend* who resists the idea of returning to therapy? What if—" She stopped suddenly, unsure of how much she should reveal.

Dr. Zuroff sat silent, her face mirroring her troubled thoughts. When she finally spoke, her voice was subdued. "In this hypothetical situation, Laney, I would suggest that you do whatever you can to persuade your friend to seek help. Urge her to take the first step."

"That's it?"

She nodded. "That, I'm afraid, is it, in regard to the hypothetical situation as you have presented it." She got up. "I wish I could do more. I hope you believe me."

Laney got up and walked to the door. "I believe you, Dr. Zuroff. It's just that . . . never mind."

Irene Zuroff stepped through a door that connected her consulting rooms with the living quarters of her duplex apartment on Maryland Drive, a quiet street in a quiet residential area of Los Angeles. She had the advantage of a location that was within walking distance of the strip of Wilshire Boulevard called Miracle Mile, appropriately named for an area populated primarily by the medical profession. And because she had had the foresight to purchase her duplex, she was not subject to the whims of fortune and unflappable corporate executives who blamed the madly spiraling real estate market and bloodsucking insurance industries for the exorbitant rental fees they were forced to charge.

After changing into a faded cotton skirt, madras blouse, and black, rubber-soled shoes, she walked into her small but carefully tended backyard. From a small potting shed, she selected several tools and, squatting on her short, sturdy legs, she methodically and calmly attacked the encroaching weeds that were attempting to infiltrate the ranks of the variegated impatiens, petunias, and begonias that held reign in her garden.

Dr. Zuroff could not remember having felt so inadequate, so confused. Laney Tolbert had appeared forthright, honest, fiercely dedicated to her friendship with Katherine Bauers.

Most probably she was. And if she was telling the unbiased truth, then Kate Bauers was truly in need of immediate help. Help that Irene Zuroff *could* offer, within certain delicate guidelines, as long as she did not violate the code of medical ethics that prohibits the solicitation of clients.

But *was* she telling the unbiased truth? Or was Laney Tolbert—the same forthright, honest woman, fiercely dedicated to her friendship with Katherine Bauers— convinced that Kate needed help, that Mark was undermining her welfare, because she needed to believe that? Had there been a cooling off, perhaps, between the two women? Had Mark inadvertently disrupted a long-time relationship simply by becoming Kate's husband? And had Laney refused to accept that redefined relationship, and instead protected herself by casting Kate's husband as the villain?

Not an unheard-of situation.

Which woman was Laney Tolbert?

Irene Zuroff pulled firmly at one particularly deep-rooted intruder and yanked it ruthlessly from the flower bed. Sometimes, the green blades were so similar that it was difficult to tell genuine growth that needed nurturing from the impostors.

Truth and illusion.

She stood up, brushed the soil from her hands, and after cleaning the tools and replacing them, she went inside.

In the end, she placed the call from her office, not her bedroom—a symbolic distinction that helped her to legitimize her action as a healer, but didn't erase all the questions.

"Who was that on the phone?" Mark asked Janine. He had heard the phone ring while he was outside checking a scratch on his BMW.

"A woman. Her name is Irene. She didn't tell me her last name; I asked. Anyway, she wanted to talk to Kate."

"Irene?"

"She had an accent. Russian, I think."

He thought for a moment, then nodded in recognition. "Kate's psychologist. What did you say?"

"I told her Kate was sleeping."

"Did she leave a message?"

"She asked me to tell Kate that she had called to offer her condolences. It seems she just learned of Barbara's death."

"I see. Nothing else? Did she ask that Kate return the call?"

"She said that Kate could call her if she wanted to."

Mark nodded. "That's fine, then. I'll take care of it."

When Sam Ryker walked out of the precinct on Friday afternoon, he was determined to leave with his mind as uncluttered as his desk. It was a holiday weekend, and he had promised himself that he wouldn't mar it with professional worries. His family deserved better.

Unlike Laney, he had long ago come to terms with the impatience that inevitably nipped at his heels during a case—witnesses out of town or ill or reluctant to cooperate; evidence to be sifted and analyzed; clues to be unearthed, chased; myriad complications that all teased "Wait." He hadn't quite mastered impatience, but he rarely allowed it to dictate his actions or disturb his equanimity.

And so, for the most part, he had a leisurely, nonlabor Labor Day weekend. He slept late each morning, enjoyed for the first time in ages the luxury of waking to an unhurried, lazy rhythm with his wife, instead of stealing out of bed in the inky night or the misty predawn gray fog; he took Linda and the girls to a Saturday matinee showing of *Who Framed Roger Rabbit?* in Westwood; he puttered around the house, fixing two leaky faucets and a squeaky kitchen-cabinet door-hinge and unsuccessfully attempting to rewire a toaster; on Sunday he rolled out the Charbroil gas barbecue into the backyard and grilled hamburgers and hot dogs for his parents and his in-laws. On Monday afternoon, while the girls were out visiting friends, he and Linda made exquisitely tender love in the king-size bed they had shared for eighteen years.

There were moments, of course, when thoughts of his cases intruded, like uninvited guests—ironically, not the cases he was being paid to solve, but the Simpson woman's death, and Dupard's: the wig, and the au pair, and Dr. Mark Bauers. Ryker liked a good puzzle, and Linda was a sympathetic listener. But even those moments were few, and he pushed the thoughts aside easily. Till Tuesday.

On Tuesday, Ryker called Morelli during his lunch break, but nothing had turned up yet with the wig. And in between following some leads on a major case he was working on—a series of robbery-homicides that had the same criminal signature—he stopped by Barbara Simpson's condominium, had the manager let him in, and looked through her personal effects.

No diary. Nothing revealing. She had received some mail posthumously, including a "You-are-a-lucky-winner!" postcard that guaranteed Ms. Barbara Simpson a new motor home, a color T.V., a camera, or a set of teflon pots if she would visit the future site of a real estate development "just minutes from Palm Springs" and attend a two-hour lecture on the exciting possibilities of becoming a member of a select recreation community.

There was a bill from AT&T and an envelope containing a Northwest Airlines ticket to St. Paul, Minnesota. Scribbled on the envelope was a phone number. Ryker took the phone bill and the envelope with the ticket and returned to the station.

Barbara Simpson had placed a large number of long-distance calls during the first week of July, just before

206

she'd been killed. *Before she died,* Ryker corrected himself. We don't know that she was killed.

But he knew. Like Laney, he was convinced.

The calls, like the ticket, were to Minnesota—some to St. Paul, most of them to places Ryker had never heard of. He called AT&T, identified himself, and asked them to trace all the calls Barbara Simpson had placed from June 29 up to and including July 6.

"There's a local call I'd like you to check, too."

"Pacific Bell will check the local call," said Lois Mummer, the woman in the business office. "This may take some time. How soon do you need this information?"

He didn't know whether the situation was urgent, but habit made him say "as soon as possible" to Lois Mummer. And to Anita Montoya at Pac Bell. The wonders of deregulation.

He still had Barbara Simpson's canceled checks. The first time, he'd been searching for an unusual amount and had found the check Simon Leicester had forged. He looked through them again. There was a $3,000 check for Dupard. Funny. Ryker hadn't even noticed it last time. He put it aside. There were also several checks, each in the amount of $150, made out to the same person: Dr. Roger Harwell.

Ryker called Directory Assistance and asked for Harwell's business number; when the operator asked him what city, he instinctively said Beverly Hills. He jotted down the number that the pleasant-sounding recording intoned, then dialed, and made an appointment to see Dr. Harwell the following evening.

At five o'clock, when Morelli called, Ryker was walking away from his desk, hoping to get home for an early dinner with Linda and the girls. The weekend had spoiled him.

"I think we got something, Sam," Morelli said. "If you want, you can still make it there today; the place closes at

207

six o'clock."

"Where is it?"

"On Hollywood, just like I figured. Just east of Highland." He gave Ryker the address. "It's called the Big Wig. And Sam—don't let 'em talk you into buying anything!"

"Right, Lou. Thanks. I'm on my way." He was happy that he hadn't told Linda he'd be coming home early; now he wouldn't have to disappoint her or the girls.

Ryker parked his unmarked vehicle in a "Loading Only" zone around the corner from the wig shop, displayed his permit on the dashboard, and headed up the street.

Hollywood Boulevard during the daytime is disappointing. Without the gaudy neon marquees that flash the electric illusion of glamor against the chimerical veil of night, it is just a street, perhaps wider than most, lined with small shops whose display windows are unartistically crammed with the items they offer: wristwatches, calculators, cassette recorders, televisions, and other electronic ware; dresses, skirts, blouses, robes, all draped on tired-looking mannequins; shoes, wigs, purses, belts, costume jewelry, exotic polyester shawls; doughnuts, orange drinks, and other fast food delights; masks, trick swords and knives, beards, and assorted disguises and paraphernalia of the grotesque.

The stars embedded in the sidewalks, each one dedicated to a celebrity, are an incongruous juxtaposition to the mundaneness of the shops. Tourists stop to point, kneel to read names they hope they will recognize. As a boy, Ryker had done the same.

The Big Wig was sandwiched between a women's clothing store and a book shop that offered adult literature. There were numerous wigs in various lengths and styles resting on white styrofoam heads that sat, expressionless, in the window, silently eyeing the passers-by. Most of the wigs were in conventional shades—blonde, brunette, black, auburn; a few in pink, chartreuse, and purple added a garish Holloween effect to the display. Ryker wondered whether they were just for show. Probably not. This was Hollywood.

Except for a short, middle-aged woman with too much make-up and long, platinum blonde hair (a wig? Ryker wondered), the store was empty. She smiled at Ryker as he approached.

"Can I help you?" Her voice was artificially breathy.

"Are you the owner, ma'am?"

"Yes. Arlette Hopper. Miss." She gazed at him admiringly, her spiky, mascaraed eyelashes stabbing the air.

Ryker showed her his I.D. "Detective Ryker, L.A.P.D."

"Oh." There was a world of disappointment in the word. "The other officer mentioned that someone else might be coming by. Just a minute, please."

A minute later she returned from the back of the shop with a woman whose long, glossy black hair and carmine lips intensified the chalky pallor of her skin.

Definitely wigs, Ryker decided. And false eyelashes, too.

Aside from the striking contrast in hair color, the women bore a strong resemblance to each other. Camouflaging the contours of their bodies were solid color caftans (black for the blonde, white for the black) that made Ryker think of ceremonial robes.

The Weird Sisters. *Macbeth* had always been his favorite play.

"Detective, this is my sister, Janette Hopper. She remembers more about the young woman than I do. I was with another customer, you see."

Ryker showed the snapshot to the raven-haired sister.

"Ms. Hopper, is this the woman who bought a brown wig from you?"

"Yes, she is," she said emphatically. "I've been thinking about it ever since that other officer left, and I can even tell you when she was here. August 15. I checked my calendar."

"How can you be sure of the date?"

"Well, I'm not *positive*, of course. But I know it wasn't last week, so it must have been the week before. And I remember we were very busy at the time, unpacking a new shipment of wigs, so that would make it a Monday, wouldn't it, Arlette?"

"Yes, Detective, because Monday is when we get a large UPS shipment. Because it's right after the weekend, you see."

"And you're certain it was the woman in this picture?"

"Yes. She was wearing glasses, but it's the same face. I'm positive of that."

"Janette has a very discerning eye. Always has had, even when she was a little girl." She smiled at her sister.

"Well, I noticed right off that she would look better in contact lenses. I said so to Arlette after she left."

"She did, Detective."

"Anyway, the reason I remember her so clearly is that I couldn't understand why she wanted a *brown* wig. It was wrong for her; a terrible choice, really. Her own hair is such a lovely shade of blonde. But she insisted." She shrugged.

"Like a 24/18/12, I thought," Arlette interjected.

"No, that's far too light. Hers was ashier, more like a 16/18." Janette saw Ryker's puzzled expression. "Those are numbers for blended shades in the blonde family."

"You're right, of course," Arlette agreed. "You do have an eye," she marveled.

"Did you find it odd that she wanted to buy a wig? You mentioned that she had such lovely hair."

"Oh, no, Detective, not odd at all. Wigs are such a convenience, you see. And buying and caring for a wig is far less expensive than constantly going to the hairdresser. That's what the public doesn't understand. But brown was just not for her. It did nothing for her skin or eyes. Black, maybe. I'm partial to black. Or red. Something with drama. I believe that everyone should have some drama in his or her life, don't you?"

"Absolutely."

"I believe in making a statement, Detective."

"I do, too," Arlette offered.

Janette smiled at her patiently, then turned to Ryker. "Right now, you're probably wondering, 'Is she wearing a wig?' Confess, Detective!" She laughed lightly.

Ryker colored. "Not at all. I haven't really thought about it."

"Don't be embarrassed, Detective. Everyone wonders. And I don't mind; I enjoy wearing wigs. And when I tell them that I *am* wearing a wig, they always ask, 'Janette, what is your *real* color?' And do you know what I tell them?"

He shook his head.

She smiled. "I tell them, 'This is my *real* color. This is the person I am today; this is an externalization of my mood, of my soul, of my essential being.' After all, Detective, what *is* real?"

Damned if I know, Ryker thought. He felt a little dazed.

He coughed. "Ms. Hopper, can you tell me what this woman was like? Was she nervous?"

"Not *nervous*." She drew out the word. "She *did* seem to be in a hurry. She didn't look around much, made her choice very quickly, and *that* is very unusual, let me tell you. And she wasn't interested in wig heads or brushes or other accessories. A mistake in the long run, Detective, because a wig needs special care, just as your own hair does." She looked at him critically.

Ryker resisted an urge to smooth his hair.

"That's true, Detective," Arlette said. "Because you see, buying a wig is a very, very important step. It can change a person's whole life! So we encourage our clients to take their time, to try on several styles and shades. We want them to be comfortable with the way they look." She turned to her sister. "I'm sorry, dear; I didn't mean to interrupt," she murmured.

"That's quite all right. Now where was I? Oh, yes. I said to her, 'Don't you want to let me style that for you? Show you the possibilities?' Because every wig has a personality, you see, that emerges once it is taken out of the box. But she said she could manage on her own."

"A lost opportunity, Detective. Janette is wonderful with her hands." She leaned forward. "You would be amazed, absolutely amazed, if I revealed the famous personalities who have bought hairpieces here because they heard of Janette's gift."

"Arlette." She frowned. "You know we can't say."

"Of course not." She looked mildly shocked at the suggestion. "I wouldn't dream of compromising the confidentiality of our clients."

"How did she pay for the wig? Do you remember?"

"She paid with cash," Janette said.

Naturally. No signature. No need to show an I.D. "By the way, did she have an accent of any kind?"

"Nooooh. Not that I recall." She looked at Arlette.

"I didn't really hear her talk that much." She sounded wistful.

"Just a few more questions. When you write up a receipt, do you indicate the style and color of the wig a customer purchases?"

"Of course, for inventory purposes. And we keep an index card for each of our interested customers where we list the same information. Often, a customer wants to reorder a wig but doesn't remember the color or the style.

212

I don't think I wrote up a card for her, though. She was in a rush, as I said."

"Could you look up the receipt for this woman's purchase? Maybe we could find out exactly which wig she bought—you know, the style number and color. For comparison purposes," he explained.

"Oh. I see what you mean. Just give me a minute; it shouldn't be hard to find." She walked behind the counter toward the rear of the shop and flipped through several books until she found the one she wanted. Ryker followed her.

"August 15. Let me see . . . we sold eight brown wigs that day, so it may take me a little time to—oh, here it is! I remember now. She bought a wig that was sitting out, the last one of a discontinued style. We had reduced the price accordingly. I think, you know, that may be why she chose it. So I'm afraid I won't be able to show you another one like it."

"That's all right. Is there a name on the receipt?"

"No. All sales are final. Health reasons. Detective, may I ask exactly why you're interested in this woman? I take it she's involved in a crime?" Her nostrils quivered slightly in eager anticipation.

Everyone should have some drama in her life.

"Possibly, Ms. Hopper. Very possibly."

"Who were you talking to?" Linda Ryker asked as she sat next to her husband on the den sofa. "The receiver's still in your hand, by the way."

"What? Oh." He looked at the receiver as though he were seeing it for the first time and replaced it. "Laney Tolbert." He had told Linda about the deputy D.A.'s wife and her interest in the case. *Cases*—Simpson *and* Dupard. Or no case at all. "I called her to tell her the developments with the wig."

213

"You could have told her tomorrow." There was mild curiosity in her hazel eyes.

"Jealous?" He smiled.

"Should I be?"

"Never." He kissed her. After eighteen years, he was still besotted with the slim, pretty, dark-blonde woman he had married. The guys at the station teased him about it all the time. It didn't bother him a bit.

"What does she look like?"

"Laney? She's very attractive, very tall. Big-boned, but not heavy, you know what I mean? Short, curly hair. Bright, good sense of humor."

"You like her." It was a fact, not an accusation.

"Yeah, I do. She's real, and she's direct. And she's very worried about her friend, Kate Bauers." He sighed.

"What's wrong?"

"It's this wig business."

"But you said the wig shop owner is willing to testify in court that the au pair bought a brown wig."

"Yeah, but so what? Like Lou said, there's no crime in buying a wig."

"But it's too much of a coincidence that she bought a brown wig and that the police found brown wig fibers in the dead man's apartment. Isn't it, Sam?"

"It could be just that—coincidence. I don't think it is, and I've just about convinced Morelli, but he can't arrest her on the basis of my thoughts. He needs proof."

"What about the bartender? Maybe you could ask him to look at the pictures again. Maybe he *can* make a positive identification."

"Number one, I called him again, just about ten minutes ago. He says he can't be sure. Number two, even if he *would* testify that she's the one who was in the bar and left with Dupard, that doesn't prove she was in Dupard's apartment."

"Well, where was she that night? What if she doesn't

214

have an alibi? Would that help you?"

"Not necessarily. Plenty of innocent people have no alibis; why would they? They don't know they're going to need one. Anyway, we don't even have enough to bring her in for questioning."

"Maybe you could figure out a different way of checking her alibi. Something indirect."

"Underhanded, you mean. Scheming. Devious. Is that what you want me to do?" He grinned.

"Absolutely, Detective Ryker."

"You're a very brazen woman, you know that?"

"Isn't that why you married me?"

"Just one of the reasons." Just one of a million.

Ryker found the address and parked directly in front of the house. Sometimes when he came home from work, he had to drive halfway down his block to find a spot. Linda always used the driveway for the Camaro.

No parking problem here; the street was almost empty. Most of the driveways, he noticed, had two cars. Lots of Mercedes, Jaguars, BMWs. A couple of Rolls Royces. There were probably other cars out of sight, in the garages. Hell, how many houses were there on the block all together? Even if every homeowner parked three cars on the street, there'd still be plenty of space.

The houses were huge, two-story affairs, each one about four times the size of his three-bedroom ranch. He could probably fit his entire lot on one of the front lawns.

Money isn't everything, Ryker reminded himself as he walked up the brick walkway to the imposing double front doors. He wondered suddenly who made up those famous adages—the haves, to prevent their lessers from envying them and their possessions, or the have-nots, to make sour grapes seem more palatable?

Bigger isn't necessarily better.

215

Vanity, Vanity, all is vanity.
Money is the root of all evil.
A good parking spot is hard to find.
Ryker grinned into the darkness.

The porch lights were on. He rang the bell and waited patiently for someone to come to the door. He wondered who it would be.

"Yes?" The male voice came through the door.

"Good evening. I'd like to speak to Mrs. Katherine Bauers."

"I'm Dr. Bauers. Kate's husband. How can I help you?"

He took his wallet from his pocket, opened it, and placed his I.D. against the privacy window. "Detective Sam Ryker, L.A.P.D."

Open, Sesame.

Chapter Fourteen

"I'm afraid my wife isn't available," Mark told the detective as they were standing in the entry hall. "Is there something I can help you with?"

"I'm not sure. This is a delicate matter, Dr. Bauers; I really think I should talk with your wife." He smiled genially.

"Too many parking tickets that I don't know about?" He grinned. "Kate doesn't have any secrets from me, Detective."

He was definitely handsome, Ryker admitted grudgingly, with a disarming, boyish quality that women probably found attractive (at least *one* did, aside from his wife, if Laney Tolbert was right). He had thick, dark brown hair—styled, no doubt; a cleft in his chin; friendly hazel eyes; a short nose with a slight bump in it (earned in a skirmish in a prep school football game?). He was tall, almost the detective's height; slim, but muscular. And he looked damn good in pleated black textured slacks and a white cotton cable knit sweater. Ryker liked pleated pants; so did Linda. But he had stopped wearing them twelve pounds ago.

Hell, he's at least ten years younger than I am, Ryker thought. And I'll bet he works out at a club three, four times a week.

"This shouldn't take long, Dr. Bauers. Is there somewhere we can sit?"

"Of course; excuse me. I wasn't thinking. We can go into my office."

Ryker followed him into a paneled room and watched with concealed amusement as Bauers seated himself in a black leather swivel recliner behind a large desk. *I'm the doctor*, his gesture announced. Ryker couldn't decide whether the need to reinstate his authority was unconscious or deliberate.

"Detective?" He pointed to a small upholstered love seat. "Can you tell me what this is about? My wife's asleep, and I really don't want to wake her unless it's urgent." He paused. "She hasn't been well lately. A death in the family."

"I'm sorry to hear that. But I'm afraid I *do* have to see her. It's just routine, I'm sure."

"What division are you with? I don't believe you mentioned it."

"Homicide." He looked uncomfortable. "The thing is, Dr. Bauers, that a man was killed several weeks ago in a hit and run, and eyewitnesses identified a blue Volkswagen as the car that hit him."

"Detective, there are thousands of blue Volkswagens in Los Angeles." His voice held patronizing patience.

"Yes, but even though it was night, these witnesses were able to give us the first three letters of the license plate and the first number: EPX4. Or ERX4. They don't agree about that second letter," he admitted. "So we've been running a computer check with the DMV, and just today, your wife's Volkswagen came up on our printout."

"That may be so, but you're wasting your time."

"Again, I'm sure this is just routine. We have a list of people that we'll be talking to, and your wife is just one of them."

"Well, you can eliminate her, Detective. You said this accident took place several weeks ago, at night?"

Ryker nodded.

"Kate hasn't left the house in almost two months, not even in the daytime. I can personally attest to the evenings. The fact is, she's usually asleep by nine o'clock. So there's no way she could have been involved in that accident."

"I see. Well, that's good to hear. Dr. Bauers, I hope you won't take this the wrong way, but I have to ask: Do you ever drive your wife's car?"

"No, I do not drive Kate's car. I have a BMW in the driveway, Detective. For some reason, I prefer that to a Volkswagen." He smiled. "Sorry. I know you're just doing your job. I just find this a little annoying."

"I understand."

"So it's all cleared up?"

"Just about. By the way, I noticed another car in the driveway, Dr. Bauers. A Mercedes."

"That's Kate's."

Ryker waited.

"Actually, the Volkswagen is just an extra car."

"You look too young to have teen-age drivers."

"We don't."

"So your wife is the only one who drives the Volkswagen?" He sounded puzzled.

"Not exactly. We have a young woman living with us. She uses it, too."

"I see. I think it would be a good idea if I spoke to her too, Dr. Bauers. Is *she* available?"

"Janine rarely goes out at night, Detective. That's the young woman's name. Janine Panetierre."

"I'd like to speak with her myself, if that's all right."

"Yes, of course. She may be sleeping, though."

"I really envy you, Dr. Bauers. Your household seems to go to bed early. I wish I could say the same. My kids are up till all hours."

Mark looked at him uncertainly. "I'll go check." He left his leather chair and walked casually out of the room. When he returned, he was accompanied by a blonde wearing jeans and a white fleece top with satin appliqués.

Ryker recognized the top. It was the same one his daughter Kelly had admired at Bullock's in the Beverly Center several weeks ago. The price tag had said $68.95. How much did au pairs earn? he wondered.

"Janine, this is Detective Ryker. He'd like to ask you a few questions." Instead of taking his seat behind the desk, he remained standing next to her.

Ryker stood up. She was damn attractive, he thought. The picture hadn't done her justice.

"How can I to help you?" she asked. Her cool blue eyes gazed at Ryker unconcernedly.

"Can you tell me where you were on the night of August 15?" He watched her carefully. Had something almost imperceptible flickered across her face at the mention of that date, or was his imagination teasing him?

"There is a problem?"

"I understand you drive the Volkswagen, Miss Panetierre."

"*Mais oui.* Yes, Detective."

He explained about the hit and run, about the partial license plate identification that the computer had matched up with eyewitness reports.

"Off the hand, I do not remember exactly where I was. What night of the week was that, if I may ask?"

Her French accent was strong. For my benefit? Ryker wondered. "A Monday night. Three weeks ago."

"Monday? A moment, please." She frowned in concentration. "Ah, yes. *Bien sûr!* I remember it very well. I was to have gone to the cinema, but Dana, *le pauvre petite,* had a fever, so I decided not to go."

"Dana is our three-year-old daughter," Mark explained.

"Your friend must have been disappointed."

"I was planning on going alone, Detective. I do not need company to enjoy the films. Sometimes, a companion is talking when I am wanting to listen, *n'est-ce pas?*"

"So you just stayed home?"

"Yes, but the television offers much that is amusing. And I wanted to be nearby. Mrs. Bauers, you see, is not feeling well, and would have difficulty going to the child if she awoke."

"And Dr. Bauers? Couldn't he have taken care of the little girl?"

"I can't be counted on, Detective. I often get emergency calls."

"Did you?"

"Pardon me?"

"Did you get any emergency calls that night?"

"Detective, I'm not sure I like the direction this questioning is taking."

"I'm sorry. I don't mean to imply anything, Doctor. I just want to be thorough. My chief tends to get annoyed if I do things in half measures, and he'll only send me back here to ask the questions I should've asked in the first place." He smiled.

"As a matter of fact, Detective, I did *not* get any calls that night."

"How can you be sure?"

"Because I remember the night clearly: Dana's fever, Janine having to cancel her plans. And I felt particularly bad, you see, because Janine has been helping out so much lately, what with my wife being ill."

"I see."

"And I can vouch for Janine's being home at night. After I finished some paper work, I joined her in the family room, and we watched T.V. till one, two in the morning."

221

"We wanted to make sure that Dana was sleeping comfortably, you see," she explained.

"Not much on that time of the morning. You a David Letterman fan, Doctor?"

"Sometimes. But we have cable, Detective."

"I see. Well, I guess that answers everything I need to know for now. You've been very cooperative, and I appreciate it."

"No problem. I don't envy your job, Detective." He led the way to the front door and opened it. "Good luck. I hope you find whoever did this."

"Oh, we will. Sooner or later, we usually get the guilty party. By the way, can you give me your office number, Doctor? Just in case my chief has any more questions. I'd hate to bother you at home again."

"I have a busy practice, Detective."

"Probably won't be necessary, but just in case."

"All right." He gave him the number.

"Good night, then."

Five minutes later, the bell rang again.

"Sorry," Ryker said after Mark had let him in.

"Did you forget something?"

"Kind of. This is kind of funny, Dr. Bauers. I was in my car, jotting down a couple of notes about our conversation, you know? I have to file a report, you see. Anyway, there I was, writing down your office number, and it's the damnedest thing."

"What's that, Detective?"

"It turns out that the victim of another homicide I'm investigating is someone you know! Can you beat that?"

"There must be a mistake. No one that I know has been killed. I certainly would have heard."

"Dupard. Franklin Dupard. Name ring a bell?"

"Not at all. I don't understand how you got the idea that I know him."

"Well, he knew you. At least, he knew your office

222

number. See, I knew that number sounded familiar, but I couldn't figure out where I'd heard it. And then I started flipping through my notebook, and there it was."

"What?"

"Your number: 555-1066. The 1066 is what got my attention. Battle of Hastings, right?"

"Where is this leading, Detective Ryker?"

"Well, that's just it. It's such a coincidence, because here I am, checking into a hit and run, and then your number pops up on another case I'm handling."

"I don't know anyone by that name. He probably wrote the number down wrong, transcribed a few digits. People do that all the time."

"I don't think so, Doctor. See, we found this mini-calendar in one of his jacket pockets, and there was a notation in it, 'Doc B.? 555-1066,' with a check next to it, like he took care of it."

"What did you say his name was?"

"Franklin Dupard. He was a private investigator, by the way. And we already talked to his doctor. Apparently, Dupard was in fine health, so I don't think he was calling to see you professionally. I know! Maybe he talked to your secretary." He nodded. "I'll call her in the morning, see if she remembers anything."

"She might, but—oh, yes, I *do* remember! A private investigator called a while back, wanted to ask me some questions about a patient. Of course, I told him I couldn't answer anything without her permission. Confidentiality, and all that. I simply forgot his name."

"Well, that clears it up, then." Ryker grinned. "Funny world, isn't it?"

"Very."

"What was the patient's name? The reason I ask, that could be a lead for us. See, we're trying to check up on all the cases Dupard was investigating. Maybe that'll lead us to his killer."

"I don't recall off hand."

"Really? Something like that, out of the ordinary, I'd think it would stay in your mind." He shrugged. "Tell you what; think about it. I'll call you in a day or so, maybe you'll have something for me. 555-1066, right? Great number. Mine is terrible; half the time I can't remember it myself. Did you have a hard time getting yours?"

"No. It's what the phone company happened to give me."

He shook his head in wonder. "Some people have all the luck."

Lois Mummer at AT&T had done her homework. She called Ryker early Wednesday morning.

"Barbara Simpson, or someone using her phone, placed a call to Mr. Jonah Kringle, in Northfield, Minnesota."

"Which number was that? I have the bill in front of me."

"The first entry. The second entry is a call to St. Paul's Office of Marriage Records; the third is to the Office of Death Records. If you look on the second page, you'll see that she called them several times. The fourth entry is to the *Northfield Daily News*. I still have four numbers to track down. I should have them by tomorrow."

"Thanks. I really appreciate your help." After he hung up, he contacted Anita Montoya at Pacific Bell, who informed him that 894-2119 was the number for Immigration and Naturalization.

Ryker sat back in his beige vinyl chair and locked his fingers behind his head. The au pair, obviously. Mademoiselle Janine Panetierre. But what had Barbara Simpson hoped to learn about her from Immigration and Naturalization? Her home address? References? He

224

doubted that they would have released that information. And why would Simpson have been interested in that?

Or maybe Barbara Simpson had simply wanted to stir up a little trouble for the Swiss girl, inform Immigration that she was working as an au pair, not just visiting an American family. Get her deported, maybe? Ryker doubted that the girl had a green card.

He closed his eyes and swiveled slowly, back and forth.

When he called Laney at the shop, he told her about The Big Wig, but not about his visit to Mark Bauers.

"Did Ms. Simpson mention to you that she was planning to call Immigration and Naturalization?" he asked.

"No. Did she?"

"I found the number scribbled on an envelope. I also found tickets to St. Paul, Minnesota."

"Minnesota!"

"Does that mean anything?"

"Mark is from Minnesota. I don't think from St. Paul, though."

"Northfield?"

"Yes! How did you know that?"

"I didn't. But Ms. Simpson made quite a few calls to Northfield, including one to a Jonah Kringle. Do you know who that is?"

"The name's familiar, but I can't place it. Let me think about it, okay?"

"Fine. Let's get back to Immigration and Naturalization. I figure Ms. Simpson was either trying to get some background information on Janine or hoping to get her in trouble." He explained his theory.

"That makes sense, I guess. But obviously, Barbara didn't say anything to Immigration, or they would've contacted Kate or Janine. Kate would've told me about it."

"Good point. So I guess it's the background info she

225

was after. What do you know about Janine, Laney?"

"Just that she's Swiss, that she's an orphan. She lived in a small town most of her life, from what I remember, but when Kate contacted her, she was living with a family in Geneva."

"How *did* Mrs. Bauers contact her?"

"Through a newspaper. Kate placed ads in several papers, some in Vienna, some in Geneva. Janine seemed the most qualified."

"By the way, whose idea was it to get an au pair?"

"Kate's."

"Not her husband's?"

"I don't think so. Does it matter?"

"Probably not. Just curious. I'm trying to get the whole picture, trying to put myself in Ms. Simpson's head. By the way, I have an appointment with her doctor this afternoon. Roger Harwell. Believe it or not, I forgot to ask what kind of doctor he is."

Laney laughed. "If anyone can help you get into Barbara's head, he can. He was her shrink. I don't know why I'm laughing," she said quickly. "Nothing's very funny, is it?"

Dr. Roger Harwell had agreed to see Ryker after his last appointment. Ryker showed up at 5:55 on Wednesday evening and waited in the small, tastefully decorated anteroom.

Promptly at 6:00, the door to an inner office was opened by a tall, ruggedly handsome man in his mid to late forties wearing what was obviously an expensive sweater in a light pewter shade, charcoal gray pants, and gray loafers. Ryker couldn't see the socks; they were probably argyle. The pants were pleated. Ryker sighed. Harwell looked as though he belonged in a Ralph Lauren ad. All that was missing was a pipe, an Irish setter, and a

226

cozy fire.

The pipe was leaning on an ashtray on the burled wood desk.

"Sit down, please, Detective." He pointed to a hunter green chenille sofa near the desk, sat in an upholstered armchair, and picked up the pipe. "Do you mind?"

"Actually, yes."

"Good for you. I encourage honesty." He replaced the pipe and tented his now idle hands. His nails were impeccably groomed. "You mentioned on the phone that this concerned Barbara Simpson. She was a lovely woman. I was so shocked when I read about her death. What a terrible accident!" He sighed. "Frankly, Detective, I'm puzzled as to why you're here."

"I'll try to explain. We know from Ms. Simpson's cancelled checks that she was seeing you professionally on a steady basis. Can I assume that since Ms. Simpson is dead, we don't have to worry about doctor-patient confidentiality?"

"No, Detective. I'm afraid you can't assume that at all. Confidentiality between a patient and a therapist doesn't end with the patient's death."

"That doesn't make much sense, does it? How can a dead person be harmed by anything a therapist reveals?"

"Well, there *is* the possibility of damaging the deceased person's reputation with his family or with the community. In either case, it would be a clear violation of trust. That's just one example. And obviously, a patient's therapy might be inhibited if he thought his therapist was bound by the confidential nature of their relationship only during the patient's lifetime."

"I guess."

"You have to keep in mind that the primary duty of the therapist is always to the patient. He has to do whatever he can to further the patient's best interests."

Ryker nodded thoughtfully. "Okay. But what if I

227

could convince you that your waiving of confidentiality would be in Ms. Simpson's best interests?"

"I'm not sure I follow you."

"The thing is, Doctor Harwell, we have a strong suspicion that Ms. Simpson's death wasn't accidental."

"I'm sorry; I still don't see your point. But without revealing anything, I *can* tell you that I find it highly unlikely that Barbara killed herself."

"Not suicide, Doctor. Murder."

He stared at the detective. "I see. Morally, of course, I'd want to help you find her . . . killer. But I don't see how revealing what she told me in our sessions will serve her best interests. I don't mean to sound crass, but finding her killer won't bring her back to life."

"True. But wouldn't she want to bring that killer to justice? Let me ask you something, Doctor. Do you think that Barbara Simpson's best interests would include the protection of her immediate family?"

"Yes. Of course."

"So it would be in her best interests to have her sister living in the same house with a suspected killer?"

"Mark Bauers?" He looked stunned.

"I have to be honest. We don't have any proof, only suppositions and weak circumstantial clues. Bauers could be totally innocent, but I don't think he is. By the way, Doctor, everything I'm telling you is confidential."

Harwell smiled weakly. "Touché, Detective." He stroked his chin. "Look, even with what you've just told me, I'm not sure what the position of the American Psychological Association would be. I could be risking a lawsuit."

Worried about your ethics or your wardrobe? "So you won't help us?"

"I probably shouldn't. But frankly, I find your argument too compelling to ignore." He sighed. "All right; let's assume that I agree to discuss Barbara with you. How would that help you?"

The pitfalls of stereotypes. Don't judge a doctor by his Beverly Hills address and his designer clothes. Ryker hid his embarrassment. "I need confirmation of what we've learned. And you may be able to help us establish a motive for her murder."

Harwell picked up his pipe and tamped the tobacco in the bowl. Ryker didn't say anything.

"Can you get me a court order requesting disclosure?" Harwell asked.

"Not at this time. We don't have enough evidence to get one." He didn't add that as far as Lieutenant Ed Kalish, head of Homicide at West L.A., was considered, *we* was *I*. Why complicate things for Harwell? But he felt a little guilty about the omission. Probably because he was in a psychologist's office. *Tell me everything.*

Harwell lit the pipe and puffed several times. He seemed lost in a haze of smoke and thought. Finally, he nodded. "All right. Go ahead."

"I appreciate your cooperation, Doctor. First of all, it would help if I had some background information. Why was she coming to see you?"

"I really don't see how that's relevant to her death. You'll have to take my word for that, I'm afraid."

"Fair enough. Can you tell me what she was like? Was she stable? A reliable judge of character?"

"She was rather brittle on the outside, Detective. Sometimes abrasive, even, with a cutting sarcasm that could be unpleasant, I suppose. But that was her defense mechanism, you see. In truth, she was a very vulnerable woman."

"Would you say she was in touch with reality?"

"In what way?"

"I mean, did she fabricate things? Twist them? Misread them unintentionally, or intentionally?"

"Detective, all of us exaggerate sometimes—and

229

Barbara tended toward the theatrical." He smiled, remembering. "But if Barbara said something, it was basically true."

"So if she said she suspected her brother-in-law of having an affair with someone, that would be the truth?"

He hesitated. "That would be the truth as far as she saw it, but that doesn't mean that he *was* having an affair. Suspicion is so nebulous, Detective, yet it can seem so powerfully real, even under normal circumstances."

"What do you mean by 'normal'?"

"Well, just that Barbara's relationship with Mark was far from normal. As a matter of fact, it was the subject of much of our therapy for the last two years."

"She didn't like Mark?"

"She hated him." His tone was matter-of-fact.

"Was there a specific reason? Did she think he was mistreating her sister?"

"She was convinced that he married her for her money, but she never indicated that Mark was mistreating Kate. And she never told me she suspected him of cheating on Kate. Detective, *was* he cheating on his wife?"

"Probably. Ms. Simpson thought so, and apparently she had some proof from a private detective she hired."

"Well, that clarifies things considerably. She was unusually tense during our last two sessions. I asked her what was wrong, but she didn't want to discuss it."

"How would she have felt about her suspicions, Doctor?"

"Confused. Quite confused. You see, on the one hand, she would have felt sorry for Kate, and her instinct would have been to protect her. But even there, she would have been troubled. What would be best? To tell Kate the truth, and destroy the illusion of her happiness? Kate has been through some terrible losses in the past three years—her first husband, her mother. Or to hope that this affair was an isolated incident."

"Would she have confronted Mark?"

He thought for a second. "Probably. She was a very direct person. And in a sense, she would have derived tremendous satisfaction from the knowledge that she had been right all along about him—of course, at the same time, she would have felt troubled about that satisfaction."

"Doctor, one last question, and this is very important: Hypothetically, if Ms. Simpson believed that her brother-in-law was not about to end his affair, do you think she would have threatened to tell her sister about it?"

"I see what you're getting at. Yes, I think she would have. And that might have helped her deal with her own feelings of rejection and inadequacy where Mark was concerned."

"Because he didn't like her either, is that it?"

He looked at Ryker, eyebrows raised. "Because they had been lovers for months, Detective. Long before Mark Bauers met Kate and took her as his lawful wedded wife, he had asked Barbara to marry him."

Kringle. The name had hovered just at the edge of Laney's memory all afternoon. The minute she got home, she headed for her bedroom and Dupard's report that had become a fixture on her nightstand.

She scanned it quickly. There it was: *Ellen Kringle.* Mark's first wife. But why would Barbara have called the Kringles? To find out if Mark had been a good husband? A faithful husband? Had Barbara been looking for proof to show Kate that there had been other Janines in Mark's life?

There was something else, some hazy, unformulated, elusive half-thought that rippled across her consciousness. It wasn't until 1:15 in the morning, while she was watching an old movie, that she finally realized what it was.

"Brian." She nudged him gently. "Brian, I have to talk to you. It's important."

He rolled over onto his back. "What is it?" he grumbled.

"It's about Mark. Don't get upset, okay?" she added quickly, seeing his yawn change into a grimace. "I want to bounce an idea off you, get your reaction."

"Fine. But make it fast, okay? I have to be in court early in the morning."

"Okay. Listen to the whole thing before you say anything, all right?" She explained what had bothered her, outlined her theory. "What do you think? Is it completely crazy?"

He was wide awake now. "My first reaction is that it's highly unlikely. I mean, what are the odds? On the other hand, until a short while ago, I thought Mark was a terrific husband." He looked at her thoughtfully. "But if what you're suggesting is true, that changes the picture considerably, doesn't it?"

"Yes. It's just a theory, though. I may be wrong."

"You're going to try to get proof, aren't you?" he asked quietly.

"I don't know. I have an idea." She looked at him.

"Laney, I know you think I'm being unreasonably overprotective when I tell you to leave this to the police. But don't you see that if you're right about Mark and Janine, you could be in danger if they find out you're meddling?"

"I'll be very careful, Brian. But I have to try. Can't you see that?"

He sighed. "Yeah. Yeah, I guess I can. But that doesn't mean I like it. What exactly are you looking for?"

She told him.

Chapter Fifteen

Thursday morning, Laney called Kate from the shop at nine-thirty, when she was sure that Mark had left for the office. She was prepared to be insistent with Janine, but Kate answered the phone.

"Hi! I'm glad you're up! I have a favor to ask."

"Sure. I hope I can help."

"First of all, is Janine taking the kids anywhere today?"

"No. I think she was planning on spending the day at home, swimming with them, stuff like that. Why?"

"Okay. This is my problem. You know the shower in my bathroom? I'm sure I've told you about it. There's so little water pressure, that it's practically like showering with an eye dropper. Well, Brian's been after me to get a plumber to take care of it. So I finally made an appointment for today—I've been trying to get hold of this guy for three weeks now—and Abby was supposed to be home to keep an eye on things, right?

"Anyway, last night Abby asked if she could sleep over Lisa's house, and she's been so terrific lately, helping out with the kids since camp ended, so I figured, why not? I arranged for a baby-sitter to watch Kim and Ned. And this morning, the girl calls and says she can't make it. She

233

probably broke a fingernail or something. So what I want to know is, do you think Janine would mind helping me out for a couple of hours this morning? She could bring Jeremy and Dana to my house; the kids would have a great time. I'll pay her, of course."

"Let me ask her. I don't see why she'd mind."

"Great! I don't want to pressure her or anything, but Brian threatened to leave me if I didn't get the shower fixed."

Kate laughed. "I get the picture. When do you need her?"

"The plumber's coming at 10:30. If she could get to my house around 10:15, that would be terrific."

Ten minutes later, Kate called Laney at the shop.

"Janine says fine."

"Great! Thanks a million, Kate."

Up to a point, everything had been true. After she hung up, Laney called the sitter. She felt a little guilty canceling her on such short notice, but she promised herself that she'd make it up to the girl next time.

Kate was in bed but awake, Anuncia informed Laney when she arrived at the house. The smiling woman bobbed down the hall and disappeared into the kitchen while Laney went upstairs.

"I'm back!" Laney entered the room, arranging her face into cheerful innocence. "Just checking up on you."

"Oh, hi." She put down the book she was reading.

"Good book?"

"I can't seem to get into it. I feel kind of jittery today. Too much coffee, I guess. What's up?"

"Surprised to see me, right? Actually, I only have a few minutes. The thing is, I almost forgot that I made an appointment for today with an insurance agent. His name is Edgar Harkum; a friend of Brian's recommended him. Harkum called me last week, said he can provide us with better coverage for less—you know the line. Anyway, I

234

didn't know how to get out of it gracefully, and I figured it wouldn't hurt to meet with him. But I thought it would be a good idea to have our policy in front of me when I talk to him. You have it in the house, right?"

"It's downstairs in Mark's office, in the bottom drawer of the file cabinet. That's where I keep all my papers. It's unlocked."

Thank you, thank you, thank you. That's what I needed to know. "Great. I'll take it with me, if that's okay."

"Let me know what he says."

"Who?"

"The insurance agent, silly. Sometimes, you're so scatterbrained, Laney! Look, why don't I come downstairs and find the policy for you."

"Oh, that's all right. I'll manage. And you really should rest, Kate. You look tired."

"That's a switch. What happened to 'Get out of bed, Kate'? Or have you given up on me?"

"Never!" She looked at her watch. "I'd really better hurry." She leaned over and kissed her. "Harkum will be at the shop in less than an hour. Somebody has to keep this business going!"

She left the room and hurried down the stairs, embarrassed by how easy it had become to slip into guile.

Flipping through the files in Mark's office, Kate blessed Kate's penchant for organization. Suspended from the side rails were ten or twelve olive green folders, each with a neatly lettered tab indicating a major category. Within each green folder were manila folders for various subcategories.

"INSURANCE" was subdivided into "Car," "Home," "Life," "Medical," and "Shop." Laney lifted out the file labeled "Shop," removed the policy, and placed it on Mark's desk. She would return it in a day or so, tell Kate that she had seen no advantage in the agent's plan. What was his name again? Harrum? No, Harkum. She'd better

235

remember it. As she was returning the manila folder, her fingers brushed against the one marked "Life." She hesitated, but left it in place.

At the front of the alphabet, she found what she wanted: "AU PAIR." A folder labeled "Janine" contained letters of recommendation from her aunt, Renee Bouchard; the principal of the Catholic high school she had attended in Chatel St. Denis; a family in Geneva named Gauthier, with whom Janine had boarded; the pharmaceutical company in Geneva for which she had worked. Laney jotted down names, addresses, phone numbers. There were also several letters from the girl herself, written on pink stationery, and a sepia-toned photograph—a graduation shot, no doubt. Laney wondered if Janine had ever been the innocent girl in the picture.

The other folder in "AU PAIR" was marked "Inquiries." In it, she found several sheets of paper; a few ads clipped from newspapers, some in what she recognized as German, some in French; correspondence from other applicants. One of the sheets was headed "Sybil Blackwood—Austria." Sybil was the one who had encouraged Kate to get an au pair, Laney recalled. The other was headed "Mrs. Brockner—Mark's patient *(avec le moustache!!)*—Switzerland." That's the one! Laney thought triumphantly. She added the woman's name to her list.

She was about to close the file drawer when she noticed "Adoption" under "LEGAL." Kate had said something months ago about Mark wanting to adopt Jeremy and Dana. At the time, Laney had thought it was a lovely idea. Now she cringed at the thought.

"What are you doing?"

It was Mark.

She shut the file drawer so quickly that she almost slammed it on her fingertips, and forced herself to turn

236

around casually. He was standing in the doorway, his body looking suddenly larger, menacing. Smile, she told herself, and felt her mouth's stiff response.

"Hi, Mark." It was an effort to speak calmly, to keep from gagging on the lump of fear that was rising in her throat. "God, you really startled me!" Her laughter sounded shrill to her ears.

"This *is* my home, Laney. My eleven o'clock appointment canceled, so I decided to see how Kate is doing. Does she know you're here?" His voice was cold, appraising.

"Of course. I told her I need the shop's insurance policy. She told me to look in the file cabinet."

She moved over to his desk and picked up the papers, hoping that her frame blocked him from seeing her slip her list of names and addresses in between the pages of the policy. She was amazed that the pages didn't rattle as she held them. "Here it is. I guess I'll be on my way."

He made no move to leave the doorway. "Why do you need the policy?" There was no pretense of curiosity in his voice, just a demand for an explanation.

She told him about Harkum. Even while she spoke, she felt as if she were outside her body, an audience alternately listening to her jabber and gauging his belief.

He smiled, finally, but his eyes remained cold. "Well, I hope you have everything you need."

He waited until she left, then checked the room. His desk drawers seemed undisturbed. The top three drawers in the file cabinet, his, were locked. The key was exactly where he always kept it. He opened the bottom file drawer, but saw nothing to indicate that Laney had searched through it.

She *had* been looking for the insurance policy, then. And her obvious nervousness? A normal reaction to his unexpected arrival? Or the guilty behavior of someone caught in the act. But what act? A frown marred the even surface of his handsome face. With an effort, he erased it and went upstairs to see his wife.

"Mark! Is everything all right?" She turned off the T.V. with the remote control.

"I had a cancellation. Aren't you happy to see me?" He smiled.

"Of course. Did you see Laney downstairs?"

"She just left. She's been around a lot lately, hasn't she?"

"I guess. She's a good friend. She came to get the insurance policy for the shop."

"So she said. Where are Janine and the kids?"

"At Laney's." She explained about the plumber and the baby-sitter problem. "Janine didn't mind a bit."

"That's fine." He walked over to her nightstand. "You haven't taken your second pill this morning."

"I wanted to talk to you about that, Mark. This new pill isn't helping at all. It makes me feel . . . I don't know, jittery, nervous."

"Your body has to get used to it. I explained that before."

"Maybe I should go back to the other ones, at half the dosage."

"This is better, Kate. You can use the other ones at night, when you don't have to be so alert."

"But I'm feeling nervous, Mark."

"Are you saying you don't trust me, Kate?"

"Oh, no. I didn't mean that. Of course I trust you."

"Well, then, just give these pills a chance, Kate. I know what I'm doing."

The minute she returned to the shop, Laney called Brian at his office. *Be in; please be in.*

His secretary answered. "He's not in court, Mrs. Tolbert; I think he's with the D.A.; I'll check."

A few minutes later, Brian got on the line. "I'm in the middle of an important meeting, Laney. Can this wait?"

"I got the information I was looking for; the name, too. I want you to call Mark's office, Brian, and check it out. Right now is best, because he's at home."

"He saw you!"

"It's all right. I told him I went to get the policy; he believed me. Will you do it, Brian? I think it's better if you call, don't you?"

He obtained Mark Bauers's office number from Directory Assistance and dialed.

"Doctors' offices. How may I help you?"

"Good morning. My name is Lewis Corcoran, and I'm with Fidelity Life. We're doing a check on a prospective policy holder, Mrs. Edith Brockner, and we need a certificate indicating that she's in good health. You should have received her written release by now."

"What's that name again?"

"Brockner. Edith Brockner."

"Just a minute. I'll check." She was back a minute later. "I'm sorry. I've checked all our files, but there is no Edith Brockner."

"Maybe I got the first name wrong. That happens."

"There's no Brockner at all, Mr. . . . ?"

"Corcoran. Are you sure? How far back do your files go?"

"A minimum of three years in active; after three years without a visit, we put them in another section."

"I can't figure this. She wrote down the doctor's name for me. Bruers."

"Did you say *Bruers?*"

"Yeah." He spelled it.

"Well, that explains it. You have the wrong doctor, Mr. Corcoran. This is Dr. Mark *Bauers*. That's why you can't find this person."

"No kidding! Well, what do you know!" He chuckled.

239

"Well, thanks for your time. Sorry about that."

He hung up and dialed the shop.

"Well?" she asked.

"You were right. There is no Mrs. Brockner; there hasn't been one. But are you sure that's the right person?"

"Positive. I distinctly remember Kate telling me that Mark kept mentioning a Mrs. Brockner—he kept making fun of the woman, said she had this horrendous mustache—how happy she was since she got an au pair. I think that's where Kate got the idea of the au pair in the first place—from the fictitious Mrs. Brockner, not from Sybil. And according to the information on the sheet I found, it was Mrs. Brockner who supplied Mark with the names of the Swiss newspapers she used to place an ad for an au pair."

"So if there isn't a Mrs. Brockner?"

"Then Mark is the one who planted the idea in Kate's head about getting an au pair. And Mark supplied Kate with the names of those Swiss newspapers. Oh, I'm sure he was very subtle, but the bottom line is that he manipulated Kate. Brian, don't you see that I'm right? It all makes sense. Mark didn't just fall for Janine and have a casual affair with her. He knew her before, brought her over here from Geneva! He engineered the whole thing!"

At one-thirty, after taking care of a few errands, Mark Bauers returned to his office. His secretary, Angela Palusky, handed him a stack of messages.

He flipped through them quickly. "That's it?"

"Uh-huh." She thought about mentioning the wrong number, but decided against it.

Laney waited all afternoon for Sam Ryker to return

her call.

"I just got your message," he told her when he called.
"I've been out in the field all day. What's up?"

"First of all, you wanted to know about Kringle. Ellen
Kringle was Mark's first wife. They were married in 1975.
The information was in Dupard's report."

That explained the call to the Marriage Records. "Did
they get divorced?"

"No, apparently she died. Dupard didn't say anything
else. Anyway, my guess is that Barbara called the
Kringles—I'm assuming the number you have is for the
parents—to find out what kind of husband Mark was.
Maybe he had an affair when he was married to their
daughter."

"Maybe. Good thinking. I'll check it out."

"I found out something else, Sam. Actually, you're the
one who started me thinking about it."

"About what?"

"Remember the other day you asked me whose idea it
was to get the au pair, Kate's or Mark's?"

"Right. You said it was Kate's."

"Well, it wasn't. I'm positive it was Mark's, but he
made Kate think it was hers. See what I mean?"

"What makes you think it was Mark's idea?"

She explained about Mrs. Brockner and the Swiss
newspapers, about Brian's call to Mark's office. "It's the
mustache that stayed in my mind. Well?"

He could hear the excitement in her voice. "You're
amazing, Laney. That's some piece of detecting."

"Is this enough to reopen Barbara's case?"

He sighed. "Unfortunately, no. The fact that Mark
Bauers invented a patient isn't a criminal offense. And it
just isn't a link that a D.A. could sell a jury. Even if we
could prove that he maneuvered his wife into placing ads
for an au pair in a Geneva newspaper—"

"I know he did!"

241

"I agree with you. But even if he arranged for Janine to answer the ad and pressured his wife into choosing Janine over the other applicants, what connection is there between those actions and Ms. Simpson's death? That's what Lieutenant Kalish will want to know."

"I don't know yet. But doesn't it change the picture?"

"Absolutely. But I'm not exactly sure how. I have to give it some thought. Okay. Let's deal with what we *do* know. Obviously, if Mark knew Janine before she came here, he must have met her in Geneva. Where did you say she worked?"

She gave him the name, address, and phone number.

"A pharmaceutical firm, huh? That's interesting. I wonder . . . Has Bauers been to Europe recently?"

"Yes, about a year ago. He went on some kind of medical convention. I wish I could say it was in Switzerland, but I just don't remember. He wanted to take Kate along, but she didn't want to leave the kids."

"When was this?"

"Well, sometime in the winter or late fall. I know it was before we opened the shop—that was just after New Year's; we knew we couldn't get ready for the Christmas rush. Kate and I had been talking about it for some time, but Mark had been against it."

"So he went in October, November, or December?"

"Not December. By then, Mark had agreed that the shop was a good idea for Kate, and we already had a lease, some inventory."

"When did he change his mind about the shop?"

"I don't know. Why? Oh, I see! You think he changed his mind so that Kate would need more help in the house. Like an au pair!"

"The thought crossed my mind."

"You're right! I don't know why I didn't see that."

"You just did. Look, I'm going to make some phone calls, see if I can find out when Bauers went to Europe, where he stayed, etcetera."

"Maybe the airlines can help."

"They probably can, but they may not be willing to without a court order. According to law, they're not allowed to release information about passengers. And the problem is, I don't think I can get a court order."

"So we're stuck."

"Not necessarily. Sometimes, it's enough if I prove that I'm with the police. If that doesn't work, I have a couple of ideas. I'll call you when I find out something. Oh, and Laney, one more thing. I want you to stay away from the Bauers for a while. I know you said Dr. Bauers believed you about the insurance policy, but let's play it safe, okay?"

"Okay." The truth was that her last visit had unnerved her more than she cared to admit, to herself or to Brian.

There were five major airlines that flew to Geneva from Los Angeles, none of them nonstop: TWA, United, American, Pan Am, and Air France. Ryker called TWA first, identified himself as a homicide detective, and asked the man who answered to check whether Dr. Mark Bauers had flown on their aircraft to Geneva, Switzerland, in October or November of 1987.

"I wouldn't have that information here. You'll have to check with our corporate office in Kansas." He gave Ryker the number. "But the office closes at five o'clock; you'll have to call tomorrow. And you'll probably have to write to them anyway. They're not allowed to release that information."

Ryker thanked him. He called the other airlines and obtained phone numbers for corporate offices in Chicago (United Airlines), Dallas (American), Rockleigh, New Jersey (Pan Am), and Paris (Air France). A lot of long-distance calls to justify to Lieutenant Kalish. He decided he would leave Air France for last.

An hour after she took the bedtime pill, Kate felt pleasantly drowsy, and for the first time that day, she was able to relax. At first, when Mark moved next to her and ran his hand lightly up and down her leg, she thought she was dreaming. It had been so long.

"You're not too tired, are you?" He smiled. "I wasn't sure if you were sleeping."

She didn't say anything, pressed herself against his naked body.

"I want you, Kate. I've missed you so much."

He undid the buttons on her gown, kissed her neck, her breasts. She ached for his touch, and it seemed like an eternity to her before he undressed her and moved her under him. Suddenly, he stopped.

"I won't break," she promised. She tightened her arms around him.

They made slow, deliberate love. It was like coming home, she thought, after a long absence.

"I've been thinking about you all day." He stroked her hair. "Do you know how hard it's been to stay away from you?"

"I know. I don't ever want to be apart again, Mark."

He kissed her. "I have a confession to make. When I came home earlier today, I thought I'd send Janine and the kids to the park. I figured we'd make love all morning."

She looked at him, surprised. "Why didn't you say something? It would have been perfect." She smiled. "And you didn't have to send them away; they weren't even home, remember?"

He shrugged. "I don't know. Somehow, when I got home, it didn't seem like the right time. Maybe it was because—" He stopped.

"What?"

"Nothing." He stroked her hair again.

"No, tell me. You were about to say something."

"I don't want to spoil the mood."

"You won't."

"All right. It's just that lately I have the feeling that Laney is spying on me."

"That's ridiculous! Laney? Why on earth would she do that?"

"I shouldn't have said anything. Look at how tense you are." He massaged her shoulder.

"No, really. I'm fine. I just don't understand why you feel that way. Laney thinks so highly of you, Mark. She always has."

"She used to."

"What does that mean?"

"Nothing. Forget it. Forget I said anything." He leaned over and kissed her again. "We have a lot of time to make up."

She edged away. "Come on, Mark. What do you mean 'She used to'?"

He sighed. "Haven't you noticed a change in her, Kate? She's very uncomfortable around me. It's not my imagination."

"But why? Did you have a fight, Mark? Is there something you're not telling me?"

"No, we didn't have a fight."

"But there *is* something. What is it?"

He hesitated. "All right." He sat up. "I wasn't going to mention this, because I know how close the two of you are, but maybe it's better if you know. The truth is, I'm convinced that Barbara mentioned her suspicions about me and Janine to Laney."

"No!"

"Yes. You mean Laney hasn't said anything to you?"

"No. You must be mistaken, Mark."

245

"I'm not mistaken. She's made little comments here and there. And she's been rude to Janine, too."

"Why, did Janine say something?"

"She was crying the other day when I came home, and I asked her what was wrong. She said Laney hates her, that she doesn't know why."

"I don't understand. That's so unlike Laney."

"And didn't you find it odd that she used her key to come in that time? I'll bet she was looking around the house. Maybe she thought she'd find my underwear in Janine's room."

"Mark, you're being silly. That's not how it was."

"I'll tell you something else. I have the feeling that Laney blames me for your condition, too. I don't know what's going on in her mind. Maybe she thinks I'm trying to keep you a prisoner in the house."

"That's crazy!"

"Well, that's how she makes me feel. Don't you think I want you to get back to normal? Do you think I'm happy knowing that you don't have the energy to get out of bed?"

"I don't know what to say, Mark. This is so sudden. I think, you know, we've all been under a lot of tension since Barbara's death. Laney, too. I mean, she's had to run the shop all by herself, and she hasn't complained about it once."

"Oh, really?" He laughed. "You have no idea how many times she's hinted that you're taking advantage of her."

"What are you talking about?"

"Twice last week she asked me how her 'silent partner' was doing."

"She's joking, Mark. You know Laney's sense of humor."

"Trust me, Kate. She wasn't joking. To tell you the truth, I'm not sure she's such a loyal friend. A loyal friend doesn't imply that your wife is weak and spoiled, that she's indulging herself at someone else's expense."

"She said that?"

"Do you think I'm making it up?"

"No. I think you misunderstood her, Mark. She told me herself that she thinks I should get off the pills. That's what you're talking about, isn't it?"

"That's part of it, Kate. She talked about the kids, how you were neglecting them, too. I can't remember everything she said. But it's obvious that she's really jealous of you, of your lifestyle. Oh, I admit she jokes around a lot, but underneath it all, the jealousy is real."

"Mark, you don't know Laney. She's not like that at all."

"Are you saying that I'm lying?"

"No. Of course not. I just think that—"

"You think I'm trying to come between you, is that it?"

"Mark, calm down."

"Don't you see what's happening? She's trying to ruin our relationship, trying to undermine the trust we have. And you're going to let her do that?"

"Mark, I don't know what you're talking about. I have no intention of letting Laney ruin our relationship."

"Well, what are you going to do about it?"

She looked confused. "What do you mean? There's nothing to do, Mark. Look, I'll talk to her, tell her how you feel—"

"No! She'll just lie, Kate. Don't you see that?" He moved abruptly off the bed.

"Where are you going?"

"I have to think."

"Please don't go. Let's talk this out."

"There's nothing to talk about. It's obvious that you think I'm wrong, that Laney's right." He shook his head. "Let me ask you something. Why do you think she's pushing you into going back to the shop?"

"She thinks I should get out of the house, get back into a normal routine. Become involved."

He shook his head. "She wants you under her influence, Kate. Believe me, if she had your best interests at heart, she'd realize that it's too soon for you to go back."

"No, Mark."

"She's meddling, Kate. She's not a doctor, but she criticizes you when you take medication that you clearly need. That I prescribed for you, goddammit! I'm trying my best to get you off the medication gradually, without throwing your system out of whack, but what the hell do I know, right?"

"Please, Mark," she begged. "Don't talk like that. You know how much I love you."

"Do you?" He looked at her. "You know, for two years I put up with a lot of crap from Barbara because she was your sister. I never complained; I never told you that I didn't want her around. Well, did I?"

"No, you never did. You were very understanding."

"You'd better believe it! Because I didn't want to come between you. But Laney Tolbert isn't your sister, and I don't intend to take any crap from her. You'd better think about that! I love you, Kate, but there's just so much I can take!"

She was too stunned to speak. By the time he had dressed and stormed out of the room, she was crying so hard that she could hardly breathe.

In the space of five minutes, she had plummeted from the heights of physical and emotional ecstasy to an abyss of confusion and despair, and she had no idea how it had happened. She had never seen Mark so angry, except for one time, more than year ago, and that had been her fault, really. She had wanted to surprise him for his birthday, so she had sent his parents plane tickets so that

248

they could come for a visit.

He had come home one afternoon, furious. His parents, he had told her, had been humiliated by her gesture.

("You made them feel like paupers, Kate. Don't you see that? What the hell did you think you were doing?"

"I just wanted to make you happy, Mark, and I want to get to know your family. I didn't see the harm in sending them tickets; you've told me so many times that they can't afford the trip."

"Did you ever stop to think about the other expenses a trip would involve? Do you honestly think my parents can afford to shut down the store to come here for a visit? And what about clothes? Don't you think my mother would be embarrassed to come here without getting a few decent outfits? Who was going to pay for that?"

"I'm sorry. I guess I didn't think it through. I meant well, Mark. Please believe me."

"I believe you, but it's going to take a while for me to calm them down. Do me a favor, will you please? Cut the Lady Bountiful routine. And don't meddle with my family, all right?")

A few hours later, he had apologized profusely, and she had put the incident behind her. That had been the only time he had ever lost his temper in more than two years of marriage. Until tonight.

She had no idea how to deal with Mark's anger toward Laney. It had erupted so suddenly, without warning. There was no point in talking to him now, in trying to refute the accusations he had hurled. In the morning, he would be calmer, more rational.

And if not? She didn't want to think about that possibility, about the implied threat that had hung in the air. *Don't make me choose,* she cried silently.

She would find a way to convince Mark that he was wrong about Laney. She couldn't believe that Laney was jealous of her, that she had been building up a reservoir of resentment about Kate's prolonged absence from the shop. Mark had misunderstood her comments, had overreacted.

Or had he?

Someone has to keep this business going.

Laney had said that just this morning. And what had she said a few weeks ago? Something about making both of them rich? But she always made comments like that, and Kate had always assumed she was joking.

Maybe she wasn't. But if that was true . . .

Suddenly, she remembered the other day, when she had found Laney in Janine's room. She had said something about looking for a nail file, and Kate had believed her. What if Mark was right? What if she had been misplacing her trust?

But that was ridiculous. Absolutely ridiculous.

She poured some water from the carafe on her nightstand into a glass and took a pill from the vial. She knew it was too early for another pill, but she didn't think it would hurt, just this once.

She didn't hear him come back into the room, into their bed, but she felt his arms around her, and then he was kissing her, whispering in her ear.

"I'm sorry, Kate. God, I'm so sorry. I don't know how I could have done that to you, put you through all that."

"It's okay. It'll be okay."

"No, it's not. I should have been more careful. Who cares what Laney thinks about me? She's your friend, and I had no right to make you doubt her."

Half asleep, she turned to him and caressed his cheek.

"I love you, Kate."

Everything was going to be fine.

Chapter Sixteen

Ryker had set his alarm for five-thirty on Friday morning. He had planned to get to the office early so that he could call the airlines before he became involved with his official cases. He had also decided to call Geneva. If Lieutenant Kalish disapproved, Ryker would pay for the call himself.

By four o'clock he was already up, and after a few attempts to go back to sleep, he admitted defeat. He lay in bed for a while, listening to Linda's soft, even breathing, watching all the furniture and accessories in the room emerge from the blanket of foggy darkness and resume their identities—first the armchair, dresser, framed mirror, Linda's needlework; then, on the dresser, a crystal perfume atomizer, a hairbrush, a silver oblong frame with a snapshot of Linda and the girls, a ceramic oval box that contained bobby pins. His wallet. His badge.

Bauers was guilty. So was the girl. Meeting the debonair doctor and the au pair had confirmed the suspicions Laney Tolbert had aroused with her convincing if bizarre theory. They were both cool, especially the blonde. But it had struck Ryker false that they had known almost immediately what they had been doing three weeks ago on a weeknight. Most people wouldn't

251

remember so easily, not without recourse to a calendar or diary or a methodical retracing of events.

And Bauers should never have admitted that he had spoken with Dupard. That had been a telling mistake. Ryker smiled again when he thought about his lucky shot—"a hit, a palpable hit"; it was the suggestion that he planned to question Bauers's secretary that had suddenly jogged the doctor's faulty memory. Not that Bauers's admission was proof of murder.

None of it was proof. That was the problem. Ryker had two people whose deaths were probably linked. Both homicides—there was no question in his mind that Barbara Simpson had been electrocuted, but there was no concrete evidence to reopen her case. If Ryker were back on his own turf at Wilshire Division, maybe he could convince Lieutenant Maynard to put some manpower on the Simpson woman's death. And at least he'd have Lewis and Moran to help him run down some leads, talk to Simpson's neighbors, check more into her past. The three always worked well together. In West L.A. he was a newcomer, on temporary loan to fill the gap left by the sudden departure of three veteran detectives. Technically, Ryker could have resisted the transfer; he had agreed as a favor to Maynard, who had said something about a promotion and an office. Maybe. Ryker wasn't looking for a promotion—he liked being a detective second grade, working in the field instead of supervising. And although the idea of having his own office had its appeal, he enjoyed the camaraderie of the squad room.

Kalish and the other detectives seemed decent enough, moderately friendly, with a "don't-expect-thanks-for-being-here" wariness toward Ryker that seemed to be thawing. Ryker knew Kalish was under pressure. He was understaffed and had several unsolved cases on his mind, including the one Ryker was supposed to be working on. If Ryker brought up the Simpson woman, he'd probably growl about wasting the taxpayers' money and laugh Ryker out of his office. Insufficient evidence.

By five-thirty Ryker had showered, dressed, and shaved. He left the sleeping house quietly and stopped at a coffee shop on the way to work to quiet the rumbling of his stomach with a muffin and a soft-boiled egg. He drank one cup of coffee, ordered another cup to go. The precinct was practically deserted when he arrived a little after six o'clock. He sat at his desk, took a sip of his now lukewarm coffee, and began making his calls.

Geneva first. There was a nine-hour time difference, the operator had informed him the night before. That meant that it was 3:00 P.M. in Switzerland. He found the number Laney had given him, got the country and city code from the long distance operator, and dialed.

"*Bonjour. LeDoux et Cie. Puis-je vous aider?*" A young woman's voice.

"Hello. My name is Sam Ryker. I'm calling from Los Angeles, California. Do you speak English?"

"A leetle. How can I to help you?"

"I'm calling to check on someone who worked for you about a year ago. Janine Panetierre."

"*Je regrette.* It is six months that I am working here. I do not know this woman."

"Is there someone else who I could talk to, please?"

"*Oui.* Monsieur LeDoux. He is speaking a fine English. I will connect you. *Un moment, s'il vous plaît.*"

Ryker waited patiently on hold until a male voice came on the line.

"Henri LeDoux. My receptionist says you wish to know something about Janine? How is she doing?"

Not a young voice. Early to mid-fifties? "She's fine, Monsieur LeDoux. I'm Sam Ryker from Los Angeles. I just need some background information on Miss Panetierre. I wanted to know how long she worked for you, that kind of thing."

"How long? Let me think. A year or more, I would say. She was, of course, a fine secretary—efficient, quick. But she was more than that. She learned the particulars of the business very rapidly, and I could see a fine future for her with our company. I was sorry to lose her."

"Did she get along well with your other staff?"

"Well, Janine, she kept to herself a great deal. Not unfriendly, you understand, but very private. To our customers, however, she was very—how do you say it?— *agréable.*"

"Pleasant?"

"Yes, pleasant. And of course she spoke the languages well."

"English?"

"*Bien sûr.* English, French, German, Swissdeutsch. I think also a little Italian. We have many foreign clients, so this was to me a grand advantage."

"Definitely," Ryker agreed. "Monsieur LeDoux, I understand that your firm deals with pharmaceuticals. I was wondering whether you are represented at medical conventions from time to time."

"But of course. This is a most important aspect of our business, a way to advertise our new products, to find out what the medical profession is needing."

"And did Miss Panetierre ever represent you at these conventions?"

"*Certainement.* With her knowledge of languages and her familiarity with our products, she was the obvious choice. And of course, if you have met Janine, you know that she is very pleasant to look at, yes?"

"Oh, quite."

"Yes. Well, quite frankly, this too is an asset, as I'm sure you can see. One can never pay too much attention to the packaging, *n'est-ce pas?*"

"Of course. Monsieur LeDoux, just out of curiosity, at these conventions, are there mostly European doctors?"

"Europeans, yes. British, South Americans, Israelis. And of course, the Americans. I must say that Janine always enjoyed most the conventions with the Americans. That is why I was not surprised when she decided to quit her job and move to America. I tried to tempt her to stay. I offered her a promotion and a considerable raise, but of course, I could not compete with her new opportunity."

"As an au pair?" Ryker was puzzled.

"*Pardon?* Ah, you are joking, yes?" He chuckled. "Janine and I, we laughed about her being an au pair, even for a short while. What a waste! But she explained that this was just to facilitate the immigration process until the happy event, and of course I wrote the references."

"The happy event?"

"Why, yes. The marriage." He paused. "Are you saying that Janine is *not* married yet? But that is most strange."

"Why is that?"

"Because that is why she left Geneva. To marry the American doctor."

"What's his name? Bauers?" Ryker asked casually.

"That I do not know. Janine, as I told you, is most private. Actually, I was surprised when she confided in me, but I think, you know, that she was so excited that she wanted to tell *someone* about her good news. I had shown her some kindness in the past; perhaps she saw me as a father." He laughed. "To tell you the truth, monsieur, if I had not been a happily married man of thirty years, I would have preferred that she look on me as something other than a father."

"Where did she meet this doctor? At a convention?"

"Exactly. About a year ago, I think. Yes, that is right. It was at the convention in the middle of October. I remember because she assured me she would not be leaving for a while—four or five months, she said—and

255

so she would have plenty of time to train her replacement. But the new girl is no Janine, that I can tell you."

"I see. Have you kept in touch with her, Monsieur LeDoux?"

He sighed. "No. That is the sad thing. I had expected to hear from her—to learn how she was adjusting to American life, to receive an invitation to the wedding. But I have not heard anything from her since she left in March. First I was surprised, then concerned. About a month after she left, I contacted the Gauthiers—the family with whom she was living in Geneva—but they, too, had not heard from her. For a long while I was hurt, but then I realized that maybe I was being selfish. Maybe Janine wanted a completely fresh start in her new life, yes? Once or twice, she had hinted to me that her life had not always been happy. She was an orphan, you see, left without any family whatsoever. Sad, very sad."

"Did you ever check again with the Gauthiers?"

"Yes. They tried sending her some mail, but the envelopes were always returned. Apparently, the address Janine had given them was incorrect. A little strange, that, but not criminal, *n'est-ce pas?*" He laughed.

"Right. Well, thank you, Monsieur LeDoux. You've been most helpful."

"Well, when you speak to her, please give her my best wishes. So she is not married yet, Monsieur Ryker? You have not said."

"Not yet, Monsieur LeDoux. But she's working on it."

Ryker had less success with the airline corporate offices. All the personnel he talked to politely told him the same thing: they would need written authorization before they could release any information regarding a passenger's travel itinerary.

People, Ryker decided, could be annoyingly law-abiding.

He waited till ten o'clock, then called Laney at the shop.

"Do the Bauers use a travel agent?" he asked.

"Yes. But I don't know which one."

"Can you find out? I'm having trouble with the airlines, and I'd like to try a different approach."

"I'll call Kate now, although I don't know what reason I'll give for asking."

"You'll think of something."

"Right."

She dialed and was relieved when Kate answered. "How are you?"

"Fine."

"I'm glad to see that you're up."

"I don't exactly sleep all day, Laney."

"Of course not. That's not what I meant. Listen, I was just wondering whether you could give me the name of your travel agent."

"Why?"

"Is something wrong? You sound odd."

"No. Nothing's wrong. I just asked a question."

"Oh. Okay. Anyway, the reason I asked about the travel agent is that Brian and I are thinking of going on one of those cruises to Mexico for a vacation. A second honeymoon."

"Really? You never said anything."

"Well, it just came up. Brian knows someone who went on one, and he and his wife had a fabulous time. I thought we could get a better deal with a reputable travel agent. I don't trust those ads I've seen for package tours—you know, seven days and six nights in a luxurious hotel right on the beach, plus all the margaritas you can drink. Then when you read the find print you find out that you're supposed to bring your own bed linen, and

257

that you're sharing a room with another couple." She laughed. "Our anniversary isn't for another three months, but I figured I'd be organized for a change."

"What about the kids? Where will they be?"

"Oh, I'll farm them out. Kim can stay with Brian's sister; Abby and Ned can be with friends. Right now it's just an idea. It all depends on how much it costs. I wish we had unlimited funds, but we don't."

"Meaning that I do?"

"Kate! What's the matter with you?"

"Nothing. I'm a little edgy."

"It's the pills, right? Kate, you have to—"

"Let me find the number of the travel agency. My address book is here on my nightstand. Here it is: 555-6442. It's called Top Tours, by the way. I always deal with a Mrs. Larkins. You can tell her that I gave you her name."

"Fine. I'll do that."

"So who's going to mind the shop while you're away?"

"You will, with Mrs. Margolin. By then, you'll be better. And I think it's only fair that you get an equal dose of her." She laughed.

"If my being away from the shop for so long is a problem, just say so, Laney."

"God, I was just joking, Kate! You know that, don't you?"

"Whatever. So how was the meeting yesterday?"

"The meeting?"

"With the insurance agent."

"Oh, right. I have so much on my mind, I forgot about it. Actually, it was a waste of time. He isn't offering anything better than what we have. But that's good to know, too, right? Anyway, thanks for the number. I'll give the agency a call."

*   *   *

258

Ryker called Top Tours and was connected with Mrs. Larkins.

"Mrs. Larkins, we're doing a survey of medical conventions and the hotels they frequent. Our computer printout came up with several names, including Dr. Mark Bauers, and listed your firm as his agent. We're trying to collect data so that we can assess how to better serve the needs of the medical community. Of course, we won't be asking anything of a private nature. We've already contacted other agencies, by the way, and they've been most cooperative."

"Well, it sounds like a good idea."

"I do have to warn you though, ma'am, that this is confidential. You can't mention any of this to Dr. Bauers or our findings will be invalidated." He could hardly believe the garbage he was inventing. He hoped she did.

"All right. What would you like to know?"

"Well, first off, what hotel accommodations were made? Did he specify a hotel, or did you suggest one? Are you partial to certain hotels, etcetera. That kind of stuff. Oh, yes. We're interested only in conventions that take place in Europe."

"I see. Well, give me a minute, why don't you, and I'll call up Dr. Bauers's file on my computer screen."

"I really appreciate this, ma'am."

"My pleasure."

Ryker doodled on a yellow pad while he waited.

"I have it now. Dr. Mark Bauers. Let me scan this. Hmmn. Here it is. But it's in 1987. Is that all right?"

"I think so. We're checking the past two years. When in 1987 was that?"

"October sixteenth through the thirtieth. American Airlines from Los Angeles to Geneva, Switzerland, via New York. He stayed at the Hotel Des Bergues, but I'm afraid there's no way of knowing whether that was his request or our suggestion."

259

"Was he pleased with the accommodations?"

"There's nothing here to indicate that he was dissatisfied. We're careful to make a note of our customer's preferences. The hotel is on Lake Geneva, by the way. It's quite beautiful, and it has several large conference rooms."

"Well, thank you so much, Mrs. Larkins. You've been most helpful, I must say. And remember, mum's the word."

"Oh, absolutely. By the way, I didn't catch your name, Mr. . . . ?"

But Ryker had already hung up.

At 12:45, Ryker took a lunch break. He grabbed a roast beef sandwich at a deli on Pico (he had wanted the pastrami, but he knew he would pay for it later). Then he drove to Third and San Vicente and found a metered parking spot. Amazing.

8631 Third Street was one of several buildings that connected via the third floor to the Cedars-Sinai medical complex. Ryker checked the directory and took the elevator to the fourth floor.

"May I help you?" The receptionist behind the window was a pleasant-looking woman in her thirties. Light brown hair, friendly eyes behind rimless glasses with a rhinestone initial in the bottom corner of the left lens.

"I'd like to see Dr. Bauers."

"Do you have an appointment?"

"No."

"Is this an emergency?"

"Oh, no. I wouldn't say that, miss. But I *would* like to see the doctor."

"I'm terribly sorry, but Dr. Bauers is with a patient, and he's booked for the afternoon. If you like, I can schedule an appointment for Monday."

"I think if you tell him my name, he'll make some time for me. Just say Detective Ryker."

Her eyes were a little less friendly. "I'll buzz him for you, Detective, but he *is* very busy."

Ryker sat down and flipped through a current issue of *Sports Illustrated*.

"Dr. Bauers will see you now."

She opened the door to the waiting room and motioned for Ryker to follow her. She was much shorter than Ryker had thought, barely reaching his chest.

Bauers was standing in front of an illuminated oblong screen, studying what appeared to be X-rays. He looked up when Ryker entered.

"Detective! I'm surprised to see you. If you had called, I would have made some time for you. As it is now, I'm late for my next appointment, so I can only give you a minute."

"I have good news, Dr. Bauers: We found the hit-and-run driver. I happened to be in the neighborhood, thought I'd stop by and tell you in person."

"Well, I wasn't worried about it. I told you there had to be some mistake. Thank you for stopping by, Detective. It was thoughtful of you. But now you'll have to excuse me; I do have a patient waiting in the examining room."

"No problem. Long as I'm here, though, there are a couple of things I wanted to discuss. I can wait till after you see your patient, if you like."

"Well, if it won't take too long, why don't you just tell me what's on your mind."

"You're sure? All right then. First, there's this crazy coincidence. You're probably not going to believe it. I know it gave me a turn."

"What coincidence, Detective?"

"That hit and run I was investigating? That was

261

Monday, August 25, right? Well, I was checking my notes on Dupard's death, and you'll never guess what I found." He smiled.

"I assume you're going to tell me he was killed on the twenty-fifth?"

"Bingo! I told you it was something! The good news for you, Doctor, is that you already have an alibi for that night, seeing as how you and the young lady were together till late."

"I don't think I like your implication, Detective."

"I didn't realize I was implying anything, Doctor. Merely stating a fact. I'm sorry you took it the wrong way."

"Fine. Forget it. Is that it, Detective?"

"There is one more thing." He took an envelope out of his pocket. "Another coincidence, believe it or not. This concerns your late sister-in-law. Do you have a minute, or should I wait in the other room while you see your patient?"

"Can you make this fast, Detective?"

"I'll try my best. See, I just happened to be going through Ms. Simpson's papers. It's routine, you understand. And I came across her bank statement. Now I think you'll appreciate the irony here, Dr. Bauers. Among the canceled checks was one made out to Franklin Dupard." He showed Bauers the check and shook his head. "Isn't that the most amazing coincidence? I said to my wife, 'Linda,' I said, 'somebody up there is having a good laugh at my expense.'"

"That *is* a coincidence, Detective."

"I knew you'd be impressed. It's something, isn't it?— Dupard is hired by your sister-in-law, and then he calls you about a patient. What are the odds of that happening?"

"Detective! It all just came back to me. *That's* how I knew Dupard! He called after Barbara's death, said she had hired him to do some surveillance on her boyfriend, Simon Leicester. She thought Leicester was cheating on her."

"I thought you said he called about a patient."

"I was mistaken. I confused him with someone else. I can't imagine why I didn't remember his call."

"Maybe you were blocking, Doctor. Your sister-in-law's death, I mean. It must have hit you pretty hard."

He looked at Ryker. "Yes. I guess I must have been."

"Funny thing, though. We checked Dupard's apartment and office. There were several files, but nothing on Ms. Simpson."

"Maybe Dupard didn't find anything on Leicester."

"Yeah, but he would have filled *something* out. A daily report, even if he came up empty. That's standard P.I. policy. He's got to show details and times of surveillance."

"Detective, maybe someone stole the file."

"Who would do that?"

"I don't want to cast suspicion on anyone, but maybe Simon did."

Ryker narrowed his eyes. "But that would mean that he knew Dupard was running a surveillance on him. How would he know that? Oh, I get it. You think Dupard called Leicester, maybe to blackmail him? And that Leicester killed him? Is that what you're saying?"

"I'm not saying anything. I'm a doctor, not a detective. But it is a possibility."

"You're sharp, Dr. Bauers. I have to hand it to you. But what would Dupard have on Leicester? That he was cheating on Ms. Simpson?"

"I have no idea, Detective. I do know he borrowed a considerable sum of money from Barbara to finance a gallery he wanted to open. Maybe Leicester thought that if Barbara got proof that he was cheating on her, she'd dump him and the gallery. He was desperate to open that gallery, you know. He forged Barbara's name to a check for $150,000. Kate's lawyer told me about it. He's the executor of Barbara's estate. The police contacted him after Leicester confessed."

"No kidding? Well, you've certainly given me a lot to think about. We'll check into this Leicester person, see if he has an alibi for August 25."

"I really have to get to my patient, Detective."

"Of course. Thanks for your help." He started to leave the room. "There's just one more thing."

"What is it, Detective?" His voice contained unconcealed impatience.

"I just had this thought. There has to be a connection between Dupard's murder and your sister-in-law, right? What if it's the other way around?"

"I'm not following you."

"What if Dupard was killed because he knew that Ms. Simpson was murdered?"

"She electrocuted herself accidentally in the tub, Detective. That was the coroner's finding. She had a habit of bathing with a radio nearby. Everyone knew that."

"Is that right? But maybe somebody made it look like she was electrocuted. Somebody who knew her habits, you see."

"I think you're reaching, Detective. Who would want to kill Barbara? The idea is ridiculous."

"Maybe not. I'll keep you posted, Dr. Bauers. I'm sure you'll want to know if I come up with anything, since this does involve your sister-in-law. And if she *was* murdered, you'll certainly want her killer brought to justice."

"Of course. By the way, Detective, my wife knows nothing about Leicester's forgery. I didn't tell her because I knew it would upset her. I don't want her bothered with any of this, either. I think I mentioned that she's not well."

"I understand. And I agree completely, Doctor. That's

why I came to you in the first place, right?"

Lois Mummer had called. Ryker found the message on his desk when he returned to the precinct. He located Barbara Simpson's phone bill and dialed AT&T.

"I traced the other calls, Detective Ryker," Lois Mummer said. "I'm following the numbers as they appear on the list, continuing from where we left off. Okay. The fifth call is to the University of Minnesota. The sixth is to the Northfield Police Department. Again, Ms. Simpson called that number two more times, as you'll note on the second page of the bill. The seventh call is to the *Lake of the Woods Clarion* in Baudette."

"Where's Lake of the Woods? I don't see that listed."

"Somewhere in Minnesota; that's all I know. Anyway, the last call on page one is to the police department in Baudette."

"Okay. Thanks a lot. You've really helped me out."

"Any time, Detective."

"By the way, what's the time difference between L.A. and Minnesota, do you know?"

"Two hours."

That meant it was four o'clock in Northfield. Ryker dialed the number for the police department and asked to speak with the chief of police.

"You want Captain Spivak," said the officer who answered. "Hold on. I'll get him on the line."

For the tenth time that day, Ryker waited.

"Raymond Spivak here. How can I help you?"

"Detective Sam Ryker, L.A.P.D. I'm investigating the possible homicide of a woman called Barbara Simpson. Apparently she called your police department several times. I was wondering if you could tell me something about the nature of her call. It might help us get a handle on the case."

265

"What did you say the name was?"

"Barbara Simpson."

"When did she call?"

Ryker checked the bill. "The first time was on July 1. Then she called you twice on July 5."

"Oh, yeah. I remember now. Right before the holiday weekend. I talked to her. She was calling about the Bauers boy. Mark, his name is."

"That's right. Can you tell me what she wanted?"

"Well, she was asking me did I know anything about his first wife. That's Ellen Kringle. Nice girl. Good family. Shame about her."

"I understand she died. Do you remember what happened?"

"'Course I remember. Terrible tragedy. She drowned. Some say it was suicide, but the official report said 'accidental death.'"

"What do you think?"

"Can't say. Didn't happen here."

"Where did it happen?"

"Lake of the Woods. That's a resort up in northern Minnesota."

"I see. Ms. Simpson called you several times, though. What was the reason for the other calls?"

"She wanted to set up an appointment to talk to me. Seemed real anxious. I wondered why she never showed up. Guess now I know."

At four-thirty Ryker knocked on the door to Lieutenant Ed Kalish's office.

"Can I see you for a minute, Lieutenant?"

"Come in, Ryker." His heavily jowled face made him look perpetually worried. "What's up?"

"Something I want to talk to you about, Lieutenant."

"Have a seat."

Ryker sat in a chair facing Kalish's desk. "Thank you. I'd like to take a few days off to go to Minnesota."

"Ryker, you know how short-handed we are. That's why you're on loan to us, for Christ's sake! This is no time to take a vacation."

"I'd be going on police business, Lieutenant. This is about the Simpson case."

"There *is* no Simpson case, Ryker. We talked about it. Unless you have new evidence that a D.A. can use in court?"

"Not yet. But I'm convinced Bauers killed her, either by himself or in collusion with his lover. I also believe that the Panetierre woman killed a P.I. that Ms. Simpson hired to investigate them. Lou Morelli at Hollywood Division has the case." He explained about the strychnine, about the woman in the bar, the wig, the identification made by Janette Hopper. "Again, I realize that's not evidence we can use, but I got Bauers to admit that Dupard called him. By the way, I've been checking into all this on my own time, Lieutenant."

"Glad to hear it." His face bore a trace of a smile.

"I've also checked into the backgrounds of Bauers and the girl." He repeated what he had learned from Harwell, LeDoux, and Raymond Spivak.

"I see you've been busy," he said thoughtfully. "So what do you plan to accomplish in Minnesota?"

Ryker explained. "So that's it. If everything works out, I can leave tomorrow and be back by Wednesday. Look, I'm willing to use a few vacation days, if that's the only way I can go. About the air fare, well, it's pretty expensive. . . ."

"You're breaking my heart, Ryker. You're really sure about Simpson?"

"Positive. And about Dupard, too."

Ten minutes later, Ryker left Kalish's office. He called Northwest Airlines and booked a nonstop flight to St.

Paul, Minnesota.

He hoped he would have better luck than Barbara Simpson.

Irene Zuroff was snipping the dead leaves off the azalea bushes in the backyard when she heard the phone ring. Sighing, she walked to the back door, rubbed the crepe soles of her shoes against the straw mat to remove loose soil, and entered her duplex. The button that was flashing on her kitchen phone told her the call was from a patient or her service.

"Dr. Zuroff speaking."

"Dr. Zuroff, I'm glad I caught you before the weekend. I left a message with your service earlier. About Kate?"

"Yes. I received your message, but my service didn't say it was urgent. I was planning to call you later this evening. How can I help you?"

"Kate really needs you, Doctor."

"You know that I cannot discuss Kate. I'm sorry."

"I understand that. But I think you should know that her situation is deteriorating. She's still listless, and lately she seems edgy, too, not at all like herself. Today, for example, she sounded very strange, but when I asked her about it, she denied that there was anything wrong."

"Have her call me. You know I would be more than happy to help her."

"That's the problem, Dr. Zuroff. I don't think she'll make the first move, even though I've suggested it again. Maybe if she hears your voice, she'll be encouraged to ask for help."

"But I *did* call. I left a message with a young woman."

"Maybe Kate didn't get your message. Or maybe the moment passed. Will you try again, Dr. Zuroff? Frankly, if she continues this way, I'm afraid to think of what might happen."

268

"What do you mean?"

"I'm not sure, exactly. It's just a feeling."

"All right. I'll call her. Please remember, though, that I cannot ask her to resume therapy."

"Of course not. I know the rules. Do you think you can call tomorrow, or would that be imposing on your time?"

"Tomorrow will be fine, Dr. Bauers."

"Thank you. I feel relieved just knowing you'll be speaking to her. Good night."

Irene Zuroff stood holding the receiver for a few minutes. She hardly seemed aware of the dial tone or the sudden silence that followed it, but when the artillery of high-pitched beeps assaulted her ear, she quickly returned the receiver to its cradle.

She brought Kate Bauers's file from her office and placed it on the desk in her study. In the kitchen, she prepared a cup of blackberry herbal tea and carried it to the desk, careful to put the cup and saucer on a mat that protected the fine cherry wood. She selected Beethoven's "Moonlight Sonata" and sat at her desk, taking careful sips of the still-hot tea, letting the tranquil rhythm of the music wash over her as she entered a few notes in the file in her neat, precise handwriting.

She forgot all about the azaleas.

Chapter Seventeen

Saturday morning was clear and pleasantly warm. After swimming his customary laps in the pool, Mark suggested to Kate that they have breakfast on the patio.

"I'll make Spanish omelettes and espresso. We haven't had espresso in ages," he told her.

"Can I help?" She yawned guiltily.

"Just put on a robe and go outside. It's too nice to be indoors. The kids have already eaten. They're playing on the swing set with Janine. Come on." He selected a pink seersucker robe from her closet, put it near the edge of her bed, and folded back her comforter. "Let's go."

"All right. It sounds like a nice idea. Give me five minutes to wash up."

When she was ready, he escorted her downstairs and out to the round, glass patio table. He pulled out a wrought iron chair and waited while she seated herself.

"I'm going to the bakery for some goodies. You sit here. I'll bring you the paper before I leave. I started the puzzle, by the way, but I didn't get very far. Maybe you can fill in a few spaces before I get back."

He returned about half an hour later and reported his purchases: fresh croissants, onion rolls, and a cream cheese pie.

"You only get the pie if you finish the puzzle," he said. "How are you doing?"

"With the puzzle?"

"That too. No, I mean in general. You look a little better, I think. You have some color in your cheeks."

"I put on some blush. Actually, I'm still tired."

"You'll be fine. Give yourself a chance. We'll work this out together. Just the two of us. Right?"

"Right." She smiled at him. She had been about to mention the pills, that they didn't seem to be helping her, but had decided against it. He was in such a good mood. It was as if Thursday night had never happened.

He brought out china, silverware, goblets, placemats, linen napkins.

"So fancy," she murmured.

"For you. Are you complaining?"

"I love it." She smiled.

In the center of the table he placed a bud vase with a yellow rose from the garden. "Be right back." He made two more trips to the house, returning with toast, eggs, freshly squeezed orange juice ("Janine prepared it earlier"), and the bakery goods.

"Breakfast was delicious," she said later.

"You hardly ate." He was sipping a cup of espresso.

"My appetite has shrunk. But it *was* delicious. And it was so sweet of you to go to all this trouble."

"I enjoyed it. Okay, let me clear the table; then we'll tackle the puzzle. Deal?"

"Deal."

After fifteen minutes, they had filled in most of the squares.

"Too bad we have to wait till Monday to see the answers." He took the classified section in which the puzzle appeared. "Did you ever look through this? It's amazing the types of business you find. Listen to this: snack machines, sheet metal, pool route, steam cleaners, car wash—there's two or three of those. Here's a bakery-donut outfit. There's an idea. Maybe I should give up my practice and buy it. Then I wouldn't have to run out for croissants and cheese cake, right?"

"We'd both look like houses within two months."

"Yeah." He grinned, then continued reading. "Hey, here's something right up your alley."

"What?"

"Shit!" he muttered.

"What's wrong?"

"Nothing. A cramp in my toe. I think I'll walk on it, get the circulation going."

"What were you looking at? You said it was right up my alley."

"Never mind. My mistake."

"What was it? Let me see."

"I said it's nothing, Kate."

"Why do you sound so strange?"

"It's the cramp. It hasn't gone away."

She looked at him. "I don't believe you. You sound upset. Give me the paper, Mark."

"All right. But you have to promise not to overreact, okay?"

"Okay."

He sighed. "I guess you have a right to know." He pointed to an ad halfway down a center column: THRIVING GIFTWARE SHOP NEEDS PARTNER. EXCELLENT LOCATION. REASONABLE TERMS. FOR INFORMATION CALL (213) 550-4646.

"That's our shop." He voice was filled with bewilderment and incredulity and the piercing hurt of betrayal. She felt nauseated.

"There must be an explanation, Kate."

"There is, an obvious one. Laney's tired of waiting for me. She wants to sell my half of the business."

"She never mentioned anything to you?"

"Nothing. I can't believe she would do this behind my back!"

"She probably planned to tell you in a while. Maybe she didn't want to pressure you."

"Why are you defending her all of a sudden? The other night you were telling me how horrible and manipulating she is."

"I was wrong to do that, Kate. I apologized for it. You've been friends for so long. You'll work this out."

"I don't know."

"Look, in fairness to Laney, she's been bearing the responsibility of the shop by herself for more than two months. You said so yourself. Maybe this is just a feeler, in case you decide not to come back."

"Then why didn't she just tell me she was overworked or worried or both?"

"I don't know what to tell you, Kate. I wish to God I'd never seen the ad."

"No. It's really better that I know. I feel pretty stupid, though. Just the other day Laney was talking about my coming back to the shop, and I believed her."

"Do you want to ask her about it? Confront her?"

"No. I'll wait. I want to see if she has the courage and honesty to say something to me. And she'll probably deny it, anyway, right?" She looked at him.

He sighed. "This is the last thing you needed. I feel responsible, somehow."

"It's not your fault. Look, do you mind if I go inside? I think I'll try to rest. Maybe it'll clear my head."

"Go ahead. It's a good idea. I'll be up to join you in a little while. I have some paperwork to finish, but I can do it just as easily in the bedroom and keep you company at the same time."

When he came upstairs, she was lying in bed, her arms rigid at her sides, her eyes wide open.

"Can't sleep?" he asked sympathetically.

"No."

"Thinking about the ad?"

"I can't get it out of my mind."

"Do you think a pill would help?"

"I took a half when I came upstairs, but it hasn't helped," she admitted.

"Maybe today you need a whole one."

"Thank you." She waited until he handed her a glass with water and a pill. "I already had a half," she reminded him.

"They're mild enough. One and a half won't harm you."

The ringing of the phone startled her.

"If it's Laney, tell her I'm sleeping."

He picked up the receiver. "Hello? Oh, yes. Just a minute, please." He covered the receiver with his palm. "It's Dr. Zuroff. She'd like to speak to you."

"Dr. Zuroff?"

"I didn't know you contacted her. I thought we agreed to wait."

"I didn't. I have no idea why she's calling."

"Oh. Well, if you want to talk privately, I can go downstairs."

She hesitated. "No, that's okay."

"You're sure?"

She nodded. He handed her the receiver.

"Dr. Zuroff? It's Kate."

"Kate, I hope this isn't a bad time. I am calling because I recently heard of your sister's death. I wanted to express my condolences."

"Thank you. That's very thoughtful of you."

Mark sat on the side of her bed and wove her fingers with his.

"I know this must be a difficult time for you. I just want you to know that I am available in case you feel it would be helpful to talk to someone."

274

"That's very kind of you." She looked at Mark. "But I don't think I need professional help right now. I'm managing on my own. And Mark is helping me get through this. He's wonderful."

"I am certainly glad to hear that." She paused. "I wish you all the best, Kate. Well, goodbye," she finished lamely.

"Thank you, Dr. Zuroff. And thank you for calling. I appreciate your concern." She hung up and turned to Mark. "She heard about Barbara's death. She wanted me to know that if I need help, she's available."

He frowned. "Isn't that unusual? For a therapist to contact a patient, I mean? I'm not even sure it's ethical."

"She's just concerned, Mark. What are you getting at?"

"Nothing. I'm sorry. I should mind my own business. It's just that I feel so protective toward you."

"Because you love me. I know that." She squeezed his hand.

"I heard you tell her that you don't need professional help. Are you sure of that, Kate? I mean, just because *I* think it's a mistake for you to resume therapy doesn't mean that you have to agree with me. If you don't think I'm helping you, if you think you need Dr. Zuroff to help you cope with Barbara's death . . ."

"You *are* helping me, Mark. Really. I don't know what I'd do without you."

"I only want what's best for you, Kate."

"I know."

"You know what I think? We've been talking about going on a vacation for a while. Why don't we set a definite date, and I'll clear my work calendar. What do you say?"

"I guess so."

"Just the two of us. No kids, no distracting phone calls, no responsibilities. We'll go to the house in Big Bear.

275

Spend a long weekend, go swimming, maybe go horseback riding. I think it'll do you a world of good."

"It sounds nice. When can we go?"

"Well, this week's out. I need more time to rearrange appointments. And I have a convention this weekend—remember I told you about it?"

"Right. I didn't realize it was so soon."

"Listen, if you don't want me to go, just say the word."

"No. It's okay."

"All right. I think we should plan for around the twenty-fifth of September. Jeremy starts school this week, and Dana goes back to play group. Let's give them a couple of weeks to get settled into their routines. Then we'll go. They'll be fine with Janine. We'll call a housekeeping service in Big Bear to send someone out to air the place out, clean it, change the bedding. We can even get the number of a local grocery and have them deliver some basic items before we get there. Like champagne."

"You're being silly." She smiled.

"It'll be wonderful, Kate. You'll see. You'll come back a changed person. I'll drive all the demons away. Trust me."

Laney called Kate twice that afternoon. Each time Kate told Mark to tell Laney that she couldn't talk. When Laney called after supper, Mark put the receiver in Kate's hand.

"You can't avoid her forever, you know," he whispered. "She won't stop calling till you speak to her."

"You're right." She picked up the receiver. "Hello."

"Oh, hi! I was getting worried about you. I called twice in the afternoon, but Mark said you weren't up to talking."

"That's right. I was resting. He gave me your messages."

"Are you feeling better now?"

"I'm all right."

"I thought I'd come over tomorrow, spend some time with you."

"Not tomorrow. Maybe another time. Call first before you come, though. I really don't appreciate surprise visits."

"What's wrong, Kate? You seem upset with me."

"Why should I be upset with you, Laney? Have you done anything that *would* upset me?"

"No, of course not." *Except for snooping around in your house, trying to prove that your husband and his lover are killers.*

"Well, then."

"Look, something *is* bothering you. It's not my imagination. Can we talk about it? Get it out in the open?"

"There's nothing to talk about, Laney, unless there's something you haven't told me. I'm feeling a little tired now. I'm going to say good night."

She hung up quickly and bit her bottom lip, barely able to keep from crying.

"She upset you, didn't she?" Mark asked. "What did she say?"

"Nothing. I just can't talk to her, Mark. I keep thinking about the ad. It's so unlike her. She's never done anything behind my back."

"As far as you *know*."

"What do you mean?"

He shrugged. "Do you ever really know a person? Maybe that's not fair, but hasn't Laney been acting a little odd lately, popping up all the time? I wonder. . . ." He shook his head.

"What?"

"It's just a thought, probably silly. I was just thinking about last week when I found her looking in the file cabinet."

"She was looking for the insurance policy for the shop."

"That's what she said. And she *did* take it with her. But she seemed very nervous, you know, like someone caught with her hand in the cookie jar. Maybe she was looking through other papers about the business."

"I *do* have most of the contracts here. Laney insisted that I keep them because she's so disorganized. But what would she be looking for?"

"Who knows? I told you it was silly."

"No, you're probably right. Now that I think about it, Laney *did* seem nervous that day." She sighed. "I'm so naïve."

"Not naïve, Kate. Trusting. It's one of the things I love about you. Sometimes, though, you end up trusting the wrong people." He hugged her. "Try to relax. Don't let this give you a setback."

She took a pill to calm her nerves, and before she went to bed she took another. She was sure Mark noticed, and she was grateful when he didn't say anything. There had been no death this time, but the sense of loss she felt was almost as painful.

Ryker had opted for the 10:45 A.M. flight to St. Paul. The one before that left at 6:45, and he hadn't relished getting up at 5:00 on a Saturday morning. Linda had been more than accommodating, insisting on taking him to the airport.

"Sorry about the weekend," he said.

"Take me out to dinner when you get back. Some place special."

"McDonalds?"

"Right." She grinned. "Does Laney Tolbert know you're going to Minnesota?"

"Uh-huh. I called her last night and told her I'm trying

to get background information on Bauers. I gave her our home number, by the way, in case she has to reach me. I'll be checking in with you as often as I can."

"Don't worry about us, Sam. We'll be fine." She kissed him warmly at the curb side, ignoring the impatient honk of the driver who was waiting for her to vacate her spot.

The flight arrived three minutes early at 4:13. Ryker had packed everything into a two-suiter, so he headed straight for the Budget car rental office as soon as he got off the plane. He had reserved an economy car—a Ford Tempo. Kalish had said not to go overboard.

Northfield was about thirty-five miles south of St. Paul. It took Ryker forty-five minutes to reach the city limits, and another half hour before he found a decent looking motel with a vacancy.

"Number 142, second floor toward the back." Mrs. Hunniker, the woman standing behind the registration desk (she was probably the owner as well as the manager, Ryker decided), handed him a key attached to a small cardboard disk. She was in her fifties, with steel-gray hair raked back into a bun, an elongated, sharp nose, thin, uncompromising lips, and wary blue eyes. A beige cardigan covered most of what looked like a polyester blouse in a floral brown and yellow print. Ryker couldn't see whether she had on a skirt or slacks. "Five dollars for a replacement key. No hotplates. No smoking in bed. No visitors overnight." She studied him. "How long will you be staying, Mr. Ryker?"

"Two or three days." He had decided not to announce his profession.

She nodded. "Check out time is twelve o'clock sharp. Anything after that, I have to charge for another day. No exceptions."

"Do you have a phone directory that I could use?"

She reached under the counter for the directory and

held it. "I can't let you take it to your room."

"I just have a few names to look up."

She released the book into his hands and stood guard while he found the addresses for Jonah Kringle, the *Northfield Daily News*, and the main police station. Ryker had the feeling that she was waiting to pounce on him in case he decided to disfigure the pages or rip them from the book. He jotted down the addresses in a notebook, pushed the directory toward her, and smiled.

"Thanks. Can you recommend a good place to eat?"

"There's a restaurant in the center of town, about two miles from here. King's Kastle, it's called. Mr. Hunniker and I go there once in a while to celebrate. Food's not bad, for a restaurant. German dishes if you want them. There's a fast food place, too, if you have the stomach for that kind of stuff, and a pizza shop." She gave him all three addresses and directions. "Kids loiter at the pizza shop all the time. Noisy. I don't like pizza."

Or kids? "Thanks again, Mrs. Hunniker."

"All calls go through the switchboard. Local calls are thirty-five cents. There's a service charge for long distance, same's you'd find in any hotel. Switchboard closes at eleven o'clock. No exceptions."

"No problem." He smiled again and turned to leave.

"There's six wood hangers in the closet. They're new. You need more, you let me know; I'll see what I can do."

Obviously, she planned to count them when he checked out. And bill him for any missing hangers. Or towels. Or toilet paper rolls. *"Thrift, thrift, Horatio!"*

In the end, after he had unpacked his few belongings and counted the wooden hangers in the closet (there *were* six), he went to the pizza shop and ordered three slices with everything on it. He wanted to think that it was because he had a craving for pizza, not because he was defying the gray-haired motel manager-owner. That would be juvenile and pointless, since she wouldn't be

280

aware of his deed. As soon as he was back in his rented car, he crunched two Tums to fortify himself against the heartburn that was sure to come.

Just "desserts," Mrs. Hunniker would say.

Ryker had bought a map of Northfield in a gas station and had confirmed directions to Jonah Kringle's street with the pizza shop owner. It was a five-minute ride, and Ryker noticed that the homes were becoming appreciably larger and more ornate as he neared his destination.

The Kringle house was a two-story brick separated from the sidewalk by a long stretch of lawn that looked velvety in the reflected light of the street lamp. Well-tended flower beds with a scalloped border hugged the walls of the house. Two red-coated figures frozen in obsequious gestures of welcome flanked either side of the steps that led to the front door.

Ryker rang the bell and waited. A moment later he heard footsteps.

"Yes?" A male voice.

"Good evening. My name is Sam Ryker, and I'm a detective with the Los Angeles Police Department."

"Yes?"

"I wonder if I could come in and speak to you for a short while."

"May I see some identification, please?"

Ryker placed his badge against the privacy window.

The door opened grudgingly and Ryker stepped into a hexagonal marbled entry hall.

"I'm Jonah Kringle. What can I do for you, Detective Ryker?"

Kringle was in his early sixties, Ryker guessed, a distinguished-looking man with appraising brown eyes, well-defined, generous lips, and still-thick, wavy, gray-white hair brushed back to reveal a patrician forehead. He was wearing dark brown slacks, a cream-colored sleeveless vest over a tan shirt, and brown loafers. He was

281

a little shorter than Ryker, and his shoulders and waist had yielded somewhat to the roundness that signals the final curtain call of youth.

"I wonder if there's somewhere we could sit," Ryker asked.

"First, why don't you tell me what you want, Detective."

"I'd like to ask you some questions about Mark Bauers."

He stared at Ryker. "I see. Very well." He led the detective to the living room and switched on several lamps. "Have a seat, please." He pointed to a green and peach brocade wing chair and seated himself on a green moiré sofa that faced a fireplace. "What exactly do you want to know?"

"Can you tell me something about Dr. Bauers's family?"

"You haven't explained yet why you're interested in Mark," Kringle said calmly.

"We're running a check on his background, Mr. Kringle."

"You came all the way out here from Los Angeles to find out background information, Detective? I find that hard to believe. You could just as easily have picked up the phone."

"You're right, Mr. Kringle. There's more to it than just a routine check. This may relate to an investigation that I'm conducting in Los Angeles. I'm afraid I can't reveal the details right now. Of course, you're under no obligation to tell me anything, but I sure would appreciate your help."

Kringle looked at him thoughtfully, then nodded.

"About Dr. Bauers's family?" Ryker prompted.

"Yes. Well, he's a local boy. Parents are Ernest and Sarah Bauers. Decent, hard-working people. They own a grocery store in the center of Northfield. Have done for

282

almost thirty years. Always pay their bills on time." He saw Ryker's puzzled look. "I supply them with their dairy products. My family's owned Kringle Dairies for three generations. Anyway, they're proud people. They've done right by their boys."

"Boys?"

"Mark has an older brother, Jesse."

"Does he live in Northfield, too?"

"Nearby."

"I understand that Dr. Bauers was married to your daughter."

"Ellen." He sighed. "That's correct. She was our only child."

"Since he was your son-in-law, you probably knew him better than most people."

"We knew him."

"Can you give me your opinion of him?"

"Mark was pleasant, easygoing. Bright, too. Earned a scholarship to Carlton. That's a top-notch college right here. Harvard of the Midwest, they call it. Mark was very ambitious. Had his heart set on being a doctor. Pre-med from the first day of classes, Ellen told us. This isn't about malpractice, is it?"

Ryker smiled.

"Sorry, I forgot that you can't say."

"Jonah?" A woman's voice floated into the living room.

"In here, Millie." He waited until a thin, fragile-looking woman joined him. Both men stood. She looked ten years older than her husband, Ryker thought. Her chin-length, straight hair was almost white, her face lined with a network of fine wrinkles on parchmentlike skin. "My wife, Millicent. This is Detective Ryker from Los Angeles, Millicent. He's here to ask some questions about Mark." He helped her onto the sofa and sat next to her.

Even with the dim lighting in the room, it was impossible to miss the spasm of pain that rippled across her face. Her lips quivered. Her eyes were a watery, faded blue. She blinked rapidly.

"I was just interested in getting a picture of what Dr. Bauers was like when you and your husband knew him," Ryker explained to her. "Was he honest, as far as you know?"

Kringle looked at him. "Mark always knew that he wanted to do better than his parents. Nothing wrong with that. Sometimes, though, I got the feeling that he wanted things faster than he was getting them. Know what I mean?"

"Can you be more specific?"

"For one thing, that scholarship I mentioned. This is just rumor, you understand. There was another boy from Mark's high school up for that scholarship. Straight A student. Mark earned a B or two along the way. Anyway, seems the principal found marijuana in this other boy's locker and wrote a letter to Carlton telling them about it. They rejected his application."

"And people thought Dr. Bauers was responsible?"

"Some did. This other boy was never in trouble before, swore up and down that he'd been framed. Offered to take a lie detector test, anything, but the principal said evidence is evidence."

"May I ask what you think, Mr. Kringle?"

"Ellen believed in Mark."

Not really an answer, Ryker thought. "Can you tell me how long they were married?"

"Less than a year," Kringle said. "They married in January of 1975. She died in August of that same year."

"August sixteenth," Millicent Kringle said. She was smoothing the pleats of her gray skirt.

"I'm sorry. It must be difficult for you to talk about it."

"Do you have children?" Kringle asked.

"Two girls."

"Thirteen years dulls the edge, Detective, but you never forget."

"Never," Mrs. Kringle echoed quietly.

"Of course. But it must be a small consolation to know that she was happily married."

"Ellen was very much in love with Mark," Kringle said. "And he was devoted to her. Everyone said so."

"I don't mean to pry, but was she ill a long time?"

"She drowned, Detective Ryker. In Lake of the Woods, a resort area, of all places." He shook his head.

"They were on vacation?"

"Ellen was under tremendous stress at the time," Kringle said. "The move to Minneapolis had taken a great deal out of her. Mark was registered at the University of Minnesota Medical School, you see, so they rented an apartment there at the end of June, when he graduated from Carlton. There were other factors, too. In any case, Mark felt she needed to get away for a while, and we have a cabin near the lake. It seemed like a good idea for them to spend the summer there."

"I begged her not to go," Mrs. Kringle said. "It's a long drive, and in her condition . . . but Mark convinced her. If she had stayed in Minneapolis, or come home for a while, she'd be alive today. I believe that with all my heart."

"We don't know that, Millie. Things happen. There's no telling why."

"It must have been terrible for you," Ryker said. "Such a shock."

"Folks will tell you she committed suicide, Detective," Millicent Kringle said, "but don't listen to them. They like to gossip, is all. And the good Lord knows they had plenty to talk about." She blinked. "But she received a proper Christian burial, Ellen did. Reverend Wilkinson saw to that."

285

"It was ruled an accidental death," Kringle said. "What does it matter what people say?"

She shook her head. "He killed her."

"Millie, don't."

"The detective should know, Jonah. That's why he's here. He wants to know everything about Mark. Shouldn't he know about our Ellen?"

"What do you mean, Mrs. Kringle? I don't understand."

Kringle sighed. "Mark Bauers didn't kill our daughter, Detective. She was taking medication to calm her nerves, you see. The Baudette police say she must have wandered, half-asleep, into the lake at night. It seems she got tangled in some weeds and drowned."

Like Ophelia, Ryker thought. *Pulled the poor wretch . . . to muddy death.*

"It didn't have to happen," Millicent Kringle said.

"My wife feels that Mark could have prevented her death."

"What kind of husband leaves his wife all alone in a cabin at night, and her feeling so poorly? Off at the library in International Falls he was, studying to be a doctor. Now that's funny, don't you think? When it was Ellen who needed the doctoring? But he killed her just as if he dragged her into the lake and pushed her under the water."

"Millicent, it doesn't do any good to blame Mark. It won't bring Ellen back. What's done is done."

"Dr. Bauers must have been devastated."

"Carried on something terrible at the funeral," Kringle said. "Blamed himself for leaving her."

"And well he should!"

"Did you keep in touch after your daughter's death?"

"Not really. It was painful for all of us. And Mark was busy with his medical studies in Minneapolis."

"What about the senior Bauers? Are you in contact

286

with them?"

"We were never close with them, Detective. The last time we saw them was at Ellen's funeral. Of course, Millicent and I bump into them once in a while in town, but we have little to say to each other. Quite frankly, we move in different circles. And then the Bauers have always tended to keep to themselves. We heard that Mark had remarried and was living in Los Angeles."

"It's surprising that Dr. Bauers moved to California, with all his family here in Northfield."

"He's not terribly attached to his family, Detective." He was about to add something but stopped. "Different families have different relationships."

Ryker rose. "Well, Mr. and Mrs. Kringle, I appreciate your talking to me. I hope I haven't disturbed you too much, bringing up painful memories."

"We understand," Kringle said. "Let me walk you to the door, Detective." He led the way to the entry hall.

"Can I call you again if I have any more questions?"

"All right." His tone was polite but not eager. "Actually, though, I'd prefer that you call me at my office." He gave Ryker the number. "As you can see, my wife is still quite upset about Mark. I don't know that she'll ever see things realistically."

"I guess I can't blame her. I assume people are careful not to bring the subject up."

"Usually. But then there are the phone calls or visits that take you by surprise. Oh, I'm not blaming you, Detective. I know you're just doing your job. But it took me a week to calm my wife down after that other woman called to ask about Mark and Ellen a few months ago."

"What woman was that?"

"Mark's sister-in-law. I don't recall her name."

"What did she want, exactly?"

"Details about the wedding, about Ellen's death. I have no idea why. She wouldn't explain. She said her

287

sister didn't know she was calling, asked me to keep her call a secret. Unfortunately, Millicent answered the phone, and by the time I took the receiver away from her, she was hysterical."

"I can see why she'd be upset."

"Yes. So was I. I don't like nosybodies. As a matter of fact, I called Ernest Bauers as soon as I hung up. Told him to call Mark in California and tell him to keep his sister-in-law or anyone else from bothering us again."

"Do you know if he called?" He tried to keep his tone casual.

"He promised he would. Seemed very upset by what I told him. Said he'd take care of it right away. I guess he did, because she hasn't bothered us since."

Chapter Eighteen

When Laney rang the bell on Sunday moring, Mark opened the door. "Hello, Laney."

"Can I come in?"

"Of course." He moved out of the doorway. "But Kate's resting."

"It's eleven-thirty in the morning, Mark. Don't you think she should be getting out of bed? Get some fresh air?"

"I'm perfectly capable of caring for my wife, Laney, and I resent the implication that I'm keeping her chained to her bed."

"That isn't what I meant, Mark."

"Isn't it?" He smiled. "Look, let's not argue. The fact is that Kate *is* resting. She didn't have a good night, and I don't think it's a good idea for you to see her."

"Why not?"

"Do you want the truth? She's upset with you. If I were you, I'd give her some space for a few days, let her calm down."

"Did she say why she's upset?"

"No. She didn't want to talk about it. But I wouldn't take it personally. She's been having some pretty radical mood swings lately. One minute she's talking about going back to work; the next she's crying for no apparent reason. I'm really concerned about her. And I have to admit that her dependence on tranquilizers is worrying me."

"Why don't you just take the pills away from her, Mark?"

"The shock to her system would be too severe. The problem is, Laney, that Kate gets hysterical when I tell her to skip a pill, or cut the dosage. I'm going to have to take a firmer hand with her, though; I realize that."

"What about one of those clinics?"

"Maybe. If things get really bad, I may have to consider one. I even called Dr. Zuroff, asked her to call Kate and let her know she's available."

"You did?"

"Why do you sound so surprised?"

"I don't know. Somehow I got the feeling that you didn't think it was a good idea."

"That was before, when I thought Kate was improving. Now I'm not so sure Kate can handle this on her own."

"Did Dr. Zuroff call?"

"Yes. But Kate doesn't want to go. She made that clear to me and to Dr. Zuroff."

"Oh." She didn't know what to say. Was he telling the truth? She could call Dr. Zuroff, but would the doctor reveal that information? "Look, can I see her? I'll take my chances."

He shrugged. "Suit yourself. Don't say I didn't warn you."

"I'm duly warned." She left him in the hall and took the stairs two at a time. The door to Kate's bedroom was open. Laney poked her head in. Kate was lying in bed, reading. "Kate? Can I come in?"

"What are you doing here?" She placed the book on her lap.

"That's a fine welcome." She laughed.

290

"I'm sorry." Her tone was cool. "But I told you on the phone yesterday that I wasn't in the mood for company."

"Well, you know me," Laney said brightly. "I don't understand subtlety." She walked over to the bed. "I had to come, Kate. I was upset by our phone call."

"I don't want to talk now, Laney. Can't you respect my wishes?"

"Not when I think there's something seriously wrong. You look awful, Kate. Have you looked in the mirror lately? You have bags under your eyes, your skin is so pale—"

"Are you done? Did you come over to insult me, Laney? Because if that's why you're here, you can leave right now."

"Kate, don't you understand? I'm worried about you, for God's sake. I'm your best friend, or have you forgotten that?"

Kate didn't answer.

"Why are you angry? Tell me, and then if you want, I'll go."

"I'm not angry. I just have the feeling that you're keeping things from me."

"What things?"

"I don't know. It's just a feeling."

"Well, I haven't done anything to betray our friendship, if that's what you mean. I'd never do that. Don't you believe me?"

"How's the shop doing?"

"The shop? Fine. Why do you ask?"

"I *am* still a partner, or maybe you've forgotten that."

"Of course I haven't forgotten. What's that supposed to mean?"

"Nothing. It must be hard running the place just with Mrs. Margolin."

"We're managing. I don't want you to worry about it."

"But it *is* hard."

291

"It's not ideal," she admitted, "but I know it's only temporary."

"Have you considered the possibility that it might not be temporary?"

"You're going to get better. It's just a matter of time."

"Would you tell me if you wanted to dissolve the partnership? Or would you be afraid of hurting my feelings?"

"This is a stupid conversation, Kate. Why are you beating this thing to death?"

"Why are you avoiding the question?"

"I'm not!"

"If I ask you something, will you give me an honest answer?"

"Of course!"

She looked at her carefully. "The day you came to look for the insurance policy. Was that the real reason you were here, or were you looking at my other files?"

Oh, God. What should she say? "Kate, that's such a strange question. Why on earth would you come up with an idea like that?"

"You haven't answered me."

"Because it's so crazy! What would I possibly be looking for?"

"You still haven't answered me, Laney."

"All right. No, I wasn't looking for anything else. I needed the insurance policy, and that's what I came for. Are you satisfied? I'm really hurt by your insinuation!" She prayed that Kate would take the sudden suffusion of color in her cheeks for anger, not guilt.

It was so sad, Kate thought. Laney had never been a convincing liar. She almost felt sorry for her. "Let's forget it, all right?" She picked up her book. It was an obvious motion of dismissal.

"You don't believe me, do you?" Why couldn't she drop it? What could she possibly accomplish except to

292

entrench herself further in deceit?

"I do. I don't want to discuss it any more."

"Well, should I stay a while?"

"Whatever you want."

"You're still angry. It's something else; I know it. It's not good to hold it in, Kate."

"When did you get a degree in psychology, Laney?"

"I'm only trying to help. Maybe if you went to see Dr. Zuroff—"

"I am sick and tired of having people tell me what to do! Stop telling me to see Dr. Zuroff, or to cut down on my pills, or to bare my emotions. I don't need Dr. Zuroff, and I don't need your interference! Mark is helping me. At least he has faith in me. For your information, we're planning on spending a week or so at our cabin in Big Bear in a few weeks, and that's all the therapy I need. I hope that meets with your approval."

"I'm sorry. It's just that . . ." She saw Kate's glare and stopped. "I guess I'll go now. Maybe I'll see you tomorrow."

"Whatever."

Kate pretended to read, and only after Laney had left the room did she put the book down. She had felt momentarily triumphant in her surge of righteous anger, but now she felt curiously deflated, empty, her buoyancy punctured by the sharp point of betrayal. There was no satisfaction in knowing that Laney had lied to her, that she had forfeited her trust, only a dull ache.

Thank God she had Mark.

Capt. Raymond Spivak, Chief of Police of Northfield, Minnesota, was younger, wider, and shorter than Ryker had pictured. He had a genial, round face, virtually unlined, with placid gray eyes and straight blond hair, cut short.

"I appreciate your coming in to see me on a Sunday morning, Capt. Spivak." Ryker had made the appointment before he had left work on Friday.

"No problem. I had a bit of paperwork to catch up on, and the truth is, you kind of tickled my curiosity. You said on the phone that this Simpson woman who called me was killed?"

"The coroner's report listed accidental electrocution as the cause of death. We think that's accurate, except for the 'accidental' part." He explained Laney's theory, outlining the circumstancial evidence linking Barbara's death with Dupard's.

"Fascinating," Spivak said. "Basically, you have no case, am I right?"

"Unfortunately, you are."

"So what do you want from me? I don't see how I can help you."

"Frankly, I'm interested in Bauers's previous marriage to Ellen Kringle. I talked with her parents last night."

"Did you, now?" He smiled. "What exactly did you tell them? That you suspected their former son-in-law of two homicides?"

"Actually, I was pretty vague. Mr. Kringle seemed pretty forthcoming. Mrs. Kringle blames Bauers for her daughter's death, says he should never have taken her up to Lake of the Woods."

"Probably wasn't a good idea," Spivak agreed, "seeing her condition."

"You mean because she was so nervous? That's what Mr. Kringle said."

"Hell, no, although that's a pretty good second reason. No, Detective Ryker, I mean because Ellen Kringle Bauers was eight months pregnant."

"I see."

"And before you do any fancy arithmetic, I may as well tell you: she was pregnant when she married Mark

294

Bauers. As far as most people are concerned, that's why she married him."

"Did she love him?"

Spivak laughed. "Who the hell knows? That was one hell of a mess they had." He looked at Ryker. "I suppose Jonah Kringle didn't mention that his daughter was engaged to someone else before she married Bauers?"

"No. Neither of them said anything. Who was she engaged to? A local boy?"

"You could say that, Detective. You surely could." He was obviously enjoying himself. "She was engaged to Jesse Bauers. Brother to Mark."

Ryker was silent.

"Gets more complicated, if you're interested."

"I'm interested."

"Ellen and Jesse were high school sweethearts. Jesse was a year older. They had everything planned out. He was going to be a veterinarian. She was going to teach music. They were going to have at least four children and buy a farm someday. Jesse was proud, you see. He didn't want to live off the Kringle money, and God knows there's plenty of that."

"How do you know all this, Captain?"

"Northfield's got a population of about twelve thousand, but it's still a small town when it comes to news. We get our average share of scandals, Detective, but this was a humdinger, seeing as how it involved the Kringles, a love triangle, a premarital pregnancy, and an unnatural death. I can't think of anything that people talked about more except for Jesse James robbing the First National Bank of Northfield in September of 1876."

"No kidding? I didn't know that."

"A little bit of local history that you can tell the wife when you go back home. Oh, I guess I should also mention that the Kringles's housekeeper comes in to us on Thursdays, and my wife's a real good listener." He

295

grinned. "Anyway, Jesse and Ellen were supposed to get married when Jesse finished vet school—he was proud, remember? And then, all of a sudden, everything fell apart."

"What happened exactly, do you know?"

"From what Ingrid says—Ingrid is the housekeeper—Mark seduced Ellen. Of the two boys, Mark's by far the better looking one, and he was always more sophisticated. Ellen was a year older than Mark, but that didn't seem to be a problem. Anyway, he gets her pregnant; she breaks off her engagement with Jesse; the next thing you know, there's a big church wedding with bridesmaids and a champagne reception for 250 people."

"And then she died."

"And then she died," Spivak repeated.

"Was she pretty?"

"Average. Brown hair, brown eyes. Cute little figure. Here. I got this file together for you, figured you'd be interested." He handed Ryker a manila folder. "You have the coroner's report from Baudette, an obituary from the *Northfield Daily News* with her picture in it. She and her husband were staying in Warroad, by the way. That's right on the lake. But the case was handled by the Baudette police."

"The cause of death was listed as accidental drowning?"

"Right. Like I told you, some say it was suicide."

"Would she have had reason to kill herself?"

"Why does someone kill himself, Detective? It's never a sound reason to you and me."

"Her father mentioned that she was very nervous."

"That she was. More than nervous, actually. Distraught. Frightened. Her parents don't know the half of it. I never told them, seeing as how I thought it would only make them feel worse."

"What do you mean?"

"People can get real ugly, Detective. I'm sure you

296

come across that in Los Angeles, too. Ellen was having a hard time living in Northfield. She was a quiet girl, you see, and she couldn't take the stares."

"Why didn't they leave Northfield?"

"Mark was finishing Carlton. That would have meant a long commute twice a day." He paused. "And then there were the letters. You've got them in that file. She came in with her husband when she got the first one. She was shaking so bad I thought she was going to fall right down. That's thirteen years ago, Detective, and I remember it like it was yesterday. Here. Let me show you." He took the file back and flipped through it. "Here they are, in the order she received them."

Ryker read them. Each letter was composed of words cut out and pasted neatly onto lined paper. They were all slightly yellowed with age, but the vindictiveness of the messages was still very much alive:

YOU ARE A SLUT AND A WHORE. GET OUT OF TOWN BEFORE WE THROW YOU OUT.

GOD DAMNS ALL SINNERS. HE PUNISHES THE CHILDREN FOR THE SINS OF THE FATHERS. YOUR BABY WILL BE A MONSTER. SAVE HIM AND YOURSELF BEFORE IT'S TOO LATE.

There were about seven letters along those two themes, each with a slight variation.

"What does this one mean?" Ryker handed a letter to Spivak.

BITCH. ARE YOU PROUD OF WHAT YOU DID TO JESSE? HE IS LOCKED IN HIS OWN HELL. YOU WILL BE TOO. INSANITY BREEDS IN-SANITY.

Spivak sighed. "I was coming to that. When Jesse learned that Ellen was pregnant with Mark's child, he tried to kill himself. Used a razor, but his mother found him in time."

"Is he better now? I think Kringle said the brother lives nearby."

"I guess you could say that. He's in Pleasant View. That's a private mental hospital just outside of Northfield. Doctors say he's pretty hopeless. He was doing better for a while, but then he heard somehow that Ellen died, and that put him over the edge."

"Jesus!"

"I speak to the director of the hospital every once in a while. Mrs. Bauers visits Jesse every week, sits and talks to him for hours. He doesn't say anything, just kind of stares at the walls."

"I'm surprised the Bauerses speak to Mark."

Spivak looked at him. "I was, too, until I found out that he's the one paying the bills at Pleasant View. I wondered why he was there. It's an expensive proposition, I can tell you. And there's a big state mental hospital not far from here, in Fairbault. Matter of fact, it's the biggest one in the state. That's where we figured Jesse would go, seeing as how the Bauers couldn't possibly afford to put him in a private place."

"So once Bauers established a medical practice, he had Jesse switched to the private hospital?"

"No. He insisted on putting Jesse in Pleasant View right from the start. Must've cost him plenty, even then."

"But where did he get the money to pay for it?"

"His inheritance, Detective. I thought you would've figured that out. Everyone knew that the day she married, Ellen Kringle would inherit $250,000 from her paternal grandmother. Makes you stop and think, doesn't it?"

298

"Are you saying that Mark Bauers married her for her money?"

"That would be a reasonable guess, Detective. Nothing anyone could prove, of course. Mark had his mind set on going to medical school, and that costs quite a bit of money. The Bauers couldn't help him out; they were already in debt trying to put Jesse through vet school. Jesse was their eldest, you see. People say he was their favorite, too. Mark could've worked, taken out loans. There's ways if you want something bad enough. Maybe he found an easier way."

"And to make sure that Ellen would marry him, Mark intentionally got her pregnant?"

He nodded. "And struck out his big brother at the same time, and took a swing at his parents, too. Who the hell knows what his main motivation was? A psychologist could have a field day with this, don't you think?"

"No kidding. But you think he married her for the money?"

"Damn right. You know what they call Minnesota? The Bread and Butter State. Guess Bauers wanted his bread buttered. But so what? There's no crime in marrying for money. If there were, the jails would be bursting more than they are now." He leaned forward. "Do you know why I'm telling you all this, Detective Ryker? Why I came in to meet you on a Sunday when I could be relaxing at home with my family? Sure, it's an interesting story, but I'm sure you've heard more interesting back home. The thing is, I know in my gut that Mark Bauers killed his wife, and it's been eating me up alive for thirteen years that there's not a damn thing I can do about it. Not. One. Damn. Thing!" He punctuated each word by banging his fist on his desk and fell back against his chair.

"What did the Baudette police find?"

"She was full of tranquilizers. Her obstetrician

299

prescribed a mild dose. He wasn't happy about it, but she was so agitated about the letters. Obviously, she took a lot more than he recommended. Name is Dr. Henry Latham; lives in Northfield. I can give you his number if you want to talk to him."

"She didn't have a doctor in Minneapolis?"

"She was planning on coming home to deliver the baby."

"How did he kill her?"

"Doped her up, walked her to the lake or carried her there. Either way, no one would see him at night."

"I seem to remember that Mrs. Kringle said he was away when it happened. That's why she blames him; she feels he shouldn't have left her daughter alone."

"He has an alibi. Her name is Marilyn Zakowski. She's a waitress in International Falls. Bauers was with her from seven o'clock to ten o'clock that night. The coroner fixed the time of death from between six o'clock to ten o'clock. It takes about an hour and a quarter to an hour and a half to drive from Warroad to International Falls. It's *Mrs.* Zakowski, by the way."

"You think she's lying to give him an alibi?"

"I *know* she's lying, Detective. Instinct. But I can't prove it. The chief of police in Baudette, Horace Treibach, spoke to her several times, tried to shake her story. I went up there myself, too, had a go at her. She wouldn't budge."

"Why would she lie to protect him? It isn't as though she was going to benefit from the crime."

"That's what I asked myself, over and over. I'm not a hundred percent sure, but this is how I figure it. One, Bauers convinced her that he's innocent, but that the police won't believe him. Two, he implies that he'll tell the husband if she doesn't cooperate. That would've scared the shit out of her. She begged us to keep this from her husband. He's a steelworker. A big hunk of a guy, the

300

way she described him. She was afraid he'd kill her if he found out. Or three, Bauers promises Miss Marilyn that he's going to marry her as soon as all the dust settles."

"Is she still in International Falls? Maybe I could go up and see her."

"Now *that* is very interesting. It seems that a couple of months after Ellen Kringle died, Marilyn Zakowski had a fatal car accident in a brand new car. Hit and run. No witnesses. I could give a wild guess as to where she got the car. She paid cash for it, by the way."

"Who found Ellen Kringle's body?"

"Bauers did. But he made sure to have someone with him when he found it. The way he tells it, he came home around eleven-thirty from International Falls. 'Oh, honey,' he calls. 'I'm home.' But his honey isn't—home, that is. So he searches the grounds, and when he can't find her, he gets real nervous, because on her bed, spread out like a deck of cards, were all those letters. So he calls the fire department. They send out two guys, and he's with them when they find the body washed up near the shore, all tangled up in some weeds."

"The Baudette police thought Ellen Kringle committed suicide?"

"Treibach wasn't sure. The way he explained it to me, it could've been accident or suicide, or maybe a combination of both. She was doped up to her eyebrows. She was frightened to death that her baby was going to be some monstrosity, some freak of nature. Dr. Latham told me that. Seems that's all she talked about during the last few months. That's why he prescribed the valium. And she got one of those letters the day before she died. Treibach saw the postmark on the envelope."

"Who do you think sent the letters?"

"Who do *you* think sent the letters, Detective?"

"Bauers?"

He nodded. "Makes sense, doesn't it? He knew exactly

what buttons to push. So maybe he didn't kill her literally. Maybe his alibi is true, which I don't believe for one minute. But even it if is, morally, the son of a bitch is a murderer. And he is sitting pretty in Los Angeles, California, the city of the goddamned angels, and Ellen Kringle is lying six feet under. It makes me sick."

"There's nothing you can do?"

"Nothing. I tested the letters for fingerprints. Zip. I nagged Treibach until he interviewed just about every tourist who happened to be in Warroad at the time. The trail is ice cold, Detective. As cold as Ellen Kringle. So I guess it's up to you."

"What do you mean?"

"Detective Ryker, you and I both know that you didn't come out here to run a check on Mark Bauers. You already suspected that he killed his first wife, am I right? You came for confirmation."

Ryker nodded. "It made sense. It explained why Barbara Simpson made all those calls, including the ones to you and to the Kringles. She must have suspected it, too. And when Kringle called Mr. Bauers to tell him about Barbara's call, Bauers probably called his son in Los Angeles and told him that Barbara was snooping around. So he had to kill her."

"It still doesn't give you proof, does it?"

"Nope."

"You know that he's going to try to do it again. He's married, right? And she's rich?"

"Loaded."

"What's her name?"

"Katherine Simpson. Kate. She has two young children from a previous marriage. She was widowed. She's an orphan, by the way."

"Figures. An easy victim. You going to stop him, Ryker?"

"I have to."

Chapter Nineteen

By the time Ryker returned to his motel room, it was almost noon. Spivak had given him a folder with xerox copies of all the papers in Ellen Kringle's file. Ryker slipped the folder into the side pocket of his two-suiter. He packed quickly—he had taken out only a fresh shirt and underwear—and checked the room to make sure he hadn't left anything behind.

Originally, Ryker had planned to fly from St. Paul to International Falls and rent a car there to go to Baudette to interview the police chief of the town. He had jotted down different flight times, calculated schedules. Now, with the wealth of information Spivak had given him, the trip wouldn't be necessary, and he wouldn't miss even one day of work. Lieutenant Kalish would be delighted.

The first seat available on a Northwest flight from St. Paul to Los Angeles, Ryker learned, was on the 5:40 flight, which arrived at LAX at 7:30. It was almost 10:00 A.M. in L.A. now. He called Linda and gave her the arrival time.

"Make reservations for dinner," he told her. "Bring the girls, too. We can go direct from the airport."

"To McDonald's?"

He laughed. "You choose. Just remember, I don't get a

paycheck till the end of next week."

"Laney Tolbert called several times. She seemed quite anxious to talk to you. She left me her home number. Do you want it?"

"Yeah. I'll call her. I have some time to kill before the flight. I figure I'll grab some lunch here and then head out to the airport."

"Save your appetite for tonight, Ryker. That's an order!"

After he hung up, he dialed Laney's number.

"Laney's not in," Brian Tolbert said. "I think she went over to Kate's house. Do you want her to call you back?"

"She won't be able to reach me. I'm checking out of my motel room now. Ask her to call me tomorrow at the station. I have a lot to tell her."

When Ryker went to the motel office to turn in his key, Mrs. Hunniker was there. She had on a different blouse (as ugly as the first, Ryker thought, if not uglier), but the beige cardigan and the guarded expression on her face were the same.

"It's 12:13," she said, and pointed to the round schoolroom clock on the wall behind Ryker. "Have to charge you for tonight." She looked pleased.

I had pizza and loved it, he wanted to retort. "No problem."

She added up his bill. "Two nights plus tax comes to $74.20. Phone calls come to $11.87; that includes three long distance. You owe me $86.07. No personal checks. I forgot to mention that."

"Master Charge?"

"That'll cost you three percent more. That's what they charge me." She calculated the addition. "That comes to $88.65."

Ryker signed the Master Charge slip and handed it to her.

"Thanks," she said. "Well, I hope you had a nice stay.

Next time you're in Northfield, come see us again."

Her smile looked a little grotesque, more grim than friendly. She was probably in pain, Ryker decided, from forcing the Chamber of Commerce farewell past her normally pursed lips.

At 10:37 on Sunday night, while Sam and Linda Ryker were making love and Brian and Laney Tolbert were watching "The Untouchables" on their VCR, Mark Bauers shut the downstairs lights off and went upstairs.

Kate was sleeping. He walked over to her bed and bent over her. Her breathing was shallow, her pulse a little slow. There was an almost full vial of white tablets on her nightstand. Kate had taken it from the medicine cabinet that afternoon. He opened the vial, counted the tablets. There were six missing. He had brought his medical bag upstairs. He switched the vial with an unstarted vial of identical white tablets that he took from his bag, and put the new vial in the medicine cabinet.

Next, he took a vial of blue tablets from his bag, opened it, removed six tablets, and placed the vial and cap on her nightstand. He flushed the six blue tablets down the toilet. Then he took the cup and saucer from Kate's nightstand and went downstairs to the kitchen. Janine was sitting at the breakfast room table, reading a magazine. She looked up when he came in.

"Did you call them?" she asked.

"Not yet," he said. "Rinse these well and put them away."

"All right."

He went back upstairs, stretched out on his bed, turned on the T.V. with the remote control, and waited.

At 11:08, after he had noted diminished reflexes and a significant drop in her respiratory rate, he called the paramedics.

He walked over to the bed. "Kate!" he called loudly. "Kate!" He pushed back her eyelids. Her eyes were bloodshot, the pupils slightly dilated. He shook her shoulders. No response. He placed her left arm around his neck and maneuvered her off the bed.

When the paramedics arrived, he was walking her up and down the length of the bedroom. Her movements were jerky, like a marionette whose strings have been severed.

"I'm a doctor. I think my wife overdosed on some tranquilizers," he told them. "I tried unsuccessfully to arouse her with painful stimuli. I don't know how many pills she took or exactly when, so I haven't given her any ipecac. I was afraid she might aspirate."

"What did she take, do you know?" the taller of the two asked.

"There's a vial on her nightstand." He pointed to it.

Mark insisted on riding with her in the ambulance that took her to the emergency room at Cedars-Sinai.

"She's going to be all right, Dr. Bauers," the resident told Mark an hour and a half later. "We pumped her stomach. We've done a tox screen on her blood. The amount she took wasn't dangerous. Her blood pressure's still low, but it's steady. She'll be tired, weak, but I don't think there's anything to worry about."

"Thank God! Can I see her now?"

"I'd wait till morning, give her a chance to rest. If all her signs are okay, she can go home tomorrow afternoon."

"That's wonderful!"

"We counted the pills in the vial. There are six missing. Do you have any idea how many pills she took just now?"

"I guess she must have taken all six. It was a new vial. She just started it this evening. Maybe she took three, two hours apart, although I don't know why she'd do

306

that. She was supposed to take one or two every four hours. But even if she took all six, I can't understand how this could have happened with such a mild dosage pill."

"I wouldn't exactly call six milligrams of Zanax low."

"What are you talking about? The pills I gave her were Valium, two milligrams. Several months ago she was on Zanax, one milligram, but only for a short while. The Zanax was too strong. I switched to Valium because it's much milder, first to a five milligram, then to the two milligrams."

"Well, somehow she got the wrong pills. The ones the paramedics picked up from her nightstand are blue Zanax, one milligram each. That means six milligrams, quite a jump from four milligrams, or even twelve, of Valium."

"But how on earth—oh, my God! I think I now what happened! This afternoon, Kate told me she needed more pills, and I told her there was another vial in the medicine cabinet. She probably took the blue Zanax instead!" He shook his head. "I knew she was a little disoriented lately, but I never dreamed she'd make a mistake like that. I feel so guilty!"

"It wasn't your fault, Dr. Bauers. Look, the main thing is that you responded in time. From the looks of things, it was an accident."

"I hope so."

"Pardon me?"

"Nothing. It's just that . . . well, Kate's been under tremendous pressure lately. Her parents are both dead. Her first husband was killed in a car accident, and her sister died a few months ago. She hasn't been able to come to terms with that. She's been anxious, fearful. That's why I prescribed the Zanax first, and then the Valium, to calm her down." He sighed. "I thought she was doing better lately. As a matter of fact, she had cut down to half the two milligram for a while, but the last

307

week, she had a setback and I didn't think it would hurt to let her take one or two of the two milligrams."

"You think she deliberately took the Zanax?"

"No! Of course not!"

"But you just said—"

"Forget what I said! I'm upset and confused. Obviously, I'm not thinking straight. It was an accident, that's all."

"Dr. Bauers, I'm going to have to report this to the police. You understand that, don't you?"

"Why? She's all right. Believe me, I've learned my lesson. I'll make sure nothing like this happens again."

"I'm sorry, Dr. Bauers. That's the law for any overdose. And to be honest, a minute ago you didn't sound convinced that it *was* an accident."

"It was. I'm sure it was."

"In any case, I have to file a report. And if I were you, I'd see that she gets some professional help right away."

"She was in therapy for a while, after her mother died, with a psychologist. Dr. Irene Zuroff. But Kate hasn't wanted to resume therapy. I don't know why."

"Well, I think you should insist, Dr. Bauers. You don't want to run the risk that she'll do it again. Next time, she might not be so lucky."

At 3:00 A.M. Mark paid the cab and let himself into the house. Janine was waiting in the family room watching a movie on the VCR.

"I couldn't sleep," she said. "What took so long?"

"They had to pump her stomach, run a tox screen. She's going to be fine."

"That's good." She walked over to him and kissed him, ran her hands down his chest. "Are you tired?"

"Not tired. A little keyed up. Let's go to your room."

308

"No. I want to go to your room, to her bed. Our bed, soon."

"The kids might get up."

"They won't. We'll lock the door."

He grinned. "Have you no shame?"

"No, and neither have you. That's why we work so well together."

Mark was at the hospital by seven.

Kate was propped up on two pillows. Her hair was disheveled. Her skin had taken on a hospital pallor, and her arms looked unnaturally thin in the wide, short sleeves of the hospital gown.

"You look fine," he said when he came in.

"Liar," she said softly. She smiled weakly. Her lips trembled. "Hold me."

He walked over and hugged her, stroked her hair. "I couldn't find a flower shop that was open."

"That's okay. The doctor said I'll be going home this afternoon. They just want to check my vital signs two more times."

"Thank God you're okay! You scared the hell out of me, Kate! Don't ever do that again!"

"I don't even know what happened."

He explained about the pills. "Didn't you read the label? Didn't you notice they were blue?"

"No. I feel so stupid. I've been so preoccupied that I guess I didn't look. We're so lucky, Mark." Her eyes filled with tears.

"Don't I know it!" He hugged her again. "You know, I think we should just forget this happened. If I were you, I wouldn't mention it to anyone, not even Laney. She gets so dramatic; and she'll probably say 'I told you so.'"

"I think you're right. She's been after me for weeks to get off the pills. How are Jeremy and Dana? Did they ask

309

where I am?"

"They were sleeping when I left. Janine's going to tell them you had severe stomach cramps but that it turned out to be nothing. Don't worry; she'll handle it without frightening them. She'll take Dana along when she drops Jeremy off at school; then she'll take Dana to play group. It doesn't start till ten o'clock today."

"Oh, no! I forgot it's the first day of school! I should be with them!"

"You'll make it up to them. They'll understand."

"I'm such a failure, Mark. Look at me!"

"Stop this, Kate! The main thing is that you're okay. We have a lifetime ahead of us to spend with the kids. Look, I wish I could spend the morning with you, but I have some patients to see in the hospital, and then I have to go to the office. But I'll be in touch, and as soon as they're ready to release you, I'll take you home."

"Okay."

"I'm going to cancel my reservations for that medical convention this weekend. I don't want to leave you alone."

"No. Please don't do that. I know you were looking forward to it. I'll just feel guilty if you don't go."

"Well, we'll see how you're doing. I can always cancel at the last minute. And I'm going to tell my secretary to clear my calendar for our trip to Big Bear. After this, you need it more than ever."

At 10:00, Mark called Irene Zuroff and left a message with her service.

At 11:55, Irene Zuroff called back.

"Dr. Bauers? The service said it was urgent."

"Kate overdosed last night, Doctor."

"My God!"

"She's all right," he added quickly. "I was doing some

310

paperwork in my office at home. Luckily, I finished early, and when I went upstairs, I noticed that she didn't look right."

"What happened?"

He explained about the mix-up with the pills.

"Why was she taking tranquilizers? They would only compound her depression."

"You're right, of course. Originally, right after Kate's sister died, I had her on an antidepressant. Elavil. But she had several side effects, said the pills weren't helping her, insisted on stopping. And after that, she seemed more agitated than depressed, so I thought the tranquilizers would help her."

"I see."

"The thing is, I told the resident in the emergency room that it was an accident. I hope I'm right."

"Do you have reason to think it wasn't an accident?"

"Not really. But she's been extremely upset lately. She had a major argument with her best friend, a woman she's known for years. That, added to Barbara's death, and the fact that she feels she's a failure as a mother and a wife . . . I *think* it was an accident, but what if I'm wrong? That's what's bothering me, you see."

"Can you get her to see a therapist?"

"You called the other day. You heard for yourself. She doesn't want help. If she won't see you, then I doubt she'll want to see anyone. She really admires you. The thing is, I don't know whether I should be worried or not."

"Well, you're alert and obviously on top of the situation. That's important. In all probability, the overdose was an accident. Let's hope so. In the meantime, I would encourage her to seek help to end her dependence on the tranquilizers."

"You're right, of course. I've been trying to wean her off them gradually, but it's difficult. She panics when I

311

tell her she has to learn to get along without the pills. I think I'll give it a few weeks, see if I can help her. If not, I'll have to consider getting outside help. A clinic, maybe. Of course, I'll watch her carefully in the meantime." He sighed. "Well, thank you for listening, Dr. Zuroff. I feel better having talked to you. Please bill me for your time."

"That won't be necessary, Dr. Bauers."

"You're very kind. I wish Kate would—well, I hope everything will be all right. It has to. I can't lose her."

Ryker and Laney met for lunch at Nibbler's.

"I didn't think you'd be back so soon. When you spoke to me Friday night, you said you might be gone till Wednesday."

"I had luck. I found out everything I needed to know in Northfield."

"You went to see the Kringles?"

He nodded. "It's a long story. Actually, before I get to that, there are several things you should know. One, I found out from Ms. Simpson's shrink that she was having an affair with Bauers before he met Kate."

"You're kidding! Barbara and Mark? But she *hated* him!" She paused. "Oh, I see. That's *why* she hated him. God, that must have been terrible for her, seeing Kate and Mark together all the time. You said 'several things.' What else?"

"I met Bauers and the au pair."

"You did? When? And why didn't you tell me all this?"

"In answer to your last question: You're over at the Bauers pretty often, right? It must be hard as hell seeing your best friend, thinking her husband is a murderer. I didn't want to put you under more pressure. As far as my visit to the good doctor . . ." He described the meeting. "Anyway, the bottom line is, they give each other alibis for the night Dupard was killed. But I did trick Bauers into admitting that he knew Dupard."

"How?"

Ryker explained. "I also hinted to Bauers that we're on to him, that we know Ms. Simpson's death wasn't accidental. At least I gave him something to think about. Maybe it'll slow him down. Next, I followed those leads you gave me about the au pair, and you were one hundred percent right. Bauers met Janine in Geneva last year."

She grinned. "I knew it!"

"It gets better. I spoke to her boss. Apparently, Janine had told him she was moving to the United States permanently, that she was going to marry an American doctor."

"Maybe that's just in Janine's head. I can't believe Mark would divorce Kate and give up all that wealth. It doesn't make sense."

"Not *divorce*, Laney. *Murder*."

She looked stunned. "He wants to kill her?"

"If we're right, he's already killed the sister and Dupard. Hasn't it ever crossed your mind that he might want to eliminate Kate and keep her money?"

"I guess I just didn't think it through. Maybe I didn't want to. I mean, I figured he killed Barbara and Dupard because they got in his way, because they were threats. But Kate? Are you sure?"

"I have no proof." He grinned. "Where have we heard that before, right? But I'm pretty sure. I suspected it before I left for Minnesota, and everything I learned there confirmed it." He told her about his talk with the Kringles and with Capt. Spivak. "So you see, when Mr. Bauers, senior, called his son and told him that Barbara Simpson was poking around, Bauers had to kill her. You're not saying anything."

"I'm speechless, which for me, is a rare occasion. Ask Brian." She shook her head as if to clear it. "I can't

313

believe that he killed his wife and unborn child. He's a monster!"

"And he probably killed this Zakowski woman, too. And he put his brother in a mental institution, although I guess Ellen Kringle would have to take some of the blame for that."

"Lake of the Woods," she mused. "What a pretty name for such a horrible event!"

"Ironic that they were on vacation. But that made it perfect, you see. Away from everyone, just the two of them."

Her face turned white. "Sam! I know when he's going to do it! I know when he plans to kill Kate!"

"What do you mean?"

"Kate told me they're going to Big Bear in a few weeks. Her cabin's right on the lake. Don't you see? It'll be the same thing all over again. He'll drown her or something like that and everyone will think it was an accident or suicide. She's depressed, she's on pills, just like Ellen Kringle was. My God! He'll get away with it, just like last time."

"We have to warn her, Laney."

"She won't listen to me, that's for sure. I didn't have a chance to tell you, but she's been acting very cold toward me the past few days, indirectly accusing me of spying on her, of betraying our friendship. I know she suspects I was snooping in her file cabinet. She won't believe a word I tell her."

"I'll tell her, then."

"She'd be destroyed, Sam. It would be such a shock coming from you."

"But she'd be alive. Someone has to tell her. It's too dangerous not to."

"Look, let's wait a few days till she calms down. Then I'll find a way to talk to her, to convince her. Maybe I'll get her out of the house, take her somewhere where we can talk privately."

"When did you say they're going to Big Bear?"

"In a few weeks."

"That gives us a little time, but not much. All right. I want to talk to Kate's lawyer first anyway. I'm assuming that Bauers stands to inherit a sizable fortune if his wife dies. If not, if everything goes to her kids, then we don't have a motive and there's no point in alarming her. I'll call you and tell you what he says."

At 3:20, Mark Bauers returned to his Third Street office.

"Any messages?" he asked Angela.

"I put them all on your desk. I rescheduled the appointments you had to cancel. Mrs. Eskers was a little upset, but I think I calmed her down. How is Mrs. Bauers?"

"Better, thank you. She's resting now. I'll see my 3:45 and the next two appointments. After that, I want to get back to my wife."

"I don't blame you. What a shock!"

"It was a terrible accident. But thank God she's going to be all right. That reminds me, I'd like you to clear my calendar from September twenty-sixth through the thirtieth. I'm going to take my wife on a much-needed vacation. Dr. Korman can take any emergencies." He started for his office.

"Oh, Dr. Bauers, there's one more message. I was just writing it out now. You have to call them back right away." She handed him the slip. "They wanted an answer right on the spot, but I didn't know what to tell them. I called your house, but your wife said you'd already left."

"You did what?" His voice was cold.

"I'm sorry. I didn't know what time you'd be back, and

315

they said they had to know by three-thirty whether you wanted them to run the ad again."

"Miss Palusky, I thought I made myself clear a long time ago about calling me at home."

"I'm sorry, I thought—"

"I told you I don't want to be disturbed at home unless it's an emergency. An emergency, Miss Palusky, for your information, is a patient who is in critical condition or dying, not a telephone call from the *L.A. Times*. I don't appreciate the fact that you called my wife, who has just been released from the hospital, and bothered her with petty details that don't concern her. Did you tell her why you were calling?"

She was near tears. She had never seen this side of him. "No. I asked for you. That's all. She told me you should be arriving at the office soon."

"Well, at least you showed a smattering of common sense. I'll be in my office."

She aimed a look of hatred at his retreating back. Goddamn doctors. Think those initials next to their names spell G.O.D. Who the hell did he think he was to rip into her like that? She was just trying to do him a favor, is all. Well, that was the last time she'd go out of her way for him! She had half a mind to quit, look for another position.

Angela was still sulking when he came out of his office ten minutes later.

"Angela, I have to apologize. I was way out of line talking to you like that."

She didn't answer.

"I don't blame you for being upset. You have every right. I know you were trying to be helpful. The thing is, I'm just a bundle of nerves about my wife. You can understand that, can't you? I really value you, Angela. You're efficient, pleasant, not to mention probably the most attractive medical receptionist in the building." He smiled. "Look, I hope you can put this behind you. I would hate to think I ruined a wonderful working relationship."

"That's all right, Dr. Bauers. I can see you're not yourself today, what with everything that's happened."

"You're a generous soul, Angela! I don't know if I would be that forgiving, but I'm glad you are."

"Forget it, Dr. Bauers. Really. It's history."

Christmas was more than three months away. She hoped he'd still remember what a shit he'd been and make up for it with a generous bonus.

"Come in, Detective Ryker." Richard Bristol stood up to welcome him. "Have a seat, please. My secretary says that when you called yesterday you told her this concerns the Bauers. I thought we'd settled the incident involving Mr. Leicester."

"This has nothing to do with Mr. Leicester, sir. That case is on the docket, as far as I know. I understand he repaid most of the money?"

"All but twelve thousand dollars. We're working out a payment schedule for the remainder. If we do, then Dr. Bauers may be willing to drop the charges."

"Dr. Bauers?"

"Yes. He's been in contact with me. Kate isn't well, you see, and he doesn't want her bothered with all of this. I think that's wise. In any case, she gave him power of attorney."

"I see."

"Of course, the district attorney may still want to proceed against Mr. Leicester."

"Maybe. Or he may get off with probation and community service. But I'm here to discuss another matter, Mr. Bristol. The fact is, I need access to your file on Katherine Bauers. Specifically, her will."

"Detective, you surprise me. You know full well that I can't release those records. I have a responsibility to protect the privacy of my clients."

"I understand that, Mr. Bristol. I have a court order, however, that instructs you to release those documents." He withdrew a folded document from his inner jacket pocket and handed it to Bristol.

Lieutenant Kalish had listened to Ryker's account of his trip to Minnesota and had finally agreed to reopen the case on Barbara Simpson. A judge had signed the subpoena early Tuesday morning.

Bristol examined the document. "I see. This seems to be in order. Still, I have great reservations about betraying my client's trust. May I ask why you're interested in Kate's will? It seems like a strange request, since Barbara is the one who died."

"Mr. Bristol, I don't mind telling you, but this is in strict confidence."

"Agreed."

"We have reason to believe that Mark Bauers killed Barbara Simpson—"

"Mark!"

"Yes. We also suspect him of the murder of a private investigator Ms. Simpson hired to find out information regarding Bauers's background and activities. There is also a police captain in Northfield, Minnesota, who's convinced that Mark Bauers killed his first wife and their unborn child."

"Give me a moment to absorb this, will you, Detective? You have succeeded in shocking me." He drummed his fingertips on his desk. "If I understand you correctly, then, you fear that Mark Bauers plans to kill his wife, too? Is that it?"

"Correct. He's been having an affair with a young woman he brought over here from Geneva. She lives in their home as an au pair. I believe he plans to marry her.

It's our belief that she's involved with the homicides. We want to warn Mrs. Bauers. But before we do that, I need information about the terms of her will."

"Very well. Let me get her file." He pressed a button on his telephone console. "Edith, get me Katherine Bauers's file, please."

A few moments later, the file was on his desk.

"Kate is a very wealthy woman, Detective, but I think you already knew that. She inherited several millions from her first husband, Evan McCallum. A fine man. Terrible the way he was killed. Anyway, she also inherited several hundred thousand dollars when her father died. Barbara inherited an equal amount. And then, when Claire Simpson died—Claire was Kate's mother—Kate and Barbara inherited her estate. Since Claire wanted Kate to have the house in Hancock Park, she gave Barbara a slightly larger share of the money."

"And when Ms. Simpson died, everything went to Kate?"

"Yes. Barbara had drawn up a will. Claire Simpson had insisted that her daughters do so. She was a wise and lovely woman, a caring mother. Frankly, I'm happy she isn't alive to see what has happened to her girls."

"Mr. Bristol, if Katherine Bauers divorced her husband, what would he get?"

"Very little. Mark signed a prenuptial agreement. If I remember correctly, Kate told me it was his idea. Claire and I were impressed by the gesture. But even if he hadn't suggested it, I would have strongly urged Kate to have him sign one."

"And if Katherine Bauers were to die? Who inherits?"

"The children get two-thirds of the estate. The other third goes to Mark. He is also the executor of the estate and trustee for the children's inheritance."

"Roughly speaking, what would you estimate that one-third to be worth?"

"Quite a bit, Detective."

"Several hundred thousands?"

"Oh, more. Kate has been investing her capital wisely. The house alone is worth in the neighborhood of one and a half million. Her inheritance from Evan and her parents has more than tripled. I would say that conservatively speaking, one-third of the inheritance would come to approximately two million dollars."

"Quite a tidy little sum. What happens if Bauers outlives the children?"

"If they die without leaving heirs, he inherits the entire estate. But you don't think . . ." He looked aghast.

"Frankly, Mr. Bristol, I wouldn't put anything past Dr. Bauers. It's amazing, though, if what we suspect is true, how easily he's manipulated everyone. As far as you know, Mrs. Simpson never worried whether he was marrying her daughter for her money?"

He frowned. "It's funny you should mention that. I don't know whether this is significant, but there is one odd thing. This has to do with Claire Simpson's will."

"What's that?"

"Well, Claire called me up once and asked me how she would go about excluding someone from her will."

"Did she say who she wanted to exclude?"

"As a matter of fact, she did. 'Hypothetically'—I remember she said that—'hypothetically, what if I wanted Kate and the children to have all my money?' she asked. 'Could you arrange matters so that Mark wouldn't be able to touch the money?'"

"Weren't you surprised by the question?"

"Of course. I asked her whether Mark had done something to forfeit her trust. She said no, that she was just contemplating the possibilities. She never brought it up again, so I assumed that she had resolved her doubts."

"When did this conversation take place?"

"I can't recall offhand. Let me get her file. I'm sure I

320

must have made a note of it."

Ryker waited until the secretary placed the file on Bristol's desk.

"Thank you, Edith." He waited until she had gone. "Let me see. Ah, yes. I wrote down the gist of the conversation. It's just as I told you, almost verbatim. It's nice to know that my memory isn't going yet." He smiled.

"What's the date of that conversation?"

"Let me check. April 14, 1987." He frowned. "That's strange. I never noticed the coincidence at the time."

"What coincidence?"

"Claire Simpson died at the end of April. That's just about two weeks after this conversation took place."

Chapter Twenty

"How did Claire Simpson die?" Ryker asked Bristol.

"She suffered a massive heart attack and died in the ambulance on the way to the hospital. Actually, that was her second heart attack. The first was a year before that."

"So her death was more or less expected?"

"Not really. As a matter of fact, we—the family and I—were shocked. The first attack had been a minor one. She'd been under a cardiologist's care since then, and she appeared to be doing well."

"Where did she have the heart attack? At home?"

"I don't recall. Detective, are you suggesting that Mark Bauers killed Claire Simpson as well? But why would he do that? Kate certainly has enough money from Evan and her father, and eventually, she would receive her share of her mother's estate as well." His tone was hushed.

"I don't know. She may have died from a heart attack, but I intend to explore the possibility. I think, under the circumstances, you can see why. Was Claire Simpson cremated?"

"Oh, no! She's buried in a family plot at Forest Lawn, next to her husband. I take it you plan to exhume the body?"

"It all depends on whether I can ascertain a motive for her being murdered. I would have to have grounds to get a court order for the exhumation, and usually, the family's permission." He rose. "Thank you again, Mr. Bristol. You've been extremely cooperative."

"Detective Ryker, for many years I've been more than an attorney to the Simpson family; I've been a friend as well. After what you've told me, I'm terribly concerned about Kate and the children. You'll inform me of any developments?"

"You can count on it."

Dr. Roger Harwell greeted Ryker affably.

"Sit down, Detective. I'm sorry I couldn't see you yesterday or this morning, but I was out of town for a few days and I had a tight schedule. What can I do for you?"

"Two things, actually. The first has to do with Mark Bauers. The second with Barbara Simpson's mother."

"I'm not sure that I have the answers you want about either one, but go ahead."

"All right. The last time I was here, I told you that we suspect Bauers of killing Barbara Simpson. We still don't have concrete proof, but the list of his possible victims has grown." He explained about Dupard, Ellen Kringle, and Marilyn Zakowski. "The thing is, Dr. Harwell, I paid two visits to Bauers. I think he knows that we suspect him of involvement with Dupard's death, and I told him we might reopen the case on his sister-in-law."

"What was his reaction?"

"He told me it was ridiculous to think that Ms. Simpson's death was anything but an accident. He didn't seem upset at all."

"I see. And what exactly do you want from me?"

"If Bauers knows that we're on to him, would he still try to commit another murder?"

"Detective, how can I answer that? I've never met Dr. Bauers. I only know about him through my sessions with Barbara. It would be totally unprofessional and highly presumptuous for me to speculate as to what Dr. Bauers would or would not do."

"Playing it a little close to the chest, Doctor?"

"Being circumspect, Detective. What if you were to tell Kate Bauers that, based on my assumptions, you've come to the conclusion that her husband is planning to kill her? That's what you think, isn't it?"

Ryker nodded.

"Well, what if she confronts her husband with my chairside analysis? Her husband could sue me for defamation of character, to say the least."

"All right. I see your point. Hypothetically, then, Doctor: A man kills his first wife and their unborn child, two women with whom he's had affairs—one of whom happened to be his sister-in-law—who pose threats to his safety and security, and has his female lover-accomplice kill a private investigator who can expose him. He seems calm and assured when the police approach him. Will this man kill again if he has the proper motivation? Like several million dollars?"

"Hypothetically, Detective, you're describing someone who may have a major personality disorder, possibly a psychopath or someone who may have psychopath-like traits."

"Which means what?"

"People like that are usually charming, sociable. They are predominantly concerned with only their needs and will do anything to satisfy them, even murder. Generally, they see themselves as superior to those around them and their behavior as natural; they show no remorse for what they have done and see no reason to adapt to the values and morals of the society in which they live. Consequently, most psychopaths resist therapy. In many cases, but not all cases, there is a history of abuse or neglect in the person's childhood."

"Like an orphan? I was thinking about Bauers's—about the hypothetical killer's accomplice."

"Possibly. Of course, most orphans don't become psychopaths. However, being orphaned and deprived of love and financial security could aggravate an already existing personality disorder. And taking that a step further, a person with psychopathic tendencies would feel that it was reasonable and natural to do anything in his or her power to remove threats to his or her security."

"My main question is, if a psychopath knows that the police are on his trail, will he commit another murder?"

"Very possibly. You see, Detective, the psychopath has a tremendous attraction to danger; the risk involved in his action would only serve to heighten his excitement."

"So he would consider, for example, arranging to have his lover live in the house along with his wife?"

"Yes. He might do that. In a way, it's like a game, Detective, and he wants to increase the challenge. And getting back to your other question, knowing that the authorities are aware of his intentions would probably not deter him, because he would derive tremendous satisfaction from outwitting them and flaunting his superiority and his criminal success. Then again, remember that the person you've described has no reason to think he'll be caught. He's been successful in all his previous crimes and has no reason to believe that he'll be less than successful in committing another crime."

Ryker nodded. "Okay. Next. You told me that Barbara Simpson was having an affair with Bauers. Did she tell anyone else about it?"

"Not her sister, of course. That was very difficult for

her, but she didn't want to ruin Kate's happiness. She *did* tell her mother."

"How do you know that?"

"It was the subject of several of our sessions. Barbara had a terrible fight with her mother about it. It seems Kate had asked her mother to talk to Barbara about her snide attitude toward Mark. When Mrs. Simpson asked Barbara to be more pleasant, Barbara let her have it."

"What do you mean?"

"Barbara had always felt jealous of Kate—in her mind, Kate was her parents' favorite, etcetera. So of course, when Kate married Mark, Barbara had to work through feelings of resentment toward Kate, too, even though she knew that Kate hadn't known anything about Barbara's relationship with Mark. When her mother interfered, all her feelings of resentment and jealousy were intensified, and she told her mother that Mark had promised to marry her."

"What did Mrs. Simpson say?"

"That infuriated Barbara even more. Her mother insisted on talking to Mark, to hear his side of the story. Barbara took that as a sign of distrust on her mother's part. In the end, she begged her mother not to say anything to Mark."

"Why?"

"Because her mother had told her that if she found out it was true, she thought Kate should know. Barbara didn't want to be responsible for that."

"When did all this happen?"

"I'd have to check Barbara's file. Is it important?"

"Very important, Doctor."

"Just a minute. I'll check." He went to a file cabinet, took out a folder, and brought it to his desk. He spent a few minutes checking backward through his notes. "Yes. Here it is. Barbara talked about that during several sessions. The first one was on April 9." He looked up.

326

"Does that help you?"

"I think so, Doctor. That clears things up a great deal."

"Laney called," Kate told Mark that evening. They were sitting in the family room. Janine was bathing the children."

"Oh? What did she want? To upset you again?"

"No. She sounded very quiet, as a matter of fact. I think she's bothered by what she's done."

"How do you know that?"

"Well, she says she has to talk to me privately. She said it's important."

"Did she say about what?"

"No. She sounded mysterious. I'm sure it's about the ad. I know Laney. She's basically too honest to keep something like this from me. She probably feels terribly guilty and wants to clear the air. I'm glad, because I do, too."

"You mean you'll forgive her, just like that? After what she's done?"

"I don't know yet, Mark. I'm still angry when I think about it. But I know we have to get this out in the open. I don't want to lose a friendship of years. What she did was wrong, but I don't think it was malicious."

"I don't know, Kate. You'll probably just get hurt again, and what will you accomplish? And I don't think she's planning on telling you about the ad. She probably just wants to mend the rift between you."

"Maybe I'll bring it up, then."

He shook his head. "I doubt she'll tell you the truth. She'll probably deny putting the ad in the paper. The best thing might be to drop it. Look, you're getting better. You'll be able to get back to the shop soon, and you can put all this behind you. You're probably right about her, you know. She wasn't being malicious, just misguided. In that case, why punish her for it?"

"I don't know."

"There's another thing you might want to consider. If you force Laney to admit what she did, she might be too embarrassed to continue your partnership, or your friendship. The best thing all around is to drop it."

"Maybe. I'll think about it for a while. I don't have to decide today. I told her I'm not up to any heavy discussions right now."

"Did you tell her about Sunday night?"

"No. Of course not."

"When are you going to meet her?"

"I told her the beginning of next week would be fine. I said I'll call her."

On Thursday night, Kate was lying in bed, watching T.V. Mark had laid out two suits, two dress shirts, dress shoes, a pair of sport slacks and a sport shirt, underwear, and a grooming kit.

"That's it, I think." He started packing everything carefully into his two-suiter. "I'll pack my shaver and toothbrush in the morning."

"Mmmm."

"You're sure you don't mind my going? If you do, just say so, and I'll cancel first thing in the morning."

"No. I really don't mind. Janine is here, and Anuncia. And I'm feeling so much better, Mark. Really. There's nothing to worry about. Anyway, you're only going for two days."

"Right. And next weekend, we're off to Big Bear. Look, I'll call you as soon as I get to the hotel so you'll have my room number."

"Stop worrying." She smiled. "Just promise me you won't hitch up with any convention cuties."

"That's a promise." He walked over and kissed her.

"I'll be back before you know it."

At a quarter to eight in the morning, he kissed Kate and the children goodbye and drove his BMW to the airport. He had decided to leave it in the parking lot rather than take a taxi.

For Kate, the morning passed slowly. With Jeremy in school and Dana in play group, there was little to do. She had tried going back to sleep after they had left the house with Janine, but found that she was too wide awake, too tense. Instinctively, she reached for the vial of pills on her nightstand, then remembered. Since Sunday night, she had promised herself no more pills. Instead, she had some toast and two slices of cheese, watched a few game shows on T.V., read a chapter in a book, and waited for Janine to return from doing the grocery shopping.

Mark called mid-morning to give her the phone number for the hotel and his room number.

When Dana came home, Kate insisted on preparing lunch for her, and played with her in the backyard. It had been so long since she had pushed her daughter on the swing, heard her squeals of "Higher, Mommy! Higher!" It was the laughter more than the fresh air that filled Kate with exhilaration.

By late afternoon, she was tired, and when Janine suggested she take a nap, Kate didn't resist. But she couldn't really sleep, and when Mark called at five o'clock, she answered the phone.

"How are you feeling?" he asked.

"I'm still all right," she told him. "Go expand your medical education. Don't gamble too much."

At eight o'clock he called again, this time to say good night to Jeremy and Dana.

"You should go to sleep early," he told Kate when she got back on the phone.

"Maybe. But I'm having a hard time sleeping, and I don't want to take a pill. I thought I'd stay up a little later, watch "L.A. Law" and the news, and then go to bed. Get myself real tired. Janine said she'd keep me company."

"Okay." He sounded dubious. "Don't overdo."

"I'll let her switch the channels."

"Very funny. You know I worry about you."

"I know. And I love you for it. Good night."

"L.A. Law" was a rerun; so was almost everything, because of the writers' strike. Still, it was better than anything else on that night. After five minutes of the news, Kate got up and stretched.

"I think I'll take a bath and go to bed. Even the news seems like reruns. Are you staying up?"

"Maybe I will watch a little Johnny Carson. I want to see who the guest host is." Janine smiled. "Are you tired?"

"Not really," she admitted. "I'm still used to taking a pill. I'm hoping that the bath will make me sleepy. If that doesn't work, I'll read a chapter in my book. It's very boring."

"Why don't I prepare some hot chocolate for you? That has always helped you before."

"You don't mind? What about Carson?"

"I don't mind at all, Kate. You know that. It will not take long."

"Only if you join me."

"Yes. All right. Why don't you take your bath first. If you don't mind, I'll just finish the news, then I'll prepare our drinks."

"Fine. I'm in no rush. The house seems lonely without Mark anyway."

About fifty minutes later, Kate came back to the den. "I'm sorry. The bath was so relaxing; I didn't realize how long I was soaking. Maybe we should forget the chocolate."

"Not at all. I will have it ready in no time."

Ten minutes later, Janine entered with a tray, which she placed on the coffee table. She handed a cup to Kate and took the other one for herself.

"It smells delicious," Kate said. She took a sip, made a face.

"Something is wrong?"

"I'm not sure." She took another sip. "It tastes a little bitter, I think. How's yours?"

Janine took a sip. "It seems all right, but I see what you mean. It is a new brand I bought today. A little stronger. Would you like a little sugar?"

"A lot of sugar!" Kate laughed. "And maybe a little whipped cream while you're at it. I think I saw some in the fridge."

"A good idea. I will get it." She returned with the sugar and the aerosol can. While Kate added two heaping teaspoons of sugar to their drinks, Janine sprayed a generous mound of cream on the surface of Kate's drink."

"Aren't you having any?" Kate asked. "Come on, or I'll feel guilty about all those calories."

"All right. Why not?" She added the whipped cream to her drink, stirred, and tasted it. "You are right. It is better this way."

"A spoonful of whipped cream and sugar makes the medicine go down," Kate laughed. "That's from a movie—kind of, anyway."

Five minutes later, Kate yawned. "Your hot chocolate was very effective. I'm feeling sleepy already." She got up. "See you in the morning, all right?"

"Sleep well." She waited until Kate had left the room, then took the tray with the cups and the teaspoons back to the kitchen. She was tempted to call Mark again, to tell him that everything had gone all right, but when she had called him earlier while Kate was taking her bath, he had told her not to call again. Too risky. She thought again of their closing words and smiled.

("Did you do it?" he had asked.

"Soon. Everything is under control. I'll check on her about a half-hour after; then I'll go to sleep."

"Sweet dreams, my angel. I'm proud of you.")

He was one of the first passengers off the plane, and he was all at once inordinately glad that he had taken his briefcase and the two-suiter on board with him. Quickly, he made his way past the LAX terminal doors and across the street to the parking structure where his black BMW was waiting.

He wondered again whether he should have gone to the conference in Las Vegas. He certainly hadn't gained much from the medical lectures he had attended. But then, he hadn't really been listening. He had been preoccupied, anxious about what was happening in his absence. He had called home twice in the early evening, had exchanged long-distance kisses with Kate, with his family, had at first accepted, then turned down, a barhopping offer from some colleagues ("Come on, Mark; cut the matrimonial cord!"). After packing his few belongings, he had watched a pathetically tedious X-rated cable T.V. offering in his room.

At 11:10, she had called.

"What's wrong?" he had asked, instantly alert.

"Nothing's wrong. I just wanted to hear your voice again. You sounded so tense before. I know you're worried, Mark, but you don't have to be. I'm fine."

"The kids?"

"Sound asleep. Stop worrying."

After the phone call, he had checked the room quickly to make sure he hadn't forgotten anything. Five minutes later he was downstairs in the lobby of the Las Vegas Hilton, paying his bill. He made it to the airport for the 11:50 P.M. flight to Los Angeles with four minutes to spare.

At 12:53, she walked quietly along the hall. Standing in the doorway, she heard a moan. She took a step into the room.

"Something . . . wrong. Please . . . help . . . me." Her voice was weak, her speech slurred.

She stood immobile, her figure almost filling the doorway. Her eyes were impassive, cold.

"Please! Can't . . . reach . . . phone. Call . . . 911. . . . Please!"

She started to leave the room.

"Why?" she cried weakly. "I was . . . so . . . good . . . to you. Like . . . sister. Help . . . me!"

She left the room, pulled the door closed behind her, and went to her room.

At 1:12 she called the paramedics. That was the way they had planned it.

At one o'clock in the morning, there was little traffic. The BMW made swift progress along the main boulevards, and twenty-five minutes after he had fastened his seat belt, he turned the corner with a mixture of eagerness and a nameless dread that suddenly overwhelmed him, even before he saw the ambulance occupying his spot in the newly cemented driveway, its sepulchral whiteness illuminated by the arching streetlamps, before he saw the flashing red lights on the two black-and-white police vehicles that welcomed him home.

He braked sharply in front of the house and jerked the ignition off. The car came to a shuddering stop. In seconds he was running up the carefully tended lawn and almost collided with the white-clothed paramedic who was sliding the stretcher and its silent occupant past the

333

gaping doors of the ambulance.

A uniformed policeman approached. "Dr. Bauers?"

"Oh, my God!" Mark cried. "Kate! Kate!" He turned to the paramedic. He was the same tall blond who had come Sunday night. "Is she . . . ?"

"We have a faint pulse, Doctor, but to tell you the truth, I don't know if she'll make it. Severe respiratory distress, blood pressure's extremely low. We've alerted Cedars to expect us."

"You have to save her! You have to! I'll never forgive myself if she dies, never! I shouldn't have gone to the convention, something told me all along, but she said, 'Go, go.' I should have listened to my instincts!"

The paramedic closed the back doors.

"Can I ride along with you?" Mark asked.

"You'd better follow in your own car."

He felt a hand on his shoulder and turned to face the policeman. He almost fainted with shock. It was Kate.

"Kate! But I thought . . . !" His eyes were wild. "Thank God you're okay! Who is . . . ?" He looked at the departing ambulance.

"It's Janine, Mark." Her voice was somber. "Let's go inside. It's chilly here."

He followed her numbly into the house, up to their bedroom.

"I don't know what happened, Mark. It's just a fluke that I found her. I couldn't sleep—you know, I've been trying so hard not to take the pills—and I went downstairs to see if Janine was up. I thought maybe we could talk. She was in the family room, lying on the couch, and she looked terrible. I knew right away something wasn't right, her breathing, her color." She looked at him. "What are you doing home? I thought you had another day of lectures?"

"I kept thinking about you, worrying whether you'd be okay. It's the strangest thing, but I had a premonition

334

that something was wrong. So I checked out of the hotel and made a late flight. When I saw the ambulance in the driveway, it was like my worst nightmare had come true."

"Poor Mark."

"But I still can't understand it. What happened to Janine? Do they have any idea?"

"They think she overdosed on something. They asked me where she could've gotten tranquilizers, and I said I didn't know, maybe from your medical bag. You left it at home, right?"

"Yes. In my office. But why would she do that?"

"I don't know. It doesn't make any sense. It's so strange, isn't it? She always seemed so stable, so in control. Although she did seem a little upset tonight when I mentioned the detective's visit."

"What detective?"

"He came by earlier in the day when Janine was shopping for groceries. To tell you the truth, I'd completely forgotten about it until just before I went to sleep. I was halfway up the stairs when I remembered. I went back downstairs to tell her."

"What did he want, do you know?"

"He didn't say specifically. But he asked me how long she'd been with us. You know what I think, Mark? I think he must be from Immigration or something. Maybe Janine was afraid that they're not going to let her stay here. Maybe there's something wrong with her visa. I don't see why that would make her do something like this, but who knows? I can't think of anything else." She shrugged. "Anyway, the detective said to tell her he'd be in touch with her in a day or so."

"What was his name, do you remember?"

"Raimer? No, Ryker. That's it. You look so shaken. I feel the same way."

"I think I should go to the hospital, Kate, see that she

335

gets the best treatment."

"Of course. And she'll feel better knowing that one of us is there. Maybe you'll be able to calm her down."

"Calm her down?"

"She was saying some strange things just before they put her in the ambulance. I couldn't understand her; she wasn't really making much sense, something about 'tell police.' I guess she was thinking about the detective." She shivered. "It's so awful, isn't it?"

"Yes, it is. Get into bed; it's chilly. I'll call you from the hospital when I know something."

There was a different resident on call in the emergency room. Mark stood up when he approached.

"I understand you're a friend of Miss Panetierre?" he asked.

"Yes. She lives with us. How's her condition?"

"Too soon to tell. She had a helluva lot of stuff in her. Tox screen shows a high level of Valium and Zanax. A potentially messy combination in itself. Any idea how she got the stuff?"

"I'm a doctor. I have prescription medication in the house for my wife. Maybe Miss Panetierre helped herself to some. That's the only possibility I can think of. Can I see her now?"

"She's in and out of consciousness, Dr. . . . ?"

"Dr. Bauers. Mark Bauers. Look, she must be very frightened, all alone in this country. She's from Switzerland, you see."

"I don't know, Dr. Bauers. She's pretty weak."

"Just for a few minutes. I just want her to see a friendly face, to know that we care."

"All right. She's in a room now. I'll take you to her."

Mark closed the door behind him and stared at the still figure in the bed. She seemed to be sleeping. He walked

336

over and studied the pattern of the phosphorescent blips that made their way across the screen monitoring her pulse rate. Once in a while they seemed to stagger, but for the most part, their progress was steady, if slow.

"Janine?" he whispered. He touched her cheek.

Her eyes fluttered open. "Mark?" A smile flickered across her face. "So glad you came."

"Of course I came! I was shocked when I found out it was you in the ambulance. What happened? Do you know?"

She shook her head lightly. "Don't know. I was careful. Kate switched cups. She knows, Mark."

"How could she know? Don't be silly."

"She wouldn't help me."

"You were probably hallucinating, Janine. Kate can't know. I planned everything too carefully. Don't worry. It's all right. There'll be another time.. The main thing is that you're going to be okay."

"So frightened."

"Don't be. I'll be with you; I'll take care of you. The police will ask you questions. Did they come by yet?"

"Not yet. I won't say. Don't worry."

"Of course you won't. I know that." He patted her hand. "You have to rest now. I'll be in the lounge in case you need me."

"I love you."

"I love you, too, Janine. We'll make everything work. You'll see. Close your eyes. I'll wait until you're asleep."

He waited a few minutes until he saw that she was sleeping. He stood up. From an inside pocket, he withdrew a small vial with a transparent liquid and walked over to the I.V. bottle connected to her right arm. He uncapped the vial and turned around to look at her. Even now, she looked quite beautiful. It was a shame, he thought. Not that he felt pity. Not that. Why should he? He was doing the only thing he could. In a strange

337

way, he thought Janine would understand. If their situations were reversed, she'd probably do the same thing.

"Planning on adding a few goodies to the I.V., Dr. Bauers?"

Mark whirled around. It was Ryker. He had emerged from the bathroom.

"Don't drop the vial, Doctor. It's evidence. Officer Reynolds!"

The door to the room opened. A uniformed policeman entered. "Yes, Detective?"

"Relieve Dr. Bauers of that vial in his hand, please. I wouldn't want him to get a cramp from holding it too long. I'll hold it for safekeeping."

Using a handkerchief, Reynolds took the vial from Bauers and gave it to Ryker.

"Please remove Dr. Bauers from this room and handcuff him." He followed Reynolds and Bauers into the hall.

"You're making a terrible mistake, Detective Ryker. I can explain everything."

"I'm sure you can, Doctor, and you'll have plenty of time to explain." In a low, calm voice, he read Bauers his rights.

"What are the charges, if I may ask?"

"Attempted murder of Janine Panetierre, for starters. I'm an eyewitness to that. And we have the vial you were about to empty into the I.V. I'm sure an analysis will reveal that it contains a tranquilizer, and in Miss Panetierre's debilitated condition, even a low dosage could finish her off. Of course, you can tell the jury that the vial just happened to be in your hand, just happened to be open. Maybe you can tell them it was for you, your morning tonic before you start rounds."

"Are you finished?"

"There's also the attempted murder of your wife. Oh,

338

you probably want to know which one, right? I don't mean Ellen Kringle. I have no jurisdiction over that, but I know that Capt. Spivak will be fascinated to hear about your latest adventures. He sends his best, by the way."

"I'm glad you're enjoying yourself, Ryker, because I'll beat this. You don't have a case at all."

"The D.A. thinks we have a case. We have a cup with hot chocolate residue that I'm sure will show some interesting results. Seems Miss Panetierre wasn't up to washing the dishes. We also found vials of Zanax and Valium in her room. I guess she was supposed to put them on your wife's nightstand after she was dead so the paramedics would find the 'evidence.'"

"This has nothing to do with me. I wasn't even home."

"We had your phone tapped, and we have the tape of a very informative call that Miss Panetierre placed to your hotel room in Las Vegas last night. 'Sweet dreams, my angel'—real romantic, Doctor, but I don't think she'll remember that when she finds out you tried to kill her. And I think you should also know that you're being charged with homicide."

"I haven't killed anyone."

"Barbara Simpson? Franklin Dupard?"

"You're crazy, Ryker. You can't tie me to those deaths. Barbara was accidentally electrocuted; I only talked to Dupard once on the phone. You have no evidence."

"Those might be a little hard to prove," Ryker admitted, "but not impossible. I'm confident a jury will see you for what you are. And there's always Claire Simpson."

"What are you talking about? My mother-in-law died of a heart attack."

"She died from an intravenous injection of atropine, *Doctor*; that triggered a heart attack. We exhumed her body. The pathologist's report is conclusive. But then, you know how she died. You administered the atropine. And as her internist, you signed the death certificate, so you knew there wouldn't be an autopsy. How convenient, Doctor. Incidentally, your wife will testify that you were the one who found Mrs. Simpson and called the paramedics. You like calling paramedics, don't you? You've been keeping them pretty busy this week."

"Kate will never testify against me. She loves me. She'll realize that you're making all of this up because you're desperate. She needs me, Detective. I'm all that she has."

"Not any more. As a matter of fact, she's been extremely cooperative. Brave, too, since she knew you were planning to kill her."

"I don't believe you! You're lying to confuse me!"

"Reynolds, take Dr. Bauers to the station, please. I'll be along in a little while. Suddenly, I feel the need for some fresh air."

Chapter Twenty-one

"Kate's in the backyard with the kids," Laney told Ryker when he arrived at the Las Palmas house on Sunday afternoon. "I'll get her."

"How is she?"

"A little tired, but amazingly okay, considering what she's been through. She's a lot stronger than I realized. Why don't you wait in the family room. You know where it is?"

He nodded. He went into the room, made himself comfortable on the sofa, and picked up a *Newsweek* from the coffee table. It had the presidential candidates on the cover. Neither one looked inspiring. He sighed, began to read.

A few minutes later, the two women returned, accompanied by the children. Ryker stood up.

"Why don't you play upstairs?" Kate suggested to them.

"Who's he?" Jeremy asked, looking up at Ryker.

"He's a friend."

"Oh." Jeremy eyed him suspiciously, then lost interest. "C'mon, Dana. Let's go upstairs. I'll let you play with my Lego. You can hand me the pieces."

"'Kay." She looked over her shoulder as she followed

him out of the room, her thumb lodged securely in her mouth.

"What did you tell them about Mark and Janine?" Laney asked Kate after they had all sat down.

"I've been pretty vague so far. I told them Janine had to go back to Switzerland. I didn't see any point in telling them she was in the hospital."

"We'll be moving her to the prison infirmary as soon as the doctors say her condition is stable," Ryker said. "Should be some time tomorrow."

"What about Mark?" Laney asked Kate. "Don't the kids want to know where he is?"

"They think he's still in Vegas. Originally, he was supposed to come back today. I just told them he's staying another day. I need some time to figure out what to tell them. I want to handle it right. Dr. Zuroff is going to help me with that. I have a session with her tomorrow morning."

"That's a good idea," Laney said. "I liked her, by the way. And I respect her ethics."

"You had her totally confused, Laney. She didn't know whether to believe you or Mark. Contrary to what you told her, he seemed so concerned. He told her he was worried that I was going to kill myself."

"That was the plan," Ryker said. "That's why he did the trial with the Zanax and 'saved' you just in time. This way, both the resident who treated you *and* Dr. Zuroff would testify that he'd been worried about you. Very clever."

"Diabolical," Laney said. "I hope he's executed."

"We may have to settle for a life sentence. It depends on how good his lawyer is. By the way, your husband wants to see you, Mrs. Bauers. I can arrange it, if you want to."

She shook her head. "Not yet. I know I'll have to face him eventually, and in a way I want to tell him to his face

342

what I think of him, but I want to take things one step at a time. The kids come first. What's happening with him, Detective Ryker? Has he admitted anything?"

"He blames Janine for everything, says she killed Barbara and Dupard because they posed a threat to her. He didn't suspect anything until I questioned him about their deaths. When he confronted Janine, she threatened to tell the police that *he* was the killer if he turned her in. He was waiting, trying to get proof. He also claims he knew nothing about her plan to kill you, insists that the phone call was totally innocent."

"Did you tell him that you know he met Janine in Geneva and brought her over here?" Laney asked. "That she told her boss Mark was going to marry her? How did he explain that?"

"We don't have proof that he was the American doctor Mr. LeDoux told me about. Bauers claims that he had a brief affair with Janine in Geneva, that she found out his address, blackmailed him into arranging for his wife to hire her as an au pair. He thought she just wanted to get to America. When he found out that she had crazy ideas about marrying him, he didn't know what to do. He was terribly frightened."

"He should have been a screenwriter," Laney said. "Some imagination. What does Janine say?"

"The opposite, of course. She hates Bauers, not only because he turned on her, but because she knows he tried to kill her. According to her, they met in Geneva, fell in love, and he promised to marry her. She swears he's the one who killed your sister, Mrs. Bauers. I tend to believe her. We'll be talking to all the neighbors, see if we can find someone who can place Bauers there that night. Maybe we'll get lucky. If not, we can still get him for killing your mother. Janine volunteered that Bauers had boasted about that, told her how simple it had been to fool everyone. She admits she killed Dupard, but she

343

says Bauers threatened to kill her if she didn't. He got the coke and the strychnine, prepared the syringe, showed her how to inject it. Everything."

"Why would she admit it at all?" Kate asked.

"The D.A.'s offering her a reduced sentence if she cooperates. And we told her we have an eyewitness who'll testify to the wig, and someone who'll testify that she was the one Dupard left the bar with."

"I thought you said the bartender isn't positive about the I.D.," Laney said.

"He's not. But Janine doesn't know that. I told her we were going to put her in a brown wig and have the witness identify her in a line-up. She caved in. Right now, she's terribly frightened." He looked at Laney. "You may be interested to know that Janine says Bauers was considering killing you as well. You were snooping around too much, getting in his way. But he couldn't see an easy way to do it without ruining his chances of getting his wife's money."

"Lucky me," she said dryly.

"Don't kid yourself," Ryker said. "You are."

"I know. I think I'm joking out of nervousness. It isn't much fun to contemplate your early demise."

"Where is Mark now?" Kate asked.

"Downtown. He'll probably be indicted Monday. I understand the judge is going to set extremely high bail."

"Thank God!" Kate said. "I wouldn't feel safe if I knew he could get near us."

"What I still don't understand," Laney said, "is how you were able to look him in the face after you found out about him. I mean, you knew he was planning to *kill* you!" She shuddered.

"It wasn't easy. All I kept thinking about was Jeremy and Dana, how if I didn't do this right, Mark could somehow harm them. You made that clear to me, Detective Ryker."

"I didn't know that he *would* harm the kids, Mrs. Bauers, but given his track record, it was a definite possibility."

"He's sick!" Laney exclaimed.

"Probably. But he knew exactly what he was doing. I don't think an insanity plea would work, and even if a lawyer suggested it, I doubt that Bauers would want to try it. He's too arrogant, too full of himself. He'd never want to characterize himself as crazy."

"This is all so strange," Kate said. "I was married to him for almost two years, and I really loved him. I can't deny that. But it turns out I didn't know anything about him—that he was married before, that he had a brother in a mental hospital. No wonder he discouraged me from getting close to his parents."

"And," Laney added, "I guess he didn't think it would be a great idea to mention that he'd killed his first wife, who just happened to be wealthy, too, and just happened to be carrying their child."

"And Barbara!" Kate sighed. "I feel terrible about that. Imagine what she felt like every time she came here, seeing us together. And the irony is, I have her to thank for my life. If she hadn't hired Dupard to investigate Mark, and Dupard hadn't gone to Laney, well . . . Mark would've gotten away with everything. No one would have known he was up to anything."

"Kate, didn't you have any suspicions at all?" Laney asked. "Didn't you find it odd that he was trying to keep you from seeing Dr. Zuroff, that he was trying to separate us?"

"I didn't see it that way. You have to understand, Laney: with Barbara dead, I felt totally isolated, totally dependent on Mark. Looking back, I can see how that was part of his plan. And when he told me about the ad—and he was so clever, you know, pretending that he wanted to keep it from me—anyway, then I was *really* alone. And that's ironic, too. Because if it hadn't been for the ad, I might not have caught on so fast, and I might not have believed any of this."

"Lucky his secretary called," Laney said.

On Monday afternoon, as soon as Mark had left the office, Angela Palusky had called Kate.

"Please don't tell your husband that I told you about the phone call," she had begged. "He's really angry about it, and when he asked me whether I'd told you who'd called, I lied and said no. If he finds out about the lie, I might lose my job. Please, Mrs. Bauers."

"What was that again? The message, I mean."

"The *L.A. Times.*"

"Oh, yes. Right. Well, don't worry about it, Angela. I won't say a word to Dr. Bauers."

The woman had thanked her effusively. In truth, earlier that afternoon, when Angela had called to ask for Mark, Kate had been so tired that she had barely heard what Angela had said. Now she thought about it.

What ad had Angela been referring to? And why had Mark been so angry? The only ad Kate knew about was the one Laney had placed about the shop, but Mark wouldn't be connected to that.

Or would he? He had been unreasonably irritated with Laney lately, almost resenting her presence. Suddenly, Kate had remembered the terrible fight she and Mark had had, how he had ranted irrationally about Laney's interference. Was he jealous of their relationship? Was that it?"

She had tested him that night, asked him whether he had received his message in time.

"You know, the one your secretary called about."

"Oh, that. A patient was a little anxious about scheduling an upper G.I. series for tomorrow. I took care

346

of it."

On Tuesday morning, while Janine was out taking the kids to school, Kate called Laney at the shop and confronted her with the ad.

"Are you crazy?" Laney had exclaimed. "Why on earth would I want to do that?"

"Mark showed me an ad in the *Times* about our shop."

"Well, I didn't put it in. Do you believe me?"

"Yes." She told her about Angela's call. "I think Mark is jealous of our friendship. I'm sure that's what it is. I feel bad for him."

"Don't."

"Why?"

She had hesitated. "I have to talk to you about something, Kate. Something important. But before I say anything, you have to promise to hear me out. And then you have to promise to listen to Detective Ryker."

"Who's that?"

"I'll explain everything. Is Janine home?"

"She'll be back soon. She took the kids to school. Why? What's going on?"

"Can you send her on an errand? Something that will take a while? I'd like to talk to you in person, and if I can arrange it, I'd like to bring Detective Ryker along with me. But we can't do it with Janine in the house."

"Laney, you're frightening me. You sound so serious."

"This *is* very serious, Kate. Please, trust me."

When Janine had returned, Kate had presented her with a long grocery list and a request.

"Robinson's is having a sale on comforters. We could use a few extra. Would you mind going there, choosing two or three? While you're there, why don't you pick up something nice for yourself. Don't argue; I insist. You deserve it for all your help."

Kate had called Laney to tell her when Janine would be leaving the house, and when Laney had arrived, she had brought Detective Sam Ryker with her. The three of them had sat for two hours in the family room. Ryker had talked. Kate had listened, incredulous, indignant, horrified, frightened. At one point, she had felt like laughing; what Ryker was saying about Mark and Janine, but especially about Mark, her Mark, was so ridiculous. She should demand that they cease their litany of accusations and leave her house.

Ryker had told her what Harwell had said, that Barbara and Mark had been living together, that he had promised to marry her.

"She could have imagined it!" Kate had cried. "She was jealous of me; she was always jealous of me."

Mark had known Janine before, Ryker had told her; they had met in Geneva, had been lovers then. Impossible, she had said; I found her through an ad. An ad that Mark arranged, Laney had said. Yes, through Mrs. Brockner, the patient with the mustache, you remember, we laughed. There is no Mrs. Brockner, Laney had said, no patient with a mustache, call Angela, she'll tell you, no Mrs. Brockner, no mustache, Angela will tell you, they were lovers, no Mrs. Brockner, no ad, just lies, lies, lies, lies, lies, lies. The word reverberated in her ears until she thought she would scream.

Did scream.

Slowly, patiently, they had explained again and again, until she had allowed the first glimmer of doubt to wedge its way into the wall of her conviction, until, finally, she was helpless in the face of irrefutable facts, papers that revealed the stranger who was her husband.

Laney had given her Dupard's report. Ryker had handed her a file. In it were pictures of Mark with his bride ("Ellen Kringle, daughter of Mr. and Mrs. Jonah Kringle, of Northfield, Minnesota. The couple will reside . . ."), a woman whose existence he had kept a secret. And letters, horrible letters that seared her consciouness with the viciousness of their aim. And a coroner's report on the same woman, her body filled with tranquilizers (like me?) and an eight-month-old fetus that had gone from one watery world to another. And her doctor's statement, she could almost hear him sighing, ". . . she was so agitated, on drugs, poor thing." (Like me!) (Not me!) And finally, the police captain's report, reluctantly burying the question mark of her accidental-suicidal drowning, letting the husband go to his unjust reward: "Insufficient evidence."

No proof, she had said, clinging to a lifeboat that was slipping from her reach, unable to allow what she had believed to be true to dissolve in vapory illusion, to disappear into a terrifying vortex of nothingness, what if you're wrong? I can't . . . What if we're right, Ryker had said, what about your children? What if . . . ?

Then, having no other choice, she had believed. And listened again. And this time, believing, she had found the ringing certainty of truth in what she heard.

"Well," said Laney now, "I still don't know how you pulled it off. I would have been a nervous wreck, not knowing when they were going to try to drug me."

"I didn't know, but Detective Ryker was right. At Big Bear, Mark would be in control. And if I refused to go, he'd just figure out another time."

"You could have thrown him out of the house," Laney said.

"That would have left everything up in the air. Maybe I would be safe, but what about Barbara? And my mother? And all his other victims? I'm not a heroine, but I just couldn't see him getting off again, scot-free."

"So you told him you and I were going to talk," Laney said. "About something serious."

"Yes. I told him I thought you wanted to confess about

349

the ad; he probably worried that you'd caught on to him somehow. In any case, he couldn't let me ask you about the ad, which is what I told him I planned to do."

"So he had to change his plans, move everything up."

"Right," Ryker said. "But Mrs. Bauers was prepared. We'd figured out that the drug would probably be in a drink that could disguise the taste. She remembered that Janine often prepared hot chocolate for her."

"I switched the cups when she went to get the sugar and the whipped cream. I was so nervous that she would taste something funny, but there was so much sugar that she didn't notice anything. Then it was awful, waiting to see if there *had* been something in my drink, hoping there was, so this would all be over soon, thinking that I could have been the one near death."

"And you can bet your Swiss chocolate that little Janine wouldn't have called the paramedics to save *you*," Laney said.

"To tell you the truth, I almost didn't call them either," Kate admitted. "I was standing in the doorway of the family room, listening to her beg for help, and I felt nothing. Absolutely nothing."

"I don't blame you," Laney said. She looked at Ryker.

"But you did call," he said.

"I couldn't go through with it. And I knew that if she died, Mark would get off. You should have seen his face when he saw me standing there!"

"He made one major mistake there, coming home early," Ryker said. "But I figure he just had to be in on it; he couldn't miss the excitement of seeing his plan come off without a hitch. And then, of course, thanks to you, we caught him trying to kill Janine. Well, that's about it, I guess. I'll keep you posted on any developments, Mrs. Bauers. I want to thank you again for your cooperation. You didn't have to put yourself in danger the way you did. I admire your courage."

"I did it for me, Detective Ryker. For me, for my children. For my family. And I should be thanking you, Detective Ryker. You probably saved my life."

"Thank Laney. If not for her persistence, none of this would have come to light. I mean that." He rose.

"I'll walk you to the door," Kate said.

"No. Don't get up. I'll see myself out. Take care of yourself, Mrs. Bauers." He looked at Laney. "See you around, Detective." He smiled lightly. And then he was gone.

"He's right, you know," Kate said. "And to think I doubted our friendship. How could I have been so blind? I owe you everything."

"Please. Don't get mushy. If you want to make up for the way you treated me, a check for ten million dollars will do. Brian said I should settle for seven and a half, but I said, 'No way, not after everything I've been through.'"

"You're impossible!" She laughed.

"How do you know I'm joking?" She laughed, too. "What are you going to do now? With your life, I mean?"

"Well, for starters, I'm coming back to the shop next Monday, so in case you've been embezzling anything, you'd better clear the records."

"That's great! What about the kids? Another au pair?"

"God forbid! No, I'm going to hire a sitter from an agency to bring Dana home from play group and stay with her till I get home. And Jeremy can go home with a carpool."

"If this were a novel, you'd have a man who's been waiting in the background since chapter six, ready to come to the rescue—you know, handsome, but not too handsome, a man of quiet strength and noble character. Someone to help you put the pieces of your life together."

"I don't want that. Oh, I'm not swearing off men.

351

Don't get me wrong, I had a wonderful marriage with Evan, and I'm sure some day I'll find the right person. But you know, Laney, I realized the other day that I've always had someone around to protect me—my parents, then Evan, then my mother, then Mark. It's time I stood by myself. I know I can do it."

"Of course you can, Kate. You'll be fine. And then, *voila!* You'll be *magnifique!*"

"No French in this house. It's absolutely *verbotten!*"

"Very well, Madam Kate."

"Shut up, Laney." She grinned.